Confusion

"Written with an ear for dialogue and an uncanny empathy for the young, *CONFUSION* yields more subtle and bewitching rewards than the "chronicle" suggested in the subtitle. Atmospheric and soaked in period detail as it is . . . it also catches the emotional reverberations of growth, love and pain in an unforgettable way."
—Elizabeth Buchan, *Daily Telegraph* (London)

"A discerning, almost addictive tale. . . . Howard has a talent for storytelling and a relish for the uncomfortable complexity of relationships. . . . *CONFUSION* is a solid, perhaps old-fashioned novel, but it is immensely enjoyable."
—Sarah A. Smith, *Literary Review* (London)

"Absorbing and well observed. . . ."
—Glyn Maxwell, *Vogue* (Great Britain)

"I have been a fan of Elizabeth Jane Howard ever since I read the opening page of her novel, *The Long View*, more than thirty years ago. . . . Her characters are always totally believable. She makes you laugh, she sometimes shocks, and often makes you cry."
—Rosamunde Pilcher

"Howard goes from strength to strength in her abilities, handling an enormous cast of characters with aplomb, wit and compassion. *CONFUSION* is a family saga of the best kind. . . . a must."
—*Tatler* (Great Britain)

Confusion

VOLUME 3
of The Cazalet Chronicle

ELIZABETH JANE HOWARD

WASHINGTON SQUARE PRESS
PUBLISHED BY POCKET BOOKS

New York   London   Toronto   Sydney   Tokyo   Singapore

This book is a work of fiction. Names, characters, places and incidents are products of the author's imagination or are used fictitiously. Any resemblance to actual events or locales or persons, living or dead, is entirely coincidental.

WSP

A Washington Square Press Publication of
POCKET BOOKS, a division of Simon & Schuster Inc.
1230 Avenue of the Americas, New York, NY 10020

Copyright © 1993 by Elizabeth Jane Howard

Originally published in Great Britain by Macmillan London Limited, a division of Pan Macmillan Publishers Limited

ISBN: 0-671-52796-7

First Washington Square Press trade paperback printing July 1995

10 9 8 7 6 5 4 3 2 1

WASHINGTON SQUARE PRESS and colophon are registered trademarks of Simon & Schuster Inc.

Cover design by Joanna Reisman
Front cover illustration by John Harris

Printed in the U.S.A.

For my brothers,
Robin and Colin Howard

Contents

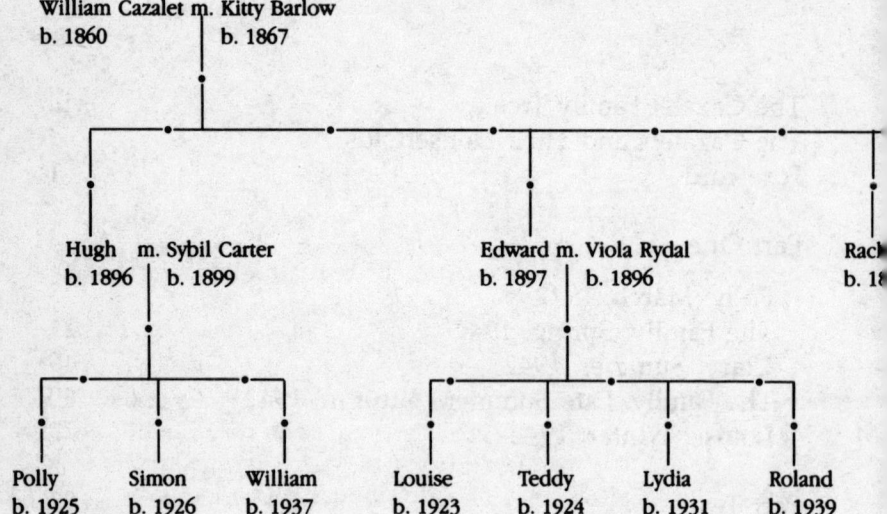

William Cazalet m. Kitty Barlow
b. 1860   b. 1867

Hugh   m. Sybil Carter   Edward m. Viola Rydal   Rac
b. 1896   b. 1899   b. 1897   b. 1896   b. 18

Polly   Simon   William   Louise   Teddy   Lydia   Roland
b. 1925   b. 1926   b. 1937   b. 1923   b. 1924   b. 1931   b. 1939

THE
CAZALET
FAMILY TREE

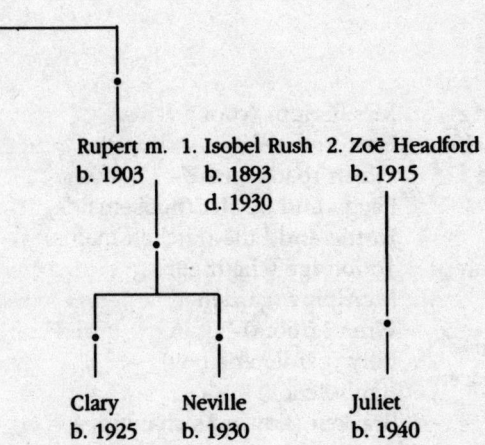

Rupert m. 1. Isobel Rush 2. Zoë Headford
b. 1903   b. 1893   b. 1915
           d. 1930

Clary   Neville   Juliet
b. 1925   b. 1930   b. 1940

The Cazalets and Their Households

William Cazalet (the Brig)
Kitty (the Duchy), his wife
Rachel, their unmarried
  daughter

Hugh Cazalet, eldest son
Sybil, his wife
Polly
Simon   } their children
William (Wills)

Edward Cazalet, second son
Villy, his wife
Louise
Teddy
Lydia   } their children
Roland (Roly)

Rupert Cazalet, third son
Zoë (second wife: Isobel died having Neville)

Clarissa (Clary)
Neville   } Rupert's children by Isobel

Juliet, child of Rupert and Zoë

Mrs. Cripps (cook)
Ellen (nurse)
Eileen (parlormaid)
Peggy and Bertha (housemaids)
Dottie and Edie (kitchen maids)
Tonbridge (chauffeur)
McAlpine (gardener)
Wren (groom)
Billy (gardener's boy)
Emily (cook)
Bracken (Edward's chauffeur)

Foreword

THE FOLLOWING BACKGROUND is intended for those readers who have not read *The Light Years* and *Marking Time*, the two previous volumes of this Chronicle.

William and Kitty Cazalet, known to their family as the Brig and the Duchy, are spending the war in Home Place, their country house in Sussex. The Brig is now virtually blind and hardly goes to London any more to preside over the family timber firm. They have three sons and an unmarried daughter, Rachel.

The eldest son, Hugh, married to Sybil, has three children, Polly, Simon and William (Wills). Polly does lessons at home, Simon is at public school, and Wills is four. Sybil has been very ill for some months.

Edward is married to Villy and has four children. Louise is succumbing to love—with Michael Hadleigh, a successful portrait painter, older than she, now in the Navy—rather than an acting career. Teddy is about to go into the RAF. Lydia does lessons at home and Roland (Roly) is a baby.

Rupert, the third son, has been missing in France since Dunkirk in 1940. He was married to Isobel, by whom he had two children; Clary, who does lessons with her cousin, Polly, but she and Polly are eager to get to London and start grown-up life; and Neville, who goes to a prep school. Isobel died having Neville, and subsequently Rupert married Zoë, who is far younger than he. She had a daughter, Juliet, shortly after he disappeared, whom he has never seen.

1

Rachel lives for others, which her great friend, Margot Sidney (Sid), who is a violin teacher in London, often finds hard.

Edward's wife Villy has a sister, Jessica Castle, who is married to Raymond. They have four children. Angela, the eldest, lives in London and is prone to unhappy love affairs; Christopher has fragile health and now lives a reclusive life in a caravan with his dog. He works on a farm. Nora is nursing and Judy is away at school. The Castles have inherited some money and a home in Surrey.

Miss Milliment is the very old family governess: she began with Villy and Jessica, and now teaches Clary, Polly and Lydia.

Diana Mackintosh, a widow, is the most serious of Edward's affairs. She is expecting a child. Both Edward and Hugh have houses in London but Hugh's in Ladbroke Grove is the only home being inhabited at present.

Marking Time ended with the news that Rupert was still alive, and with the Japanese attacking Pearl Harbor. *Confusion* opens in March, 1942, just after Sybil has died.

PART
ONE

Polly

March, 1942

The Room had been shut up for a week, the calico blind over the window that faced south over the front garden had been pulled down; a parchment coloured light suffused the cold stuffy air. She went to the window and pulled the cord; the blind flew up with a snap. The room lightened to a chill grey—paler than the boisterous cloudy sky. She stood for a moment by the window. Clumps of daffodils stood with awful gaiety under the monkey puzzle, waiting to be sodden and broken by March weather. She went to the door and bolted it. Interruption, of any kind, would not be bearable. She would get a suitcase from the dressing room and then she would empty the wardrobe, and the drawers in the rosewood chest by the dressing table.

She collected a case—the largest she could find—and laid it on the bed. She had been told never to put suitcases on beds, but this one had been stripped of its bedclothes and looked so flat and desolate under its counterpane that it didn't seem to matter.

But when she opened the wardrobe and saw the long row of tightly packed clothes she suddenly dreaded touching them—it was as though she would be colluding in the inexorable departure, the disappearance that had been made alone and for ever and against everyone's wishes, that was already a week old. It was all part of her not being able to take in the forever bit: it was possible to believe that someone was gone, it was their not ever coming back that was so difficult. The clothes would never be worn again and, useless to their one-time owner, they could only now be distressing to others: or rather, one other. She was doing this for her father, so that when he came back from being with Uncle Edward he would not be reminded by the trivial, hopeless belongings. She pulled out some hangers at random: little eddies of sandalwood assailed her—together with the faint scent that she associated with her mother's hair. There was the green and black and white dress she had worn when they had gone to London the summer before last, the oatmeal tweed coat and skirt that had always seemed either too big or too small for her, the very old green silk dress that she used to wear when she had evenings alone with Dad, the stamped velvet jacket with marcasite buttons that had been what she had called her concert jacket, the olive green linen dress that she had worn when she was having Wills—goodness, that must be five years old. She seemed to have kept everything: clothes that no longer fitted, evening dresses that had not been worn since the war, a winter coat with a squirrel collar that she had never *seen* before . . . She pulled everything out and put it on the bed. At one end was a tattered green silk kimono encasing a gold lamé dress that she dimly remembered had been one of Dad's more useless Christmas presents ages ago, worn uneasily for that one night and never again. None of the clothes were really nice, she thought sadly—the evening ones withered from hanging so long without being worn, the day clothes worn until they were thin, or shiny or shapeless or whatever they were supposed *not* to be. They were all simply jumble sale clothes, which Aunt Rach had said was the best thing to do with them "although you should keep anything you want, Polly darling," she had added. But she didn't want anything, and even if she had, she could never have worn whatever it might have been because of Dad.

When she had packed the clothes away she realized that the wardrobe still contained hats on the top shelf and racks of shoes beneath the clothes. She would have to find another case. There was only one other—and this time it had her mother's initials upon it, "S.V.C." "Sybil Veronica" the clergyman had said at the funeral: how odd to have a name that had never been used except when you were christened and buried. The dreadful picture of her mother lying encased and covered with earth recurred as it had so many times this week; she found it impossible not to think of a body as a person who needed air and light. She had stood dumb and frozen during the prayers and scattering of earth and her father dropping a red rose onto the coffin, knowing that when they had done all that they were going to leave her there—cold and alone for ever. But she could say none of this to anyone: they had treated her as a child about the whole thing, had continued till the end to tell her cheerful, bracing lies that had ranged from possible recovery to lack of pain and finally—and they had not even perceived the inconsistency—to a merciful release (where was the mercy if there had been no pain?). She was *not* a child, she was nearly seventeen. So beyond this final shock—because of course, she had *wanted* to believe the lies—she now felt stiff with resentment, with *rage* at not being considered fit for reality. She had slid from people's arms, evaded kisses, ignored any consideration or gentleness all the week. Her only relief was that Uncle Edward had taken Dad away for two weeks, leaving her free to hate the rest of them.

She had announced her intention of clearing out her mother's things when that question had been mooted, had refused absolutely any help in the matter; "at least I can do that," she had said, and Aunt Rach, who was beginning to seem marginally better than the rest of them, had said of course.

The dressing table was littered with her mother's silver-backed brushes and a tortoiseshell comb, a cut-glass box containing hairpins that she had ceased to use after having her hair cut off, and a small ring stand on which hung two or three rings, including the one Dad had given her when they were engaged: a cabochon emerald surrounded by small diamonds and set in platinum. She looked at her own ring—also an emerald—that Dad had given her in the autumn last year. He does love me, she thought, he simply doesn't realize how old I am. She didn't want to hate *him*. All these things on the dressing table couldn't just go to jumble. She decided to pack them in a box and keep them for a bit. The few pots of cold cream and powder and dry rouge had better be thrown away. She put them in the waste-paper basket.

The chest of drawers had underclothes; two kinds of nightdresses, the ones Dad had given her that she never wore, and the ones she bought that she did. Dad's ones were pure silk and chiffon with lace and ribbons, two of green and one of a dark coffee-coloured satin. The ones she had bought were cotton or winceyette, with little flowers on them—rather Beatrix Potter nightdresses. She ploughed on: bras, suspender belts, camisoles, camiknickers, petticoats in locknit Celanese, all a sort of dirty peachy colour, silk stockings and woollen ones, some Viyella shirts, dozens of handkerchiefs in a case Polly had made years ago with Italian quilting on a piece of tussore silk. At the back of the underclothes drawer was a small bag, like a brush and comb bag, in which was a tube that said Volpar paste and a small box with a funny little round rubber thing in it. She put these back in the bag and into the waste-paper basket. Also in that drawer was a very flat square cardboard box inside which, wrapped in discoloured tissue paper, lay a semi-circular wreath made of silver leaves and whitish flowers that crumbled when she touched them. On the lid of the box was a date, written in her mother's hand. "12 May 1920." It must have been her wedding wreath, she thought, trying to remember the funny picture of the wedding on her grandmother's dressing table with her mother in an extraordinary dress like a tube with no waist. She put the box aside, it not being possible to throw away something that had been treasured for so long.

The bottom drawer contained baby things. The christening robe that Wills was the last to have worn—an exquisite white lawn frock embroidered with clover that Aunt Villy had made—an ivory teething-ring, a clutch of tiny lace caps, a silver and coral rattle that looked as though it had come from India, a number of pale pink unworn knitted things, made, she guessed, for the baby that died, and a large, very thin yellowing cashmere shawl. She was at a loss: eventually she decided to put these things away until she could bring herself to ask one of the aunts what to do with them.

Another afternoon gone. Soon it would be tea-time, and after that, she would take over Wills, play with him, bath him and put him to bed. He is going to be like Neville, she thought—only worse, because at four he'll remember her for a long time, and Neville never knew his mother at all. So far it had not been possible to explain to Wills. Of course they had tried—*she* had tried. "Gone away," he would repeat steadily; "Dead in the sky?" he would suggest, but he still went on looking for her—under sofas and beds, in cupboards; and whenever he could escape, he made a journey to this empty room. "Airplane," he'd said to her yesterday after repeating the sky bit. Ellen had said she'd gone to heaven, but he had confused this with Hastings and wanted to meet the bus. He did not cry about her, but he was very silent. He sat on the floor fiddling listlessly with his cars, played with his food but did not eat it and tried to hit people if they picked him up. He put up with her, but Ellen was the only person he seemed to want at all. In the end he'll forget her I suppose, she thought. He'll hardly remember what she looked like; he'll know he lost his mother, but he won't know who she was. This seemed sad in a quite different way and she decided not to think about it. Then she wondered whether not thinking about something was the next worst thing to not talking about it, because she certainly didn't want to be like her awful family, who, it seemed to her, were doing their damnedest to go about their lives as though nothing had happened. They hadn't talked about it before, and they didn't now; they didn't believe in God, as far as she could see, since none of them went to church, but they had all—with the exception of Wills and Ellen, who stayed to look after him—gone to the funeral: stood in the church and said prayers and sung hymns and then trooped outside to the place where the deep hole had been dug and watched while two very old men had lowered the coffin into the bottom of it. "I am the Resurrection and Life," said the Lord, "and he who believeth in me shall not die." But she *hadn't* believed, and nor, as far as she knew, had they. So what had been the point? She had looked across the grave at Clary, who stood staring downwards, the knuckles of one hand crammed into her mouth. Clary, also, was unable to talk about it, but she certainly did not behave as though nothing had happened. That awful last evening—after Dr. Carr had come, and given her mother an injection and she had been taken in to see her ("She is unconscious," they said, "she doesn't feel anything now," announcing it as though it was some kind of *achievement)*, and she had stood listening to the shallow, stertorous breaths, waiting and waiting for her mother's eyes to open so that something could be said, or at least there could be some mutual, silent farewell . . .

"Give her a kiss, Poll," her father said, "and then go, darling, if you would." He was sitting on the other side of the bed holding one of her mother's hands, which rested, palm upwards, against his black silk stump. She stooped and kissed the dry tepid forehead and left the room.

Outside it was Clary who took her by the hand and led her to their room, flung arms around her and cried and cried, but she was so full of rage that she could not cry at all. "At least you could say goodbye to her!" Clary kept saying in her search for comfort of some kind. But that was the point—or another of them—she *hadn't* been able to say goodbye: they'd waited until her mother was past recognizing or even seeing her . . . She had extricated herself from Clary, saying that she was going for a walk, she wanted to be alone, and Clary had agreed at once that of course she would want that. She had put on her gum boots and mac and walked out into the steely drizzling dusk, up the steps in the bank to the little gate that led into the copse behind the house.

She walked until she reached the large fallen tree that Wills and Roly used for some mysterious game and sat upon a piece of the trunk nearest the torn-up roots. She had thought that here she would cry, would give away to ordinary grief, but all that came out of her were loud gasping sighs of fury and impotence. She should have made a scene, but how could she have done that in the face of her father's misery? She should have insisted upon seeing her that morning after Dr. Carr had left and said that he would come back in the afternoon —but how could she have known what he would do when he came? *They* must have known but, as usual, they had not told her. She should have realized that her mother was going to die at any moment when they got Simon back early from school. He had arrived that morning, and *he* had seen her, then she had said that she wanted to see Wills and they had said that that was enough until later in the day. But poor Simon hadn't known that it was the last time for him either. He hadn't realized: he simply thought she was terribly ill, and all through lunch he had told them about how one of his friends' mothers who had almost died of an appendix miraculously recovered and after lunch Teddy had taken him out on a long bicycle ride from which they hadn't yet returned. If I had spoken to her—if I had said *anything,* she thought, she might have heard me. But she would have wanted to be alone with her to do that. She had wanted to say that she would look after Dad, and Wills, and most of all, she had wanted to say, "Are you all right? Can you bear to die, whatever it means?" Perhaps they had cheated her mother as well. Perhaps she would simply not wake up—would never know her own moment of death. This awful likelihood had made her cry. She had cried for what seemed a long time, and when she got back to the house they had taken her mother away.

Since then, she had not cried at all—had got through the first awful evening when they had sat through a dinner that nobody had wanted to eat, watching her father trying to cheer Simon up by asking him about his sports at school until Uncle Edward took over and told stories about *his* school; an evening when everyone seemed to be searching for safe ground, for wan and innocuous little jokes that you weren't meant to laugh at, but were rather to get them through from minute to minute with the trappings of normality; and although underneath this she could detect the oblique and shallow shafts of affection and concern she had refused to accept either. The day after the funeral, Uncle Edward had taken her father and Simon off to London, Simon to be put on a train to go back to school. "Must I go back?" he had said, but only once as they had said of course he must, it would soon be the holidays and he mustn't miss the end of term exams. Archie, who had come down for the funeral, proposed after dinner that they play Pelman patience on the floor in the morning room, "You too, Polly," and of course Clary joined them. It was freezing cold because the fire had gone out. Simon didn't mind—he said it was just like school, everywhere except the san, which you only got into if you were covered with spots or nearly dead, but Clary fetched cardigans for them, and Archie had to be dressed in an old overcoat of the Brig's, the muffler Miss Milliment had made that had not been considered up to standard to send to the Forces and some mittens that the Duchy used for practising the piano.

"The office I work in is boiling hot," he said, "it's turned me into an old softy. *Now*, all I want is a walking stick. I can't sit on my haunches like you lot." So he sat in a chair with his bad leg stretched out stiffly, and Clary turned the cards he pointed at.

That had been a kind of respite: Archie played with such ferocious determination to win that they all became infected, and when Simon did win a game he flushed with pleasure. "Damn!" Archie said: "Dammit! One more go and I'd have cleaned up."

"You're not a very good loser," Clary had observed lovingly: she was no good at that herself.

"I'm a wonderful winner, though. Really nice about it, and as I usually win hardly anyone sees my bad side."

"You can't win *all* the time," Simon said. It was funny how Archie behaved about games in the kind of way that made them say the grown-up things to *him*, Polly had noticed.

But later, when she was coming out of the bathroom she found Simon hanging about in the passage outside.

"You could have come in. I was only cleaning my teeth."

"It's not that. I wondered if you could—Could you come to my room for a minute?"

She followed him down the passage to the room that he usually shared with Teddy.

"The thing is," he said again, "you won't tell anyone, or laugh or anything, will you?"

Of course she wouldn't.

He took off his jacket and began loosening his tie.

"I have to put something on them, otherwise they hurt against my collar." He had unbuttoned his grey flannel shirt and she saw that his neck was studded with pieces of dirty sticking plaster. "You'll have to take them off to see," he said.

"It will hurt."

"It's best if you do it quickly," he said, and bent his head.

She began cautiously, but soon realized that that wasn't kind, and by the time she'd got to the seventh piece, she was holding down the skin of his neck with two fingers and tearing quickly with the other hand. A crop of festering spots was revealed—either large pimples or small boils, she didn't know which.

"The thing is, they probably need popping. Mum used to do it for me, and then she put some marvellous stuff on them and sometimes they just went away."

"You ought to have proper plasters with a dressing under them."

"I know. She gave me a box to go back to school with, but I've used them all up. And of course I can't pop them—can't see them to do it. I couldn't ask Dad. I thought perhaps you wouldn't mind."

"Of course I don't. Do you know what she put on them?"

"Just marvellous stuff," he said vaguely. "Vick, do you think?"

"That's for people's chests. Look. I'll go and get some cotton wool and proper plasters and anything else I think might be good. Won't be a sec."

The medicine cupboard in the bathroom had a roll of Elastoplast that had yellow lint on one side of it, but the only stuff she could find to put on the spots was friar's balsam with hardly any left in the bottle. It would have to do.

"I've got another style coming as well," he said when she got back to him. He was sitting on his bed in his pyjamas.

"What did she put on that?"

"She used to rub them with her wedding ring and sometimes they went away."

"I'll do the spots first."

It was a disgusting job, made worse because she knew she was hurting him: some of the spots were oozing, but some simply had hard, shiny yellow heads that eventually spurted pus. He only flinched once, but when she apologized, he simply said, "Oh, no. Just get all the stuff out you can."

"Wouldn't Matron do these for you?"

"Lord, no! She hates me anyway, and she's nearly always in a bate. She really only likes Mr. Allinson—the PT Instructor—because he's got muscles all over him, and a boy called Willard whose father is a lord."

"Poor Simon! Is it all horrible there?"

"I loathe and detest it."

"Only two more weeks and you'll be home."

There was a short silence.

"It won't be the same, though, will it?" he said and she saw his eyes fill with tears. "It's not my foul school, or the beastly war," he said as he ground his knuckles into his eyes, "it's my wretched style. They often make my eyes water. I often get that with them."

She put her arms round his stiff, bony shoulders. His awful loneliness seemed to be boring a hole in her heart.

"Of course, if one has bee used to getting a letter from the same person every week, and then one isn't going to get them any more, it stands to reason it would feel a bit funny at first. I think anyone would feel that," he said with a kind of bracing reasonableness, as though he was minimizing somebody else's trouble. Then he suddenly burst out: "But she never told me *that!* She seemed so much better at Christmas and then all this term she's been writing and she didn't say a word!"

"She didn't tell me. I don't think she talked about it to anyone."

"I'm not anyone!" he began and then stopped. "Of course you aren't either, Poll." He took one of her hands and gave it a little shaking squeeze. "You've been wizard about my beastly spots."

"Get into bed, you're freezing."

He fished in the pocket of his trousers, which lay on the floor, brought out an unspeakable handkerchief and blew his nose.

"Poll! Before you go, I want to ask you something. I keep thinking about it—and I can't—" He stopped and then said slowly, "What *happens* to her? I mean, has she just *stopped?* Or has she gone somewhere else? It may seem idiotic to you, but the whole thing—death, you know, and all that—I can't think what it *is.*"

"Oh, Simon, I can't either! I've been trying to think about that too."

"Do you think," he jerked his head in the direction of the door, "*they* know? I mean, they never tell us anything anyway, so it might be just another of those things they don't see fit to mention."

"I've been wondering that," she said.

"At school, of course, they'd go on about heaven because they pretend to be frightfully religious—you know, prayers every single day, and special prayers for any of the Old Boys who've got killed in the war, and the head gives a talk on Sundays about patriotism and being Christian soldiers and being pure in heart and worthy of the school and I know when I get back he'll mention heaven, but anything they say about that seems to me so idiotic that I can't think why anyone would want to go there."

"You mean, all the harp playing and wearing white dresses?"

"And being *happy* all the time," he said savagely. "So far as I can see, people simply grow out of happiness, and *they're* against it anyway, because they keep on making one do things that are bound to make one miserable. Like being sent away to school for most of your life, just when you might be having a good time at home. And then wanting you to pretend you like it. That's what really gets me down. You have to do what they want all the time and *then* you have to pretend to like it."

"You could tell them, I suppose."

"You couldn't tell anyone at school!" he exclaimed, aghast. "If you said anything like that at *school* they'd practically kill you!"

"Surely not all the masters are like that!"

"I don't mean the masters. I mean the boys. Everybody's trying to be the same, you see. Anyway," he said, "I just thought I'd ask you about—you know, death et cetera."

She had given him a quick hug and left him after that.

Now, she thought, even before she played with Wills, she would write to Simon, having silently resolved then to take over the weekly letter to him at school. She pulled down the blinds in her parents' room, picked up the box with the trinkets and took it to the bedroom she still shared with Clary. As she walked along the passages to the gallery over the hall, she could hear the variously distant sounds of the Duchy playing Schubert, the gramophone in the day nursery playing the now deeply scratched record of "The Teddy Bear's Picnic," a work that neither Wills nor Roly ever tired of, the Brig's wireless that he used whenever he didn't have anyone to talk to, and the spasmodic rasping of the old sewing machine, being used, she supposed, by Aunt Rach sides-to-middling sheets—an interminable occupation. It was Friday, the day when Dad, and Uncle Edward now that he was back in the firm, usually came down for the weekend, only this time they wouldn't, as Uncle Edward had taken Dad away to Westmorland. Except for that, everybody was getting on with their lives as though nothing had happened, she thought resentfully, as she searched for some writing paper for Simon's letter, which she decided to write in bed as it was slightly warmer than anywhere else could possibly be (the fire was not lit in the drawing room until after tea—another of the Duchy's economies).

She decided that the best thing was to give Simon as much news as possible about everyone. "Here is news of people in order of their age," she wrote: this meant beginning with the remaining great-aunt.

Poor old Bully went on *again* about the Kaiser at breakfast: she's in completely the wrong war. Apart from him—the Kaiser, I mean—she talks a lot about people who nobody even knows who they are, which makes any sensible response difficult. And she spills even valuable food like boiled eggs all down her cardigans so Aunt Rach is always having to wash them. It's funny, because we're all used to Miss Milliment's clothes being like that, but it seems pathetic with Bully. The Duchy gives her little jobs to do but she usually only does half of them. [She was going to put "She misses Aunt Flo *all the time*" but decided not to.] The Brig goes to London to the office three days a week now. He tried not going at all, but he got so bored, and it was so difficult for Aunt Rach to think what to do with him, that now she takes him up in the train and then to the office, and once a week she leaves him there and goes off to shop and things. The other days he plans his new plantation of trees that he's going to plant in the big field on the way to where you and Christopher had your camp and listens to the wireless or gets Miss Milliment or Aunt Rach to read to him. The Duchy doesn't take much notice of him (although I don't think he minds), she simply goes on practising her music and gardening and ordering meals although there are so few things left to have on our rations that I should think Mrs. Cripps knows them all by heart. But old people don't change their habits, I've noticed, even if to you or me they seem to be very boring ones. Aunt Rach does all the things I've already said, but in addition she's awfully nice to Wills. Aunt Villy is *plunged* in Red Cross work and also does some nursing at the Nursing Home, I mean real nursing, not like Zoë, who simply goes and sits with the poor patients. Zoë has got quite thin again and spends all her spare time altering her clothes and making Juliet new ones. Clary and I both feel really stuck. We can't think what to do with our lives. Clary says if Louise was allowed to leave home at seventeen, we should be too, but I've pointed out to her that they'd only send us to that stupid cooking school that Louise went to, but Clary thinks that even that would broaden our minds, which are in danger (she *says*) of becoming unspeakably narrow. But it also seems to both of us that Louise has become *more* narrow-minded since she's been in the world. She thinks of nothing but plays and acting and trying to get a job in radio plays for the BBC. She behaves as though there isn't a war or at least not for her. Between you and me, she is pretty unpopular with the family, who think she ought to go into the Wrens. There is fuel rationing now—not that it *can* make much difference to us, as the only coal is used on the kitchen range. Simon, when you come back I'm going to take you to see Dr. Carr because I bet you he could get your spots better. Must go now because I promised Ellen to bath Wills as she finds bending over the bath very bad for her back.

Love from your loving sister, Polly

There, she thought, it wasn't a very interesting letter, but better than nothing. It occurred to her that she didn't really know much *about* Simon, as he had always been away at school and in the holidays had gone about with Christopher or Teddy. Now, with Christopher working on a farm in Kent, and Teddy having this week joined up with the RAF, there would be nobody for him in the coming holidays. His loneliness that had struck her so hard the evening after the funeral struck her again: it seemed awful that the only things she knew about him were those that made him miserable. Ordinarily, she would have talked to Dad about him, but now this felt difficult, if not impossible: one of the things that had happened in the last few weeks had been that her father seemed to have got further and further away from anyone until by the time her mother actually died, he seemed shipwrecked—marooned by grief. Still, there was always Clary, she thought, she was full of ideas; even if a good many of them were no good, their sheer quantity was exhilarating.

Clary was in the nursery giving Juliet her tea—a long and rather thankless task; crumbs of toast and treacle lay thickly on the tray of her high chair, on her feeder and little fat, active hands, and when Clary tried to post a morsel into her mouth, she turned her head dismissively. "Down now," she said again and again. She wanted to join Wills and Roly, who were playing their favourite game, called accidents, with their toy cars. "Just have some milk, then," Clary said, and proffered the mug, but she simply seized it, turned it upside down onto her tray and then smacked the mess with the palms of her hands.

"That's very naughty, Jules. Give me a nappy or something, could you? I do think babies are the *end*. It's no good, I'll have to get a wet flannel or something. Watch her for me, would you?"

Polly sat by Juliet, but she watched Wills. She had seen how he had looked up from his cars when she opened the door and his face had changed from sudden hope to a lack of expression that was worse than obvious despair. I suppose he does that every time someone opens the door, she thought: how long will it go on? When Clary returned she went and sat on the floor beside him. He had lost interest in the game and sat now with two fingers in his mouth and his right hand pulling the lobe of his left ear; he did not look at her.

She had been thinking earlier that, really, her mother dying was perhaps worst for Simon because his particular loss had not seemed to be recognized by the family; now she wondered whether it was not worst of all for Wills, who was not able to communicate his despair—who did not even understand what had happened to his mother. But then I don't either—any more than Simon—and *they* just pretend that they do.

"I think that all religions were invented to make people feel better about death," Clary remarked as they were going to bed that night. This—to Polly rather startling—statement came after they had had a long discussion about Simon's unhappiness and how they could make his holidays better.

"Do you really?" She was amazed to find that she felt slightly shocked.

"Yes. Yes, I do. The Red Indians with their happy hunting grounds—paradise or heaven, or having another go as someone else—I don't know all the things they have invented, but I bet you that was why religions started in the first place. The fact that everyone dies in the end wouldn't make any single person feel better about it. They've *had* to invent some kind of future."

"So you think that people just snuff out—like candles?"

"Honestly, Poll, I don't know. But the mere fact that people don't *talk* about it shows how frightened they are. And they have awful phrases like 'passed away.' Where the devil to? They don't know. If they did they'd say."

"You don't think then . . ." She felt rather hesitant about the enormity of the suggestion. "You don't think they actually *do* know, but it's too awful to talk about?"

"No, I don't. Mind you, I wouldn't trust *our* family a yard about that sort of thing. But people would have written about it. Think of Shakespeare and the undiscovered bourne and that being the respect that makes calamity of so long life. *He* knew far more than anyone else, and if he'd known he would have said."

"Yes, he would, wouldn't he?"

"Of course, he might have made that just what Hamlet thought, but people like Prospero—he'd have made *him* know if *he'd* known."

"He believed in hell, though," Polly pointed out. "And it's a bit much to go in for one without the other."

But Clary said loftily, "He was simply pandering to the fashionable view. I think hell was just a political way of getting people to do what you wanted."

"Clary, lots of quite serious people believed in it."

"People can be serious and wrong."

"I suppose so." She felt that this conversation had gone wrong several minutes ago.

"Anyway," Clary said, tearing her rather toothless comb through her hair, "Shakespeare probably did believe in heaven. What about 'Good night, sweet prince, and flights of angels sing thee to thy rest'?—that wretched Jules has got treacle into my hair—unless you think that was merely a courtly way of saying goodbye to your best friend."

"I don't know. But I agree with you. I don't think anyone else really does. And it has worried me rather. Lately." Her voice shook and she swallowed.

"Poll, I've noticed something quite important about you so I want to say it."

"What?" She felt defensive and suddenly extremely tired.

"It's about Aunt Syb. Your mother. All this week, you've been sad about her for *her*—and for your father, and Wills, and now for Simon. I know you mean all that because you are kind and much less selfish than me, but you haven't *at all* just been sad for yourself. I know you are, but you aren't letting yourself be because you think other people's feelings are more important than your own. They aren't. That's all."

For a moment Polly caught the grey eyes regarding her steadily in the dressing table mirror, then Clary resumed tearing at her hair. She had opened her mouth to say that Clary didn't *understand* what it was like for Wills or Simon—that Clary was wrong—before a warm tide of grief submerged any of that: she put her face in her hands and cried, for her own loss.

Clary stayed still without saying anything and then she got a face towel and sat opposite her on her own bed and simply waited until she had more or less stopped.

"Better than about three handkerchiefs," she said. "Isn't it funny how men have large ones and they hardly ever cry, and ours are only good for one dainty nose blow, and we cry far more than they do? Shall I make us some Bovril?"

"In a minute. I spent the afternoon clearing up her things."

"I know. Aunt Rach told me. I didn't offer to help, because I didn't think you'd want anyone."

"I didn't, but you aren't anyone, Clary, at all." She saw Clary's faint and sudden blush. Then, knowing that Clary always needed things of that kind to be said twice, she said, "If I'd wanted anyone, it would have been you."

When Clary returned with the steaming mugs, they talked about quite practical things like how could they—and Simon—all stay with Archie in the holidays, when he only had two rooms and one bed.

"Not that he's asked us," Clary said, "but we want to be able to forestall any silly objections on account of *room*."

"We could sleep on his sofa—if he has one—and Simon could sleep in the bath."

"Or we could ask Archie to have Simon on his own, and then us at another time. Or you could go with just Simon," she added.

"Surely you want to come?"

"I could possibly go some other time," Clary answered—a shade too carelessly, Polly thought. "Better not talk about it to anyone or Lydia and Neville will want to come as well."

"That's out of the question. I'd rather go with you, though."

"I'll ask Archie what he thinks would be best," Clary replied.

The atmosphere had changed again.

After that, she found herself crying quite often—nearly always at unexpected moments, which was difficult because she did not want the rest of the family to see her, but on the whole, she didn't think they noticed. She and Clary both got awful colds, which helped, and lay in bed reading *A Tale of Two Cities* aloud to each other as they were doing the French Revolution with Miss Milliment. Aunt Rach arranged for her mother's clothes to be sent to the Red Cross, and Tonbridge took them in the car. When her father had been away with Uncle Edward for a week, she began to worry about him, about whether he would come back feeling any less sad (but he *couldn't* be, could he, in just a few days?) and, above all, about how to *be* with him.

"You mustn't," Clary said. "He will still be very sad, of course, but in the end, he'll get over it. Men do. Look at my father."

"Do you mean you think he'll marry someone else?" The idea shocked her.

"Don't know, but he easily might. I should think remarrying probably runs in families—you know, like gout or being short-sighted."

"I don't think our fathers are at all alike."

"Of course they aren't *completely*. But in other ways they jolly well are. Think of their voices. And the way they keep changing their shoes all day because of their poor thin feet. But he probably won't for ages. Poll, I wasn't casting aspersions on him. I was just taking human nature into account. We can't all be like Sydney Carton."

"I should hope not! There would be none of us left if we were."

"Oh, you mean if we *all* sacrificed our life for someone else. There'd be the someone else, silly."

"Not if we *all* did it . . ." and they were into their game, founded on the rhetorical question that Ellen used constantly to ask Neville when he behaved badly at meals. "If everyone in the world was sick at the same time it would be very interesting. I should think we'd all drown," he had said after consideration, thereby, as Clary had pointed out, neatly making a nonsense of the whole notion. But almost as soon as they embarked upon playing it, they both—separately—recognized that it had lost its allure, their sallies were feeble and they no longer collapsed in giggles over them. "We've outgrown it as a game," Clary said sadly. "Now all we have to look forward to is being careful not to say it to anyone else, like Wills or Jules or Roly."

"There must be other things," she said, wondering what on earth they could be.

"Of course there are. The end of the war and Dad coming back and being able to suit ourselves because we'll be too old for them to boss us about and white bread and bananas and books not looking old when you buy them. And you'll have your house, Poll—think of that!"

"I do, sometimes," she answered. She sometimes wondered whether she had outgrown the house as well, without, so far as she could see, growing *into* anything else.

The Family

Spring, 1942

ARE YOU GOING to London, Aunt Rach?''

"I am. How on earth did you guess?"

"You're wearing your London clothes," Lydia answered, and then after careful scrutiny added, "I honestly think you look *nicer* when you aren't in them. I do hope you don't mind my mentioning the fact."

"Not at all. You're probably right. It's ages since I had any new ones."

"What I mean *is,* I don't think you ever looked your best in them. You would probably be the kind of person who ought to wear a uniform so that you were the same all the time. Then one could just notice whether your eyes were happy or not." She was hanging about in the passage by the open door to Rachel's room watching her as she packed an overnight suitcase. "Clothes age you," she said finally. "Unlike Mummy. I think clothes youthen her—her best ones, that is."

"Don't kick the skirting board, darling. The paint will come off."

"A lot of it's off already. This house is getting most dilapidated. I wish *I* was going to London."

"Darling, what would you do when you got there?"

"Go and stay with Archie like the lucky others. He'd take me to the cinema and out to a huge exciting dinner and I could wear my christening present jewellery and we could have steak and chocolate cake and crème de menthe."

"Are they your best things?" She was trying to decide whether she needed to pack bedroom slippers or not.

"They *would* be if I ever had them. Archie said they had meat in his ship every day. It's bad enough being a civilian, but being a civilian *child* . . . In restaurants it's bound to be different. It's ghastly bad luck to be living in a place where there aren't any. You don't wear make-up either, do you? *I* shall. I shall wear very black red lipstick like film stars and a white fur coat except in summer. And I shall read frisky books."

"What kind?"

"You know. It's French for not very nice. I shall tear through them by the dozen in my spare time."

"Talking of spare time, oughtn't you to be with Miss Milliment?"

"It's the holidays, Aunt Rach. I should have thought you would have noticed that. Oh, yes. And I shall ask Archie to take me to the Chamber of Horrors at Madame Tussaud. I suppose you've seen them?"

"I must have, I suppose, but years ago."

"Well, what kind of horrors are they? Because I'd rather know before I went. Neville pretends he's been. He says the floor is running with blood, but I'm not tremendously interested in blood. And he says there are moaning sounds of torture but he is not at all a truthful boy so I am none the wiser. So what are they?"

"It's ages since I went there, my duck, I don't remember—except a tableau of poor Mary Queen of Scots being executed. But I expect Mummy will take you to London some time during the holidays."

"I doubt it. She only takes me to Tunbridge Wells—for the dentist. Do you know something silly about Mr. Alabone? When you go into his room, he's always standing by the chair, and he takes two steps forward to shake you by the hand. Well, the carpet has two worn-out places where he takes the steps and they really look squalid and if he varied his gait it wouldn't happen. You'd think that someone intelligent enough to make holes in people's teeth would know that, wouldn't you? I did mention it to him, because with the war the chances of his being able to get a new carpet are rather slim, if you ask me. But he simply said, 'Quite, quite,' so I knew he wouldn't take any notice."

"People seldom take advice," Rachel said absently. The times that she had begged Sid not to live on sandwiches, to take a lodger who would at least contribute to the household expenses and perhaps do a little cooking were foremost in her mind. "I *like* to have the house to myself. Then, when you come, my dear love, *we* can have it to ourselves," was all that Sid would say to that. Today, tonight, would be one of those—increasingly rare—times. Perhaps I ought to learn to cook, she thought. Villy has learned, after all, but then Villy is so *good* at tackling entirely new things.

"Why are you taking so many handkerchiefs? Are you expecting to be awfully sad in London?"

"No. But the Duchy always made me take six for a weekend, and a dozen if I was going away for a week. It has just become a habit. One had to have a clean one every day, you see, even if one hadn't used it."

"So if you went away for a month you had to have forty-eight handkerchiefs. If you went away for three—"

"No, no, then they would get washed. Now go and see if you can find Eileen for me."

"Okey-doke."

Alone, she looked at her list. On one side of it were the things she had to see to before she caught the train. On the other, the things she must try to get done in London, when she'd finished her day at the office, where she sat in a black little room doing accounts and listening to the repetitive woes of the staff, who had early found her the perfect repository for all their troubles. At least she would not be accompanied by the Brig, who had had a cold that had turned into bronchitis and had been forbidden by Dr. Carr to leave the house until he was better. Miss Milliment would keep him occupied. He was editing an anthology on trees, and she was doing so much of the work that really, Rachel thought, she deserved to be part-author. But Aunt Dolly was to be looked after by the Duchy and Eileen, which meant Eileen, as Aunt Dolly preserved an entirely fictitious independence in front of her sister and would admit no help. It would be Eileen who would have to stand around for hours, searching for garments that Aunt Dolly wished to wear. Rachel felt she must warn Eileen that many of the searches would be fruitless, since Aunt Dolly often chose clothes that she could not have possessed for many years. "The best thing is to say that they are in the wash," she told Eileen. "Poor Miss Barlow's memory is not what it used to be. And just choose whatever you think most suitable."

"Yes, m'm."

"And her medicines. She's frightfully keen on taking them, which means that when she forgets, she's liable to have a second dose. It's best if you give them to her with her breakfast and then take them away—you may put them in my room. She also has one yellow pill at night.''

"And what about her bath, m'm? Will she be wanting me to draw that for her?''

"I think she will prefer to wash in her room." Rachel felt she could hardly expose Aunt Dolly's deep aversion to baths—she alleged that they were dangerous and that her father had forbidden her to take more than one a week. "She will go to bed after the nine o'clock news, so you need not be late. Thank you, Eileen. I know I can rely on you.''

That was another thing done. What a fuss just for two nights, she thought, but then, when I am in the train, I shall be able to look forward to two lovely evenings. She and Sid had been dogged by bad luck for weeks now. First, of course, because of poor Sybil, and then the Brig falling ill, and the Duchy had had a frightful cold which meant she could not go near him. And then Simon had come back for the holidays and Polly had been worrying her—altogether, it had been impossible to leave the house for more than her hours at the office. But somehow Sid didn't seem to understand that she had obligations to the family—and to the house, come to that—that *had* to come before pleasure. Their last argument about this, in a tea-shop near Rachel's office where Sid had come for a miserable sandwich, had been really rather *painful,* and afterwards, although of course she had never told Sid, she had cried. The only place to do that had been the very nasty ladies' lavatory at the office, on the sixth floor of the building where the usual lav paper was pieces of the *Evening Standard* cut into squares and attached to the wall by a piece of string, and the pipe leading to the cistern leaked. Sid either assumed that she *wanted* to go back to Home Place to look after Wills and Aunt Dolly and the Brig (which, in a way, was true because she wanted to do what she felt was right), or worse, she accused Rachel of not caring about her— sometimes, as on the tea-shop occasion, both. She knew that Sid was lonely, missed her teaching at the boys' school, although she had recently taken one or two private pupils which helped her precarious finances, and found the ambulance station extremely boring a good deal of the time but, after all, one could not expect life to be anything but dull and tiring in war-time. And that was the least of it. When she thought of Clary's vigil for her father, from whom, of course, nothing had been heard since the little Frenchman Pipette O'Neil had brought those scraps of paper back with him, and of the degree to which poor Hugh was shattered by Sybil's death, of Villy now having to face her son becoming a fighter pilot and seeing less and less of Edward; when she thought of poor little Wills and Polly and Simon each in their different way trying to come to terms with the loss of their mother . . . when she thought of all or indeed *any* of these things she felt that being bored or lonely or actually rather often exhausted was hardly comparable, or deserving of complaint. She does not always think of others, she thought, reverting to Sid: it was a serious indictment. She went in search of the Duchy, whom she found in the drawing room, mending china at the card table, which was spread with newspaper.

"I'm off now, Duchy dear. Anything I can get you in London?"

"Not unless you can find a new kitchen maid."

"Is Edie leaving?"

"Mrs. Cripps tells me she wants to join the Women's Air Force. She is so cross about it that Edie's petrified and bang went another of the Copeland plates. As she says, Edie only breaks the best."

"Have you spoken to Edie?"

"Not yet. But in any case I shouldn't feel justified in asking her to stay. I rather admire her for wanting to serve her country. She came straight from school to us. She has never left the village. I think it's rather brave of her. But, of course, Mrs. Cripps is beside herself. I shall have to find a replacement, drat it, but goodness knows how. Is Mrs. Lines still operating, do you know? That rather good agency—in Kensington, wasn't it? They might have someone. After all, kitchen maids are usually below the call-up age. You go, darling, or you'll miss your train. But you might see if Mrs. Lines *is* still going, and ask them. If you have time."

"I will. And don't forget to remind Tonbridge to pick up the piano tuner."

"I won't."

At least she didn't ask me to go to the Army and Navy Stores to get anything, she thought. The Duchy patronized very few shops and was convinced that any others were no good. She bought household linen from Robinson and Cleaver; her own clothes, acquired very occasionally, from Debenham and Freebody; material from Liberty, and practically everything else from the Army and Navy, which, being in Victoria Street, was not near anything else. As she had not been to London since the war began she relied upon her daughters-in-law and Rachel to provide her with her modest but none the less exacting requirements.

"Have you your gas mask, Miss?"

"Thank you, Tonbridge. It's packed."

As she settled into the back of the car, with Tonbridge tucking the old felt-lined fur rug over her lap, she thought how extraordinary war *was*; the juxtaposition of the gas mask and the fur rug seemed precisely to mirror what most of life was now like. Or like for the useless, stay-at-home people like me, she then thought. I do nothing to help end the war; I do nothing useful except trivial things that anyone else would probably do better. The depression that had descended upon her when she had finally realized that her beloved Babies' Hotel had had its day descended yet again. The hotel had returned to its London home briefly after the Munich business, but then a combination of shortage of funds and shortage of girls who wished to train as nurses had gradually overwhelmed the whole enterprise. Matron had retired to look after an aged father, the replacement had been unsatisfactory, and by the time the blitzes on London began the whole thing had come to an end in the nick of time, since the premises—then mercifully empty—had received a direct hit. But it had been the last, indeed the only time that she had felt she had some sort of career. Now she was forty-three, too old to be called up and unable—or unwilling—to volunteer for anything more than supporting her parents and any others of the family who might need her. And then, one day, eventually her dear parents would die, and then she would be free to live with Sid. Then she would be able to look after Sid, make her happy, put her first, share everything with her. When, as now, she was by herself, it seemed sad that she could not talk about this future with Sid, but when they were together, the fact that this future depended upon her parents' death somehow made it impossible to mention, let alone discuss.

In the train, she decided that she would buy Sid a gramophone, something she had never been able to afford. This idea made her feel suddenly far happier: they would have such fun choosing records together, and Sid would have it to assuage her loneliness. She would get a good machine, one of the ones with a large horn and thorn needles that were supposed to be less hard on records than the steel ones. She would go to HMV in Oxford Street in her lunch hour to choose one, and might very well be able to take it straight to Sid that evening in a taxi. It was a splendid idea—almost a solution.

"Honestly, darling, as soon as I've had this baby, I'll simply have to find somewhere else to live. Apart from the fact that the cottage is far too small for the boys, it isn't even really large enough for Jamie and a baby. And poor Isla can't have anyone to stay."

She did not add that her sister-in-law was driving her mad, because she knew that people not getting on with each other simply embarrassed him.

They were lunching in a small Cypriot restaurant off Piccadilly Circus which he had described as convenient and quiet. Its convenience escaped her, but it was certainly quiet. Apart from a couple of disconsolate-looking American officers, there was nobody there. For lunch they had had rather tough chops surrounded by rice and tinned peas. It wasn't at all the sort of place he usually took her to and she wondered, as she had when they walked in, whether he was embarrassed at taking somebody so conspicuously pregnant out to lunch. She had said she could not drink wine, and now, after the meal was over, the waiter brought her a carafe and poured some water into her glass. It was tepid, and tasted of chlorine. The hard chair on which she was sitting was extremely uncomfortable. On the wall—painted a rather dirty yellow—in front of her was a poster with an impossibly blue sky, a mountain with a ruin on top and in the foreground a ferociously smiling Greek Orthodox priest. The waiter arrived with small cups of Turkish coffee, upsetting the three paper carnations that stood in a vase on the table. He righted it with a flourish and then laid a saucer with two lumps of Turkish delight upon it in front of her with a benevolent smile directed at her belly. "On the house," he said, "for Madame."

"I'm sorry, darling," he said. "It wasn't much of a lunch. But I thought we'd rather go somewhere quiet, where we could talk. This coffee is perfectly beastly. I shouldn't drink it."

But they hadn't talked much, she thought.

"What about Scotland?" he now said.

"I couldn't *live* there! They wouldn't want me."

"I thought you said that they did."

"That was only immediately after Angus died. They felt they had to *offer*. They'd have been appalled if I'd agreed." She felt panic rising. He *couldn't*—surely he wouldn't—try to ditch her now.

"I thought it might be a temporary solution for the older boys," he said.

Burying anything else he might have thought, she said, "Well, it would be, in a way. But it means I wouldn't see them."

There was a pause.

"Darling, I feel so utterly *useless*. It's just a bloody awful situation. I ought to be looking after you—and I can't."

Relief flooded over her. "I know you can't. I do understand."

His face brightened. "I know you do. You're a marvellous person." He started to tell her, for the hundredth time, how he could not possibly leave Villy, but luckily the waiter came with the bill and he became occupied in paying it while she went in search of the lavatory. As she repaired her face—she really wasn't looking her best, had overdone her make-up in the morning—she felt self-pity besieging her like a fog. They had nowhere to go, nowhere where they could quietly spend the time until she had to catch her train; the perm that she had had that morning in Brook Street (her excuse to Isla for escaping to London) looked tight and artificial and not at all as though it would ever be a success; her back ached from the uncomfortable chair and her best shoes had made her feet swell. The thought of being driven to the nursing home by the local taximan when the time came to have the baby, possibly unable even to *tell* him that she was going and then being visited by Isla, who would go on and *on* about its likeness to Angus and indeed the whole Mackintosh family, filled her with a kind of irritable despair.

And then the awful uncertainty of what to do next—where to live and how to find the place; she was nearly in her eighth month and would have to get on with that. It all seemed too much. She seemed to be surrounded by discretion and loneliness and lies . . . This would not do; she must not give up; she decided to be confident and sanguine, but just a touch helpless over practical matters. She gave her nose a final admonishing dab of powder and went to rejoin him.

"I was thinking," she said brightly, "that the best thing would be for me to find a flat in London. Or possibly, even, a small house. I don't quite know how to go about it but I'm sure that it would be the solution. Where do you think I should look?"

They discussed this with animation while he drove her to Vigo Street, where he parked outside Harvey and Gore and took her in to buy her a present.

"Amethysts," he said. "I'm sure you could find us some nice amethysts, Mr. Green." And Mr. Green, who thought the only thing wrong with Mr. Cazalet was his not having a title, rubbed his hands and produced an array of battered leather cases, inside the bruised velvet of which lay various brooches, pendants, necklaces and bracelets of amethyst set in gold, sometimes with pearls or diamonds, and one with tiny turquoises that Edward particularly liked. "Try it on," he said.

She did not want a necklace—when on earth would she wear it?—but she unbuttoned her coat and the top of her blouse and bared her neck, which fortunately, humiliatingly, turned out to be too large for the necklace. Mr. Green said that some chain could be put at the back to enlarge it, but Edward said no, try something else. What she wanted was a ring, but she sensed that this would be the wrong thing to ask for. The time he had driven her from Lansdowne Road and dumped Villy's jewel box on her lap and, because it was not locked, all the jewellery spilled out, came suddenly into her mind, and she felt envious and desolate. For a moment she wondered quite madly whether he had *strings* of women who had had his children—whether the unctuous Mr. Green was utterly used to visit upon visit with different women . . .

"Darling? Look! What about this?"

It was a collar of graduated oval stones set and backed in gold, heavy and simple and handsome. She sat, and it was fastened on her and admired and he asked her whether she liked it and she agreed that she did.

"If Madam is not absolutely sure . . ." Mr. Green had years of experience of ladies being bought things that they did not like or want, or being bought one thing when they would much rather have something else.

"The only thing is that I don't know when I would wear it."

But he simply said, "Nonsense, darling, of course you'll wear it." And when Mr. Green retired to wrap it up, he leaned over her and whispered, "You can wear it in bed with me," and his moustache brushed her ear.

"Well, it certainly makes a glamorous alternative to Utility nightgowns," she managed to say.

"Darling, you don't have Utility nightgowns!"

"No, but I soon shall have. The government has said no more embroidery on lingerie."

"Rotten bastards. Perhaps we'd better buy you some of that before the shops run out."

"They need coupons, darling, and everybody's short of them."

He had finished writing the cheque and Mr. Green returned with a carefully sealed white package. "I hope Madam has much pleasure wearing it," he said.

Outside the shop she said, "Darling, thank you so much. It's a marvellous present."

"Glad you like it. Now, I'm afraid, I'd better take you to your train."

They drove down Bond Street to Piccadilly past the bombed church, round the boarded-up statue of Eros and into Haymarket. "MALTA GETS THE GEORGE CROSS!" was the main headline on the billboards. The buildings round Trafalgar Square had sandbags piled against their lower windows. Outside Charing Cross station an old man was walking slowly up and down with a board strapped to his back that said: "The End of the World is Nigh." Starlings intermittently clouded the air. They arranged for her to come up the following week and he would give her lunch and help her to find a flat.

"Darling, I wish I could take you down myself. But Hugh expects to go with me on Fridays—you know how it is."

"That's all right, darling. Of course I understand."

She understood, but it didn't stop her minding.

"You're the most understanding girl in the world," he said, as he put her in the train and handed her the paper he had bought for her. "Afraid there wasn't a *Country Life*."

"Never mind, I can read all about Malta getting the George Cross."

He bent to kiss her and then, as he straightened up, began fumbling in his pocket. "I nearly forgot." He put three half crowns onto her lap.

"Darling! What's this for?"

"For your taxi because I can't take you home."

"It's far too much. It won't be more than five bob."

"The third one is the Edward medal for bravery," he said. "For enduring that really ghastly lunch—and everything. I must fly, I'm late for Hugh already."

Her eyes filled. "Fly," she said.

After he had gone and the train had begun to lumber slowly over the river, she sat looking out of the window (there were other people in the carriage by then) trying to sort out the confusion she felt about him. Resentment, anger, even, that she should have to have this baby without his public support, that she should have so much financial anxiety, all the business of having to find somewhere to live, setting up there by herself with four children to worry about—she didn't know how on earth she would be able to pay the school fees for the three boys, let alone this new one. Angus's parents had offered a small sum for the eldest, but they had no money either, simply the same ideas as Angus had had about Eton being the only suitable school. Frustration: here she was after a four-year affair—*more* than four years, actually—and no nearer getting him to leave his wife and marry her, although I didn't always want *that,* she thought. When she had first met him she had simply fallen head over heels; he had seemed the most attractive man she had ever met, and Angus, she had recognized then (how funny that it hadn't occurred to her before), was absolutely no good in bed at all. He had been rigidly romantic, had taken up with her because she had reminded him of an actress he had seen and adored in a play by Barrie, but when it came to sex he embarked upon it seldom, apologetically and as speedily as possible in the dark, as one displaying an unfortunate but undeniable weakness which he wished to involve her with as little as he could contrive. Edward also seemed to consider that sex was largely for men, but, when the first-time rapture had worn off, although she had had to admit that he did not seem to apprehend her feelings with the attention to detail that would have been satisfying, he *enjoyed* himself so openly and so much that she had fallen back upon a kind of maternal indulgence with him. He undressed and admired her, he never failed to say afterwards how marvellous it had been for him and how wonderful, in every way, she was, that she had found it quite easy to lie back and think not of England but of him. And he had given her a very good time in other ways. Apart from the restaurants, the dancing, the presents, and the feeling that being with him was like one of the birthdays he always claimed to be having, she was attracted by his desire for her—by the obvious fact that he was attractive to nearly every woman he met but had stayed with *her,* which gave her a sensation of power and identity. Of course there had been times when she had wondered how faithful he *was,* but here her slowly growing long-term ambitions about him intervened. To be broadminded about any possible—although unconfirmed—lapse seemed the best policy. Since Angus had died the reasons for wanting to be married to Edward had become so diffused and so uncomfortably complex that, when any of them arose, she bundled them up into dark corners beneath the protective umbrella of what she evolved to herself as her undying love for him. Of course he was her great love: she had had one if not two of his children; she had spent four years patiently being available for him whenever he wanted her; her entire life had revolved round his presence, his absences, his needs and his restrictions. She had never looked at anyone else, and she was forty-two and so, she felt, was unlikely to start now. She *was* deeply, irrecoverably devoted to him. When, as now, some demonic shred of doubt tried to voice itself—that there was something, somehow, not quite right about the affair—she banished it: if there was anything wrong she was determined not to find out what it was. She loved him, that was all that she was prepared to know.

"*Did* you tell her?"

"I couldn't, old boy—I really couldn't. I fully intended to, but for various very good reasons, it simply wasn't practicable." Then seeing his brother's face, which was full of accusing incredulity, he said, "She's having a baby any minute, for God's sake—"

"You never told me that!"

"Well, I'm telling you now. I simply can't upset her. Anyway," he said, moments later, "she knows the form. I've never lied to her."

There was a silence. He had managed to get as far as Lea Green without having this conversation by talking feverishly about an office matter where they were not in agreement, but he had known that Hugh would ask him. Just as he knew that any minute now he'd ask the next question.

"Is it yours?"

"Yes."

"God! What a mess!" Then he noticed that his brother, extracting a cigarette from the packet with one hand while gripping the steering wheel with the other, was shaking and, with an effort, he added. "Poor old boy! It must be a nightmare!" and with a further effort, for he could not imagine that one would have someone's baby if it was not so, he said, "You must be very much in love with her."

And Edward answered gratefully, "You bet! I have been for a long time."

After that, as they drove back to the house that did not have Sybil in it, Hugh said no more on the subject.

"My dear Miss Milliment! *When* did this happen?"

"Oh—a little before Christmas, I *think*. I know there was still quite a remarkable display of berries on the holly, and those snowdrops outside the table door were not out, so I think it must have been about then. I used my suitcase as a prop and it seemed to serve quite well for a while, until, as you can see, it has unfortunately given way under the strain."

It had indeed. The moment Villy had entered Miss Milliment's room in the stables' cottage, she had realized that it was not only her bed (the breakdown of which was the reason for her visit) that needed attention, it was all the furnishings, indeed, practically everything that Miss Milliment possessed. The wardrobe door hung drunkenly on one hinge and was open to reveal Miss Milliment's clothes, the same clothes that she had arrived with two years ago and that were not only palpably in need of cleaning but that she expected were, in many cases, beyond repair. The room had been hurriedly furnished then: the Duchy had arranged it, but her Victorian attitude about the bedrooms that were occupied either by grandchildren or servants meant that it had never contained more than the barest necessities and they had been composed of furniture that would, in any other circumstances, have been thrown out. Villy remembered that she had asked Miss Milliment whether she had a bedside lamp and a table to write at, and, when Miss Milliment had admitted that she had neither, had had these things sent over to the cottage. But she had never come to see for herself. She was ashamed.

"I am so sorry, Viola dear, to be such a nuisance."

"You aren't at all. It is my fault." She was kneeling by the bed trying to prise the jagged broken leg out of the suitcase whose lid it had penetrated, leaving the mattress sloping uncomfortably almost to the ground. "It must have been most dreadfully uncomfortable: I can't imagine how you slept a wink." She was unable to shift the broken leg and guilt about the whole situation made her say: "You really should have told me before!"

"I expect I should. In any case, it is not your fault, Viola. I cannot allow you to feel that."

And Villy experienced the fleeting sensation of being back in the schoolroom on those occasions when she had said one thing and felt another, and it had always been perceived.

She spent the rest of that day reorganizing Miss Milliment's room. This entailed first tackling the Duchy. There was plenty of furniture stored from Pear Tree Cottage that she could easily have taken without saying anything to her mother-in-law, but for another most embarrassing fact that had gradually emerged, which was that the servants had not been cleaning Miss Milliment's room, had done no more for her than place clean sheets at the bottom of the narrow cottage stairs each week. Her other laundry had been ignored, and Villy found the dank little bathroom full of stubbornly damp bloomers, vests and stockings that had been washed by Miss Milliment in the bath, but her capacity for housework, due to her age, bulk, short-sightedness and inexperience, had been negligible: the room was extremely dirty and smelt of old clothes.

"I'll clean out the room, Duchy dear, but I really think one of the maids ought to make her bed and dust, et cetera."

The Duchy was angry and rang for Eileen. "Servants have always been naughty about governesses," she said.

"I shouldn't have thought that either Dottie or Bertha was old enough to have experienced a governess before."

"No, but it is tradition. They will have heard about them from Mrs. Cripps or Eileen. But don't *you* bother, darling. The maids can spring clean the room."

"As a matter of fact, I'd rather do it myself." She did not say that she couldn't bear Miss Milliment's pathetic squalor to be exposed to them, but the Duchy understood.

"Perhaps that would be best," she said. "Ah, Eileen, would you send Dottie and Bertha to me, please?"

Dinner-time that day in the kitchen was a tense affair. Dottie and Bertha were full of defiant and martyred excuses: nobody had *told* them to clean in the cottage, how were they to know? Nobody had told her to cook for a governess, either, Mrs. Cripps retaliated, but it stood to reason that anyone living in had to be catered to. Eileen said a number of times that it was nothing to do with her and she believed in minding her own business, but she couldn't help feeling sorry for the poor old lady. Bertha burst into tears and said whatever happened it was always her fault. Tonbridge reminded them that there was a war on, as a consequence of which, although moving furniture was not his place, he had naturally lent a hand with it when asked. Edie said nothing at all. If she so much as opened her mouth these days, Mrs. Cripps snapped her head off or made sarcastic remarks about people who left other people in the lurch simply for a bit of excitement and to doll themselves up in a uniform. She'd be gone in four weeks, she said to herself, and then they wouldn't see her for dust. Apart from Madam's plate, she'd broken a pudding basin, two cups and a jug that Madam used for flowers, as she jumped every time Mrs. Cripps called her and things just slipped from her hand. Tea was drunk and very few remarks were passed.

By lunch-time Villy had emptied the room of everything; Miss Milliment's possessions were laid upon a dust sheet on the floor of the small neighbouring bedroom, and she procured a bar of soap, a scrubbing brush and a pail. It was then that she discovered that the electric water heater in the bathroom had broken down and realized that poor Miss Milliment had been doing without hot water for goodness knows how long. She went back to the house and rang the builder for an electrician, borrowed Ellen's electric kettle from the nursery and set about the fairly unpleasant business of sweeping and then scrubbing the floor. The state of Miss Milliment's wardrobe appalled her, and she resolved to take her to Hastings or Tunbridge Wells to replenish it. She must have accumulated a number of clothes coupons by now, and if shops no longer contained garments that would fit her, they could buy some material and get it made up. Sybil would have helped in this, she thought, recognizing yet again how much she missed her. She had never been able to have much of a relationship with Zoë, and of course she was fond of both the Duchy and Rachel, but with Sybil she had been able to gossip, discuss their children and their own youth, their early married days and sometimes reminiscences that stretched back to before they had become Cazalets. Sybil's brother had been killed in the war; her mother had died in India when Sybil was three and she had been brought up almost entirely by a devoted ayah and her father's household servants until she reached the age of ten, when their father took her and Hubert back to England and left them there in the charge of his married sister, who despatched them both to boarding schools, where both were profoundly homesick. The holidays had only been better because they had each other, never getting on with their cousins: "We have our secret language, Urdu, which, of course, they couldn't understand, and so they hated us and my aunt blamed us for not getting on with them." She remembered Sybil's rather flat, very English voice when she said this, and had added that they spoke it far more than they did English, which they regarded as a foreign, boring grown-ups' language. But when she asked if Sybil could still speak it, she had said no—never since her brother died. He had died just before the Armistice: she had been in the throes of her grief when she had met Hugh.

She had become very close to Sybil in the last weeks, ever since the morning when she had gone into her room to see if she wanted breakfast in bed and found her sobbing.

"Shut the door!" she had cried. "I don't want anyone to hear." Villy did so and sat on Sybil's bed holding her until she had finished and said: "I thought I was getting better—but I'm not." There was a silence, and then, with eyes fixed upon Villy in such a way that she could not look away, she said: "I'm not, am I?" Before Villy could bring herself to reply, she said suddenly: "No, don't tell me. I don't want to know. I promised Hugh that—just because I've had a couple of bad nights . . . for goodness' *sake*, Villy, don't tell him I've been so low. Don't say *anything*—to *anyone*." And she, who knew that Hugh knew but had had a similar promise exacted from him, could only acquiesce in the marital labyrinth. She had talked to Dr. Carr—trying to get him to get them to talk to each other, to face reality, she remembered she had said because he had instantly replied: "Oh, Mrs. Cazalet, they're each facing *reality*. But they each think they are doing that for the other one. I wouldn't dream of interfering in that. They each think it's the last thing they can do for the other, you see." She was silenced. He had added that he could see she was doing a good job with the nursing.

She'd done her best. The one day a week that she had worked in hospitals for the Red Cross before the war had taught her much that was of use. Blanket bathing, turning the patient in bed and bedpans, all things that gradually became necessary, and Sybil preferred her to any other anxious, amateur kindness . . .

She had felt useful as, indeed, and of course to a lesser degree, she supposed she did now. She wondered whether Miss Milliment would have told anyone else about her bed or the lack of hot water. But there certainly would have been someone else; Edward would have married someone who would have had his children, engaged servants, ordered meals and gone to parties with him. Except now there were no parties to go to, and when she saw Edward, which was not even every weekend, they were hardly ever alone. Not that she particularly wanted *that*; one of the things she had noticed during this last year had been that Edward seemed less keen on all the bed stuff, which had been something of a relief. It did happen occasionally, of course, but she could see that there would come a time when it would probably hardly happen at all. When they retired for the night these days they seemed to have little to say: there were desultory conversations about the children; she had tried several times to get *him* to give Louise a good talking to about how irresponsible it was to go on trying to get work in the theatre—a grossly overcrowded profession if ever there was one—when she ought to be doing something for the war effort. He made excuses, tried to change the subject and once, when she got cross about it, simply said that Louise would be called up anyway when she was twenty, which was only a year away, and why shouldn't she have some fun while she could? Which seemed to her to be a thoroughly frivolous attitude to have about one's daughter.

Louise . . . She was really becoming quite out of hand. She insisted upon living in London, where, although she said she was always to be on the point of getting some theatre job, it never actually happened: she had done one or two small parts in broadcast plays, but otherwise she was always talking of the auditions she went to, and the people she met who were considering her for a part. She went about London with her hair streaming down her back, in *trousers*, most of the time wearing far too much make-up. Villy had had what seemed to her the extremely sensible idea of Louise living with Jessica in the grandparents' house in St. John's Wood but, much to her chagrin, neither Louise nor (more surprisingly) Jessica had seemed at all keen on the notion. Jessica had made all kinds of excuses, the main one being that she did not want the responsibility, and Louise had declared that she simply couldn't bear to: she was going to share a flat with her friend Stella and be free to do as she liked. And before she could object to this, Edward had anted up the thirty shillings for rent and Louise had moved in. And goodness knows what they get up to, Villy thought— staying up all night probably and not making themselves proper meals. And then there was Michael Hadleigh. His mother, Lady Zinnia, had rung up once enjoining her not to allow Louise's heart to be broken by her son, which she had added, was constantly happening with girls. "But what on earth can I do about it?" Villy had asked herself. She felt ambivalent about Michael: on the one hand, Louise was far too young to be seriously pursued; on the other, he was a damn sight better than those awful actors she had got involved with in Devon. But he was far too old for her, and in any case she was not old enough for anyone—yet. More likely to turn her head than break her heart, Villy reflected bitterly: hearts were secretly (and rather horribly) a sore subject for her and, like most sore subjects, one that she dwelt upon a very great deal. There had been an accident in London that she had found so shocking that even now—weeks later—she was quite unable to think clearly about it, as when she tried she seemed prey to a kind of double vision, of how something that she had imagined would be wonderful, and what had actually happened.

It was to do with Lorenzo, of course. He had sent one of his rare postcards (inside a envelope), inviting her to a concert he was conducting in a church in London where, he said, a small choral piece of his own was to have its first performance. She was enthralled at the prospect. He had, rather surprisingly, asked her to ring him at home to say whether she could come—ordinarily it would have been out of the question as the jealousy (unnecessary, of course) of poor Mercedes was invariably inflamed by the most innocent telephone calls to her husband. But Mercedes turned out to be in hospital "so I am able to invite you to supper after the concert," he had said. This meant staying the night in London. Her first thought had been to stay with Jessica, who she felt was rattling about in their parents' house in St. John's Wood, but when she had rung once and got no reply, she had second thoughts. If she stayed *there*, Jessica might say she wanted to come to the concert as well and that would spoil everything. Hugh would have her. She would go up in the morning, do some shopping, perhaps have lunch with Hermione and then go to Hugh's house to bath and change for the concert. She arranged with Rachel and Zoë that between them they would do everything that Sybil required, obtained a latch key from Hugh and settled into a few days of glorious anticipation of her treat. An evening with Lorenzo, a concert, supper alone with him (they had only ever managed one tea together when he had so enchantingly accompanied her half-way to Sussex in the train), time, at last, in which they could discuss all the romance and despair of their attachment, their previous and lifelong commitment and their mutual integrity. She spent two evenings trying on her clothes to see what would be most, as she put it to herself, suitable, decided that nothing would really do, and planned a delicious excursion to Hermione's shop. After all, she had not had anything new to wear since before Roly. She rang Hermione, who said, what perfect timing, she had just got her summer collection into the shop and added that she would provide lunch. Those days of waiting until *the* Thursday made her realize how entrenched she had become in routine and duty, how beset by insignificant but necessary detail and how tired it had all made her feel. For those three mornings she woke full of energy and resolution, looking forward to each day that brought her meeting with Lorenzo nearer. She told Edward, of course, that she was coming to London, and exactly what she was going to do and he was nice about it—said he hoped she'd have a splendid time and gave her twenty-five pounds to buy "the dress you'll want but feel you can't afford." But everyone was nice about it. "I must say you're extremely *sparkly*," Lydia remarked when Villy was trimming the split ends of her long hair. "I always thought grown-ups had fun all the time, but you don't, do you? You hardly have a *speck* of fun. I suppose having such a good character is a bit of a drawback. Mum! You know that awful very very old lipstick you only used to wear for going to the theatre, the very dark red one in a gold case that there's only about a quarter of an inch of left?"

"How do you know so much about my lipstick?"

"I just happened to see it. One day. When I happened to be near your dressing table. Well. I wondered if you would sort of *lend* it to me. You never wear it any more and Louise said it was the wrong colour for your skin anyway."

"What do you want it for?" Even Louise's remark did not irritate her in her present mood.

"To practise with. I mean, one day, quite soon really, I'll be wearing all that kind of thing and when I do I definitely don't want to look like a beginner. So I just thought I could practise, you know, in the evenings when nobody would notice."

Why not? she thought. The children did not have much fun either: no parties with conjurers and crackers or treats about London. "But you must only do it in the evening before you have your bath," she said.

"I absolutely faithfully *promise*." It would mean having more baths than she cared for, she thought, but it was worth it.

Eventually, at last, it was Thursday morning. "You deserve a treat," Sybil had said when she slipped in to say goodbye to her. "It's sad you won't be dining with Hugh, but you'll have breakfast with him. And you'll be able to tell me truthfully whether Mrs. Carruthers is looking after him properly."

"You're not to worry about *anything*," Rachel had said. "Just enjoy yourself."

"I shall!" she had exclaimed. She felt joyful—and quite unlike her usual self.

It was a beautiful day: the sun shone, the sky was clear with small skittish white clouds, forsythia glistened in back gardens. She caught the train that people working in London caught and it was full of people reading their morning papers. "Princess Elizabeth registers for war service," she read over someone's shoulder. I must buy some scent, she thought. Her old bottle of Coty's L'Origan had gone dark brown and smelt only as though it had once been scent. She wore a very old black and white printed frock that she had bought from Hermione before the war; for some reason, she always felt that when she went to buy clothes there she must wear something previously bought from her. She didn't have a decent pair of stockings, but had packed some old beige silk ones in case she was unable to buy any new. Beige went with anything, she thought, a trifle uncertainly; pale stockings had always been the thing when she was young, and she had found it difficult to change. Her mother had always said that the peachy shades favoured before the war were *extremely* common: it was palest beige for the young, and pale grey for the old. Hermione wore flesh-coloured stockings, but she was the kind of person who could have worn any stockings—even *black* ones—and look both glamorous and well bred. She thought—not for the first time—of the occasion when Diaghilev, tapping one of her knees with his cane, had said, "Pas mal, ma petite, pas mal." This, considering that he thought a woman's knees the ugliest part of her anatomy, had been praise indeed. But, of course, it was usually ankles that people went on and on about and hers were definitely *not* good. But Lorenzo, who never seemed to take his burning eyes off her face, would not notice them. Their relationship, she thought happily (then), was literally on a higher plane.

The session with Hermione was utterly enjoyable, bounded only by how many clothes coupons she had, although Hermione mentioned in passing that they might be able to make the coupons go a little further than they had been designed to do. "Of course, we only do it for our favourite customers, don't we, Miss MacDonald?" and Miss MacDonald, who must hardly ever have needed any clothes coupons at all since she seemed always—for years now—to be wearing the same tailored pinstripe coat and skirt, smiled obediently and said, "Of course we do, Lady Knebworth." She tried on dozens of things—well, probably about a dozen, but some things she put on twice so it seemed like dozens. Hermione seemed to know how starved she'd felt for new clothes, and encouraged her to try things, even when she knew they would not really suit. "I must be sensible!" she kept saying as she stroked the most beguiling dark blue chiffon blouse that tied in a large floppy bow at the neck.

"Well, darling, if you had the navy suit, and really you *must*, you look a dream in it—you could have the blouse which would see you right through the summer, and then *somewhere*—fetch it, would you, Miss MacDonald—we have a perfectly divine sharkskin shirt, rather manly with cufflinks that you could wear with the suit in the autumn. And after *that*, any old cashmere . . ."

She bought the suit. And a crêpe dress that was a kind of mushroom colour trimmed with a dull orange velvet ribbon with padded shoulders and a cape sleeve. She bought both blouse and shirt, and finally a summer jacket or short coat made in a soft silvery colour that was neither blue nor grey. And Hermione *gave* her two pairs of stockings that were as fine as cobweb; they were made of nylon, she said, and had been sent from America. "Americans are so amazingly generous—I get absolutely deluged with them," she had said. She also most kindly showed her how to put them on, which was helpful as they were so thin that Villy had felt they would snag if she touched them. "You turn the foot part inside out, like this, and whatever you do sit *down* when you put them on. But they're marvellous: they last far longer than ours. I've never understood the patriotism of bare legs—especially with the ghastly regulation length of skirts these days."

The morning cost her forty-four pounds—Hermione's clothes were always priced in guineas—but she felt elated rather than extravagant. "Miss MacDonald will pack them up for you while we have lunch."

Lunch was at a little restaurant that Hermione described as her standby. They seemed to know her very well there, and rushed to serve them. "Don't bother with the menu," Hermione said. "They'll bring us much nicer things if we don't."

They began with some sort of pâté—"It's probably made of field mice or hedgehogs, but it tastes delicious"—followed by grilled trout and a salad. Hermione made them wrap up the trout carcasses for the shop cat, a stray that she had found weeping, she said, in Hyde Park. "Riddled with worms and covered with fleas, but such a darling. She gives poor old Miss MacDonald fearful hay fever, but it can't be helped." Hermione was known for being kinder to animals than employees, although she inspired devotion in both.

"Is Edward taking you somewhere nice tonight?" she enquired when they got to coffee.

"He's away, in Liverpool, I think, looking at a shipment of wood. I came up for a friend's concert," she added, as airily as she could manage, but felt herself beginning to blush.

Hermione regarded her with cool grey eyes. "What a good thing," she said.

After lunch she said she would like to do a little shopping in Bond Street and collect her clothes in a taxi afterwards. She bought make-up and a new swansdown powder puff in a chiffon handker-chief and a stick of solid eau de cologne for Sybil to rub on her forehead. There wasn't any scent to be had except lavender water, the only scent that her mother had approved of for girls. But I feel like a girl, she thought. It was strange and delightful not to find that a visit to London must entail a wearisome family shopping list: Start-rite shoes for Wills and Roly, summer vest for Aunt Dolly, esoteric haberdashery for the Duchy (fearful things like dress preservers), BBs for Clary and Polly, a hunt for razor blades for the men, who were always short of them these days—oh, all that stuff that would have taken the whole day and left her exhausted. She was *not* going to survey the dusty house in Lansdowne Road; she was not going to have an uneasy lunch with Louise when the conversation would have consisted in her asking questions that Louise did not wish to answer. She was *not* going to see Jessica in St. John's Wood, which would have entailed criticism of her sister—Jessica seemed to have a series of small voluntary jobs that she could do when she pleased and not when she didn't—and would have ended in resentment and envy. None of any of that. Instead, she bought presents: a café au lait straw hat for Lydia with a wreath of cornflowers, buttercups and poppies round it. Jacqmar scarves for Rachel and Zoë, lavender water for the Duchy, a box of chocolates for Aunt Dolly and Dinky cars for Wills and Roly.

In the taxi, after she had picked up her clothes from Hermione and was bowling along Bayswater Road thinking how much prettier Kensington Gardens looked now that they had taken all the little railings away from each side of all the paths, she remembered that she had bought nothing for the girls: she would have to do that in the morning.

The taximan helped her into the house with her boxes and parcels. "I can see it's Christmas for some," he said. "We don't know what the hubby's going to say to all that, do we? Oh, well, it's what women are for, isn't it? Men make it, the ladies take it. *I* don't know. Thank you, madam."

Hugh's house was tidy, and reasonably clean, but it had the neglected air of a house hardly used. The spare room was on the top floor and there was a bathroom on the half landing below it. When she had bathed and dressed in the navy suit and chiffon blouse, she decided that she wanted, needed a drink. As the time to go to the concert drew nearer, and therefore seeing and subsequently being with Lorenzo, she had begun to feel nervous. Hugh would not mind her taking a drink, indeed he had said how sorry he was that he couldn't get back in time to have one with her before her concert.

The shutters were closed in the drawing room and the drinks cupboard contained a number of bottles that had clearly not been used for some time, and were mostly almost empty, but she found a little gin left in one and a sticky bottle of Angostura, so she made herself a pink gin and took the glass back upstairs to fill with water from the bathroom. Armed with this and a cigarette, she tackled the business of her new make-up. She overdid it, wiped it all off with cold cream and started again. Her second attempt was not much better: she realized that she had not really *looked* at her face for some time (and for her, looking meant criticism). Now she could see that her lips had become much thinner, which she supposed must have happened when she had had to have practically all her teeth out; that the lines that ran down from each side of her nose to her mouth were not only more pronounced but reached down below it which in repose gave her an air of discontent. She smiled, but the smile seemed artificial, which it was; she could find nothing to smile at. Her eyes and her cheekbones were the same and, of course, she still had her widow's peak which grew maddeningly a little off centre. Her hair was whiter, which was an improvement on the oyster-shell colour it had been for years, and it was comfortingly thick and naturally curly. Her face was one which was better when animated. She was not, never had been, the classic beauty that Jessica was. These unsatisfactory reveries were interrupted by a sudden fear that she would not get a taxi at the rank in Ladbroke Grove, and would be late for the concert.

But she did, and she wasn't.

The concert was well attended; the church was nearly full and the choir—about sixty of them, already in place—were sitting in three rows in a semi-circle round the space where the orchestra was to be situated. They all wore white shirts and long black skirts or trousers according to their sex. They all looked tired, but since nearly all choirs were amateur they would have done a full day's work before coming to sing and, in any case, the light shed from the high brass chandeliers was not flattering. She looked at the thin piece of paper with the programme mimeographed in purple ink upon it. Purcell, Bantock, Clutterworth, she read, *The Temptations of St. Anthony*. The players— not very many of them; it was a chamber orchestra of minimal size—were taking their places, and then *he* appeared in his black tailcoat and white tie. There was a small flurry of applause and as he turned to the audience to acknowledge it she thought she saw her, but she was not sure.

"Indeed I saw you at *once*," he said, "my Good Angel," and he squeezed her hand again so that her rings hurt. They were sitting in a taxi by then—alone at last.

"Where are you taking me?" she asked, full of excitement at the thought of their candlelit supper in some discreet restaurant.

"Aha! You will see, you will see," he replied, and she smiled indulgently—he seemed as excited as a boy, or as she was.

When the taxi stopped and he was paying it off, she recognized that they were in fact in Curzon Street, very near Hermione's shop, at the entrance to Shepherd Market. It would be too odd, she thought, if he was to take her to the same restaurant where she had had lunch.

"Give me your darling hand."

He led her through the wide arch into a narrow little street—everything was dark—through a doorway that seemed to be open, since he used no key, and up two flights of narrow and steep stairs.

"Where *are* you taking me to?" she had said, trying to sound merely curious and amused, but she could hear her voice and it did not sound like either of those things.

"This is our chance for a little privacy, my angel," he had answered as he fumbled with a key to a door on the landing they had reached. He switched on the light to reveal a small and cluttered room, its windows covered with blackout blinds, its floor crowded by a table, two chairs and a large divan bed without a cover. The table had two Chianti bottles with candles stuck in them, plates and glasses, there was a gas fire with a meter beside it and, above, a mantelpiece littered with dusty postcards. In one corner she observed a very small sink with an electric water heater, a draining board on which stood various pieces of unwashed crockery. He was busy with matches—lighting the fire and the candles on the table, little drifts of dust spurting from the shaggy carpet as he bustled about.

She stood uncertainly by the door, where he had relinquished her hand: she felt utterly confused—as though she might be on the brink of being quite out of her depth—with also an element of sheer disappointment. She had imagined a cosy, charming, romantic restaurant for their tête-à-tête, not this squalid little bed-sitting room with its stale and faintly nauseating air, but then *he* seemed so happy and excited and was almost pathetically doing the hostly honours: he was removing a paper napkin from a plate on the table to reveal a small pie and a pair of tomatoes and then rushing to the draining board by the sink where stood a bottle of wine in a bucket, and as he unwound the wire from the neck of the bottle she realized that it was champagne. Now he was advancing to the table, took out the handkerchief with which he had mopped his brow at the end of the concert and wrapped it round the bottle, "Hold out a glass, dearest, or we may lose some," and eased the cork till it emerged with a soft thud. "Ha *ha!*" he cried, as though amazed by his achievement. He filled both glasses to the brim and went down on his knee to hand her one of them. "At last!" he said, gazing at her with an ardent devotion that was both thrilling and familiar.

"Sit down, dear lady"—he had taken her hand again and was leading her to the divan—"it is more comfortable than those kitchen chairs."

He sat beside her. "Here's to us," he said huskily. They drank. The champagne, while not actually warm, was far from cold. He had put her at the pillow end of the divan, and she noticed that the sheet and pillow-case were distinctly grey. The thought occurred to her that perhaps he could not afford to take her out to dinner and that this was the best alternative he had been able to provide, and she said how grand it was to have champagne with which to celebrate his first performance that evening. "*Our* first performance," he said as he poured them more champagne. As she did not quite understand what he meant—was he going to dedicate *The Temptations* to her? (an intoxicating thought)—she smiled back at him and agreed when he suggested she should take off her jacket: the room was indeed becoming rather warm. Was he staying here while his wife was in hospital, and how was she, by the way?

No, no, he wasn't staying *here*, he had simply borrowed the place for the evening from a very good friend who was on tour. Mercy was having something done to her sinuses, he added, nothing serious, but they had been causing her trouble.

"But tonight we can leave all those cares behind us. We are as free as air. Oh, my beloved, if you only knew how much I have been longing for this night! Put down your glass and let me caress you!" and he seized her glass, put it on the floor and taking her head in his hands, proceeded to shower her face with kisses. He began in a romantic manner with her forehead, then her eyes, but when he reached her mouth she began to feel nervous and to fear that he might get carried away.

"We must be—" she managed to say, but he stopped her with surprisingly muscular lips, at the same time pushing her down so that she was half lying on the bed. "We can have our supper afterwards," he said.

Then, at last, and of course, she realized what he was up to—the reason that he had brought her to this awful little room. For suddenly not only the room, but the whole thing seemed awful: there ensued the most unseemly struggle, as she fought him off, sat upright, reminded him of all the responsibilities that they both had to other people, and how they had *agreed* that there was nothing to be done but endure them. To begin with he had simply responded as though she was shy—*coy* even, he had suggested (she was not flattered by this suggestion); but when she said that they had always known that their love must be platonic, he retorted that so far as he was concerned, that was simply because they had had no opportunity for anything better. It was not as though they were intending an *elopement*; he was the first person to see the impracticability of *that*; therefore a little roll in the hay which nobody would ever know about could surely do no harm? "I love you madly," he added.

"I love Edward," she had answered. This pair of half truths reassured neither of them. He was beginning to take offence, and *she*—she felt that everything was shattered, degraded from pure, romantic devotion to mere *lust*. It was disgusting; looking at him now, a little sweaty sulking man—how could she have attributed to him so much nobility and charm?—she felt a kind of confused despair, as she recognized that most of her relationship with him had been conducted in his absence. He was not, could never be the creature of her dreams. Her only desire was to go—to get out of this place.

He did not make that easy. He alternated offers of food and more drink with oblique accusations—nothing in her behaviour could possibly have led him to suppose that she did not like him—and, worse, kept reverting to the light-hearted romp theme. This both wounded and incensed her: the idea that she should ever be the object of somebody's passing fancy was so offensively at odds with the idea of her own nature, that she found it suddenly easy to get to her feet, announce her departure and refuse to allow him to see her to a cab.

It took her some time to find her way out of Shepherd Market which, though dark, seemed to be full of subterranean clubs, tarts placed at as regular intervals as lamp-posts, snatches of distant singing with the surging crescendos that implied drunkenness. It was very cold, the streets were full of sudden corners—the other side of one of them she nearly ran into a pair of American officers who had stopped to light cigarettes which was how she saw what they were.

"Excuse *me*, lady," one of them said. "Would you care for a drink?"

"No, thank you," she replied, and then something made her add, "I'm looking for a taxi," whereupon one of them said, "Brad! Let's find the lady a taxi."

And they did. Walked her to Green Park, waited with her until an empty cab came along, hailed it and put her in.

"Thank you very much," she said; she wanted to cry then from this unexpected kindness.

"Enjoy your ride." They stood watching, she saw, as she drove away.

In the cab she prayed that Hugh would have gone to bed, or that, as it was so early, he had not yet come home. But, of course, he was there, anxious to give her a drink and enquire after her evening, to talk to her about the next step in Polly's education. It was midnight before she was able to plead fatigue and escape to bed where she thought that after all the whisky she would mercifully just pass out, and this happened, but all too briefly: she woke to find that she had slept a mere two hours. The whisky after champagne on an empty stomach had done their worst: she had a raging thirst, her head ached, and when she put on the light and staggered down the stairs to the bathroom waves of nausea overcame her and she was painfully sick. Humiliation succeeded the nausea, and she sat shivering in bed, sipping water and miserably going over every detail of the ghastly evening. Of course she blamed him more, for flirting with her and calling it love; for being such a cheap little sham, as she put it. "A roll in the hay—a little fun on the quiet—*harmless* fun," as though making love to her would be of no consequence to either of them! He whom she had thought understood and appreciated her so well, had really had no more regard for her than he clearly had for any woman he thought might be available. She cried—with difficulty since she also felt so angry and humiliated. For months she had lived in a dream world inhabited by this secret life which she had been able to enjoy because its consummation had been out of the question. The private conviction from which she had always suffered, that her life was some kind of tragedy since the essential element had been missing, returned to her now in all its dreary familiar force. To be mutually in love and to have to renounce it was one thing; to discover that the frightful disparity of their feelings for each other precluded what she thought of as love was another. It was clear now that he had felt merely lust, a sensation that she recognized as a weakness common to many men, but which had never meant anything at all to her.

The idea that he should expect her to take off her clothes and lie in that bed with its squalid, anonymously used sheets kept recurring, filling her with a kind of enraged shame. Why had she not realized when she walked into that awful little room what he intended? It was true, of course, that he *had* agreed with her that their feelings for one another could never "come to anything," but lurking in the back of her mind was the embarrassing fact that this had only been mentioned once, on the day that they had had tea together at Charing Cross and he had accompanied her part of the way home on the train; all other allusions to it had occurred during her imaginary conversations with him. This was the hardest part to bear since it made her feel such a *fool* . . .

At least, she thought, as the train rumbled slowly out of Charing Cross and over the river, nobody need ever know; it could hardly have been an episode that *he* would wish to recount to anybody.

"I kept you up too late," Hugh had said at breakfast (tea and toast that he had burned, rather, under the grill and the bright yellow margarine that Mrs. Cripps used only for cooking at home). "I'm afraid the marmalade has run out."

At the station, he tucked one of her dress boxes under his arm and carried her case with his good hand. "Tell Sybil that I'll be down tomorrow evening," he had said as the train began to move. Then he had smiled his very sweet, rather melancholy smile and added, "And bless you for all your nursing."

This tribute brought tears to her eyes. At least I am of some use, she thought, as the contrast between how she had felt coming over this same bridge yesterday and how she felt now overcame her.

Lydia came with Tonbridge to the station to meet her. "I wanted to be the first person to see you," she said. "Goodness, Mummy! You *do* look tired! Did you have a lovely time?"

"Yes, thank you."

"Well, if you ask me, pleasure doesn't seem to agree with you. You looked much better before you went."

"Don't be silly, darling. I just had rather a bad night."

"Anyway, I'm terrifically pleased you're back."

She was moved. Here was another person who needed her. "You'll be saying in a minute that nothing at home's the same without me," she said.

But Lydia instantly replied, *"It's* the same. I'm not."

Clary

Summer, 1942

Don't you think, Archie, that politicians particularly say very silly things? I mean, nobody would think for a moment that you'd *train* people to play tiddlywinks—certainly not millions of grown-up American men. I have my doubts about public utterances generally. They are a bit like shouting something boring to extremely deaf people, aren't they?"

It was being a thoroughly grown-up evening, and she didn't want him to think that she didn't know about conversation—particularly as Polly wasn't helping at all: she simply smiled and chose things to eat and ate them. She looked awfully pretty in a pale yellow dress with a lace collar and a little black taffeta bow with streamers.

"But, then, Harry Hopkins is a very unserious name for a politician, isn't it? He sounds much more like somebody from Ridgways Late Joys."

"He does, indeed. That was fun, though, wasn't it?"

"Oh, *yes!* It was. Was it really like Victorian music hall?"

"Well, even I am not old enough to have been to that, but yes, I think it's probably a fair imitation. Who did you like best, Poll?"

She thought, and a strawberry fell off her spoon, but not into her lap like it would have with me, Clary thought, just onto her plate again.

"I am so fond of pleasure that I cannot be a nun," Polly said. "I thought Nuna Davey was wonderful and it was a really funny song."

"We have a rather ghastly cousin who wanted to be a nun once," Clary informed him. She had spilled strawberry ice-cream—that went with the strawberries—down the front of her dress just above where her napkin was, of course, and before that, during the hors d'oeuvres, a bit of Bismarck herring had slid off her fork and landed on a different bit of the plain dark blue velveteen that Polly had advised her to wear: "You look your best in plain things," she had said, but it was now *un*plain in a most unfortunate way. She found it very difficult to think *and* talk *and* eat at the same time, and whereas at home one could do these things in comfortable turn, out to dinner in a posh restaurant she felt one was meant to manage all three. But I just haven't had the practice, she thought.

"I thought Leonard Sachs was marvellous, too. Making things up to say all the time, and answering people back and being funny. I should like to go every night."

"But since she's been nursing, she's reputedly fallen in love with a frightfully wounded patient, and of course if she marries him, being a nun will be out of the question." She gave Polly a severe glance for changing the subject. Polly smiled apologetically and stroked her hair. They had both had perms—their first—when Archie had invited them to London. Polly's had been a terrific success, Clary thought: she had set it in a thick page-boy bob with a delicate little fringe curling round her forehead, but hers had gone into awful ripples like a cheap doll's and she hated it. It was funny: she had never minded about anything like that before. She looked up from her plate, and found Archie regarding her.

"I suppose you feel I've changed the subject," she said, "but you didn't seem awfully interested in American politics."

"Let's *not* talk about the war," Polly said. "People do all the time and it doesn't make it any better. One of the reasons why we wanted to see you without the children was that we wanted to have a very serious conversation with you."

She agreed with this. "And it would have been impossible with *them*."

"Of course, Simon isn't exactly a child, but he's away at school. Anyway, his interests are different. But Neville and Lydia . . ." Polly left their hopeless immaturity to his imagination.

"It would have been simply a children's outing, and *we* take *them* on those," Clary finished. "It's absolutely no fun for us, I can tell you."

"Right," Archie said. "Let me just order the coffee and then we shan't be interrupted. Would anybody like a Grand Marnier?"

"Yes, please," they both said, and then Clary added, "You see, a case in point. If you'd offered us that in front of them there would have been an awful rumpus with them saying it wasn't fair and why couldn't they have one when, of course, they are far too young."

"*Far* too," Polly agreed.

When the coffee and liqueurs had arrived, and Archie had offered them both a cigarette, which they both refused—Polly because she had promised her father not to smoke until she was twenty-one, and Clary because she had tried one and need never try one again—Polly said, "You explain, Clary, you're far better at it than me."

So she told him how it was felt that they were getting too old simply to do lessons any more with Miss Milliment, but that although there was general agreement about that, there was no agreement at all about the alternative. "The Duchy thinks we could perfectly well stay at home and help with the children and have French lessons with a ghastly person who lives quite near whose breath smells and who laughs at absolutely everything, and Aunt Villy and Aunt Rachel think we should go to the same cooking place that Louise went to to learn cooking and household management when neither of us is in the least interested in any of that, and Polly's father thinks we should learn shorthand and typing so that we can be useful when we're called up, and Miss Milliment thinks that we ought to work frightfully hard and try to get into a university—at least that's something she wished *she*'d done, instead of like the others, just making us do things they've *had* to do, and Aunt Dolly thinks we ought to get married to some nice man—" She started to giggle. "I *ask* you! Of course, she only got asked what she thought out of politeness . . ." She had run out of people, "and that's what *they* all think," she finished.

"And what do you both want to do?"

She looked at Polly who said at once, "You go first, Clary."

Not for the first time that evening, she wished that she had Archie to herself, because she didn't feel that Polly wanted the same things. However, she did her best.

"What I *want* is to get a huge lot of *experience*. I'm just running out of any at home, you see. I mean, anything new I learn is nearly always from books, which is interesting but it isn't the same, because if those things happened to me I don't know if I would have agreed that that's how it was. Polly says she doesn't know what she's here *for*, and I'm coming round to agreeing with her. About me, I mean. We're not like Louise, you see. She's always wanted to be an actress."

"You could be a writer," Polly reminded her. "You used to say that was what you wanted to be."

"Well, I'm not so sure now. I have the uneasy feeling that people have already written everything. I do write, of course, but Louise does that too. She's always writing plays, but it's not her main thing. So I feel extremely muddled about it all. But *not* knowing doesn't mean I want to be frog-marched into some boring enterprise that they think would be good for me. What they mean is that it would be safe and dull and wouldn't actually be bad. I'm not very interested in safety."

"One thing we thought," Polly said, "would be for Clary and me to have a little house in London where we could live on our own."

"What would you live *on?*" Archie enquired.

"Oh, easy! We both have allowances now. Forty-two pounds a year each. If we didn't buy clothes and things, we could easily pay for food and electric light and all that sort of thing. And if it wasn't enough," she added seeing Archie's face, "we could get jobs in a shop."

"Or, *you* said," Polly reminded her, "that bus conductors get two pounds ten a week and with the war going on like this they would probably take women to be them."

"And Poll says she wants to go to parties because we never have much since we were children."

"Well, *you* want to go to them too."

"Only to meet people in more walks of life," she said.

Afterwards, she thought that Archie had been a very good listener. He never interrupted, or pooh-poohed anything. He made them go through the cons of each idea that had been presented: "You've only told me the pros," he said, "and they might be because you haven't noticed the cons."

So they went through it all. It was agreed that they didn't want to stay at home, but learning French would be a good thing wherever they were. They agreed that it *might* be useful to learn how to cook, but it wasn't only cooking, it was learning how to interview servants and ironing ghastly complicated clothes they would never have. "Anyway, Polly doesn't want servants in her house when she has one, and I may easily become a socialist because they are keener on being fair to people, and we can always eat out of tins or make sandwiches which we both adore." They could neither of them see much of a pro in the domestic science school. When it came to learning shorthand and typing they were on weaker ground. Archie pointed out that when they *were* called up, having some skill like that would almost certainly give them a better chance of an interesting job. "Although," she had said, "I don't think women are allowed to *do* any really interesting jobs. They're allowed to get killed in a war, but not to do any of the killing back. Another injustice for you."

"You know perfectly well, Clary, that you would absolutely loathe to kill anyone."

"That's not the point. The point *is* that if women had an equal responsibility about wars, we probably wouldn't have them. That's my view."

"She half wants to be a pacifist—like Christopher—and I agree with that in a way," Polly said. "But she also wants to be able to fly aeroplanes and be in command of a submarine, which, you must agree, Archie, isn't very logical."

"All the same, I do sort of see what she means," Archie replied.

Clary glowed: the most understanding person she had ever met. "One can have contingency wishes," she said; she was trying to lick her fingers in an unnoticeable manner, but she saw them both watching her. "Isn't it extraordinary how Grand Marnier gets on the outside of the glass? It's surprising there's any left inside at all."

Archie said that leaving aside how they would like life to be, they had to consider what it was, and perhaps, given the status quo, they might consider a secretarial course useful. The university idea was ruled out. "We haven't even passed School Cert," she said, "and I have the feeling that for years and years we've been learning all the wrong things to get us to pass that."

"It's just poor Miss Milliment wanting us to have what *she* wanted," Polly said. "She's far brainier than us. She has *taught* us things," she added, "it's just that mostly they aren't of the kind that would pass exams."

"Where are we going now?" she asked as they walked down the dark narrow street from the restaurant.

"Home, I thought. Did you have any other ideas?"

"I slightly—only *faintly*—hoped we might be going to a night club."

"I'm afraid we aren't tonight. I don't belong to one, you see. But if you're very keen, I'll join one and take you at a later date."

"I'm not all *that* keen. Only Louise went on and on about it, and she went once after going to the Late Joys. I suppose you couldn't take *two* women to one, anyway."

"Why not? I should think it would be twice as much fun."

"It would be very awkward for the person you weren't dancing with," Polly said. "They might get kidnapped."

"That would be me," she said at once. "I'm rotten at dancing. I can't really see the point of it."

"We didn't go to a night club," she wrote in her diary. "Just as well, really, as they are reputed to be extremely boring places—only much good for people who want to drink a lot and be in love."

She looked at this for some time wondering what either of these things would be exactly *like*. It seemed to her that you could do either or both anywhere, you didn't have to go to a night club for them, so there must be something else about NCs that wasn't mentioned. Oh, well. It was probably all part of the general conspiracy—a club as well, really—that neither she nor Polly seemed able to get into, and probably never *would* get into until they'd had some of the mysterious experiences that were never talked about, except with each other. It couldn't be simply connected (as they had once thought) with age: they were both seventeen and if that wasn't grown up, what on earth was?

Archie's flat is very nice [she wrote]. We spent the night there. He kindly gave Polly and me his bed, and he slept on the sofa in his sitting room, which wasn't long enough for him, poor Archie, and he said his neck felt like a coat hook at breakfast. I *knew* that Polly and I should have had separate evenings with him, and then one of us could have had the sofa and he could have stuck to his bed. But although it is quite small, and it was a furnished flat, he has somehow made it nice and like he is. He showed us a cupboard in the passage in the hall crammed with the bits of furnishing he couldn't bear. There was an awful lampshade with ships in full sail on it, all dark parchment and coffee-bean coloured ships, and a boxful of china rabbits all pale blue and getting larger and larger but otherwise the same, and a carpet with what Archie calls post-Picasso zig-zags all over it in fruit juice colours—things like that. But Archie has put red baize tablecloths over the worst tables and he bought an amazing picture by a painter called Matthew Smith—terrific reds and deep blues of a rather fat person asleep which he's hung over the fireplace and he painted the walls white himself which makes it all much lighter. The bathroom has a salmon and black bath which apparently was once fashionable. He says the only thing to do is to laugh at it, but there was rose geranium Morny soap and the water was far hotter than at home. For breakfast we had toast and potted meat and tea. Then Archie had to go to his office which is in the Admiralty. So Polly and I washed up breakfast and tidied everything up and then we went shopping and prowling until it was time to have lunch with Uncle Hugh at his club. Clubs again. His is called the In and Out because of it having two openings to the drive in front of the main door. Although there aren't being any raids on London at the moment, it does look very dusty and *tired*. We decided to go to Piccadilly Circus and see if Galeries Lafayette had anything nice we could afford—Poll bought her lemon dress there for five shillings so it can be a good place. On our way there, we sort of talked about Archie but only in a very superficial manner. For instance, I said I wondered how he ever did any shopping if naval officers aren't allowed to carry parcels, and Polly said they must change into their civilian clothes, or get their girl friends to do the shopping for them. I said I didn't think that Archie had a girl friend and Polly said how did I know, had he told me? He hadn't actually mentioned the subject, but of course if he had there would have been signs. Poll instantly said what *sort* of signs and I couldn't think of them, except pots of cold cream in the bathroom. Anyway, I said, people always talk about the person they're in love with—look at the way Louise goes on and on about boring Michael Hadleigh, and for all we knew Archie might be too old to have affairs. "He's not too *old!*" Polly cried. "He's actually, anyway, extremely *young* for his age."

But all through the morning Archie seemed to be in both our minds, because we kept referring to him—or rather, I think it was mostly Poll: she kept saying things like how did he have dinner every night as he didn't have a cook, and what did he do at weekends when he didn't come down to our house, and wondering what he did when he went to the Admiralty. All things she could have asked him herself, as I pointed out to her. She didn't answer.

The shopping wasn't a success. Galeries Lafayette didn't have anything we wanted; a shop called Huppert at the bottom of Regent's Street had a very pretty pink silk blouse that Polly longed for, but it was six pounds, "an astronomical sum for something that would only dress half of you!" she said sadly. I offered to lend her half the money, but she said better not, better to save the money for when we were living in London. We decided to walk to Uncle Hugh's club which faced Green Park. It was an interesting walk—past Fortnum and Mason and a very grand-looking bookshop and then a bombed church. There was ragwort and loosestrife growing out of bits of it as well as on the ground. We were rather early for lunch so Poll said why didn't we go and sit in the park opposite and we could decide how to tackle her father at lunch about us living in London. But I said I wanted to go into the Ritz because it was the poshest hotel and I'd never been inside it. "I'll just go to the lav," I said, "and if they don't seem to like me just doing that, I might have a gin and lime."

Poll was simply terrified by the idea and it made her angry. "It's stupid," she said. "People don't just walk into hotels—"

"Yes, they do! It's what they're for!"

"*Unless* they are going to stay in them. *Please* don't. I beg you not to."

So I didn't. Instead, we went and sat in Green Park and, after a bit of not talking, talked about how we could get our house. I said I thought it might be a good idea if Polly said she wanted to go to an art school, as the very word school seems to have a reassuring influence on the nervy grown-ups. Polly said the worst hurdle was if Uncle Hugh wanted us to live in his house with him and Uncle Edward.

Oh, well. We had a delicious lunch—crab salads and a wine called Leebfrowmilk, German, so of course I can't spell it; Uncle Hugh said it was a hock, whatever that may mean. He was very nice and treated us in a totally grown-up way *until* it came to us having a house whereupon he became all slippery and we'll-seeish, which in both our vast experience of this behaviour usually means no. He did say how lovely it would be for him if we lived in his house, and I could see Polly weakening which weakened me, because after all he *is* her father, and if Dad made the same proposition to me, of course I'd live with him. Of course I would. Only it wouldn't be the same, of course, because there would be Zoë. Perhaps she would stay in the country with Jules, and then it could be just Dad and me. And then Archie could come and live with us . . .

But for me to stay (with Polly) in Uncle Hugh's house will not be like that, and will certainly curtail our freedom, as I pointed out to Polly going back in the train. She said we'd have to see—a thoroughly Middle-Aged Remark—mutton talking lamb, I said to her, and she had to agree. But she said we could lobby some of the others although I haven't much hope of that producing the desired result: Aunt Villy is rather *snappy* these days, and Aunt

Rach doesn't ever seem to think things should be done because they might be *fun*, and Zoë has no real influence over anyone excepting Jules and that poor RAF man who is in love with her, if you ask me. And the Duchy—she can't help being old-fashioned as she is so old—thinks we don't need to go anywhere or do anything.

I don't plan to have any children, but if by some chance I do, there are some resolutions I shall make. No MARs like "we'll see," "it depends" or "all in good time". And no subjects that can't be talked about, and I shall *encourage* them to have adventures.

She read over what she had written to see whether it was right to put into the journal she was writing for Dad. Most of it was. She left out some of the bits about her and Polly and Archie, and the bit about living with him in his house, but Zoë being also there. Instead, she put in bits about the family, so that he would know as much as possible what had happened to them.

Ellen [she wrote] is getting pretty old. I suppose rheumatism makes people seem older than their years, and I don't know what Ellen's years are because she says it is none of my business, but she is very creaky and all the yellowish bits of her hair have gone, and it is now a sort of foggish white. Also, she has specs that Aunt Villy took her into Hastings to get, but she does not like wearing them except for sewing. She does look after Wills and Roly and Jules a lot of the time but Eileen helps her with the ironing because her legs won't stand it, she says. On her day off, she tends to put her feet up—not a very day-offish sort of thing to do. It must be fearful getting really old: it's extraordinary to think that we're doing that all the time without actually noticing. I wonder how much I have changed in two years since you last saw me, Dad. I mean, except for getting taller—I am half an inch at least taller than Zoë—I don't feel to myself to have changed much. I did have my hair permed last week, because Polly was having hers done and she thought it might make mine more interesting. It hasn't, at all. Instead of being straight as well as an extremely boring dark brown colour, it turned into sort of ghastly wiry waves that ended in fainting corkscrews, and every time I washed it, I had to wind those awful curlers that are made of something like lead encased in dark brown stocking stuff that hurt and dig into your head whichever way you lie in bed. So I got the hairdressing lady in Battle to cut it all off. She had to cut it quite short all over my head so now I look a bit like a golliwog as it sticks up everywhere. I don't seem to suit the ladylike things. Make-up, for instance. Polly, who is *immensely* pretty, now looks terrifically glamorous if she puts on eye-shadow and mascara and lipstick and stuff. I look idiotic. The mascara goes straight into my eyes and then they water and it runs down my face and the eye-shadow gets into that crease of my eyelid and I can't keep lipstick on for a second. Polly says you open your mouth and sort of pop the food in like a letterbox, but I forget. And powder seems to make my nose shinier in a luminous way. I think I'll just have to be like Aunt Rach and not wear any. So, Dad, in spite of that loony remark you made about me being beautiful—that day when we were getting water from the spring—I'm afraid I'm not turning out like that. I'm not like Polly. I was just about to write that she seems to be getting over her mother's death, but it seems a meaningless phrase to me. I don't think people ever *get over* something as terrible as that; it just slowly stops being the only or main thing in their mind, but when they remember it, they *feel* the same. Of course, what it amounts to is that I don't know what she is feeling because of not being her. But this is what makes people so interesting, don't you think, Dad? Most of the time one hasn't the slightest idea what other people are feeling, and sometimes one has the slightest idea, and I suppose, occasionally, one actually knows. Miss Milliment, with whom I have discussed this point, says that morality, or principles of one kind or another, are what is supposed to hold us all together, but they don't, do they? There was a huge air raid on a German city called Cologne last month (we are bombing the Germans all the time now, but this was an especially large raid with 1000 bombers and people were quite pleased and bloodthirsty about it). But either killing people is wrong or it isn't. I don't see how you can start making exceptions to that sort of rule; you might as well say that it isn't wrong, after all. I do find it terribly confusing. I do talk to Archie about this sort of thing when I am alone with him, but, of course, when we went to London and stayed with him, I never was. Polly *hates* talking about the war, she gets upset and keeps going off the track—like pointing out all the people we know who *wouldn't* kill people. When Archie came down for a weekend in the Easter holidays there had been a raid on a place in France called St. Nazaire—not so far from where *you* were, Dad, when you wrote me your love, and I felt he was very sad about something, and in the end he told me. They rammed this destroyer against the lock gates and so, of course, they couldn't get away from the Germans and they had mined the ship so that it would blow up at a certain time, and they invited many German officers on board for a drink before they were to be taken prisoner (the English, I mean—goodness! writing can be tricky) and so of course dozens of the Germans got blown up with the English. Archie knew one of them. Hardly anyone got away. Think of them all pouring out gins and being jolly and counting the minutes till they knew there would be the explosion. Archie said it was a kind of courage that made him feel very small. He says the Germans are just as brave—there's no difference, really. I can believe that because I've been reading a very good awful book called *All Quiet on the Western Front* which is about the First World War from the Germans' point of view. You would have thought, wouldn't you, that after so many people *knew* how awful and revolting and frightening war is that they'd agree not to have any more, but I suppose only a minority read books like that and the others get old and people don't believe them. Don't you think there is something quite wrong about our life span? If we lived for 150 years and didn't get too old for the first hundred, then there would be time for people to get sensible before they got like Lady Rydal or just too set in their bad old ways.

Oh, Dad, I can't help wishing you could say things back to me. Sometimes I feel that. Naturally I would rather you were at home and going to the office and coming down on Fridays and making jokes. The latter are rather few and far between these days. That's because you were always the funniest. *Are* . . .

This was getting out of hand, she thought. If Dad reads this when he comes back, I don't want him to feel I'm *anguished* or anything. Here she stopped altogether, because she found she was crying.

The Family

Late Summer – Autumn, 1942

Good Lord! Bit young, isn't she?"

"She's nineteen."

"He's a lot older, though, isn't he?"

"Thirty-three. Old enough to keep her on an even keel."

"Do you like him?"

"Hardly *know* him. I'm going down to Portsmouth tonight to discuss things. Sorry I can't dine with you, old boy, but he's going to sea again tomorrow and it's the only chance for us to meet."

"That's all right. Of course I understand. Good luck. Will you be back in time for the meeting with the Board of Trade? Because I'd quite like it if—"

"I'll be back. Two thirty, isn't it? I'll be back in time to have a bite with you first."

"Fine. Come to my club. Then we can walk to the meeting."

"Darling, how too too thrilling! Of course you must let me make the dress. She'd look divine in lace and luckily one doesn't need coupons for it. When is it to be?"

"Rather soon. In four weeks, actually. He has some leave then, so it seemed sensible. Could I stay a night with you? I've got to meet the in-laws to make some plans and I'm slightly dreading it."

"Are they not pleased?"

"They *seem* pleased. I said I thought she was a bit young, but Lady Zinnia seemed to think that was a good thing."

"She must be in favour, darling, I'm sure of that."

"Why?"

"It wouldn't be happening if she wasn't."

"Oh."

"She utterly adores Michael. *He's* angelic—you'll love him."

"Well, of course I've *met* him. He's been down to stay once or twice."

"No, I mean the Judge, Peter Storey. Her husband. I used to know him years ago. He's a charmer. When do you want to come?"

"As soon as you can have me. There's going to be so much to do."

"You are happy about it, aren't you? I can't help feeling a bit responsible as I introduced them."

"I think so, but she does seem terribly young . . ."

"Oh, Kitty dear, you must be *so* relieved. It began to look as though she was going to be left on the shelf like yours truly, didn't it?"

"Dolly dear, it's not Rachel who is getting married, it is Louise."

"Louise?"

"Edward's eldest daughter."

"That poor motherless child! Surely she's too young."

"No, Dolly, you're thinking of Polly. This is Villy and Edward's child—Louise."

"Well—I still think she's too young. And I shall need a hat. Flo used to be so wonderful with hats. I always said she could make a hat out of anything. 'Give you a few yards of petersham and a *waste-paper basket* and you'd concoct something that would surprise me,' I used to tell her. It was a gift. I do hope the engagement will not be a *long* one. Dear Mama always said that long engagements were such a *strain*."

"No, it will be short."

"Although, myself, I've always thought that a long engagement would be so comfortable. One would feel that one's future was settled, but one could not have any of the difficulties of marriage, which I am told can be *most* trying. I hope they won't live in London—the Zeppelins are a constant anxiety these days.

"What on *earth* for?"

"People just do, when they reach a certain age."

"Catch me!"

"You haven't reached the age—by any means."

"Weddings are just for girls."

"They can't be. You have to have one of each for them. You'll have to go to this one, as a cousin, and I shall *certainly* have to go as a sister, and quite likely a bridesmaid."

"Will there be cake?"

"You won't like it, it'll have marzipan."

He groaned. "I'll take my penknife."

"People don't take penknives to weddings, Neville. You'll be able to wear your longs. And there'll be champagne."

"I can't *stand* champagne. Will there be ginger beer?"

"I have not the *faintest* idea," Lydia answered, in her mother's most crushing voice.

"And then he asked you?"

"Yes."

"And you said yes?"

"Yes."

"Are you excited?"

"*Excited?* I don't know. Sort of—"

The telephone rang.

"If it's Kit or Freddie I want to speak to them," Stella called after her as she went to the telephone.

Stella heard her yelling "Yes?" in her best Cockney (last night they had all played charades and she had been raucously funny as a mum whose child had got a chamber-pot stuck on his head) and then her talking quite ordinarily, but too quietly to be heard. It was Saturday, and as they did not have go to their typing school, she decided to have one more cup of coffee before tackling the ghastly sinkful of washing up from last night.

When Louise came back she was flushed, but subdued.

"It was *The Times,*" she said.

"The newspaper?"

"Yep. Wanting to know about my being engaged to Michael Hadleigh."

"Gosh! I didn't know he was as famous as that."

"Nor did I, really. Have you got a fag?"

"Afraid not. We smoked the lot last night. I'll go and get some, if you like."

"No—I'll go."

"When are you getting married?"

"In about four weeks. Michael gets some leave then."

"In four weeks you'll be Mrs. Michael Hadleigh."

"Yes. It *is* exciting, but it also feels—" She stopped, because really she wasn't sure.

"What does it feel like?"

There was something reassuring about Stella's familiar curiosity, which provoked in her, as it always did, her most careful honesty. "I'm not sure. Stupendous—and also a bit unreal. As though I was two people: one who it is happening to, and one whom it couldn't possibly be happening to. It's rather amazing that he should want to marry me, don't you think?"

"No."

"Oh. I think it is. His family's frightfully glamorous, you know. They know hundreds of famous people—he could marry anyone."

"Anyone could marry anyone, you fool. I don't think that's how it works."

"No, it doesn't. He says he loves me."

"Are your family pleased?"

"I think so. When I told my mother, she simply said, didn't I think I was too young! Of all the idiotic questions . . ."

"And your father?"

"I don't care what he thinks. But, of course, he approves of Michael because his father was a hero in the last war."

"How simplistic."

"Isn't it?" It wasn't a word she had ever encountered before, but she could see at once what it meant, and it seemed just right for her father. "I shall miss 'Mon Debris' terribly, though. And being with you." She looked fondly round the dilapidated little hole, once part of the coal cellars that now served as a kitchen in their basement flat. "Back in a minute."

But after the front door had slammed, and in the ensuing silence, Stella, with pictures of her mother—quenched, entrapped on a velvet sofa in an overheated room from which she could only escape by nostalgia and the poetry of her youth—rubbed the unexpected angry tears from her eyes. She has already gone, she thought, and she won't ever really be back.

"Five pounds of the finest flour—the dear knows where I get that, it's all the same flour nowadays—three pounds of fresh butter—I might as well fly—five pounds of currants, do you hear that, Frank? Two nutmegs, mace, clove, well, at least I've got them, sixteen eggs, a pound of sweet almonds and one and a half pounds of candied peel.

For the life of me, I do not see my way at all—I'm at my wit's end, really I am!''

"You could make a Utility cake, Mrs. Cripps—Mabel." He always found it difficult to call her Mabel when she was wearing her specs, which had thick steel rims and made her look cross even when she was in a good mood, which was not, at present, the case.

"A Utility cake? For Miss Louise's wedding? You must be out of your mind if you think I'd entertain such a notion for a minute. For *one second*," she added. "Marge and dried eggs, when it will be known that the cake came from this house? Well-known people will be partaking of this cake, Mr. Tonbridge, and I'm not having aspersions cast at it. On it. Either I shall make it of the proper ingredients, or it will not be made at all. Those are my last words on the subject," she added untruthfully as she continued to ruminate for the rest of the day with a ferocity that brooked no further suggestions from him or anyone else.

Life had not been easy lately. It was true that she had achieved an Understanding with Frank, whom she still called Mr. Tonbridge in front of the others, but that had occurred before Christmas over eight months ago; and his divorce from That Woman, Ethyl her name was, didn't seem to be getting on at all. This was partly because the letters—and they seemed few and far between—that Frank's lawyer sent were never, or hardly ever, answered although a Mr. Sparrowgrass had once written back to say that he had no instructions from his client and therefore was unable to instigate proceedings. "But you're the one to do the proceedings," she had said. "*She's* the one who's gone off, she's the one to blame." Then he'd started up with some nonsense about doing the gentlemanly thing by Ethyl, letting her divorce him. But supposing she didn't want to, Mrs. Cripps had thought to herself. Supposing she wanted the house *and* the man she had got off with *and* Frank to fall back on if things went wrong? She hadn't dared to say that to him, but she had gone on worrying about it. He was ever so reserved with her—wouldn't put his arm round her except in the dark when they were alone, and how often was that? He hadn't any confidence, she could see that—needed building up in more ways than one, but it was rather like how he was with food; she could feed him three square meals a day and endless snacks in between them and he didn't put on an ounce, was as scrawny as ever. Meanwhile she wasn't getting any younger and sometimes she longed for him to throw his weight about more, be masterful like they were in films, instead of the jerky little pounces he sometimes made when he'd had a drink or two at the pub, or they were in the cinema, and once on the pier at Hastings in the evening. Of course, he knew ever such a lot about the war and history and all that; she knew he was quite clever because she couldn't understand half of what he said sometimes: he had opinions about things and she liked a man to have them, and he'd bought a wireless that they listened to in the evenings and he told what he thought about what they said on it. But none of this seemed to be getting them anywhere, and having been engaged once before in her life—long before she came to work for the Cazalets—and he jilting her at the last moment, something she *thought* she never thought about any more, had, none the less, made her wary and more anxious than she would otherwise have been. Mrs. Fellows, the cook she had been kitchen maid to in those days, had warned her about Norman, but she hadn't listened—she'd done things with him when she was young and silly and knew no better, which she did now, that it made her blush to think of. No man was going to make free with *her* out of wedlock ever again, she had vowed, when she had got over the awful fright of thinking she was in the family way. Norman—he'd been a groom at the place she worked— had just gone off to sea one day without a *word*. It had been a shock, made worse when she discovered that the lodgekeeper's daughter had the same idea about him. In the servants' hall they said that he'd got too many girls' fathers after him and that was why he'd gone to sea. *Her* father had been killed in the war—the one before this—so he wouldn't do no chasing and, anyway, she was a hundred miles from home. That had been her first place—she hadn't gone out to work until she was fourteen, because with five other children and a job cooking at the cottage hospital her mother needed her at home. Mrs. Fellows had been ever so strict but she'd given her Standards that she'd been thankful for ever since, as she always told the succession of girls she'd trained, but oh dear, *they* weren't what they used to be. The last girl—the one before Lizzie, that Miss Rachel had got from London—had been a real little madam, no respect for her elders, painting her fingernails and hanging her knickers on the line where the men could see them; she hadn't lasted a fortnight. Now with Lizzie—who was Edie's youngest sister—at least she had respect, you couldn't hardly hear a word she said and she did what she was told, although she was very slow and didn't get through things like Edie had. "We have to make allowances, Mrs. Cripps,"

Mrs. Cazalet Senior had said, which reminded her that she would have to go and see Mrs. Edward about the cake. She left Frank finishing the custard tart and buttoned up the straps on her shoes.

Mrs. Edward, who was making lists in the morning room, understood the problem at once and said she would ask everyone, including Lieutenant Hadleigh's family, whether they could contribute some rations for the cake. People in the services could often help about things like that, she said, and she also seemed to understand that they must do so quickly, as a cake of that kind needed time to settle after baking. "Although some people are using artificial wedding cakes—just to be looked at and not eaten," she said.

Concealing her shock and disgust at such a notion, Mrs. Cripps had said that this would not do for Miss Louise, and when Mrs. Edward had agreed with her, she felt emboldened to put in a word for Frank who was working himself up about it.

"Mr. Tonbridge was hoping he would be driving the bride to church," she said.

"Oh! Really I don't know, Mrs. Cripps, the wedding is to be in London, you know, so that it is easier for people to get to it."

Mrs. Cripps knew that. Information, often contradictory, sometimes invented, about the wedding, poured into the servants' hall: Eileen provided a good deal from waiting at table, Ellen from what Mrs. Rupert told her, the housemaids from airy suppositions made to them by Clary and Polly. She knew that the wedding was to be in Chelsea and the reception held at Claridge's Hotel; she knew that a Lady Knebworth was making the dress and several other items, and that Mrs. Lugg from Robertsbridge was making some of the underwear, of curtain net Eileen had remarked, but trimmed with some of Mrs. Senior's lace. She knew that Miss Lydia and Miss Clary and Miss Polly were to be bridesmaids and Mrs. Rupert was making their dresses, that four hundred people had been invited and that there had been pictures in *The Times*, and in the paper that Mr. Tonbridge read it had said "Hero's Son to Wed." Dottie had suggested that the King and Queen might be present, but she, Mrs. Cripps, who in far earlier days, when she was second cook in a big place, had once made and rolled the hot-water pastry for game pie for a shooting lunch at which His Majesty's father—his late Majesty—had shot and was therefore regarded as an authority on the subject, had snubbed her at once; Their Majesties would think twice before they went to weddings in the middle of a war, she had said, and Dottie should not get silly ideas above her station. The fact that the wedding was to be in

London had come as a great blow to all of them: Dottie had cried, Bertha had stopped trimming their hats and Eileen had got one of her sick headaches. Mrs. Cripps had felt that her station required her to preserve an impassive demeanour, but nevertheless told Frank that she thought it a great shame: girls always used to be married at home, and if this wasn't Miss Louise's home she would like to know what was. So it was with very great delight and no small surprise that she received the news now that everybody, the whole household, was to attend the wedding; that they were all to go up to town in the morning, lunch would be provided at the Charing Cross Hotel and they would go in cabs to the church. "But Tonbridge will be driving Mr. and Mrs. Cazalet and Miss Barlow to London that morning, Mrs. Cripps, so you will have to be in charge of the rest of the staff. Lunch will be at twelve o'clock which will give you plenty of time to get to the church by two thirty. I shall include Ellen and the two little boys in your party."

"Yes, madam." This was a relief, as Ellen knew London and she did not.

"After the reception, you will all return in a train. I think there is one at six, but there is time to arrange that."

This meant that they would all be going to the party after the wedding. "Everybody will be very pleased, I'm sure," she said.

"Darling, if I was you, I would be counting my blessings. It's a match that even our poor mamma would have approved of. And *she* would certainly not have thought Louise too young. I must say that I wish I was in your shoes. Angela shows no sign of an engagement to anyone and she was twenty-three last month. And, after all, you never *wanted* her to go on the stage."

"No, but he is fourteen years older than she is. Don't you think that that is rather a lot?"

"It simply means that he is old enough to look after her. How are you getting on with his family?"

"Quite well, I think. We've had to do a good deal of liaising over plans. The Judge wanted it to be a dry wedding. He felt it would be more patriotic."

"Goodness! What did Edward say?"

"He went white to the lips and said no daughter of *his*, et cetera. Of course, *I* had to tell them, but Lady Zinnia took it quite calmly. I think she has taken rather a shine to him."

Villy had dropped in for tea after taking Louise to have a fitting with Hermione and doing various other errands about London. She had made the arrangement ahead so there were no farcical problems like there had been the time before when she had just turned up, Jessica thought, and then thought it funny that she had not mentioned Lorenzo. She had been there for over two hours now; tea had developed into sherry while they went through all the family news, taking turns as they had always done, and according each other the ritual sympathy expected. Teddy had nearly finished his initial square-bashing in the RAF and was then likely to be sent somewhere for further training. "But the actual flying part they do abroad, in Canada or America. I must say I dread that."

"Oh, darling!"

Christopher was still working in the market garden. He had acquired a second-hand caravan where he lived with his dog. "I *never* see him! He simply loathes London!"

"Oh, darling!"

Lydia was doing quite well with Miss Milliment, but she was going to have to wear a brace on her teeth and probably have one out as her mouth was overcrowded; and she was quite dreadfully untidy and never stopped talking and mimicked everybody. "And she's picked up some dreadful language—from Neville, I think—and they have the most *morbid* obsession with death—they've been playing cemeteries all the summer and keep looking for things to bury."

"Darling, it's only her age. What is she, about twelve? Well, she'll soon grow up."

Nora was nursing and had fallen in love with a nineteen-year-old airman whose back had been broken before he bailed out of his plane. "He'll be in a wheelchair for the rest of his life, but she is determined to marry him."

"Darling! You never told me!"

"Well, I suppose I didn't believe it would go *on* at first, but it has—for nearly a year. Would you believe it, it is *he* who doesn't want to marry her!"

"Goodness!" Villy tried to put the right amount of shocked surprise into her voice. "At least it would put paid to the idea of being a nun," she said.

"Oh, I think she's over *that*. She's far too bossy for *that*."

There was a pause, and then Villy, having groped for the most delicate way to phrase it, asked: "If she *does* marry him . . . would there be the chance of offspring?"

"I haven't liked to ask. I *imagine* not—" She fell silent, and for moments both sisters were occupied by the kind of thoughts that, naturally, neither of them would dream of voicing. Villy lit another cigarette, and Jessica poured them both more sherry.

"How is Raymond?"

"Oh, tremendously involved in his secret work at Woodstock. As it *is* secret, of course, he can't tell me anything about it. But he seems to work fearfully long hours, and they live in some hostel so there is built-in company in the evenings. It's ironic, really. When we had no money, he wouldn't have dreamed of doing a steady job with a salary—always wanted to run his own business and they always came to grief, and now when money isn't so tight, there he is, in a steady job with a salary."

"He did do the school job."

"Yes—after the mushrooms failed. But that was largely so that Christopher could go to that school as we only had to pay half fees. I think he will be one of the people who will be quite sad when the war finally does come to an end. Going back to Frensham with nothing to do will be dull for the poor lamb."

"The end of the war seems a long way off." Villy sighed. "Michael was involved in that raid on Dieppe last week."

"*Was* it meant to be the beginning of the invasion?"

"Apparently not. No—Michael told Edward that it had been mounted because they had to find out what it would be like, but it must have been hell. We could hear the guns all day in Sussex—eerie and horrible. All we could see were the planes going over. Of course, Louise will have a very anxious time. Michael seems always to want to be in the thick of things."

Jessica sighed. "I suppose we are really rather lucky."

"*Lucky?*"

"To have escaped all that kind of thing. I mean, we married men who'd come *back* from the war. We didn't have to worry about whether they'd be killed."

"I can't say that I feel particularly lucky," Villy said stiffly, and Jessica thought: There she goes—*just* like Mamma, she has to be the tragedy queen . . .

"How's Edward?" she asked with deliberate brightness.

"All right. Dead tired." She looked at her watch. "Gosh! I must fly. Can I call a cab? I've got to get to Hugh's to change. Edward and I are dining *chez* Storey—the wedding again. Thank you so much, darling. It was a lovely respite."

From what? Jessica asked herself, when Villy had gone. Without apparently having made the slightest effort, Villy had achieved this desirable marriage for her daughter. It was true that Louise was very good-looking, but Angela, though perhaps not so striking, was lovely with large, well-spaced features and an admirable figure, a statuesque girl with an air of remoteness that dear Mamma would deeply have approved of. But perhaps she was *too* remote: ever since that most unfortunate business with the BBC producer, nothing seemed to have happened to her. To begin with, this had been a relief, but now it was becoming a little worrying. She had left the BBC and got some job in the Ministry of Information which meant that, although she had registered for war service, she had not yet been called up. She shared a flat with another girl and Jessica hardly ever saw her. Her dreams of a débutante who married the right sort of person, had her picture in the front of *Country Life* and subsequently went to all the right sort of parties had faded. Now, she thought, she would be relieved if Angela married anyone at all.

"Well?"

"If you are asking me about the evening, Zee, I thought it both pleasant and sensible."

"Pleasant because?"

"They are a nice couple. The backbone of English society."

"Ah! Of course you are right. I suppose I've always preferred the more decorative, less useful parts."

"He is an attractive man, surely? And a brave one. Two MCs and a recommendation for a Victoria Cross in the last war."

"Really? I didn't know that."

"And she is a pleasant woman."

"Oh, yes. Most wives are that. The number of pleasant wives I have had to put up with! Thank God you left politics. It has cut down the number of women one *has* to have to dinner."

He passed a fond hand over her wonderfully thick silver-white hair. "But, my darling Zee, if you had your way, there would *be* no women at all to have to dinner. There would be you—and a world full of handsome, entertaining, daring men. With just a few broody hens kept well in the background."

She smiled slightly, but her eyes were sparkling. "Tell me, what was sensible about the evening."

"I thought we got a great many of the tiresome wedding arrangements sorted out without either argument or acrimony, and I am told that this is seldom the case."

"It was very good of you to say that you would share the cost of the reception."

"We are inviting so many people that it seemed to me right. And he is your beloved son. And you are one of the few women on whom it would be no good practising the cant of losing a son and gaining a daughter."

She indicated that she wanted to get up from the sofa on which she was lying.

"Although you do like her, don't you, darling?"

"Little Louise! Of course I like her. I am delighted with her. So funny and charming and so *very young!*"

She was on her feet now, and he put his arm in hers as they began the slow progress to their respective bedrooms.

"And I shan't lose my son," she said. "Nothing but death would achieve it. And I have no intention of dying. I want to see my grandson far too much for that."

Louise

Winter, 1942

Wʜᴇɴ sʜᴇ ᴡᴀs alone, which was very nearly all the time these days, and when she was not completely inert—she would try to put the pieces of herself together into some recognizable shape so that she could sort of *see* what she was. At the acting school they had spent hours discussing characteristics of people—facets of their personality, aspects of their nature, quirks of behaviour or temperament. They had discussed characters in plays, of course, and over the weeks had condemned "bad" plays that had characters who were merely two-dimensional—cardboard cut-outs with no depth. Then, when she had talked about this with Stella and had trotted out all their theories, Stella had said: "Of course, that's why Shakespeare and Chekhov are the only playwrights with genius. Their characters are more like eggs. However you approach their surface they are never flat, always tailing mysteriously off round a corner that isn't even a corner, but at the same time you can always imagine the whole shape . . ."

But she, although she was not merely a character in a play, did not feel at all like an egg; more like a bit of crazy paving, or part of a jigsaw puzzle. She did not feel like anyone she could recognize; even the disparate pieces of paving or jigsaw seemed hardly to belong to her, were more like a series of bit parts that she had become accustomed to, and was therefore good at playing. Mrs. Michael Hadleigh was one of them. The fortunate young wife of a glamorous man who, according to Zee, had broken innumerable hearts. People wrote "Mrs. Michael Hadleigh" on envelopes; it had been the caption to the photograph taken by Harlip that had appeared shortly after her marriage in *Country Life*. Receptionists in hotels called her that. This person had gone through a fashionable wedding with photographs of it in most of the newspapers. "I look like a new potato in white lace!" she had wailed, knowing it would make Michael's family laugh. This person wore the gold watch that the Judge had given her as a wedding present and a turquoise and diamond ring that Zee had given her for her engagement. She had new luggage stamped L.H. in gold on the white hide. At Claridge's, she had been given a room in which to change from the white lace to the suit Hermione had made her for going away—a pretty creamy tweed with a wide-spaced thin scarlet check on it, a straight short skirt and a short-sleeved jacket with light scarlet buttons. She had emerged from the lift to walk through the wide entrance to the hotel that was thronged with family and people she had never seen before in her life, to the Daimler where Crawley—the Judge's chauffeur—was waiting to drive them away. Her topcoat had been forgotten, and Zee sent Malcolm Sargent for it. "Kind Malcolm will get it," she had said, and he did. Mrs. Michael Hadleigh was the person who was eyed appreciatively by admirals, some of whom had sent huge packing cases full of what had clearly been valuable but was now shattered glass. These had been difficult to thank for, as in the worst instances, the fragments made it impossible to know what the object had originally been. "Thank you so much for sending us all that lovely glass," she had written to one of them. A large number of people—many of them distinguished—were delighted to meet Mrs. Michael Hadleigh, and congratulated Michael with varying degrees of elegance and gallantry on his charming young wife. Sometimes she felt a little like a conjuring trick, the white rabbit he had so cleverly produced from nowhere. Mrs. Michael Hadleigh only seemed to come to life when there were other people present.

Then there was the child bride. Her youth was endlessly harped upon, by senior naval officers, by friends of Michael, many of whom were even older than he. This also applied at Hatton, where she discovered they were to spend half of their honeymoon. "A week on our own, and then we'll stay with Mummy," Michael had said. She *was* the child: arrangements were announced to her with the ostensibly indulgent, slightly teasing admonition that she would like whatever it was, wouldn't she? It would have been churlish to disagree, and she never did. Part of being the child bride was everybody approving of her—a *good* child bride . . . So—they had spent a week in a cottage lent to them by a godmother of Michael's who lived in a large house in Norfolk. The cottage was pretty, with a reeded roof and a large open fireplace in the sitting room where they also ate. Lady Moy, the godmother, had arranged for somebody to cook and clean for them, and when they arrived, that first evening, it was to the enticing scents of a log fire and roasting chicken. Crawley brought in their suitcases, touched his cap and left, and when she had served them their chicken and shown them the damson tart lying on the trolley, the cook, who said her name was Mary, also left and they were alone. She remembered that she had thought, "This is the very beginning of my married life—the happily ever after bit," and wondered what that would be like. And Michael had been full of the most charming admiration, telling her again and again how lovely she had looked as a bride and how lovely people had *told* him she was. "And just as lovely now," he had said, picking up her hand and kissing it. Later, when he had poured two glasses from the bottle of hock Lady Moy had left for them, he had said: "Let's drink to us, Louise and Michael." And she had repeated the toast, and sipped the wine and then they had had dinner and talked about the wedding until he had asked her whether she would like to go to bed.

Afterwards, when she slipped out of bed to put on one of the nightdresses her father had given her when she was fourteen that were still her best, she thought how lucky that this hadn't been the first time, because at least now she knew what happened and was more or less used to it. She had, in fact, been to bed with Michael four times before: the first time had been awful because it had hurt so much and she'd felt she couldn't tell him as he seemed so enthusiastic. The other times had been better in that it hadn't hurt, and the beginning of one time had even begun to be exciting but then he had started to put his tongue in her mouth and after that she had a sort of black-out and felt nothing. He didn't seem to notice, though, which at the time had seemed a good thing, but, and it happened gradually, during that first week of the honeymoon, she began to feel that it was odd that although he kept saying how much he loved her, and kept telling her how he was feeling and what was happening to him throughout his lovemaking, he didn't seem to notice much about her. In the end she wondered whether the sharp sweet thrill—as though something was starting to open inside her—had actually occurred.

That first night, however, she simply felt relieved that it didn't hurt and he had seemed to enjoy it; she also felt suddenly dog tired, and fell asleep moments after she got back into bed.

In the morning she woke to find him making love to her again and then there was all the novelty of having a bath together and getting dressed and a delicious breakfast with eggs and honey, and after it they went for a long walk in the park where there was a lake with swans and other waterfowl and then woods. It was a perfect September morning, mellow, balmy and still. They walked hand in hand, saw a heron, a fox and a large owl, and Michael did not talk about the war at all. During the week, they went and had dinner at the big house where Lady Moy and a companion existed in a state of elaborate decay. Most of the house was shut up and the rest of it seemed implacably cold; it was the sort of house, she thought, that made you want to go out of doors to get warm. Lady Moy gave Michael a beautiful pair of Purdey guns that had belonged to her husband and two watercolours by Brabazon. "I'll have them sent over to you," she said; "And *you*," she later said to Louise, "I could hardly choose a present for someone I had not seen. But now I've met you—and by the way, Mikey, I think you've done very well for yourself—I know what to do." She rummaged about in a large embroidered bag and produced a small watch of blue enamel edged with pearls that hung from an enamelled bow with a brooch pin behind it. "It was given me by my godmother when I married," she said. "It does not keep very good time, but it is a pretty thing."

During dinner Lady Moy asked Michael about his ship and he told her a great deal about it. She tried to be, and then to look, interested but the number of guns with which a new MTB was going to be equipped was not a subject to which she could contribute.

It was not until they were about to leave, and Lady Moy asked them about their plans, that she learned that they were to spend the second week of Michael's leave at Hatton.

"Mummy is so longing to see us. And we thought it would be nice for her if we went."

"I'm sure it will be."

She found Lady Moy's eyes upon her but she could not interpret their expression. "I must kiss you too," she said after she had embraced Michael.

They walked back down the drive to their cottage in the dark.

"You never told me we were going to Hatton!"

"Didn't I? I must have. I'm almost *sure* I *did*. You don't mind, anyway, do you?"

"No." She was not at all sure.

"You see, darling Mummy is not very well, and she worried so frightfully about me that it seemed—she loves *you* very much, you know. She told me that she couldn't imagine a better mother for her grandson."

She was aghast.

"We're not actually *having* one, are we?"

He laughed, and squeezed her arm. "Darling, you'll be the first to know that. There's always a *hope*."

"But—"

"You told me you wanted six. We have to start somewhere."

She opened her mouth to say that she didn't want them immediately—now—and shut it again. His voice had sounded teasing—he wasn't serious.

But the subject was resumed at Hatton. She got the curse when they had been there four days, and although Zee didn't talk to her directly, this resulted in various messages. She had fairly bad stomach cramps, and Michael was very kind to her, tucking her up in bed with a hot-water bottle after lunch.

"You are sweet to me," she said, after he had bent down to kiss her.

"You are my little darling wife. By the way, Zee told me one useful tip. When you're OK again, after we've made love, it helps if you prop your legs up with a pillow. It gives the sperm a better chance to meet an egg."

She swallowed: the thought that he had been discussing all this with his mother suddenly nauseated her.

"Michael—I'm not at all sure that I *want* to have a baby so quickly. I mean, I do want them in the end, but I want to get a bit more used to being married first."

"Of course you do," he said heartily. "But that'll happen in no time, believe me. And if, by any chance, the other thing does happen, nature will take over, and you'll feel fine about it. Now you have a lovely snooze, and I'll wake you up in time for tea."

But she didn't sleep at all. She lay and worried about why they wanted her to have a baby so badly, and felt guilty that she didn't feel as they did.

The rest of the week was passed with music and Michael drawing her and beginning an oil painting, and jokes and games with neighbours and a dance and the Judge reading aloud to them, and they all treated her with teasing, affectionate indulgence and she was the favoured, petted child bride. Conversation at meals was exhilarating: the family jokes involved being better read and having a far larger vocabulary than she possessed. She had asked the Judge, whom she had learned to call Pete, if he would make her a reading list.

"He was *delighted*," Michael said when they were dressing for dinner that evening. "You do fit in so well with my family, my darling."

"How did you know I had asked him?"

"Mummy told me. She was very touched that you asked *him*."

Whenever people came to lunch or dinner, they would ask Michael about his ship, and he always told them, usually at great length. She noticed that however often he talked about the superior merits of Oelikon guns to the Bofers or Rolls, Zee listened with rapt interest as though it was the first time she had heard him on the subject. Privately, she found these conversations very boring, more boring even than when they talked about the war more generally: the battle for Stalingrad, which was on the news every night, and the bombing raids on Germany.

During all this time, which was actually very short, only two weeks, excitement, like a heat haze, had obscured most of any other feeling: she had married her wonderful, glamorous Michael, who, although he was so much older and famous and brave, had chosen her. It was exciting, if you have never thought much of your appearance or brains, if you felt, as she felt then, that you had not been properly educated, to be told from morning till night how beautiful, clever and talented you were. It was a fairytale, and she was the fortunate princess who at nineteen had already embarked upon her "ever after."

They left Hatton at the end of the week, and went by train to London. Michael had to go to the Admiralty and they arranged to meet at Waterloo station.

"What will you do with yourself, darling?"

She hadn't thought. "I'll be all right. I might try to get hold of Stella, but they don't like you ringing students at Pitman's. If I can't get her, I'll go to the National Gallery."

"Have you got any money?"

"Oh! No—no, I'm afraid I haven't."

He thrust his hand into his trouser pocket and pulled out a wad of notes. "There."

"I won't need all that!"

"You never know. You might. I'll deal with the luggage."

They kissed. It was enjoyable (she did not then know *how* enjoyable) to part knowing that they would meet again so soon.

She tried to ring Stella from a telephone box but could not get her, so she went to the National Gallery where Myra Hess and Isolde Menges were playing two pianos. In the interval, when she was buying a sandwich, she saw Sid talking to a very old man with thick white hair and a walking stick. She was just about to walk over and make herself known, when she saw a youngish woman, or girl, in fact somebody probably no older than she, leaning against the wall at the end of the sandwich table and staring at Sid with a look of such intense, moony devotion that she wanted almost to laugh. What Aunt Jessica used to call a pash, I suppose, she thought. At that moment, Sid saw her, smiled and beckoned.

She was introduced as Louise Hadleigh to the man with white hair and the man said, yes, he recognized her. "You married my old friend Zinnia Storey's son a few weeks ago. How is Zee? Now she is in the country so much, I hardly ever see her."

Fumbling about to shake hands, he dropped his stick. Instantly, the girl leaning against the wall had leapt forward, bent down and picked it up.

"How kind!"

The girl blushed—her forehead looked damp, Louise noticed—as Sid said, "Well fielded, Thelma," and introduced her to them as one of her pupils. Then the interval was over, and everyone began leaving the basement where the sandwiches were served for the resumption of the concert.

"Please give my love to Zee," the man said and she smiled and said yes, she would. But as she would not be seeing Zee for she did not know how long and had not the faintest idea who he was there was no chance of that, she thought.

When the concert was over, after the lovely and expected comforting encore of "Jesu, Joy of Man's Desiring," she wondered what to do. There were no pictures to see at the gallery: they had all been removed to a place or places of safety. She walked out into Trafalgar Square. There was sun, but it was without heat, and the sky was an unclouded cool blue decorated by the glinting barrage balloons that floated serenely—like gigantic toys, she thought. It was two hours until the train, and she wondered what to do. Michael had given her a wad of pounds, there must be at least ten of them; she felt rich, and free—and then, with no warning at all, extremely frightened. "What am I to do with myself?" "Why am I here?" "What am I for?" A host of small, darting, preposterous queries that seemed to come at her from nowhere and were only dwarfed by their quantity. To answer any of them—even to consider them—spelled complete danger: she would not attempt any reply; she must do something, think of something else. I'll go to a bookshop, and buy some books, she thought and, furnished with this sensible and practical purpose, she caught the bus to Piccadilly that stopped outside Hatchard's.

By the time she had bought three books and hailed a cab to take her to Waterloo her spirits had risen. She was not going tamely home to Sussex to be criticized by her mother and asked to do boring things by the rest of the family. She was catching a train with her husband and then a boat to the Isle of Wight where they were to stay in an hotel—something she had never done in her life before. She was Mrs. Michael Hadleigh again, and not whoever it was who had been struck by some idiotic panic on the steps of the National Gallery. It would have been nice to get hold of Stella, but she would write to her.

But, she quickly discovered, life in that hotel, and subsequently in other hotels, in Weymouth and Lewes, was not at all as she had imagined. Michael went off at eight in the morning and she was left for the day, day after day, with nothing whatever to do. The Gloster Hotel had a particular disadvantage, made worse because, to begin with, it had seemed like an incredible luxury. There was always lobster for lunch and for dinner. Occasionally there was something else, usually not awfully nice, but after a week or so, she took to having whatever it was. She got bored with lobster; and started to hate it. She read books, and went for walks in the town, but the place was stiff with troops, and the whistling and inaudible, but undoubtedly rude remarks made her dread going out. Then one day she went into a greengrocer to buy some apples and, without the slightest warning, seemed to lose her balance, everything went black, and she came to on the ground surrounded by a smell of earthy hessian. Someone was bending over her and telling her she would be all right, and asking her where she lived, and she simply couldn't think. Her head was propped against a sack of potatoes and she'd laddered her stocking. They gave her some water, and she felt better. "The Gloster Hotel," she said. "I can easily walk there." But a kind woman took her back there, got the key of her room for her and helped her upstairs. "I should have a little lie-down if I were you," she said when Louise thanked her. After she had gone, she did lie on their bed, on top of the slippery quilt. It was half past eleven by her gold watch that the Judge had given her. Michael would not be back until six in the evening. She felt shocked and suddenly violently homesick. She began to cry and when she had finished and blown her nose on one of Michael's large white handkerchiefs she lay on the bed again. There did not seem to be any point in getting up.

After that she would lie in bed in the mornings, watching Michael shave and dress with what seemed to her a heartless speed and pray that something would happen that would stop him going. The ship he commanded was a new MTB still on the slips on the Medina river and he was passionately excited by everything to do with her. Every evening he came home full of news about its progress (she had learned to call it "she" but privately she thought of the ship as "it"). They had dinner and then he drew her and then they went to bed and he made love to her and it was always exactly the same and she tried not to disenjoy it. She did not tell him how lonely and aimless—well, bored really, she felt, because she was ashamed of these feelings. There were no other naval wives staying in the hotel, there were no other women there: people came and went; they seemed to be the only long stayers in the place. When she told him about fainting in the greengrocer's shop, he smiled and said, "Oh, *darling!* Do you think it might be—"

"What?" She knew what he meant, but she was so appalled at the idea that she wanted to gain time.

"Darling! A baby! What we've been trying to have!"

"I don't know. It might be, I suppose. People are alleged to faint at such times. And feel sick in the mornings. But I haven't felt in the least sick."

Shortly after that, she did meet a naval wife, a lady much older than herself whose husband was commander of a destroyer and she suggested that Louise come and help her at the Mission to Seaman. "We're always short of willing hands," she said; "there's bound to be something for you to do, my dear."

So from nine until twelve each morning she either helped in the canteen, or made up endless bunks. This last entailed stripping the sheets off the old ones—generally extraordinarily grey and concealing beer bottles, odd socks and other detritus. This coincided with her starting to feel sick in the mornings. When Marjorie Anstruther discovered her retching over a sink, she sent her home to lie down, saying she *quite* understood, and that Louise had been a little Trojan to stick it out. So that was the end of that. She *was* pregnant, and she had gradually come to think that perhaps this was as it should be: if one got married and had nothing else to do, one was meant to have babies. Although the prospect still secretly terrified her, she managed to seem cheerful about it, and very soon a letter arrived from Zee, saying how delighted she was with the news (which Michael had telephoned to her).

She spent her mornings feeling sick and sometimes being it and mostly otherwise in bed, but at noon, as regular as clockwork, a single German reconnaissance plane came over the island and thence to Portsmouth, and all the ships lying in what she had learned to call Cowes Roads let off every anti-aircraft gun at their disposal. They never hit the plane, but the noise was very great, and Michael had told her always to be on the ground floor on these occasions. So she would put on her overcoat and creep down—braving the nauseous fumes of boiling lobsters—to the hall, where pieces of glass dripped disconsolately from the roof down onto the tiled floor, while she read very old numbers of the *Illustrated London News*. After about fifteen minutes, the plane sheered off. Then she would go back to her room and sometimes she would collect her things and go along the passage for a bath. She had come to dread the lonely lunches in the hotel dining room and usually went out to the town to a cake shop that sold buns and very solid Cornish pasties that were mostly potato and onion. She had run out of books to read quite quickly, but there was a bookshop, and she spent hours there choosing, but they didn't seem to mind. She read novels by Ethyl Mannin, G. B. Stern, Winifred Holtby and Storm Jameson, and then one day she saw a second-hand copy of *Mansfield Park*. It was like meeting an old friend unexpectedly and she could not resist buying it. After that, she bought all the others, in spite of the fact that she had a whole set at home in Sussex. They engrossed and comforted her more than anything else and she read them all twice. When she wrote to Stella, it was largely about what she was reading. "By the way, I'm pregnant!" she put at the end of one letter. The exclamation mark was meant to make it sound exciting. She thought about telling Stella what she felt about this, and what life was being like for her, but found she could not bear to do it. It meant thinking about things seriously, and she felt too confused and altogether unsure of everything to try. Also, she was afraid it might clear things up in a way that she might find unendurable. As long as she played her part (and she *was* in love with Michael—look at how she *hated* him going every morning and practically counted the hours until his return), it would be a kind of betrayal to say that she was finding life difficult—or boring. "Intelligent people are never bored," Zee had said at Hatton during her honeymoon. "Do you agree with that, Pete?" And the Judge had replied that it might imply a certain *dimness.* She must never be *dim.*

By the middle of November, Michael's ship was ready, and Zee and the Judge came to Cowes for a night, as Zee was to launch her. Rooms were booked for them at the hotel, and Michael got off work early to meet the ferry at Ryde.

Dinner was at the Royal Yacht Squadron—very grand—because Zee knew an admiral who was a member and who invited them all.

"Dear little Louise! You are looking splendid. Pete has brought your reading list."

At dinner there was the dreaded lobster and Michael talked with unflagging enthusiasm about his ship. "I can't *wait* to see her!" Zee exclaimed and Louise saw Michael basking in her enthusiasm. It transpired that the Admiral, whom they called Bobbie, had not been going to be present at the launch, but by the end of the evening Zee had got him to say he would come.

But the next morning, Louise, apart from a particularly virulent bout of sickness, had a sore throat and a temperature.

"Poor darling! Better stay in bed, though. Can't have you getting ill. I'll get them to send you up some breakfast." After a long time, tea in a scalding metal pot, two pieces of leathery toast and a pat of bright yellow margarine arrived. The tea tasted of metal and she could not face the toast at all. It was all too much. Just when something was actually *happening* she couldn't go, was doomed to yet another dreary lonely day, only worse than usual, as she felt so awful. She got out of bed to go to the lavatory—an icy interlude; there was no heat in the bedroom. She put on a vest and some socks and went back to bed with some aspirin which sent her to sleep.

Michael came back in the evening to say that he was sleeping on board as the ship was starting her trials early the next morning. Zee and the Judge had left, but Mummy had been marvellous at the launching, and they had had a jolly lunch.

"Poor darling, you still look rather mouldy. Mrs. Watson says she sent somebody upstairs to see if you wanted any lunch, but you were asleep. Shall I get them to get you something for supper?"

"Couldn't you have it with me?"

"Can't, I'm afraid. I'm expected back on board. The flotilla commander is dining with us."

"When will you be back, then?"

"Tomorrow evening, I expect. But, I told you, darling, while the trials are on life will be hectic. I shan't be able to sleep ashore all the time. We've been extraordinarily lucky, you know.''

"Have we?"

He had been collecting his shaving gear and cramming it into a brand new black leather briefcase.

"Darling, of course we have. My Number One hasn't seen his fiancée since Christmas. And our coxswain hasn't even set eyes on his latest son who is nearly six months old. I don't say we *shouldn't* be lucky, I want you to be the luckiest girl in the world, but it doesn't do any harm to recognize one's blessings. Most officers I know couldn't afford to have their wives in an hotel. Do you know where my pyjamas are?"

"Afraid I don't." She was so miserable at the thought of a night *and* a whole day entirely alone that she sounded sulky.

"They must be somewhere! Honestly, darling, try to think."

"Well, usually the chambermaid puts them under the pillow when she makes the bed. But she didn't come in this morning."

"Oh, well, I'll take some new ones."

But when he got some out, they proved to be almost without buttons.

"Oh, damn! Darling, you might have looked them over when they came back from the laundry. After all, it isn't as though you have an *awful* lot to do."

"I'll sew them on now, if you like."

"They aren't there to sew on. You'll have to get some."

He took her Royal Yacht Squadron burgee brooch, presented by the Admiral the previous night to celebrate Michael's being made an honorary member. "I should think I'm the only naval officer who does up his pyjamas with one of these. I must fly now." He bent to kiss her forehead. "Cheer up: don't get *too* gloomy." At the door, he blew her another kiss. "You look very cosy," he said.

After he had gone, and she was sure that he wouldn't be coming back, she had wept.

When she was better he had suggested that she go to her home for a bit while he finished the trials. "Then, when I know where we'll be sent, you can join me again."

She did not demur. Homesickness—not quite, but nearly—as bad as she had had as a child had been assailing her, and she would lie in bed after he left in the mornings, longing for the familiar, shabby house that was always so full, the sounds of so many lives going on; the gasping squeak of the carpet cleaner, the wheezing grind of the nursery gramophone alternating "The Grasshoppers' Dance" with "The Teddy Bears' Picnic"; the steady rumble of the Brig dictating, the insect whirr of the Duchy's sewing machine, the smells of coffee and ironing and reluctant log fires and damp dog and beeswax . . . She went through each room in the house furnishing them with the appropriate inmates. Everything that had either bored or irritated her about them before now seemed only to make them more charming, dearer and more necessary. Aunt Dolly's passion for mothballs, the Duchy's belief that hot paraffin wax was essential for burns, Polly and Clary's determination not to be impressed by her being so much more grown-up than they, Lydia's uncanny impersonations of anyone she chose to emulate; Miss Milliment looking exactly the same, but none the less mysteriously older, her voice gentler, her chins even softer, her clothes encrusted with random pieces of ancient foods, but her small grey eyes, magnified at certain angles by her narrow, steel-rimmed spectacles, still so unexpectedly penetrating. And then, a complete contrast, Aunt Zoë who contrived to look glamorous whatever she wore, whose years now in the country had not at all altered the impression she gave of being fashionable and pretty. And darling Aunt Rach whose uttermost word of approval was "sensible"—"such a sensible hat," "a really sensible mother": "I am going to give you a really *sensible* wedding present," she had said. "Three pairs of double linen sheets." These were all at home with the many other presents, waiting until she and Michael had a home of their own, although God knew when that would be. Perhaps it was entirely the war that was making life seem so strange. Going away to the cooking school and then to the rep had seemed like logical excursions from home—all part of growing up and preparing for her great career on the stage. But being married had changed everything —in many ways that she had not envisaged. Leaving home was a much more final business when one married. As for her career, not only was there no sign of the war ever coming to an end, when she supposed she might resume it, but there was the problem of having children as well. Her mother had stopped dancing when she married: had never danced again. For the first time, she wondered what that had been like for her, whether her mother had minded or had *chosen* just to be married. But somehow, in her nostalgic dreaming about Home Place and her family, she could not, or did not want to, include her parents: there was something—and she did not want to find out what—that was vaguely . . . uncomfortable. All she knew was that in the weeks before the wedding, she had come to dislike being alone with her mother nearly as much as she disliked being alone with her father—although not exactly, if at all, for the same reasons. This had been confusing, because she could see that her mother was trying very hard to do everything to make the wedding a success. She had been endlessly patient about the fittings for the dress and her few other clothes, had *given* her clothes coupons, had even asked her whether she wanted her friend Stella to be a bridesmaid. *Stella* hadn't wanted to—had been gently adamant—and it had been a question of choosing which of the girls; in the end it had been Lydia and Polly and Clary. Zoë and her mother and the Duchy had made their dresses of white curtain net that her mother had dyed in tea so that it was a warm cream colour. Pure silk ribbon was still available in London shops. Aunt Zoë had chosen the colours, pink, orange and dark red, and she had sewn the ribbons together in strips to make sashes. The dresses had been plain, high-waisted, with low round necks and a deep flounce round the bottom—"Like little Gainsboroughs," the Judge had said when he saw them outside the church. There had been an awful lot of work in the short time between the engagement and the marriage and most of it had fallen upon her mother. But besides all her organizing, the letter-writing, the arrangements and the discussions, she had sensed something about her mother that she simply could not bear: it had made her cold, sulky, irritable; she had snapped when asked perfectly ordinary questions and then felt ashamed but somehow unable to apologize. In the end she discovered what it was: the night before the wedding her mother asked her if she "knew about things." She had instantly said, yes, she did. Her mother had smiled uneasily and said, well, she had supposed that Louise would have learned all about that sort of thing at that awful acting place, adding that she would not have liked her to enter upon marriage "unprepared." Each allusion made the whole thing seem nauseating and the allusions, she had realized, were only the tip of the iceberg. In a fever of revulsion and anger it had seemed to her then that her mother had been thinking of nothing else all these weeks, and not only thinking but *wondering*, ruminating, imagining her in bed with Michael, employing the most disgusting curiosity about something which had absolutely *nothing* to do with her! (As though one married people simply to go to bed with them!) After that bit of the evening, her mother could say nothing that did not have some sickening double meaning. Yes, she *should* go to bed early, she needed a good night's sleep as tomorrow was going to be such a day. "You must be fresh for it." Well, she had thought, when she had finally escaped to her room in Uncle Hugh's house for the night, in twenty-four hours I shall be miles away from her. It will never have to be like this again.

She had managed not to be alone with her father at all until the day of the wedding when he turned up just as she had finished dressing with a half-bottle of champagne. "I thought we might each have a glass," he had said. "Dutch courage, don't you know." He looked very dashing in his morning dress with the pale grey silk tie and white rose in his buttonhole. By now she was feeling nervous, and the champagne seemed a good idea.

He eased the cork out of the bottle and caught the fizz in one of the glasses. He had put them on the dressing table and now she saw him looking at her reflection in the mirror. When he saw that she saw, he looked away and filled up both the glasses.

"Here you are, darling," he said. "You can't possibly know how much happiness I wish you."

There was a small silence while he handed her her glass. Then he said: "You look—most awfully pretty." He sounded humble— almost shy.

"Oh, Dad!" she said, and tried to smile, but her eyes pricked. Nothing more could dare to be said.

"To my eldest unmarried daughter," he said as he raised his glass. They both smiled at each other: the past lay between them like a knife.

It was when she got back to Sussex that these scenes recurred— when she was alone, when she was not playing one of her parts.

"Do you feel different being married?" Clary had asked the first day.

"No, not especially," she had answered—the lofty, older cousin.

"Why not?"

The simplicity of the question confounded her.

"Why should I?"

"Well—I mean, you're not a virgin any more to start with. I don't suppose you'd tell me what that's like, would you?"

"No."

"I thought not. I do see how writers get circumscribed by having to rely on direct experience nearly all the time. Or *reading* about things, which is not at all the same as someone telling you."

"You're far too inquisitive, in a *morbid* way. A bit disgusting to boot," she added.

But Clary, having suffered countless accusations about her curiosity, had become adept at defending it.

"It isn't like that at all. It's simply that if you are really interested in people and how they behave you get every sort of thing to be curious about. For instance—" But Louise had seen Zoë on her bicycle in the drive and had gone downstairs to meet her.

"*Honestly!* I'm sick of people accusing me and then not listening to anything I say," Clary grumbled later to Polly as they were waiting in the day nursery for Ellen's kettle to boil so that they could fill their hot water bottles. "It isn't just a question of whether she's a virgin or not, I'm just as curious about prisoners, and nuns and royalty and childbirth and murder and things like that—*anything* that either hasn't happened to me or couldn't ever happen."

"Royalty's the only one of them," Polly pointed out: she was used to these discussions.

"No—what about your favourite song? 'I am so fond of pleasure that I *cannot* be a nun.'"

"I don't know how fond of pleasure I am," Polly said sadly. "We really don't get enough of it to find out."

She had not wanted to announce her pregnancy at home but she felt so sick the first morning that she couldn't get up for breakfast. Lydia was sent up to see why she hadn't come down.

"It's nothing. I must have eaten something."

"Oh, poor you! It's probably that horrible meat loaf we had last night for supper. Do you know what Neville thinks? He thinks Mrs. Cripps puts mice and hedgehogs in it. He thinks she might be a witch because of her black hair and her face is practically luminous in the dark. Even toads, he thought she might put—squashed, you know— he thinks that might be the jellyish bit you get on the outside—toads' ooze—"

"Oh, shut *up*, Lydia."

"Sorry. I was only trying to think what it could be. Shall I bring you up some tea?"

"Thanks, that would be lovely."

But it was her mother who arrived with tea and toast, and she seemed to know at once without Louise saying a thing.

"Oh, darling! How *exciting!* Does Michael know?"

"Yes."

"He must be pleased."

"He is—very."

"Have you been to a doctor?"

"No."

"Well, Dr. Carr is awfully good. Eat the toast, even if you don't put anything on it. Toast and water biscuits are the thing for morning sickness. How long . . . ?"

About five weeks, she thought. It seemed like for ever.

In the end she stayed nearly a month at home, by which time Dr. Carr had confirmed her pregnancy. Everybody assumed that she was delighted at the prospect. The only person she came near confiding in was Zoë. She was helping to put Juliet to bed. "You give her her supper while I clear up," Zoë had said. They were alone in the nursery: Wills and Roly were being bathed by Ellen.

Juliet sat in her high chair. She wanted to feed herself, which was a messy and inconclusive business. "No, Jule do it," she repeated whenever Louise tried to take the laden spoon from her.

"Goodness! She'll need another bath."

"Oh, I'll just sponge the worst bits off. One has to let them learn."

"I don't know anything about babies."

Zoë looked at her quickly and waited for her to say something else, but she didn't. She often found herself trying not to cry these days.

"Listen," Zoë said as she came across the room to sit at the table by Louise and the high chair, "neither did I. And it's *terrifying* because everybody seems to assume that you do."

"And that you're thrilled," Louise said in a muffled voice.

"Yes."

"And *you* weren't?"

"Not the first time—no. And then everyone kept saying I should have another one and I didn't want to."

"But you did."

"Not then, not immediately. Hang on, Jules. Let me clean you up a bit first.

"But when I finally did have her—it was wonderful. It was—well, with Rupert gone, she just made all the difference. I had been dreading something happening to him so much, it seemed like the worst thing in the world that could happen, and then it happened—but at the same time, there was Jules."

"Chockat!"

"No. Onto your pot first."

But Jules did not agree with this. She lay on the floor, arched her back and set about a luxuriant tantrum.

Louise watched while Zoë dealt with this. Finally, Jules was on her pot with a small piece of chocolate. "It usually turns out to be a compromise."

"Aunt Zoë—I—"

"I'd much rather you dropped the Aunt. Sorry! What?"

"I just wanted to say I hadn't realized about—what an awful time you must have had."

"Why should you have? You were a child. And, anyway, it's far harder for you. I didn't start until I'd been married for about five years, and Rupert wasn't *in* the war then. You're doing it all at once."

In some ways this conversation was comforting; but in other ways not. Perhaps, like Zoë, she would feel quite differently about a baby once it was *there:* on the other hand, and for the first time, she came up against the dreadful prospect of Michael getting killed.

A few evenings later when he rang her up, which he did from time to time, he told her that he could get away for a night and proposed coming to Sussex. "We've had a bit of engine trouble and so I'm leaving them to it for a day or two."

She felt light-hearted with excitement, everybody was very pleased for her and the whole family entered into preparations to welcome him. The Duchy procured a brace of pheasants for dinner; the Brig spent the morning choosing and decanting port; Lydia had a row with Polly about wearing their bridesmaids' dresses for dinner (Polly thought it was unsuitable but Lydia, who had tried to wear hers for lessons, for tea on Sundays and sometimes secretly after her bath was determined). "It is perfectly the proper thing to wear for dinner," she said, "and it will remind Michael of old times—his lovely wedding and all that."

"You won't *be* at dinner," Polly had said.

"I shall! Louise! You'll let me be, won't you, as your sister?"

But before Louise could reply, their mother had said she was afraid it was out of the question. There was not enough pheasant to go round: Aunt Dolly would be having a tray upstairs, and Aunt Rach had said that she found pheasant a wee bit indigestible and was going to stick to veg.

"Couldn't I be at dinner and have a boiled *egg?*"

"No, you can't. Miss Milliment is having hers on a tray in the nursery. You may have yours with her."

"Thanks very bloody much."

"That'll do, Lydia. I've told you not to use that word."

"It'll only be an ordinary old dinner," Clary said when Villy had left the room.

"It wouldn't be ordinary to me. I don't *have* dinners as a rule. I seem to be in a class by myself for misfortune. It doesn't seem to have struck them that we might all get bombed before I reach the age to have any privileges at all. I shall have had a completely wasted life."

Clary and Polly exchanged weary, consciously adult glances but then made soothing noises of comfort and commiseration. But Louise had recognized the faint irritation in her mother's voice and found herself in sympathy. Lydia was only trying to get the rules changed: all children did that—why, even *she* had done the same thing ages ago. Being at home certainly made her feel older although not the same age as anyone else in the family.

Michael arrived that evening by train, and she went to meet him with Tonbridge who now called her "Madam." He drove her so slowly to Battle that she thought they would be late, but they weren't. She had only to stand a minute at the door of the ticket office when the train shuffled in. Although it was dark, small chinks and streaks of dark yellow light were emitted by the train as doors opened and some passengers twitched aside the blackout in a hopeless attempt to see where they had arrived. Stations had been without names for so long that most people were used to it, and simply counted the number of stops, but there were always a few anxious strangers.

"Fancy seeing you here!"

"Oh—I just thought—if I meet enough trains, I'm bound to know *someone* getting off one of them."

He put his free arm round her and gave her a hug before a kiss. "I'm not 'arf glad to see you. How's His Nibs?"

"Who?"

"Our babe."

"Fine."

"Darling girl! Have I missed you!"

The feeling of excitement and happiness came back. He was wearing his greatcoat that smelled faintly of diesel oil and salt and camphor with the collar turned up round his neck; the badge on his cap glinted slightly in the darkness when he turned his head towards her. They sat, holding hands, and made grown-up conversation for the benefit of Tonbridge.

"News is good, isn't it? Good old Monty."

"Do you think we're actually winning the war?"

"Well," he said, "it would seem that the tide is turning. The Russians are holding on in Stalingrad. North Africa is definitely our biggest victory so far. But we've still got a long way to go."

"What's wrong with your ship?"

"We've been having trouble with the port engine. Each time they think they've got it right and then it packs up again. So now they're having a really serious overhaul. There have been other things, of course. But the crew is shaking down nicely. Little Turner packed us some cheese for you, it's in my case. I've scrounged a tin of butter as well. So I hope I'll be popular."

"You would be, anyway," she said. "They're all longing to see you. Lydia wanted to wear her bridesmaid's dress in your honour. Do you think you could draw Juliet? It would be so lovely for Zoë."

"I might at that. Not easy because at that age they don't keep still. You're my best sitter, darling. Which was Juliet?"

"My smallest cousin."

"She was ravishing. I'll have a go. Haven't got very much time, though."

"When do you have to go back?"

"Tomorrow afternoon, I'm afraid."

What he did not tell her then, what only came out at dinner—it seemed to her almost by accident—was that he wasn't going back to the ship the next day, he was going to go on a bombing raid over Germany. "They're going to pick me up at Lympne, which seems to be the nearest airfield to you, but it's devilish small for a Stirling. However, they say they can just about manage it. That would be super," he said when Villy offered to drive him there. "It would be lovely to have a family send-off."

"Why on earth are you going in a bomber? They haven't told you to, have they?"

"No. I just thought it might be fun. And I'm rather interested in camouflage at the moment. Said it would be useful to me to make the trip. And they agreed."

Pride forbade her letting the family know that this was news to her so she was silent. But once they were on their own, undressing for bed, she said, "Why didn't you tell me?"

"I was going to tell you. I have."

"I can't think *why* you want to do that. You might—you might get—"

"No, darling, that's very unlikely. Where's the bathroom, darling? I've rather lost my bearings."

She told him and he went. Alone, remnants of news bulletins kept bombarding her: "Three of our aircraft missing"; "Two of our bombers failed to return." He was mad to go if he didn't have to; of course it was dangerous. It wasn't fair that he should risk his life—on purpose, as it were—when he had married her and was so keen on having a family.

"Does Zee know?" she asked when he returned. (That might stop him: she was sure Zee would be against it.)

"Yes. Of course she doesn't like the idea any more than you do, darling, she loves me too, you know. But she just put her arms round me and gave me a hug and said, 'You must do what you want.'

"Actually," he said, smiling at the recollection of it, "she said, 'A man's got to do what a man's got to do.' She is amazing—she really is."

"You *saw* her last night? Did she come to Cowes, then?"

"No. She came up to London for the night. There was a play of Jack's she wanted to see."

"Jack?"

"Jack Priestley. So we went to that. Jolly good it was. We both thought of you and how much you would have enjoyed it."

It was all too much. He had two—no, *three* nights' leave and he had chosen to spend the first with his mother and the third on a bombing raid over Germany. She burst into tears.

"Now, darling," he said, "you mustn't upset yourself. You really mustn't. This is war, you know. I shall have to do all kinds of things that involve a certain amount of danger, that's what war is. You must learn to be brave."

The next morning he spent half of it drawing Juliet, and the other half teaching her a code so that if he was taken prisoner he could send messages about his escape plans in apparently innocuous letters to her. He wrote out a specimen of the code in his beautiful clear writing and told her to lock it up somewhere safe. "Unless you can memorize it," he said. "That would be best, of course."

Then there was lunch—fricassé of rabbit and gooseberry fool—but she found it difficult to eat anything, listening dumbly to the usual family discussion about who was to come on the excursion to the airfield. Lydia was determined to go and Wills wanted to see the aeroplane, but as she would not have been alone with him in any case, she did not very much care. Michael had brought some petrol coupons with him (he must have planned to get the lift, she thought); it seemed as though all of his arrangements about life were unknown to her until they happened. She sat in the back of the car with him with the children wriggling and chattering in front. She had become very passive, and simply concurred in everything, but inside she felt cold and heavy with fear. In an hour, she thought, he would be gone, and she might never see him again, and he seemed unaware, unconscious of what this meant. To spend your last hour with someone who was map-reading, while "I spy with my little eye" went on in the front of the car seemed bizarre.

Eventually they reached the windswept but bright green grass runway, and everybody got out. It was raining, not hard but steadily. Michael was saluted by a very young man in RAF uniform and they were conducted to the hut, which smelled strongly of the paraffin stove that stopped it being entirely cold.

Here was an officer who said he was the station commander, adding that he was amazed that a Stirling was going to land there: "I must say I rather doubt whether it *can*."

For a moment she imagined it falling—swooping away, and not managing to pick up Michael, after all. But a second later the throbbing sound of the engines could be heard and, surprisingly soon, there it was. It looked enormous. It did one circuit over them and then came in at the far end of the runway, finally stopping right at the other end, with its blunt nose almost in a hedge.

"Right," he said, "here we go. I mustn't keep them waiting." He kissed his mother-in-law affectionately, bent down and kissed Lydia on the cheek and she blinked and went pink, nodded to Wills who was transfixed by the Stirling and finally turned to her, put his hands on her shoulders and gave her a kiss on her mouth of the kind that is almost over before it has begun. "Keep your pecker up, my darling," he said. "I'll ring some time tomorrow. Promise."

Her mother took the two children to the car: Wills had broken out into a roar of despair when he realized that he was not going to get *into* the aeroplane. She stood and watched him climb up into the bomber, watched them pull the narrow stairway up into it after him, watched the door, or hatch, or whatever it was, slam shut removing him from sight, watched the huge unwieldy plane turn and then taxi away down the runway.

"The wind's east," the station commander said. "They'll go out to sea and then turn and come back over us. You can wave to them then."

So she waited a few minutes to do that, wondering whether he could see her, whether even if he could see her, he would be looking.

Her mother was very kind to her in just the right way: she made it clear that she thought it was hard, but she did not go on about it.

Lydia wanted to go and have tea in a tea-shop in Hastings, "As we've come all this way. To make it a proper treat."

Villy turned to Louise who was sitting in front beside her. "Do you want to do that, darling?"

She shook her head. As so often nowadays, she was perilously near tears.

"We'll go home, then."

They drove home in the dusk, and that evening she stayed with the family to listen to the nine o'clock news. "French fleet has been scuttled by their crews in Toulon harbour," it began, but eventually it got to heavy raids having been carried out on Kiel and Cologne the previous night. Then she realized that she wouldn't know anything about the raid Michael was on until he rang up. So the aircraft that were being reported missing could have nothing to do with him. Soon, as she was unable to bear the atmosphere of covert sympathy, she escaped to bed where she had what her family would have called a good cry. She had begun to be afraid that Michael did not love her, and that he would be killed.

PART

TWO

The Family

New Year, 1943

Bᴜᴛ Hᴀᴘᴘʏ Nᴇᴡ Year all the same.''

There was such a silence, that she said, ''Darling, you *know* how disappointed I am. Or perhaps you don't.''

''No, I don't think I do.''

''Well, I am. But I simply can't abandon poor old Dolly with nobody to look after her.''

Nobody! Sid thought. The house is chock-a-block with people and servants. What does she mean ''nobody''? Aloud, she said, ''I suppose if I broke my leg, you'd come and look after me?''

''Darling! You *know* I would.'' Irony was not part of Rachel's make-up. The eager sweetness of this response brought tears of love and resentment to her eyes. The little respite—it was hardly even a holiday—of Rachel's spending two nights with her in London was foiled, like so many other anxious, hopeful plans that they made these days. Usually it was the Brig, the old despot, who frustrated them; now it was Dolly with flu. It could easily have been the Duchy. There would always be some old person for Rachel to look after, an endless succession of them, until *we* too are old . . .

''You can't possibly come down?''

''You know perfectly well I'm on call. I didn't do Christmas so I have to do New Year's Eve.''

''All right, darling. I quite understand. I'll be up at the end of next week, anyway.''

''You always say things like that.''

"Do I? What I meant was, I have to go to the dentist. I think I've got that abscess coming back on a tooth. So I've made an appointment."

"Is it hurting?"

"Off and on. It's nothing to worry about. Aspirin keeps it at bay. I must go, I'm afraid. Villy is waiting for the phone. Happy New Year again. Why don't you ring up that poor girl and have her to supper?"

When she had rung off, Sid thought, why not? She was so fed up and *used* to being disappointed, so tired from endless hopes being frustrated and deferred, so exhausted by the chronic general jealousy that Rachel's, in her view, excessive unselfishness so constantly presented—which always brought with it the nagging fear that her importance to Rachel was waning or had never really existed in the first place—that the idea of spending the evening with someone who clearly worshipped her was a kind of balm. Somebody, at least, cared to be with her, would understand if she was suddenly called out to the ambulance station, would wait until she returned and would certainly appreciate the modest feast that she had collected to enjoy with Rachel and that she certainly would not have had the heart to eat alone. All the same, she felt unsure about whether ringing Thelma would prove to be a good thing. It was all very well to give her free violin lessons—that much she felt she owed the poor little thing. And taking her to the odd concert had also seemed appropriately kind. But asking her to supper would place the relationship on a different footing and it might not be one that she would feel able to sustain. She felt sorry for Thelma—how could one not? Thelma's parents had both been killed: her father on a North Atlantic convoy, her mother in an air raid on Coventry. She seemed without any other family, and struggled to live on a succession of ill-paid part-time jobs. Sid had been introduced to her by the forcefully kind lady who ran canteens for various ambulance stations. This girl had come to clean her house, she had said but, really, she was a very gifted musician. Mrs. Davenport, returning to her house unexpectedly, had caught her playing the piano quite *amazingly* well. Of course *she* didn't know *anything* about music, but she could tell *instantly* this girl had a gift . . . And the girl had told her that the piano was not really her instrument—she considered herself to be a violinist.

Of course, she had agreed to hear the girl, whose musical talent proved to be nothing remarkable. But she had seemed so willing, so eager to learn and her sense of identity so clearly rested upon the idea of being a professional musician, that Sid, who missed teaching more than she had realized, took her on. Thelma had been grateful—

extravagantly, pathetically so. Sid was constantly getting little gifts—bunches of violets, bags of sweets, packets of cigarettes and, with them, a stream of cards. She also worked exceedingly hard at her violin practice between the weekly lessons. When Rachel's niece got married and Sid had gone to the wedding, Thelma produced a quantity of newspaper cuttings about the event that Sid, whose interest in it had been chiefly centred upon the pleasure of seeing Rachel, had sent on to her: "From my indefatigable little pupil," she had written. "But I dare say somebody in the family might like to see them." Of course she felt sorry for Thelma, but not perhaps quite sorry enough to spend New Year's Eve with her. No, she would dine alone.

Just as she had decided this, the telephone rang and it was Thelma asking if she might bring a small New Year's gift? In seconds, Sid found that she had not only invited her to supper, she had suggested that if they were to see in the New Year, Thelma had better bring things for the night. As Thelma lived in a room near Waterloo and could not possibly have afforded a cab home, this seemed a small practical kindness. "What Rachel would certainly have done," she said to herself. She felt tired and dispirited, selfish and resentful, and not disposed towards festivity of any kind. She would be forty-four when the New Year was a week old and felt as though she would never stop living from hand to mouth with not very much in her hand.

"Darling, you shouldn't say that. It's not going to be New Year for another four hours at least."

"I shall probably say it every time I have a drink. Which tonight will be rather often."

"Bad week?"

"A *sodding* awful week."

"Hugh again?"

He nodded. "I don't know what's got into the old boy. He's always been as stubborn as a mule, but these days, whatever I say, he deliberately takes the opposite view. And then sticks to it. Nothing will shift him."

Before Diana could reply, wails broke out from upstairs.

"I'll have to go up. Darling, just relax. Have another whisky. I might be some time getting him off. Have a little snooze: there's plenty of time before dinner. Put another log on the fire, darling, would you?"

The logs were in a large rush basket by the enormous open fireplace. He hoisted himself out of his chair with caution; the cottage was full of beams and the last thing he wanted was a crack on the head. She had made the place very cosy: the room, which occupied nearly all of the ground floor, was sitting and dining room combined; there was a tiny kitchen which contained a Raeburn stove, a sink and a draining board, and a door that opened into an icy larder. The main room was crowded with a sofa and two armchairs, all rather battered, a scrubbed table which was set for dinner, a dresser on which the china was kept and at the far end, near the front door in front of which an old carpet had been hung to exclude the worst draughts, a play pen with rag books, bricks and several stuffed animals who lounged with a kind of stoic abandon against its bars. Jamie's tricycle was parked at that end of the room, together with his gum boots. Apart from the fire, the room was lit by a large oil lamp that stood on the dresser, further crowding the room with pools of mellow gold and mysterious twilight angles of shadow. In the daytime, its small, heavily recessed windows made the room rather dark; at night, it came into its own. It was good to be here, he thought. At home there would be Hugh, and either we'd have another row, or we'd bottle everything up for the weekend.

He poured himself another drink. He didn't feel like dropping off; he wanted to go through the whole thing on his own, when he could perhaps manage not to feel quite so angry that it clouded his judgement. Right. They had taken long enough to pay the compensation for the war damage to the wharf: there had been months of assessments, overseeing stock books, paperwork of every imaginable kind, but in the end they had paid—a hundred per cent both for repair of the property and the value of the stock held there. That had seemed fine. But then, out of the blue, at the end of that tax year, the firm had been faced with excess profits tax on all of the stock, as though they'd *sold* it, which meant, in effect, they were not getting its value at all. They'd made the tax allowable profit on timber that had been sold, but this was *stock*, worth the best part of two hundred thousand pounds: paying EPT on that effectively meant that it couldn't be replaced on the money left. He was so damned angry that he'd gone to lawyers at once, although Hugh had said there was no point. They would simply have to pay it, he said—again and again. The lawyer had been pretty feeble: said that if they fought it, it would undoubtedly have to go as far as the Lords since it would be setting a precedent or, at best, attempting to stop one being set. He'd talked to the Old Man, who had suggested they speak to a friend of his in the Board of Trade. "Find out whether this has been happening a lot, or whether we're a one-off case," he had said. The Old Man's friend had said, of course, that it wasn't really his department, but had also more or less intimated that he thought they ought to grin and bear it. Hugh had been gloomily triumphant. "Told you it wasn't the slightest use, simply a waste of time and money," he had said. But *he* felt that there was too much at stake for them to take it lying down. That money represented their trading future and, given that hardwoods were rising in price steadily, by the time they came to renew stock they would anyway be unable to match the stuff that had been destroyed in the bombing. The EPT was the last straw. So, this morning he had had one more go at Hugh about fighting the whole thing. It was not only *their* money, he had said, there was also the principle: it was patently unjust for the Government to turn the compensation for damaged stock into some sort of trumped-up profit, to treat it as a sale. Hugh had seemed to agree with this, but then he had reverted to the high costs of employing the right kind of lawyers to act for them, the enormous waste of time, the fact that they were understaffed and that this would be a disruption lasting for months, "on top of which," he had finished, "we have absolutely no guarantee of success. We could simply be even more out of pocket and have made fools of ourselves."

Hugh had been sitting at his desk when he said this, playing with a paperweight, picking it up and dropping it from the height of an inch or so back onto his desk. And *then*, and this is what had made Edward see red, he had added, "In any case, I've had another talk with the Old Man, and he's dead against it. So it's two against one, I'm afraid."

"He *wasn't* against it before!"

"Well, he is now."

"You know perfectly well you've put the case in such a way to him as to make him agree with you."

"I told him what I thought, naturally."

"It seems to be the greatest possible pity that you should see fit to talk to him behind my back."

"Does it? I thought you were rather in favour of doing things behind people's backs."

This oblique, but unmistakable reference to Diana enraged him so much that he had got to his feet and left Hugh's office, slamming the door behind him. Damned cheek! Ever since he'd had that awful conversation with Hugh who had almost persuaded him to ditch

Diana, and then, for obvious reasons, he hadn't, there had been a smouldering disapproval coming from Hugh that he'd found it very difficult to stand. Because, of course, from a conventional point of view, Hugh was right. But he seemed to take no account of feelings—either his or Diana's. He was in love with her; she had had his child; he couldn't abandon her now. He couldn't think beyond now about that. But Hugh had no right to bring *that* into a discussion, or argument, about business. *There* he was indisputably right. Not for the first time, he wished old Rupe was with them, but then, and also not for the first time, he remembered that Rupe would agree with enthusiastic sympathy with whoever was talking to him. I'll have to tackle the Old Man, he thought. He had to go back anyway, tomorrow, had only wangled this night off by saying there was an RAF do that he had been invited to and couldn't refuse. It was a good thing, really, that Diana had finally decided against living in London. This cottage, half-way between the wharf and Sussex, had been a far better idea, although he supposed it must be a bit lonely for her at times. But she had chosen it, or rather, one of Angus's rich friends had offered it to her for almost nothing; it had been a keeper's cottage on his family's estate. God, what a mess everything is, though, he thought. He didn't *want* to quarrel with Hugh; he loved the old boy, and he knew, he felt, better than anyone, how hard Sybil's death had hit him. The last time he had felt really close to Hugh was when he had taken him away afterwards. God knows why he had chosen Westmorland. He thought it ought to be somewhere that they had never been to before, but he hadn't reckoned on the weather. It had rained practically every day. They had gone for long wet walks taking packed lunches from the small hotel; played darts in the evenings, listened to the news on the radio in the bar, had a game of chess and gone to bed early, although it was clear that Hugh was not sleeping much. To begin with he had seemed stunned, was very silent, although from time to time he would say things like "I can't tell you how grateful I am to you for seeing me through this bit of it," and then his eyes would fill with tears and he would stop. Then, gradually, he began to talk about Sybil, despairing, feverish ruminations about whether she could have been saved: if they had found out about the cancer earlier, if she had *told* him when she began to feel ill, if they had operated sooner . . . "In the end, you know, we talked about it," he said. "I discovered that she had known how ill she was for months. She was very sick one night; she made herself eat an ordinary dinner to please me. She was very upset because she said she hated me having to clear it all up: I told her that being able to do *anything* for her was a joy, a blessing, some kind of relief, and then when I had got her a clean nightdress and was helping her get into it, she told me that she knew she was dying, and she knew I knew. 'I want to be able to say anything to you,' she said, 'because soon I won't be able to say anything at all.'"

They had talked, he had said, as though they had just met, uncovering layers about each other, like onion skins, she had said and when she became too tired to talk, he would read to her: she especially liked poetry, which had never meant much to him. "To tell the truth," he had said, "I often read pages of the stuff without really knowing what was going on. But as I got used to it, sometimes I'd suddenly see what the chap was on about and actually it was very good—very *telling*." He'd bought one or two of her favourite books with him, he said, and was working his way through them, but it wasn't the same. In the end, she had got so weak from the bloody pain, that she'd just wanted him to sit with her and not say very much. But a couple of days before she had died when she'd just had a shot of something and wasn't feeling too bad, she'd said did he remember when they were in St. Moritz, which, of course, he did and she'd smiled and said, "Tell me about it," and he had. There had been a long silence after that. Remembering Hugh's face as the shadowy little smile of reminiscence came and went before it could reach his poor haunted eyes, he felt a return of the familiar, protective love that he had always had for this older brother. There was something rigid, inflexibly unworldly, honourable and innocent about Hugh that needed protection, he thought. At the moment it was the inflexibility that he was up against. Oh, well, he mustn't be too impatient with the old boy.

"Sorry to be so long. Jamie wants you to say good night to him." She had changed into a dark blue velvet housecoat thing that made her skin look very attractive. "I've got Susan off, so don't let him get too excited and make a noise."

Jamie lay flat on his back with the blanket up to his chin.

"Hallo, old boy."

"Hallo, old boy." He thought for a moment and then added, "I'm not actually old. Well, I am *old*, but I'm not as old as you. You must be very very very *very* old."

"Well, yes, I suppose I am." He was certainly feeling it this evening.

"How old *are* you?" he asked, as though this question had long been lying between them.

"Forty-six."

"Forty-*six!* Good God!"

"Jamie, I don't think you should say that."

"My grandfather, who lives in Scotland, says it all the time. He even said it about a wasp on his marmalade at breakfast. And he says it all the time he's reading the paper. So of course I've picked it up. Mrs. Campbell who cooks there says it's astonishing what I pick up. If you pick things up you can't help it," he explained.

"What do you think of your new sister?"

He pretended to consider. "I really don't like her. I'd much rather we'd had a dog. I don't like her because she's ugly and stupid you see."

"Oh well," he said, as he got up from Jamie's bed, "I expect you'll like her when she's older."

"I *don't* expect. Will you read me a story?"

"Not tonight, old chap. I'm going to have some dinner now."

"Tell *her* to say good night to me. *Order* her."

As he left the room, Jamie called, "Uncle Edward! If I *shot* her, would I get beheaded?"

"I should think you jolly well might."

"Good God!"

"He didn't mean you, of course, he meant Susan."

"I know *that.* He's fearfully jealous, poor lamb."

"But he wouldn't do anything awful to her, would he?"

"He might try to," she said calmly. "You have to try and imagine what it's like to be him. Supposing, just as an example"—her voice became mellow with reason—"suppose you suddenly took me back to Home Place one day, and told Villy that although, of course, you loved her, I would be living there with both of you henceforth. How do you think she would feel?"

"Don't be absurd. Naturally she wouldn't like it."

"That's an understatement, surely. She'd be fiendishly jealous. I know I would be."

In the short silence that followed, she noticed that his eyes had become as bleak as blue marbles.

"I'm afraid I really can't see the parallel," he said at last.

"I only meant that that is how Jamie feels about Susan. I'll get our stew."

It wasn't all she had meant at all, he thought. It was as near as she dared to get to telling him what she felt. He knew that he should take the bull by the horns but, as dear old Rupe had once said, when you did that you had to bear in mind the fact that you were still faced with the rest of the bull.

"Well, now! Happy New Year, little girl."

"Happy New Year." For a minute, she did not know where she was, but she had learned to lie low on these occasions, knowing that, one way or another, she soon *would* know.

"Boy! That was some night we had ourselves. How are you feeling?"

She tried to sit up and her head started pounding, like a huge piece of cumbersome machinery. She relapsed onto the pillow and shut her eyes to try to stop the room rocking.

"Poor baby! Now you just lie there and Uncle Earl will fix you something."

That was it! He was the one she had met in the Astor last week when she'd had the row with Joe Bronstein because she'd wanted to go home and he wouldn't. Earl had come over to their table and somehow—magically—sorted things out. In no time she had found herself being taken home in a taxi to her flat, where he had escorted her to the door, made sure she got in and then left her in peace. The next morning a large bunch of red roses arrived with his card, that had Colonel Earl C. Black on it and a note with his telephone number that said how much he would like to see her again. She was fed up with Joe, who had proved to be as predictable as everybody else in bed and more tiresome than many out of it, so now here she was, in the Major's flat, she presumed, though she could remember nothing of how she got there. Never mind. If she kept absolutely still, kept her eyes shut, the pounding grind in her head did seem to be getting less . . .

". . . now, then, Angie honey, sit up . . ."

"What is it?"

He was holding out a glass that contained some brownish red liquid.

"Honestly, I couldn't. I feel awful."

"I know, sweetheart, but this will make you better. Trust Earl." He put an arm round her shoulder and hoisted her up, and held the glass to her mouth. She couldn't feel worse, she thought, and therefore obediently swallowed the peppery sharp, slippery mixture although it made her retch.

"That's my girl," he said. He put the glass down and draped her shoulders—which were bare, she realized—in his striped pyjama jacket.

"You just sit for a while and then you'll feel fine. A hot shower and you'll feel better still."

"Have you by any chance got a toothbrush I could use?"

"I do," he said. "Do you want to go to the bathroom before I take my shower?"

She did. She got out of bed and tottered across the room clutching the jacket round her—it came nearly to her knees.

When she returned and had climbed gratefully back into bed, he was wearing boxer shorts. She watched him as he walked about the small beige bedroom selecting clothes. He was a barrel-chested man, with broad shoulders and wiry hair that rioted over his chest like grizzled scrub. He had a wide low forehead from which more grizzled but copious hair sprang in a pronounced peak. His eyebrows grew in a militant manner like small brambles, his muscular arms with thick wrists were hirsute like his legs. He must be quite old, she thought— at least forty. She wondered whether he had made love to her (she still called it that), but she wouldn't ask. Surprisingly, she *did* feel better. Across the room, her dress from last night was carefully draped upon a small brocaded chair.

He said it was time for her to shower and conducted her to the small bathroom—even turned it on for her. "There's a robe on the back of the door," he said, "you can wear that."

She looked awful. The bathroom mirror with its heartless little light above (there was no window in the bathroom) revealed a pallid face with dark rings of smudged mascara round her eyes and streaks of other make-up running down her neck. Her usually smooth and shining hair looked matted and dark as though she had sweated all night, her eyebrows, plucked so that they needed a pencil to delineate them were just two shadowy half moons. Next to the basin was a towel rail on which were her underclothes: stockings, suspender belt and knickers—all recently washed. Oh, God! Tears of humiliation filled her eyes: she could not remember anything except that they had been sitting in some night club new to her—dark, as they all were—at a tiny rocking table that had bottles and glasses on it. "Happy New Year," he had said, and she just remembered the feeling of total despair that had surged up in her, threatening even her party smile as she had gulped down her drink to quench it. That was all. She couldn't remember a thing after that. She couldn't even remember feeling drunk, a sensation both disagreeable and familiar, but she must have been—very drunk—if she had such a blackout. I must stop, she thought, try something else, get away, find something different—a new life. I can't go on like this. But the bleakness of any alternative seemed terrifying in its openness: she could do absolutely anything without it making any difference. Meanwhile, somehow she must get through the next hour, clean herself up, rejoin him and apologize and creep home, away from the whole squalid incident. She took off the pyjama jacket and stepped into the shower, which although it nearly scalded her, was somehow comforting. Hot water was not often available in her flat: Carol, the girl with whom she shared it always seemed just to have had the only hot bath the geyser afforded. While she was drying herself, she thought of the flat. Carol would be asleep if she was there: she worked at the London Palladium and always slept until about three in the afternoon. Angela's bedroom, the smaller of the two, looked out on a black brick wall and tiny courtyard in which the overflowing dustbins of a restaurant were lodged. They had smelt awful last summer. It was about the fourth place she had lived in: girls she had shared with had been called up, got married, found a job somewhere outside London, and since they always seemed to be the main tenant of wherever it was, and she couldn't afford to live in any of them alone, she had moved on. She still had her job at the BBC—six nights on and three off—so one way or another, all of her life was conducted after dark. There was a tiny kitchenette in the flat, but she never bothered to cook: when she was working, she ate at the canteen, and on her nights off people took her out. She spent her salary on clothes, make-up, having her hair done, and taxis. The advent of the Americans in London had meant that there always seemed to be someone who wanted to take her out. She found them far easier than Englishmen. They were usually lonely, didn't ask questions about her family, were generous, producing wonderful stockings made of nylon, scent, unlimited cigarettes and drink, tins of butter and Spam (which she exchanged for black market clothes coupons) and once a marvellous length of green silk sent from New York with which she had had a beautiful dress made. They were also usually married, or engaged to someone back home, and although these facts were seldom volunteered, she had become very good at discovering them. To begin with this had worried her, but it didn't any more. They were miles from homes to which, possibly, they might never return, cut off from everything they knew, and they simply wanted a good time. Their ideas of what this might be varied, but not much. She felt as though she, too, was miles from home, or rather that she had not got one at all; Frensham was being turned into a convalescent place, and ever since her mother had interfered over the Brian thing she had not gone to St. John's Wood. Her father was safely tucked away in Woodstock; Christopher, the only one of her family for whom she felt the warmth of love, was sweating away at some nursery garden in Sussex—he hated London and so she hardly ever saw him. She had gone to her cousin's wedding in the autumn, and it had felt extraordinary to be with all the Cazalets again, simply accepted as one of their family, sitting in a pew with her parents and Christopher and Nora and Judy. Sitting there, waiting for Louise to walk up the aisle on Uncle Edward's arm, she realized how isolated from the family she had become, how shocked they would be if they knew about her life now: sleeping all the morning, pottering about her dreary little room, mending stockings, and ironing and painting her nails; in the afternoon bathing and dressing and going out evening after evening with men she hardly knew, drinking clubs, restaurants, night clubs, necking in taxis, sometimes bringing someone back with her (but not often; she was ashamed of her room and did not like anyone to see it)—if she was going to go to bed with whoever it was, she preferred it to be on their ground, the anonymity of an hotel room.

In the months after Brian had left her, and after the abortion, she had clung to the idea of love. Love, that had been so painful twice—with Rupert and then with Brian—was still to be her goal and salvation: if she continued to seek it, surely one day it would occur. Meanwhile she had to get through the days and nights. Her job was a lonely one: often she hardly spoke to anybody excepting the junior programme engineers on the other side of the glass screen in the studio, and the people in the canteen who doled out her breakfast. She loved dancing: it created an illusion of intimacy; to be in somebody's arms in a dark place with slow music was a kind of drug; being admired, being wanted, soothed her, made her feel less worthless. She learned how to please . . . anyone, really—excepting herself. She did not go the whole way with everyone by any means, and made choices; but deep down she felt that admiration had to be paid for, and she dealt with that by calling it only an interim, *until* she met the wonderful as yet unknown person who would transform her life. It was the war, she told herself: it made everything different, harder and, if one was not very careful, unspeakably boring. But as the months had dragged by the idea of love receded; she was no longer very sure what it was, and one still had to get through life. She had been afraid that she would get called up but when the time came, she failed the medical—something about her chest, they said; it hadn't bothered her and so she wasn't interested, just deeply relieved. For at least a week after that, her life had seemed wonderfully free and easy, glamorous even, but it soon slipped back into a kind of limbo where nothing seemed important enough to be more than a boring, or less boring, way of getting through time.

He was knocking on the bathroom door. "Coffee's up," he was saying.

She had rinsed her hair under the shower and combed it out. Her face, devoid of make-up, was still faintly flushed by the hot water. She couldn't look worse than she had before the shower, she thought, and it didn't matter, anyway. She would drink the coffee, clamber into her damp underclothes and freezing skimpy little frock and get him to put her into a cab. That would be that.

The coffee was laid out on a small rickety table in the sitting room. It *was* a flat, he had, she realized, not an hotel room or suite. The coffee was very strong and good. When he pushed the sugar bowl towards her and she shook her head, he said, "Take some. I haven't got any food here, and you've got nothing inside you. Don't feel bad about it, sweetheart. You had a dose of hooch. That stuff was real bad: we won't go back there again."

"What about you, then? Did you—"

"I was drinking Scotch. You had gin—that was the trouble."

"I'm really sorry—"

"Don't be. It was just lucky it wasn't the both of us. It was a bad joint."

But her mind was full of humiliating scenes—of her passing out, being sick, being unable to control herself in any way—and not being able to remember any of it, made it somehow far worse . . .

"I think I should go," she said. "If you could get me a cab?"

"I had a better plan," he said. "Someone has lent me an automobile. I'll take you home, wait while you get into some warm clothes, and then I thought we'd drive out into the country some place—and have us a square meal." And before she could respond, he added, "In case you're worrying about whether I took advantage of you last night, let me tell you that I did not." He put a large hairy hand over hers on the table. "Cross my heart and hope to die. Nothing happened. OK?"

"All right," she said. She still felt embarrassed, but also now relieved: she believed him about last night, which didn't mean that she trusted him otherwise.

"All right, that's enough of the Happy New Years," Archie said. "Now what about the resolutions?"

They were in the drawing room. The older members of the family had gone to bed: the Duchy and Miss Milliment had bad colds; Rachel had succumbed to her toothache immediately after the chimes of Big Ben had announced the New Year, "I can't kiss any of you, darlings, my face feels like a boiling *marrow*," she had said, trying to smile but looking ghastly, Clary thought. Edward and Villy were in London celebrating with Hermione. So Archie and Hugh were left with the children—allowed to stay up down to Lydia, who had promised to go to bed when Archie made her. Everybody had kissed everyone else and wished them a Happy New Year.

"Couldn't we play charades?" Lydia thought they might take longer than resolutions.

"No, Archie said resolutions. How many do we have to have? One, or as many as we like?"

"I think three each," Archie said. "What do you say, Hugh?"

"What? Oh, by all means, three. Whisky?"

"Thanks." Lydia seized his glass and carried it over to her uncle. She was hell bent on pleasing, hoping that resolutions might *lead* to charades.

"What are they?" Neville said. "I mean what sort of thing?"

"Oh, good ones, of course," Polly said. "Like being kind to your enemies."

"That's a silly idea. They wouldn't *be* my enemies if I was kind to them."

"Well, they are meant to be good," Archie said. "I mean constructive, you know, vaguely *improving*."

Someone suggested writing them down, and Lydia flew to the card table and got out the old score pads and pencils that people used for anything from bridge to racing demon.

"Five minutes," Archie said. "And then everybody can read out their own."

"Or other people's," Clary said. "Oh, yes—we could muddle them up and then a person takes one and we all have to guess whose it is. That makes it far more interesting. Oh, do let's do it that way!"

"You win," Archie said. "Put another log on the fire or I shall freeze to death before your very eyes."

There ensued a fidgety pencil-chewing silence.

"I've finished," Lydia said. "I've thought of wonderful ones. Really good and kind."

"You do realize you've jolly well got to do them, don't you?" Simon said. His efforts had made him feel extremely hot. However hard he tried to think, all he came up with was "Kiss Miss Blenkinsopp," a resolve he felt better left unsaid. She was the art mistress at school—old, of course, but far younger than the masters and absolutely wizard to look at with black hair and scarlet lips and a wispy fringe that she kept pushing out of her marvellous eyes with a long white hand that had turquoise rings on it. "Learn to draw," he put.

Neville was also having problems. He was planning to run away from his horrible school, but he couldn't decide where *to*. If the war finished, he could probably get a job as an inventor. Meanwhile, he considered living with Cicely Courtneidge whose record about ordering two dozen double damask dinner napkins entranced him however often he played it.

Clary did hers, which were intensely boring, she thought, and then went and fetched a hat from the gun room in which they could put their pieces of paper.

"Hurry up," she urged the slow ones.

"Time's up." Archie put his paper in the hat and handed it round. He was the first one to read. "'Be kind to old people,'" he read. "'Give all my money away. Save someone's life.'"

"That's mine," Lydia said, which anyone could have known by the smug look on her face.

"Idiotic," Neville said. "You don't want to save *anyone's* life, you fool. Hitler's? Would you save his life?"

"No-o. But I'm most unlikely to meet *him*. A good person's life, of course."

"So you'd go up to someone who was falling out of an aeroplane and say, 'Are you good?' and depending on their answer, and of course they wouldn't tell the truth however wicked they were, you'd save them? I never heard anything so stupid in all my life."

"I don't think she meant it quite like that," Archie said mildly.

"Well, the money bit is idiotic too. She's spent all her Christmas money so it would only be a shilling a week. How will you be able to give me a birthday present if you give all your money away? Or," he added broad-mindedly, "a birthday present for anybody else come to that."

Lydia was trying not to cry, frowning and holding her bottom lip in her teeth.

"You're far too horrible to give a present *to*," she said. "You can see how difficult it is to be good with someone as wicked and awful as Neville about," she appealed to the rest of them.

"I think we should just read the papers and people listen." Archie handed the hat to Polly.

"'Not smoke so much. Be more patient with people. Help the Duchy with the garden.' That must be you, Dad." There was a moment's silence, and then she said, "I think you're awfully patient with people. I really do."

Archie noticed them smile at each other, she aching to comfort, he, acknowledging but comfortless: there was the same feeling of pain in the room as there had been earlier, when Clary had wanted to drink to absent friends, meaning her father but the implication had gone further than she had intended.

"Your turn, Clary," he said briskly.

Clary unfolded the piece of paper she had chosen and read with elaborate scorn. "'Finish the war! Leave school! Have lunch with Cicely Courtneidge.' We know who *that* is! Wrong end of the stick as usual. Honestly, Neville. It's not meant just to have things you'd *like* in it. Or things like the war stopping which you couldn't possibly *do!*"

"They're what I resolute. I'm not going to change them."

"You can't leave school till you're years and years older," Lydia said. "And as you aren't Prime Minister, thank the Lord, you can't stop the war. And Cicely Courtneidge wouldn't dream of having lunch with an unknown *boy*. I agree with Clary."

"We agreed not to comment on people's resolutions," Archie said. "Hugh?"

"'Learn to draw. Learn to write poetry. Invent something.' Heavens, Poll, is that you?"

"It's me," Simon said. He had gone scarlet.

"Goodness. What interesting things, Simon," Polly remarked.

"It's very difficult to learn to write poetry," Clary said. "I have a feeling you have to be born to do it. And I should think we'd have noticed by now if you had a vestige of talent."

"Clary, that's rather crushing."

"It wasn't meant to be."

But Polly said, "Yes, it was."

"Come on, finish the game," Archie said. "It's time we all went to bed."

"What about charades?"

"Nobody wants to play them except you. Come on, it's your turn to read."

"'Learn French. Stop biting my nails. Mend my clothes before they get unmendable,'" Lydia read. "That must be you, Clary. You're the only one who *seriously* bites nails."

"She only bites her own," Neville pointed out. "I think she ought to be allowed to do that. If she bit other people's you could be against her."

"Your turn to read, Neville," Archie said.

"'Go swimming. Learn Russian. Do some drawing.' I don't see how swimming can be a resolution." He *liked* swimming: why on earth hadn't he thought of that?

"It's you, Archie, isn't it?"

"Yep. I hate swimming in swimming baths. It's to get my leg better. I feel like a tiger in a cage. Up and down, to and fro."

"When we come to London, I'll come with you," Clary said. "We can have interesting conversations, and you won't notice how boring it is."

"Well, I'm for bed," Hugh said, as though he had been waiting for the earliest possible moment to say it.

"Oh, *must* we?"

"Nobody's read me," Polly said.

"Oh, darling Poll!" He sat down again. "Read away. I really want to know."

"It isn't for me to read," Polly said. "But there's not much point, because you'll all know it *is* me."

"We still want to know," Archie said.

"I haven't read anyone's," Simon said, and took the paper.

"'Learn to cook. Teach Wills to read. Tell the truth.'"

"You see? It wasn't at all interesting." She was clearly very hurt.

"Yes, it was," Simon said, with embarrassingly obvious loyalty.

"Bed," Archie said. "Everybody do all the right things. Put the guard in front of the fire. Put the cat out. Be quiet on the stairs. Give me a hand, Poll. No thanks, Lydia, I'd rather have Poll."

"What does he mean 'cat'? Flossy'll be in the kitchen. She wouldn't like us to put her anywhere."

"It's a figure of speech, Lydia," Hugh said. He had kissed Polly, and put his hand on Simon's shoulder. "Good night, old chap." Kissing his children made him want to cry. This time last year, he thought, she was here. She was just beginning to feel rotten again, but she was *here.*

"Do you think it *will* be a Happy New Year?"

"Oh, I think it's bound to be better. We've got the Germans on the run, you know, now. Monty's doing a *marvellous* job. I shouldn't be surprised if El Alamein won't prove to be the turning point. And they're getting *nowhere* in Russia. Nobody who invades Russia reckons with the winter. *And* we're giving them merry hell on their home ground. Yes, I think we can definitely say that nineteen forty-three will be happier. For us, God bless us." He smiled kindly at her, and said, "Is your husband away at the wars?"

"Not any more. He was briefly in the RAF but then he had to go back to manage the family business." Then she found herself saying, "Of course, he fought in the first war . . . in the Fifth Army."

"With dear old Goffy? Very fond of *him.* Well, it must be nice for you to have him home."

It would be, she thought, if he was. His non-appearance at Hermione's party had caused her, first, anger, then embarrassment, and finally anxiety. Where *was* he? He wasn't at his flat, and his shaving things weren't there either. He wasn't at home, because she'd rung on the pretext of wishing them a Happy New Year, and if he had been, of course they would have said so. But "Have a lovely party," Rachel had said, "you both deserve some fun together." She hadn't told *them* he wasn't with her. But, of course, she had to tell Hermione. She'd rung her from the flat.

"Darling, how tiresome for you. Never mind, perhaps he'll simply turn up here. Oh, don't worry about *that.* I've got two spare men coming anyway."

She was sitting next to one of them now. Colonel Chessington-Blair was a rotund pink little man in his early sixties. He reminded her of a cork, bobbing up to the surface of every conversation saying all the first things that had come into other people's heads in the brisk understated way that almost transformed them into original utterances. He worked in what he called the war house; one could not imagine him out of uniform.

When the ladies withdrew and most of them had gone to Hermione's bedroom, Hermione had linked an arm with her to stay her from joining the others and said, "You were divine to be so sweet to old Piggy. I could see he simply adored you." Then she said, "Don't worry about Edward. Something must have come up and I expect he tried to get hold of you. You know what telephones are like these days."

"I'm not worrying."

"Why don't you stay the night here? It couldn't be easier, and you know how frightful it is getting cabs on this sort of occasion."

She said, no, she'd rather go to the flat. (*What* could possibly have "come up"?)

It was nice to be wearing evening clothes, being in London, being at a party, but every time she started to enjoy these things, the mysterious absence of Edward intervened, and she felt cross and frightened. Supposing something awful had happened to him? She hardly knew whether she *least* wanted it to be his fault that he wasn't there, or not his fault at all.

Polly and Clary

Spring, 1943

THERE WAS A small, magical patch of time between being completely asleep and becoming awake that she had begun to notice ever since they'd gone to London. It had no prescribed duration, always felt tantalizingly short since it began to fade the moment she became aware of it. Sometimes she thought it was the very end of a dream, since not only her heart and thoughts but her body had a weightless light about them—a kind of serene detachment that still possessed joyous response to something that was already mysteriously slipping into the past, dissolving into distant memory and mist until it seemed either forgotten, or never known at all. Dreams could be like that, she knew. They could be like telegrams, or the most significant lines of a poem—so crammed with a fragment of truth that for a moment they seemed to illuminate the whole of it. But dreams did not always contain joyful messages: they could convey anything from anxiety to nightmare—she knew that. Her recurring nightmare—only once told to Clary—about trying to kiss her mother's forehead and it simply melting into the pillow, had a kind of rigid horror that no amount of repetition rendered powerless. But this patch was more as though she was flying in some sunlit element, alighting upon her own body, and then entering it to discover that her wings had disappeared. She was ordinary Polly lying flat on her back on the top floor of her father's house in London. Next door, would be Clary, profoundly asleep until physically shaken. Perhaps, she thought, it only happened because she was sleeping alone: at Home Place she had always shared a room with Clary, and sometimes Louise as well.

At least Clary had her own room—bed-sitting rooms they were called, but for Polly living in her father's house, with the kitchen three floors down in the basement was *not* the same as them having their own flat, which had always been their plan. But when it came to the point and she had discovered that Dad had always thought they would live with him, and when *he* had discovered that they had meant to find their own place and she had seen his intense disappointment congeal to good-natured acquiescence, she knew that she could not persist. *"You* can find a flat," she had said to Clary, "but I simply can't. It's the first time I've seen Dad at *all* pleased or excited about anything since Mummy died. He so hates being alone in the house without her. You do see, don't you?" And Clary, shooting her a look compounded of disappointment, exasperation and love, had said immediately, "Course I do. And I wouldn't dream of having a flat without you in it." Her face always showed all of her feelings however careful her voice was about them.

And Dad had been sweet about everything. They were to have the top floor to themselves. "You could make bed-sitting rooms as they are quite large," he had said. "And you have your own bathroom on the half landing. And I'll have a telephone plug put on the top floor. I expect you'll want to ring up your friends. And if you want to have a party with them, I can always be out. You must just tell me what you want in the way of furniture. I expect the rooms need painting as well. You must choose the colours you would both like." He talked and talked about it, and when Clary said could she bring all her books from home, he said of course, and when he saw how many there were, he'd have bookshelves made for them. It was as though he wanted them to live there for ever.

They got furniture from all over the place. Aunt Rach said they could have curtains from Chester Terrace because the ones that were there were so flimsy and awful and no good for blackout.

Now, after barely three months, they had got into a routine. They went to the secretarial course at Pitman's five days a week, bicycling there four of the days, but on Fridays they went by bus, because of going straight on after work to catch a train for Sussex. Clary wanted to stay in London for the weekends, and sometimes she did, but Polly felt that she ought to go home to see Wills. He was not especially glad to see her, but she felt that if she stuck at it he might get to be. He liked her if she did everything he wanted, and so she spent cold afternoons pushing him on his fairy cycle, helping him build nameless structures with the family Meccano, and reading him *Winnie-the-Pooh*. He had become a disconsolate tyrant, determined upon having everything that he did not really want, using the innumerable gratified whims like leaves to cover the secret body of his loss. So, he would insist upon wearing one red sock and one blue; he would not eat his mashed potato until he had transferred it to his mug; he filled his bed with fir cones many of which had mysterious names; he had awful bouts of simply opening and then slamming doors. Aunt Villy was teaching him to read, but he would only do it if she let him wear a hat. It was almost a year now, but she knew that he still missed his mother, although the aunts seemed to think he was getting over it. So she went because of him. She went also because of her father. He loved meeting her at the station, buying her a paper to read (when Clary was there he always bought her one as well). He usually went to sleep half-way through the journey while she sat trying to learn her grammalogues. The weekends were always the same. They were met by Tonbridge who told them of any minor misfortunes that had occurred during the week—they sometimes had bets together about who these would be about—and then they would get a few of his opinions, couched as questions, about the war. At the house, the smells—so familiar when she had lived there that she had not noticed them—were of damp log fires, the Brig's pipe smoke, beeswax and occasional wafts of food cooking as Eileen barged back and forth through the baize door laying the dining room for dinner. Upstairs, the smells changed to lavender, Wright's Coal Tar Soap, shoe polish, clothes drying in front of the nursery fire, and the sounds were either of children having baths, or of people trying to make them. She would go to her room to get into a warmer jersey for supper: they no longer changed for dinner excepting on Saturday night when she always wore her pale green brocaded housecoat made of curtain material by the aunts for her birthday last year. After supper, they would all listen to the news and then she and Clary would play bezique and racing demon. She always missed Clary when Clary stayed in London, and on top of missing her, she could not help feeling envious: Clary used to go to the cinema with Archie and sometimes the theatre, and got taken out to meals. Apart from the treat side of it, she was alone with Archie which Polly felt was a treat in itself. Of course, *he* came for the weekend sometimes, and you could bet that Clary never stayed in London *then*. What it amounted to was that *she*, Polly, never had evenings alone with Archie but then, she kept reminding herself, she had responsibilities and Clary had none. All the same, the old niggling thing of this not being fair attacked her: of course she knew by now that things weren't, but that did not in the least prevent her wanting them to be.

Today was Friday, and they were both going home, because Archie was coming, because on the Saturday it would be a year since her mother died—a fact that Dad didn't mention, but that everybody else in the family was acutely aware of. A kind of opposite of a birthday, she thought, a deathday, but really it was no worse that her mother had been dead for three hundred and sixty-five days than three hundred and sixty-four, or -six. She was glad that Simon would still be at school. "But I'm only glad because it would be worse for him if he wasn't, I'm not really *glad*. I'm not really glad about anything," she said to Clary as they waited for the bus to go to Pitman's.

Clary agreed.

"Nor am I. I think life is frightfully depressing. If nearly everybody is having a worse time than we are, I can hardly see the point of it."

"I suppose it *is* just the war?" she said.

"How can we know? We haven't the faintest idea of what it would be like if there wasn't one."

"We can *remember* it. It is only three and a bit years since peace."

"Yes, but then we were children. Subject to all kinds of petty rules made by Them. And now that we're becoming Them, there simply seem to be more rules."

"Like?"

"Well," Clary considered, "I mean, neither of us *wants* to get awfully good at typing and shorthand. We didn't spend our childhood *wishing* we could type at sixty words a minute."

"It might be useful to you if you're going to be a writer. Look at Bernard Shaw."

"He invents his own kind, I believe. And that was just because he wanted to. But generally men don't have to learn typing."

"They have to join up and kill people," she said sadly. "The trouble is that we haven't worked out what we believe in. We just go on in a dreary unbelieving muddle."

The bus came then. When they were on it, Clary said, "Disbelieving is different from unbelieving. What don't we believe in?"

"War," Polly said promptly. "I absolutely disbelieve in war."

"That doesn't do any good, though, because we've got it."

"Well, you *asked* me. You think of something."

"God," Clary said. "I don't believe in God. Although, actually, it occurred to me that there might be a whole lot of them, and that's why there's such a mess—they don't agree with one another about anything."

"I can't be against war," she said—she'd been thinking. "The fact that we've got it is neither here nor there. I'm against the *idea* of it. Like Christopher."

"He didn't last. He went off to join up. It was only because there was something wrong with his eyesight that they didn't take him."

"He went, *not* believing in it, because he thought it wasn't right to let other people do the dirty work. He had principles."

"Ah now, do you believe in *them?* If so, which ones?"

But they'd reached Lancaster Gate and the peeling, blistered pillars of the stuccoed house in which they were to spend the next six hours pounding their typewriters steadily to what Clary called Hastings pier music, learning to write "Dear Sir, Thank you for your letter of the 10th inst." in a cabalistic scrawl, and struggling with double-entry book-keeping, which they both simply loathed. "It seems madness to me," Clary had said after the first day of it. "Either one hasn't *got* any money to put in the columns, or else one has masses, in which case there would be no need."

"It won't be *our* money we're putting in, stupid, it'll be our rich powerful employer's."

The day was punctuated by a lunch hour when they consumed Spam sandwiches and cups of pink-brown tea that tasted of the metal pot. There was a basement room in which students could spend the lunch hour and sandwiches were sold there for those who wanted them. So far they had not found any of their fellow students enlivening; they all seemed deeply earnest about the work, and as it was an intensive course there was in any case little time to fraternize. Usually, they managed to go out at lunch-time, taking their sandwiches to eat in the park. This morning, however, a new student had joined the classes who looked very different from the rest. To start with, she was very much older, but almost everything else about her was different too. She was immensely tall—she towered above everyone else—but she had long, narrow hands and feet and elegant ankles. Her iron grey hair was cut in a careless bob and cut shorter on one side of her forehead, and she wore a black cardigan rather carelessly embroidered with buttercups and poppies. But it was her face that entranced them both. Unlike everyone else, she wore no make-up at all, her skin was uniform olive with very fine, dark eyebrows that arched over eyes of an amazing colour that they could not agree about.

"Sort of pale greyish green," Clary said.

"Bluer than that. Aquamarine, would you say?"

"I might *say* it, but it would be no good if one wrote it. It wouldn't really *describe* them."

"I'd know what it meant."

They decided to eat their sandwiches in the basement room in the hope of getting to know the new student, but she was not there. Her absence whetted their curiosity.

"I think she's foreign."

"We know that. We heard her say thank you to Miss Halton."

"Well, I think she's minor royalty from some central European court."

"Or she could have been imported by some American general. I bet they're allowed to bring their mistresses abroad with them. You know, like Stanley taking cases of port with him when he was exploring in Africa."

"Honestly, Clary, that's not at all the same thing."

"She could be royal *and* someone's mistress."

"I must say she doesn't at all look like a wife."

"She was probably married off in her youth to some frightful Prussian brute. Then all her children died of TB because the castle was so cold and she ran away and escaped." Clary had recently come upon a copy of *Moths* for a penny on a second-hand book stall and had become immersed in Ouida which had affected her observations of people. "She journeyed overland for weeks dressed as a peasant and then stowed away on a ship to come here."

"I don't think she'd *stow* very well," Polly said. "I mean, she's a bit too remarkable to merge into any background. And large," she added, after thinking about it.

When they went back to the classroom for the second typing session, she still wasn't there.

"Next time we see her, let's ask her to supper with us."

"All right. Do you think she'd get on with Dad?"

"You said he said he would be out if we wanted to have our friends."

"I know—but—"

"Oh, Poll, we have to start having our own lives."

"OK. But she is pretty old—his sort of age. If she's really terrifically nice, she might make him a suitable wife." And as Clary snorted with disagreeing despair, she added, "I don't mean he should be at the first supper. I just mean if we think she's OK we might introduce them."

"I don't see much point in that. They're both too old for sex, I should have thought."

"You don't *know* that. Do you think Archie's too old for sex, then?" There was a dead silence during which she noticed that Clary's forehead had become pink before she answered, "Archie's different."

He was, she thought, of course he was. He was the most different person she had ever met.

13 March 1943

This is Saturday afternoon, Dad, and it is raining and quite cold as well, so I'm sitting on my bed at Home Place with the eiderdown over me writing to you. It's awful: I realize that I haven't written anything since before Christmas. That is partly because of us moving to London—Poll and me to Uncle Hugh's house which has meant such a change in our lives that I don't seem to have had much time. That isn't true: there *has* been time—only I haven't felt like writing much at all. Christmas was OK, I suppose. Roly and Wills and Jules loved it and so did Lydia and Neville, but I think I am beginning to feel a bit bored of it. Neville tried to give me a rat he has got tired of at school. Who could possibly want a rat *brought up by him?* I said that. He gave Polly a jig-saw which we knew had five bits missing. He simply won't use his pocket money on presents and all *he* wanted was money. Some people gave it to him, but there was quite a lot of disapproval in the air.

Well, after Christmas we went to London as we have to go to an Intensive Course in Typing and Shorthand at Pitman's so that we shall be of some use when we are called up. I was looking forward madly to us having our own flat, but in the end we had to go to Uncle Hugh because Poll said he was so wanting us to, and she feels he is frightfully lonely without Aunt Syb. I saw her point . . . If it had been you, Dad, I would have felt just as Poll did, so of course I had to agree. We have a room each on the top floor and our own bathroom, but we have to cook in the basement so by the time we have carried food up to our lairs everything is cold. But we can make tea in the bathroom which is something. Uncle Hugh was very kind about letting us paint the rooms *and* he had some bookcases made for me which go all along one wall which is a good thing because I got my room the wrong kind of yellow and can't be bothered to paint it again. Aunt Rach said we could have some curtains from Chester Terrace as Aunt Syb never got around to having any on the top floor, and she took us to Chester Terrace to choose some. She said she would make them fit the windows which is jolly decent of her. It was odd going back there, Dad. Everything is covered up—all the furniture—and the shutters are down and there are hardly any lights to put on. When we went in there was a faint damp darkish smell, like wet prayer books. The curtains were all packed in tea chests in the Brig's study with labels on them saying which they were, but of course I could only remember the drawing room ones—the huge white roses on dark green shiny chintz and the oatmeal ones with blue birds on them that were in my bedroom when I stayed there while you were marrying Zoë when I was nine. I didn't tell you, Dad, but honestly that was the most miserable time of my life. I didn't believe you were coming back to fetch me, you see: I thought they were simply trying to soften the blow when they said you were. I stole half a crown out of the Duchy's bag to get bus tickets to go home, but then I remembered that Ellen had taken Neville to stay with her family and that there would be nobody to let me in. I thought all this in the hall just as I was going—and then I realized that there was nowhere to go *to*. That was the worst of all. I felt so furious I wanted to break everything up and I got the Brig's swordstick out of its walking case and I bashed through the iron scroll grid at the glass on the front door to break it. I did break one bit, but I was crying and they came and found me. Aunt Rach came and I kicked her and shouted that I was trapped and there was nowhere to go and I wished I was dead. I can see now how good she was about it all. She didn't punish me although I slightly wanted her to because I wanted everything to go on being simple and bad. She took me into the Brig's study which was the nearest room and held me till I stopped crying and talked to me about you getting married and about people having honeymoons which meant being on their own for a bit, and then she gave me a calendar—I remember it had *Timber Trades Journal* at the top of it—and she marked the day it was on it, and then marked the day you were coming home and gave me a red chalk to mark off the days—ten more of them—and I couldn't *not* believe her then. That afternoon she took me to a very grand tea at Gunter's with ices and hot chocolate and she bought me a bag of their special lemon drops to take home. I remembered all this because the curtains we were to choose were in the Brig's study, and all the glass had gone from the front door and there was wood instead. That evening—after the treat at Gunter's—the Duchy cut out a piece of linen for me to embroider a pyjama case for you, but I was rotten at embroidery and it never got finished. Anyway, I certainly didn't want the blue bird curtains and Poll, who chose the white roses, suggested that I have blue velvet ones. It's funny, Dad, you were in France then, but you did come back. And in the end, of course, you'll come back again. But it *is* a long time that you've been gone this time, isn't it? It's no good my having a calendar because it might easily be more than another year. I go on writing this just as much for me as for you, because it helps me to remember you—I mean *more* of you. One of the difficult things about it being so long since you went—two years and nine months now—is that although, of course, I do think about you a lot, I seem to remember *fewer* things about you. I go over them again and again, but I keep feeling that there are other things I no longer remember. It's as though you were walking slowly backwards from me into the distance. I *hate* it. If this is what people mean about their grief getting less, I don't want it. I want to remember you as completely and sharply as I did the evening the man rang up to say you were missing; as much as when Pipette brought the amazing note you wrote me which I keep in the secret drawer of the desk Poll gave me. Do you remember when you took the skin off my hot milk and ate it? I often think of that.

This is Sunday. I don't think I mentioned that Archie is here this weekend which is good because he seems to get on well with everyone and cheers people up, even poor Uncle Hugh who I think you would find awfully changed, Dad. He's got rather quiet and fidgety—he's always picking things up and putting them down again as though he's surprised to find whatever it is in his hand, and even when he's smiling or someone has made a joke, his eyes look shocked and a bit haunted. I think his heart is broken but Poll said the other day that she hoped he'd marry again. I should have thought at his age that this was very unlikely. The trouble is that with the war we don't meet anyone much, and certainly nobody kind and faded which would be best for him I should think.

Once, I didn't go home—well, several times, actually—for the weekend but one time I spent the whole weekend with Archie. It wasn't a plan; it just turned out like that. He asked me to go to a film with him on Saturday afternoon. He didn't *exactly ask* me: it was when he came to supper with Uncle Hugh and Poll and me and I said I was going to see what a weekend in London would be like and I must admit I said it would be fun to go to a film with him, and he said righty-ho, Saturday afternoon. But then on Friday evening when I got back to the house on my own because Poll had gone to Charing Cross to meet Uncle Hugh it all felt rather silent. I was feeling a bit gloomy because I'd forgotten to buy any more bread and there was only a very stale bit to have with my cheese ration, and I was creeping about in the dark putting up the black-out because the air-raid wardens are devilish about anybody showing a light and shout, "Put out that light!" from the street and ring the bell to tell you again. Anyway, the telephone rang and I answered it and it was Archie. He said he supposed he'd interrupted me getting dressed for my party. What party? I said. He said, "I didn't think you'd be staying up for the weekend unless you had a party."

I told him I didn't know anybody so I couldn't be going to one, and he said, "Come to a very small party indeed with me then. Get a taxi and come to my flat any time after seven." Wasn't that wonderfully kind and cheering of him? I missed Poll then because she's so much better than I am at knowing what to wear for going out, but actually I've only got one decent dress that Zoë got me for Christmas which is bottle green velveteen, a bit of a change from the dark blue one that I had for ages and this one has a square neck and sleeves just to my elbows so it is a bit more adult than the old blue one. I cut my hair to get rid of a perm that just went on being frizzy whenever it rained and, anyway, I couldn't bear sleeping on those awful iron curlers that dig into your head at night so now it's just straight again like it always was and Polly gave me an old tortoiseshell slide she found in a junk shop for Christmas, which is much nicer than it sounds. Polly usually helps me with my make-up and I had to have several goes at it. In the end I just used some green eye shadow of Poll's that doesn't suit her so she wouldn't mind, and her dark blue mascara which is very difficult to put on without getting the brush in your eyes and lipstick called Signal Red which it jolly well is only it comes off if I even eat a biscuit. I gave up rouge because my face went so red from rubbing things off—in fact I had to put out the lights and hang my head out of the window to get my face back to its normal colour which is actually a sort of khaki-fool colour, I mean khaki mixed with cream, not really a good *face* colour at all. Poll is really lucky to be so beautifully pretty.

Archie has changed his flat to a much nicer one in South Kensington. It is in a tall dark red house looking onto a square but inside it is really nice. He has a gramophone like the Duchy's with an enormous horn made of some black and gold stuff like papier-mâché, I think, and he has those triangular wooden needles that you have to clip to sharpen after each record. Very modern and jolly expensive, I should think. Anyway, he was playing it when I arrived. We had gins—I had lime in mine—while he finished playing that Schubert quartet that the Duchy loves so much. He said I looked very smart when he hugged me, so at least he noticed. He took me out to dinner at what he called his local restaurant: it was a Cypriot one where you get lamb chops and rice and then a delicious pudding of little fried honey balls and Turkish coffee—but you have to be careful not to drink the muddy part. But we had a most interesting conversation about a new idea called the Welfare State invented by someone called Sir William Beveridge. It is going to mean that everything is much fairer and OK for everyone with free schools and free doctors and hospitals. I think it is an extremely good idea because charity is so patchy and although our family is rich compared to many, most people hardly have anything. We started talking about it because I said that when I earned money I planned to give half of it away to poor people (when I'd first thought this Neville heard and said I could give it to him as he was always poor). But Archie said that we would all pay more taxes which would mean we would be doing our share. He said he thought that after the war even Conservatives would see that things should be fairer and that if everybody had the same opportunities there would be far more people who were clever and useful. I asked him then if he was a Socialist and he said, yes, he was, although he didn't talk about that much at Home Place, which he described as a hotbed of Tories. He said he had a great respect for Mr. Attlee and hoped he would be Prime Minister which I should have thought very unlikely as Mr. Churchill is so deeply popular. After dinner, Archie said he'd take me home to Ladbroke Grove, but on the way there he said was I sleeping alone in the house, and when I said yes, he said he didn't like the idea of that and perhaps I'd better stay with him. Of course it was far more enjoyable to do that, so I collected some things from there while he waited in the cab. We went back and he made some cocoa with dried milk which if you put sugar in was not too bad—well, he said that, but I thought it was delicious—and he asked me whether it was nice being in London. I told him then about it being not what I'd imagined—living with Uncle Hugh which doesn't feel at all the same as having our own place would be. Also, I said it had made us realize that we didn't *know* anyone much outside the family and he sympathized with that. I pointed out, for instance, that he was probably the first Socialist I'd ever met, which is pretty feeble, considering my age. Then he said he would take me to dinner with some friends of his the next night—the man is a sculptor who lives with a Spanish woman. He met her when he was fighting in the Spanish Civil War against Franco. He'd known them before the war because they used to live in France. I asked if he'd known you, and Archie said he thinks you met once when you were staying with him, but he's not sure. Then he said we'd better go to bed as we had a lot to do the next day. That was Friday. It was one of the best evenings of my life, and the best thing about it was that it wasn't *just* that one evening—there was the whole of the next day.

In the morning we had rather burned toast and Marmite and tea and he asked me what I would have been doing if I'd been on my own and I said spend the morning in Charing Cross Road that is absolutely full of bookshops and many of them second-hand ones. Poll doesn't ever want to do that; she likes shops that have some of everything in them. Archie said what a good idea, and we took a bus and went.

Here, she paused. Quite suddenly, the gap between the kind of day she had spent with Archie and how she felt about it seemed enormous. It had not seemed like that at the time: if it had, she would not even have got this far in her description of it to her father. It was now, sitting in her bed at Home Place writing very fast with her mind racing ahead of the words on paper, that she had got past those serenely happy hours browsing and searching through the rows of battered books propped against one another on the rickety tables in the bookshops, past the visit to the Redfearn Gallery where Archie had made her look at pictures by a painter called Christopher Wood whom he very much admired, and lunch, spaghetti in an Italian restaurant where men ate with napkins tucked into their collars below their chins to the moment when Archie opened a new packet of his cigarettes, started to take one and then said: "I'm so sorry, darling Clary, want one?" And she had looked up from the proffered packet to the friendly attention of his eyes, had shaken her head and said: "Uncle Hugh has promised Poll and me gold watches if we don't smoke before we're twenty-one."

"That's that then," he had answered. "How old are you now?"

"I'll be eighteen in August."

"Three and a half years to go. I keep forgetting how young you are."

"Seventeen and a half isn't particularly *young*."

"Of course not. Well, I think you're absolutely splendid for your age." He made his curious little suppressed croak of laughter which meant, she knew, that he was amused, but before she could feel hurt he pushed it over the top, teasing her.

"Splendid," he repeated. "I mean, on your feet all the morning, got your own teeth, hearing unimpaired—you're a *wonderful* old thing for your age."

So. If she remembered *just* that it was the old Archie teasing the old Clary that would be familiar and simple. But what she discovered now, when she remembered it, was that other things seemed to have arrived, to *keep on* arriving with increasing density each time she went over that scene. They couldn't be memories, because she hadn't noticed them at all at the time—they must be her imagination—she was turning something real that had happened into something else. "I'm so sorry, darling Clary, want one?" and then looking up from the cigarettes to his eyes, pale grey, affectionate, intent upon her. This was the bit that she kept returning to and each time his exact tone of voice, the expression in his eyes, the way that his long narrow mouth twitched but did not quite smile became more sharply imprinted, bringing with it a shaft of happiness so unalloyed, so brilliant, so complete, that she lost all other senses. Recovering, she would reflect of this pure violent happiness that it was entirely new to her; in all her life she could not remember anything comparable, and yet sometimes she had thought herself happy, or else she had not thought about it at all. But then she would want more of it and play the scene again. At the time, she had not felt anything, or anything very much; affection for Archie, gratitude for being treated as a grown-up and given the chance to choose whether she had a cigarette or not. But as the weeks went by, since that weekend, she began to recognize that she *had* been aware of something new and strange at that moment; it was as though, for a split second, she had sensed something approaching to knock her out, as swift and powerful as a tidal wave, and somehow managed to avoid it.

I got some jolly nice books [she wrote], all second hand, so you might have read them. Novels: *Lost Horizon* by James Hilton—about Tibet—*Death of a Hero* by Richard Aldington—about the First World War—*Sparkenbroke* by Charles Morgan and *Evelina* by Fanny Burney. Then I got *Grey Wolf* in a Penguin edition about someone called Mustafa Kemal and Keats' letters and a very *thin* book of poems by Housman. I had to stop there because I couldn't carry any more and Archie, who was in his uniform, says that there is a law against naval officers carrying paper parcels. I suppose you knew that, Dad.

In the evening Archie took me to dinner with the sculptor and his Spanish wife. She isn't actually his wife, but they live together. He is quite old (I mean older than you and Archie) and he's Jewish, which is why he left France. He had to go to the Isle of Man at first and so did Teresa because they were foreign. She is dark and not thin at all, but rather glamorous in a fruity sort of way; she reminded me of a black cherry with long dangly earrings. I do think earrings are pretty; it's a pity people don't wear them more. She cooked an amazing dish of mussels and rice and chicken: the rice was yellow and smelt and tasted delicious and we had wine. They live in one huge room that had a stove with glass doors to it. Louis, he's called. Louis Kutchinsky. The most interesting thing about them is that they're Communists which was very exciting as I've never met one before. He belongs to something called the Peace Pledge Union, but in spite of that, he's quite keen on having us joined up with the Russians. Archie teased him about war being all right if the Russians were in it, and he said his opinions had changed since the news about what the Germans are doing to Jews in Poland, and everywhere else, he said. He said they were trying to exterminate them but they couldn't be doing that, could they? I mean you can't kill off a whole race of people—there must be thousands and thousands of them—how could they possibly do it, even if they were so wicked as to want to? I asked him if he was a religious Jew, and he said no, but that didn't stop him feeling Jewish any more, he said, than an English person wouldn't stop feeling English if they weren't a Protestant. But mostly he and Archie talked (and he talked a jolly sight more than Archie), and I simply listened and Teresa sewed. He had a bad leg, like Archie—he got his in Spain—Archie said that between them they could run a three-legged race but he didn't know what that was. Archie asked him what he was working on, and he said he'd given up sculpture because he had no commissions and the materials were difficult to come by so he had taken to drawing. "An encyclopaedia of hands," he said. He showed us a whole collection of drawings, mostly done with charcoal, of hands—clasped, clenched, praying, playing the piano, just lying on a table, sometimes the backs, sometimes palms, not the same person's hands doing those things, but all kinds. They weren't all in charcoal, also some in pencil and some in inks of different colours. There were dozens of them, and sometimes he'd had several goes on one page. Archie looked at them for ages and he didn't talk while Archie was looking, but I noticed he watched him all the time to see what Archie thought and I could see he minded. Occasionally, Archie asked him whose hands they were and "a pianist" "a surgeon I knew" "the woman at the paper shop" "a neighbour's child" "anyone who will lend me their hands," he said. At the end of looking, Archie said he admired them *profoundly* and it was a new kind of portraiture. When we left—which was pretty late—Mr. Kutchinsky hugged Archie and then gave him a sort of terrier shake and said: "You should come to dinner at least once a week—my audience of one."

Here she stopped again, remembering Archie taking her arm in the black street, walking to the King's Road in search of a cab which did not materialize until they'd got so far, Archie said, it was easier to walk the whole way. He had told her about Louis, who he said was Hungarian, and Teresa, who he said was not married to him because she had been married when Louis met her, but her husband used to beat her up, so Louis had kidnapped her and brought her to France. They had had a child but it had died, and she couldn't have any more, but he said they were happy together and well suited. Louis could be a demanding partner and she liked to look after him. Half of her had listened to this and half of her simply enjoyed the walk in the dark empty streets with Archie limping beside her. "So there are your first Communists," he said. "Not so very different from other people."

She wrote, "Oh, by the way, Dad, he *hadn't* met you. He was very sorry that he hadn't. He said he was looking forward to meeting you after the war. I thought that was nice of him."

That wasn't quite what she meant, she realized: it wasn't nice of him to want to meet Dad; what had been—more than *nice* was the way in which he had accepted that after the war Dad would be there to meet. Sometimes about this, her heart failed her: it now seemed so long since he had vanished—and so long until the war could possibly come to an end. People talked about a Second Front, which meant invading France, but nothing ever happened about it, and even if it happened, it wouldn't be the *end* of the war, although it might be the beginning of the end. What was it Mr. Churchill had said some time ago? "Not the beginning of the end, but perhaps the end of the beginning"? She couldn't remember exactly. The awful thing was that a lot of the time she got absolutely *sick* of the way the family listened to every news bulletin, and read the paper from cover to cover and then talked about what they had heard and read.

She didn't want to write any more. The next day she and Archie had gone to Richmond Park and then they had made lunch in his flat of tinned steak and kidney pudding—absolutely delicious, she thought. Then Archie took her to a cinema in Oxford Street that showed old French films and they saw *Le Fin du Jour* with Jean Gabin, who she had never seen before, a marvellous film, and she thought that going to French films might be the best way of learning French. When they reached the Corner House at Marble Arch for an early supper, she asked Archie what he thought of that.

"I think it would be a good idea if you both learned something else besides shorthand and typing," he said. "Polly ought to do some drawing. If she went to an art school—in the evenings, for instance—she'd meet some people or her age." What about me? she had thought, but she hadn't said anything about that. Instead she had found herself saying, "Polly is so beautiful, she'll just marry someone, I think. I don't think she wants to be a painter really."

And he had answered, "She is as pretty as paint, I have to agree."

She had asked him then if he thought that beauty or prettiness was important, and he had said that it had its place. Then he had paused and looked at her consideringly: "But what stops it becoming a lethal kind of *yardstick*," he said, "is that everybody has different ideas about what constitutes either beauty or prettiness, or whatever you want to call it. It is one of nature's little tricks for getting people to mate, but on the other hand I can't imagine going overboard for a lady who had fourteen rings round her giraffe-like neck" (they had been looking at "Believe It or Not" by Ripley in the *Sunday Express* at breakfast that day).

"That doesn't count. That's something people do because it's fashionable—like tight lacing or people in China having bound feet. I meant just how they are in the first place."

"They don't often stay like that, though, do they? Of course you're right—the giraffe ladies aren't an example. Well done, Clary. But you, for instance, permed your hair not so long ago—I must say you look far better with it straight. And while we're on the subject, I don't think putting stuff on your face really suits you."

"That's because you're against make-up."

"No. I think it does suit some people—"

"Polly looks lovely whether she wears it or not."

"Yes, I agree she does. But she doesn't *need* it."

"What you mean," she said, suddenly feeling rather hopeless, "is that there are two kinds of people who it's not worth doing things to—the fearfully beautiful ones and the ones like me."

There was a short silence. They were sitting opposite each other at the small marble-topped table and she felt hot and miserable and the horrible beginnings of tears.

"Clary, I wouldn't want you to be in any way different. I like you exactly as you are. You look just right to me."

"You must have very bad taste in people, then," she said as rudely as she could manage.

"That's rather hard. Let me remind you—as I'm sure Miss Milliment would have put it because I bet you *haven't* read him—of what Congreve said, or made one of his characters say, a man to a lady anyhow: 'That she should admire him as much for the beauty he commends in her as if he himself was possessed of it.' Put that in your pipe and smoke it."

She struggled with this for a moment: "You mean, she should admire him for having such discrimination? Well, I think you're just trying to be *tactful* or something. Dad once said I was beautiful, and for a bit I jolly nearly believed him because, as you know, he has terrifically good taste in things—but actually he was just trying to make me feel—less—*ordinary*."

She looked up and he was watching her.

"And did he succeed?"

"I told you, for a bit . . . I wouldn't like you to think that I *envy* Poll—or grudge her being so marvellous to look at. It's just that sometimes I wish"—she shrugged to make it seem trivial—"well, *you* know. I mean, people will have to fall back on my character, won't they, which is no better than Poll's incidentally, in fact it's probably worse, but ordinary people have to have *better* characters to make up for looking ordinary. You know, like you said once about someone with a Cockney accent having to be better than someone without one to become an officer in the Navy. I'm not sure if I feel up to that."

She fell silent, but he went on listening, so she said: "Once, when he was about six, I was playing that game with Neville where you have to say what you would most like to be. And I said I'd like to be kind and brave. And Neville stretched his eyes as though I'd told a whopping lie and then looked at the ceiling and said *he* would like to be rich and pretty. And immediately I felt that that was what I wanted to be, really, I'd just made up the other things to sound good."

There he was—looking at her in her thoughts again, but this time was not like the other: this time his eyes, which seemed to see and to tell so much, were fixed upon her with an expression that she could not bear (for one awful second it had crossed her mind that he was sorry for her, an idea so humiliating and detestable to her that she had dismissed it utterly and at once without an alternative). What she said was: "You look extremely soppy to me. What on earth are you thinking?"

And he had answered at once, "I was trying not to laugh."

She had been so grateful for this (people certainly weren't *pitying* somebody while they were trying not to laugh at them) that she was able to change the subject without confusion. "Do tell me," she had said, "all that you know about *brothels.* They seem only to get mentioned in fairly old books. Are they still going on? You know what our family is like about things like that. They simply will not discuss them. So I go on being none the wiser."

But sometimes, as now, sitting in bed with the eiderdown round her shoulders, what she had so briefly felt about that second expression of Archie's recurred and the humiliation flooded her like a blush. If he ever started to feel *sorry* for her it would be the end of everything. "It would be an impertinence so profound that I should never recover from it," she wrote in her journal before she could stop herself, and then read it with dismay. She certainly didn't want Dad to read that because it really didn't go with anything else she had written; on the other hand, it did seem to her rather an interesting and *mature* remark and one that she did not feel should be lightly jettisoned. In the end, she rubbed and then crossed it out most thoroughly, and then wrote it in the notebook that Poll had given her for Christmas to write out ideas for books.

The Family

Summer, 1943

Having something to look forward to only served to emphasize the featureless desert that she felt her life had become, and having lunch with her brother-in-law which would once have been nothing more than a mild—a very mild—diversion, now assumed the proportions of adventure. She decided that she would catch an early train and go to Mr. Bayley in Brook Street to have her hair cut, then she would go to Liberty's where Zoë had recently bought a very pretty striped cotton bedspread with which she had made both herself and Juliet frocks. No coupons were required for bed linen or furnishing materials, but it was not easy to find anything suitable. She had decided not to stay the night: ever since that ghastly dinner party with Hermione that Edward had clean forgotten about, she had hated his dreary little flat. She couldn't think why he kept it. It was a mean, modern, cramped sort of place; its décor reminded her of the captain's cabin in a battleship (although why on earth she should make that comparison she could not imagine—she had never been in any captain's cabin anywhere). Anyway, the paint was all sleek greys, the carpets, fitted, were the colour and texture of porridge. The minimal furniture was "modern," that is to say its designer had been keen on its looking unusual at all costs. The drawers had no handles, but declivities so shallow that it was nearly impossible to get the purchase to open them; the taps, likewise, had no graspable spigot, rather a moulded top that eluded spiral pressure. Although Edward had imported a larger bed in place of the single divan, it still wasn't large enough for both of them; it meant that they had to sleep touching each other all night, something she had never liked very much. Anyway, Edward was away—on a visit to Southampton where they had recently bought a wharf—so there was not much point in her staying up. None the less, she had been, she was, looking forward to getting away from Home Place just for the inside of a day. Although the house was full of people she felt isolated. She missed Sybil far more than she had thought she would; she missed Rupert, who, like the rest of the family, she privately thought dead; she missed her pre-war London life, even though at the time she had thought it dull; she even missed her sister Jessica and the long summer visits she had made when she had been poorer and somehow more accessible than she ever seemed to be now.

On the whole there was not much time for nostalgia or introspection. McAlpine's arthritis meant that not only was the garden far too much for him, but also that his temper had become such that no boy recruited from the dwindling supply available stayed longer than a few weeks. Last summer she had taught herself to use a scythe and cut all of the orchard, which had gained his grudging respect. "I've seen worse," he had remarked. After this, she spent at least two afternoons a week on outside maintenance: she had taught herself to prune the fruit trees; she sanded and repainted one of the green-houses; and, of course, on wet days there was always wood to be sawn and stacked. "You must not exhaust yourself," the Duchy had said, but that was exactly what she had wanted to do, the whole of last year ever since last spring which now seemed such a very long time ago. But apart from—*that* (she now never allowed herself to mention his name), last year had been hard in other ways. After the row with Edward about his forgetting Hermoine's party during which she had heard herself make the classic denunciation of his general lack of concern, he had spent an unusually long time making love to her, and she had been so wrought up and then exhausted by pretending to enjoy it that it was not until the next morning that she remembered she had taken no precautions. So when, the following month, she missed her period she naturally thought herself pregnant, and this time, unlike with Roly, she actually felt glad at the prospect. It would be her last baby, she would be able to share her pregnancy with Louise who was also in the family way. But when she told Edward she sensed that he was not wholly enthusiastic, although he wouldn't voice any objection. "Good Lord! *I* don't know . . . Do you really think you should . . ." were some of the things he said. When pressed, he had eventually said that of course *he* was pleased, it was only that he wondered if perhaps she wasn't getting on a bit for having another baby. Of course she would be if it was her first, she had answered, but she was perfectly healthy, there was really no reason why she shouldn't . . . She toyed with the idea of going to London to see Dr. Ballater, but in the end she went to Dr. Carr. She went to his consulting room in his house, because she didn't want to tell the family anything until she was *absolutely* sure, but by now it was the second month and she felt she knew. "I'm sure I *am*," she had said to Dr. Carr, "I just wanted to confirm it with you."

He had given her a sharp look from under his rather shaggy eyebrows and remarked that it was a bit early to be sure . . .

After he had examined her and asked her a good many questions, he had said that although it might not be to her liking, he thought it far more probable that she was embarking upon the menopause than that she was pregnant. He could be wrong, he added, but it was clear that he did not think so.

"After all, Mrs. Cazalet, you are forty-seven, you have four fine children as it is. Don't you think, in any case, it's a wee bit late to start again?"

"Surely it's too early for all that!" She was aghast at the idea.

"People vary about it. You tell me that you started menstruation late, and the later starters are usually earlier to finish."

She felt herself flushing; she found it embarrassing even to hear any words connected with the whole revolting business. He mistook her revulsion for disappointment and talked encouragingly about her prospect of becoming a grandmother (Louise had twice been to see him). "You are young enough to get the full benefit of grandchildren," he had said, but Villy had always regarded comfort as a means of minimizing the authenticity of her distress in the first place and was therefore hostile, or at least impervious to it.

Of course, this visit was shortly followed by incontrovertible evidence that she was not pregnant, and she spent the rest of the winter much depressed. Edward's relief at the news had irritated her and she had several times said how pleased he must be, but she did not mention the disgusting alternative.

One way and another it was good to have the small excursion to look forward to. She would go and see Louise too, of course, who was still in the nursing home where she had had her baby the previous week. Michael had telephoned the news—he had managed to get a few days' leave—and she had offered to go up at once, but he had said much better to wait until his leave was up and Louise might be feeling lonely. And then Raymond had rung her. It was a very bad line and he sounded both portentous and faint. He would so very much like to see her, he said twice: she was the only person who, he felt, might be able to give him advice . . . This remark with its doubled-edged attractions—her vanity was soothed, her curiosity aroused—settled the matter: she had agreed to meet him at the Arts Theatre Club in Great Newport Street at a quarter to one. She put on last year's blue suit with the chiffon blouse (it was quite sunny and warm) and caught the train.

She was early and he had not arrived, so she sat in the densely populated and very small dusky area that was half passage, half room on the ground floor and watched people booking theatre tickets and meeting each other for lunch, until Raymond suddenly loomed beside her, bending down to present her with his huge pale face that gleamed almost phosphorescent in the gloom.

"My dear! My train was late. Awfully sorry." His cheek was damp, his moustache like thistles. He took her arm. "Shall we go straight up? Have a drink and all that?"

He led the way to the large pleasant dining room.

"A table for two—name of Castle," he said in the tone of elaborate courtesy he reserved for what he considered to be his inferiors. It was one of the things she had not noticed before, but now recognized as his habit.

"And we should like to order drinks immediately—if you would be so kind."

The drinks arrived, he offered her a cigarette and began laboriously enquiring after the health of everyone in the family, receiving her answers as though they were exactly what he expected, and she began to see that he was nervous.

"I suppose it is no use asking you anything about your work," she said.

"Fraid not. Of course one likes to feel useful—to have found some sort of niche. And I do feel that it is up to *somebody* in my family to make some contribution to the war effort."

"Oh, Raymond! Christopher is working for a farmer and, goodness knows, we need food grown here, and Nora, they say, is a simply wonderful nurse, and hasn't Angela moved from the BBC to the Ministry of Information? And, after all, Judy is just a child. And—" But here she came to an end. She could not honestly think of anything useful that Jessica was doing, or ever had done, and this was when she realized that she was not being mentioned.

"And as for Jessica," he said as though he had heard her thoughts, "her contribution seems to be adultery." There was a short silence: the word lay like a scorpion on the table between them.

Then he said, "For one awful moment I thought that perhaps you might have known. That everyone knew excepting me. But you didn't, did you?"

No, she said, she didn't. She was so shocked—she had always assumed that she and Jessica felt the same about things like that— that although her mind seethed with questions, each one on its own seemed too trivial to voice.

"Are you *sure*?" she eventually managed to ask.

"Dead sure." And then he began answering the questions without her having to ask a single one.

He'd known for nearly a month now. When he'd first found out, his instinct had been to go and confront her at once, but he'd not dared to do that. "I wanted to kill her," he said, "I was honestly afraid of what I might do. She's been lying to me so much, you see. I felt such a fool. Also, there were some things I didn't want to know. Supposing she thought she was in *love* with the bastard, for instance, or supposing she wasn't—it had just been a roll in the hay—I didn't know which would make me feel worse. Then I discovered that it had been going on for quite a long time—"

"How long?"

"Oh, well over a year. *I* don't know—it could be much longer. She got to know him when we were still at Frensham. Of course, you know who it is by now, don't you?"

She began to say no, she didn't, but before the words were out of her mouth a horrible thought assailed her, a doubt, suspicion that in a second congealed to sickening certainty.

"Oh, *no!*"

"My dear! I'm sorry if I've shocked you, although I quite understand your feelings. It *is* shocking. A decently brought-up woman who has been married for twenty-seven years—*happily* married I always thought . . ."

She drank some water while he droned on and his face, which had briefly obscured to a dizzy blur, slipped jerkily back into focus. So, too, did all kinds of small matters—things said, or not said, the way Jessica never asked her to stay, did not seem to want to come to Home Place, had not wanted Louise to stay with her and then that curious time when she had dropped in at St. John's Wood and Jessica had behaved so oddly . . .

He was on to what he thought of Clutterworth now—suddenly he seemed unable to stop repeating his name. "If *Mr.* Clutterworth thinks that being a musician entitles him to behave in this manner . . . and, what is more, if Mr. Clutterworth thinks he can get away with it, Mr. Laurence Clutterworth is in for a serious shock. I've half a mind to get in touch with that wretched wife of his to see if she knows what is going on . . ."

If it has been going on for over a year, I was not even his first choice, she thought, as the humiliation she had thought buried from that ghastly evening in Soho came flooding back. Oh, God! Supposing he told *her* about it afterwards!

But there was worse to come.

"Tell me," he said, leaning over the table towards her. "Tell me, how on earth can *any* decent woman—I nearly said *lady*—think for a moment of falling in love with a greasy little worm like that? Let alone . . ." Here his complexion became suffused with embarrassment. "Let alone contemplating getting—physically involved with such a creature? Can you at all understand it? I mean, am I being obtuse, or what?"

Fortunately, he did not seem to expect an answer, was so immersed in angry rumination that any question was rhetorical: all she had to do, she thought, was sit and endure the floodgates of his rage and shock—for beyond all his clumsy, cliché-ridden language she could sense, as her Red Cross experience had taught her, that he *was* in shock—until somehow lunch would be over. She stopped trying to eat, lit a cigarette, stared at her plate and tried to let the ultimate humiliation of hearing somebody who she at least *thought* she had loved being described in terms that were compounded of coarseness and brutal reality wash over her. This numb, mindless reverie came abruptly to an end because he seemed to be asking something . . .

". . . what you think I should do?"

"*Do?* What do you mean?"

"I mean, about talking to her. I must confess that I really don't know what would be the best way to tackle it."

She looked at him in astonishment. His anger seemed to have evaporated; he had now a nervously furtive, conciliatory air. Before she could reply, he exclaimed, with wholly unconvincing spontaneity: "I know! Well, that is, if you feel you could . . . Have a word with her?"

He stuck at it throughout all protestations: what should she say? What did he want her to say? What, in fact, did he want? He thought she might find out what Jessica really *felt*—perhaps she might even talk to the feller's wife—get her to remove him from the scene or something. Beneath all the earlier bombast of which there was now no sign, she recognized that he was anxious, craven, and very much afraid. In the end, and in order to escape, she said she would have to think about it, and he wrote out his address and telephone number at Woodstock so that she could get in touch with him. By the time they parted outside the Arts Theatre Club it was four o'clock and she had to run to Charing Cross to catch her train.

Neville and Lydia, who had most mistakenly complained of not having anything to do, had been sent to fill up the drinking trough for the horses in the field. This entailed filling two buckets, one each, from the hose outside the stables and staggering through the arch in the wall, along the narrow cinder path past the potting shed, the compost heap and the broken-down kennel, along a grassy track that had huge sunbaked ruts in it to the trough just inside the gate that led to the horses' field: it was a long walk. They had done four journeys and the trough was still only half full.

"It's partly because Marigold is drinking it all up behind our backs," Neville complained.

They had had their usual, almost mechanical grumble about the task immediately after they had been told to do it—gone through the unfairness of being made to work in their holidays, especially on such a hot afternoon when nobody else was, they bet. They went contemptuously through the grown-ups' indolent and paltry activities: the Duchy machining, Aunt Zoë reading to ill people at the nursing home, Aunt Rachel sewing, Aunt Dolly (Bully) *having a rest*—they rolled their eyes at each other in a paroxysm of sarcastic amusement—Aunt Villy off in the *car* somewhere to fetch something or other . . . "They're all sitting *down*," Neville said.

"Hardly exhausting, my dear," Lydia agreed. "Why doesn't Mr. Wren do this? Wait for me, I've got to change arms."

"He doesn't do anything except chop a tiny bit of wood and go to the pub in the evenings. Tonbridge has to fetch him home sometimes because he can't walk properly."

"He's intoxicated with drink," Lydia said.

"But what does he do all day? I think we ought to find out."

"Oh, Nev! He can be quite frightening—especially if you wake him when he's asleep."

"Well, he can't run as fast as we can on his little spindly legs."

They had reached the field again. The old chestnut was drinking from the trough. She put up her head suddenly and knocked Lydia's bucket over so that the water ran into the hard-backed ground and disappeared at once.

"Oh, God!"

"You should have got her head out of the way first. We shall have to do this practically the whole afternoon and you'll have to do an extra one."

"I might not have to."

"We'll see," Neville said in Ellen's voice.

They had begun trailing back, easier with empty buckets, and they were free to notice other things; the old buddleia by the kitchen garden gate, for instance, that was swarming with butterflies; Flossy, asleep on a most unsuitably narrow piece of wall with her tail hanging down, "like the Speckled Band," Neville said—he had become very keen on Sherlock Holmes. When, at last, they got back to the stable door with the hose that had been wired onto the tap beside it, they both simply went and sat on the mounting block for a rest.

"Well, this afternoon settles one thing. When I'm grown-up I shall be a freelance."

"What's that?"

"It means you don't have to do anything you don't like."

"But what does it *mean?*"

He hadn't the slightest idea, but he was damned if he would let her know that.

"There is a South American snake," he began in his lecture voice, "extremely poisonous called a Fer de Lance. It comes from that. The snake only bites people if he feels like it, you see."

She knew that he was extremely interested in snakes and read everything he could find about them, so she accepted this at once. "I expect in France a freelance would actually *be* fer de lance," she said. "I shall ask Miss Milliment."

"I shouldn't, if I were you. Miss Milliment's knowledge of reptiles has always struck me as rudimentary." He was using another voice now—a master at his school, probably. She wanted to point out to him that to copy unknown people's voices wasn't very funny, but she wanted to keep on the right side of him because then he might waive her doing the extra bucket.

"What do you think of Mussolini?"

"I hardly ever think of him and, anyway, now he's deposed he doesn't count any more. Listen, I've got an idea."

Her heart sank. She knew it would be to do with Mr. Wren. It was.

"I'm going to creep up the ladder into the hayloft, and if he's asleep, I'm going to give him a little squirt from the hose and ask him why *he* isn't carrying water to the horses. You can watch."

"Supposing he *isn't* asleep? He might . . ." She mouthed the rest of the sentence, "he might be *listening* to us." She imagined him listening, smiling his grim, tight little smile and getting ready to pounce on Neville as he reached the top of the ladder . . . "He might topple you off," she said.

"I'll be careful. I'll call out to him first. If he answers, I won't go right up the ladder."

"Let's finish our job first." Perhaps by then it would be tea-time, and Neville was always hungry so he wouldn't miss that.

"You can go on, if you want to." He got off the block and picked up the hose. The stable door was ajar. He pushed it open and disappeared into the gloom.

"Mr. Wren! I say, Mr. Wren!"

She heard him calling. There was a silence. She got off the block and followed him.

"Unwind the hose for me, I'm going up."

She did as she was told, and then her fear prompted her to look in the loose-boxes in case Mr. Wren was hiding in one of them. But they were bare except for an old nest in one of the iron mangers bracketed to the wall. The walls were whitewashed and laced with ambitious cobwebs, as big as fishing nets at Hastings; they had not been repainted for a long time. She looked into all four boxes. Each had a small round window placed high in the wall—no good for a horse to look out—and most of the glass was cracked and dirty; a dusty twilight prevailed. She could hear that Neville had reached the top of the ladder: his footsteps were loud on the boards of the loft above.

"He's not here," he called. "He must be out. Take the hose, could you?"

Going back to the foot of the ladder, she noticed the tack room door. It was shut: he might easily be there. As he took the hose she pointed silently to the tack room and then moved towards the stable door so that she could escape if Mr. Wren suddenly pounced out at them. But he didn't.

When Neville was down again, he regained the hose. "I bet that's where he is all the time," he said.

The latch on the door was stiff and creaked as he lifted it.

"Yes! He's asleep, as usual."

She joined him, staying in the doorway. The tack room had a brick floor. There was a small iron grate with a mantelpiece on which was propped a cracked mirror. The walls beside it had faded rosettes pinned to them that Louise would have won in her gymkhana days. The window had a piece of sacking nailed over it, but some of it had rotted so that it only made half of a curtain. The room had a different smell from the rest of the stables: damp leather and musty old clothes. Mr. Wren lay on a camp bed in the far corner. He was partly covered by a horse blanket, but his legs, covered in brown leather gaiters and dark toffee-coloured boots, stuck out.

"Mr. Wren!" Neville said in a teasing voice.

"Neville, don't—" she began to say, but it was too late. He gave her one of his bland, gleaming looks that she knew meant total defiance, squeezed the trigger on the hose and played it lightly over the reclining figure. It did not move.

"He *is* fast asleep," Neville said, but he let her take the hose from him.

But she had gone right up to the bed.

"He *isn't*," she said. "His eyes are wide open. Do you think he's possibly—you know—*dead?*"

"Gosh! *I* don't know. He doesn't look pale enough. Feel him."

"*You* do it."

He leaned over and put his hand gingerly on the old man's forehead. There were drops of water on it, but the skin felt cold. "I'd better try and feel his pulse," he said, trying to sound calm, but his voice was shaking. He pulled the blanket back: Wren lay in his dirty striped collarless shirt, his braces hitched to his breeches; his right hand was clutching a yellowing piece of paper. When Neville picked up his wrist, the piece of paper slipped sideways and they saw it was an old photograph out of a newspaper of their grandfather on a horse whose bridle was held by a young man in a tweed cap. "Mr. William Cazalet on Ebony with his groom," it said. His wrist, just bones with skin round them, was cold as well. When he let go, it dropped back onto the bed so quickly that it almost made him start. Tears rushed to his eyes.

"He must be dead," he said.

"Oh, *poor* Mr. Wren! He must have died awfully suddenly if he didn't even have time to shut his eyes." Lydia was crying, which he was glad of because it stopped him.

"We must go and tell them," he said.

"I think we ought to say a prayer for him first. I think the people who find people who are dead *ought* to do something like that."

"Well, *you* can stay and pray if you like, I'm going to find Aunt Rach."

"Oh, no, I don't think I will," she said hastily. "I'll come with you and pray on the way."

They found Aunt Rach and told her and she and Villy went to see him and then Dr. Carr came and then a black van from Hastings took Mr. Wren away, and during all this Neville and Lydia were told to keep out of the way, "have a nice game of tennis or squash or something." This infuriated both of them. "When *will* they stop treating us as though we were children?" Lydia exclaimed in her most die-away grown-up's voice.

"If it hadn't been for us he might have stayed there for days and weeks and months. Even possibly *years*. Until he was just a skeleton in his clothes," Neville said, and immediately wondered where the rest of him went.

"Actually, they would have found out because Edie takes him a plate of dinner with a lid on it every day. She would have noticed the plates piling up," Lydia said. She was wondering what happened to the *body* part of people. But I shan't ask Neville, she thought. She bet he wouldn't know, and would simply *make* something horrible *up*. By mutual consent, they went through the green baize door to the kitchen, where they regaled the servants—a most satisfactory audience—with an extremely dramatic account of the affair.

". . . and what we were both wondering," Neville said when eventually they could think of nothing more to tell, "is how do you *shut* a dead person's eyes?"

Mrs. Cripps said that she didn't think that was a very nice question, but Lizzie, in her rather hoarse whisper, used when she (rarely) conversed in front of Mrs. Cripps, said that you put pennies on their eyelids.

A really useful thing to know, Lydia said, when they were washing their hands for supper, but Neville said not awfully, because they didn't come across dead people very often.

"I'm thirteen," he said, "nearly, and this is the first one I've ever met. And Clary hasn't ever. She *will* be mad with jealousy."

Lydia, who had been feeling it for some time, said that she was shocked by how heartless he was being about poor Mr. Wren.

"I'm not actually heart*less*, but I have to admit that I don't feel very heart*ful* about him. I'm sorry for *him* he's dead, but I don't feel sorry for *me*, that is."

"I know exactly what you mean," Lydia said. "He did go about in a sort of silent bad temper most of the time. But Mummy says that he was awfully sad about the Brig having a car instead of horses to go about on. Especially when the Brig got too blind to go riding. I can see that those sort of things blighted his life."

His funeral happened a week later, and the Brig and the Duchy and Rachel and Villy all went to it.

In September, it was time for Zoë to make the visit to her mother in the Isle of Wight again. She went every three months, stayed three or four days, or a week if she could bear it. In the spring and summer, she took Juliet, but as Juliet grew older, taking her became more of a problem. Her mother could not deal with a small active child for more than about half an hour, and Jules, at three, was far too young to be left to herself, so Zoë found it increasingly difficult to divide her time between them to the satisfaction of either.

This time, Ellen had agreed to look after her, and Villy was going to be there to keep an eye on things.

"I'll only stay three days," Zoë said.

The Duchy had once suggested that Zoë might like to have her mother stay at Home Place, but Zoë—appalled at the idea—had quickly said that her mother couldn't travel so far alone, and that if she, Zoë, was going to fetch her, she might as well stay with her, and the Duchy, who understood perfectly that for some reason Zoë did not want her mother to come, and also knew that the older one got the less one wanted to move from familiar surroundings, had immediately desisted.

Now she had packed—winter nightdress because Cotter's End, the cottage that she was going to owned by Mummy's friend Mrs. Witting, was always cold, hot water bottle because the bed she slept in there seemed most of the year to be damp—she had never got over her first visit when steam had risen from it after she had put her bottle into it—a packet of ginger biscuits (meals were dainty in the extreme) and a mac in case any of the windy walks she went for when she felt the need to escape were wet. She had also a box of marshmallows for her mother whose favourite sweet they had always been. She took sewing and knitting and *Anna Karenina*, a novel that Rupert had introduced her to just before he had been called up and that she had, to her surprise, enjoyed very much. She always took some such book with her on these occasions to absorb her during the long evenings after her mother and Maud had gone to bed. She took a bottle of sherry for Maud, as every time she went a small sherry party was arranged so that she could be shown off to neighbours and friends. This occasion entailed a dress and a precious pair of stockings—she only had two unworn pairs left.

The case, when full, was horribly heavy and, with the war, there were hardly any porters, but Tonbridge carried it for her onto the train to London.

It was a relief to be on her way. Leaving Jules was always hard; when she had been smaller, Jules had hardly noticed, it was *she* who had suffered. Now, in fact all of this year, Jules minded if she even went to London for the day, although Ellen said that she settled down very quickly afterwards. And with Wills and Roly, she really wasn't an only child. Although she will be *my* only child, I suppose, she thought. The prospect of being on her own for several uninterupted hours on end, practically the only aspect of these journeys that she looked forward to, had begun: she could afford the luxury of thinking only of herself, in terms that various members of the Cazalet family would brand either selfish, or morbid, or both. What was to become of her? She was twenty-eight: she could not spend the rest of her life at Home Place, working as a part-time amateur nurse, looking after Jules, helping the Duchy, making and mending clothes, washing, ironing, looking after the invalids of the house—the Brig and Aunt Dolly—listening to interminable bulletins of news about the war on the wireless. The war, which everyone said was likely to be over in a year or two, would finish some time after the Second Front was launched, although nobody expected that to be before next spring; however, the end, which had once seemed unimaginable, was definitely in sight. What should she do then? Years of adapting herself to the continuous warm throb of family life that her in-laws seemed to find so natural and necessary, had sapped her initiative: the thought of going back to the house in Brook Green on her own with Jules seemed bleak. For she no longer expected that Rupert would come back, and in the train, she felt free to acknowledge this. At home, she was surrounded by people who, even if they secretly agreed with her, could not admit it; if by nothing else, they were all in thrall to Clary's unwavering faith that he was alive. This could only stop with the end of the war, when he did not come back and even Clary would have to believe that he was dead. She had, of course, felt a wonderful relief when that Frenchman had brought the news of him, and the messages for her and Clary. She had wept with excitement and joy. But that was two years ago—two years without a sign that he was still alive. This summer the head of the French Resistance had been tortured to death by the Gestapo. It had been on the nine o'clock news; nobody had said a word, but the room became full of unnameable anxieties. She remembered wondering how long anyone would continue to hide him if being found out meant that they risked torture before death. Clary had not been present on this occasion.

Since then, she had tried, and usually succeeded, to put all thoughts of him out of her mind. She would never, never have admitted this to any of the family, as she knew they would either not believe her, or would think that she was unnaturally cold and selfish. Perhaps she was, she now thought. But the fact remained that she was in what seemed to her an interminable limbo: she was not a widow, nor what the family, satirizing the Brig, called a splendid little woman whose husband was a prisoner of war. She might be any of these, indeed, must by the nature of things be one of them, but what could she do or feel when she did not know which? So she had taken refuge in the present, the minutiae of daily wartime life that was full enough of mundane problems to occupy and fatigue her. Her escape had become reading novels—preferably long, old ones. There were a number of them to be found in the house, carelessly stuffed into shelves all over the place; they had never been arranged and nobody knew where any particular book might be, except the girls who had their own bookshelves in their room, so each novel she read was a discovery, sometimes deeply enjoyable, sometimes almost unreadably dull. As, to begin with, she had the simple idea that all these books, being classics, must therefore be good, she was confounded by the struggle she had to get through some of them. A conversation with Miss Milliment, however, altered this sweeping view: through her she discovered that the nineteenth century had its crop of pot boilers, books that Miss Milliment described as being like the curate's egg (did she not know that saying? it meant good in parts), novels that had been admired for their sociological significance, as well as some masterpieces, "although, sometimes, masterpieces, as I'm sure you know, can also be boring." After that, she would ask Miss Milliment about the books she found, before she embarked upon them. "One has also to remember," she had remarked in her gentle, diffident voice, "that even very *good* writers will produce work of varying quality, so you may admire one novel very much and feel nothing for another." She wondered whether, if there had not been a war, and if Rupert had not gone away, she would ever have found out that she enjoyed reading novels—probably not.

Archie had asked her to lunch with him on her way through London, but she had some shopping to do for her mother and it had been arranged that she should lunch with him on her homeward journey instead. It would be nice to have Archie to herself, she thought, and really exciting to lunch in a restaurant. She had packed her new green tweed skirt and the jumper she had made to match it for the occasion. She *liked* Archie, although she did not find him attractive—thank goodness, she thought now, because falling in love with one's husband's best friend would obviously be a very stupid thing to do and ever since the ghastly incident (it had shrunk, with time, to that) with Philip Sherlock, she had shied away from the very idea of flirting with anyone. No, Archie was almost family now; he knew all about everybody because they all confided in him: he alone knew that she thought Rupert was dead and did not make her feel either guilty or heartless about it.

In order to buy the particular bust bodices and camisoles that her mother wanted, she had to go either to Ponting's in Kensington High Street, or to Gaylor and Pope in Marylebone. Her mother had said that if one shop did not have what she wanted, the other was almost certain to, presenting the alternative as though this would make the task easier. In fact, the shops were so far apart that without a car she would not have time to visit both: she chose Ponting's because she could go all the way there on a number nine bus, a long ride that cost fourpence. She left her luggage at Charing Cross. Kensington Gardens looked far larger and more like a country park with all its iron railings gone. She remembered the boring walks that she had occasionally been taken on by a collection of people whose names she could hardly remember who looked after her when her mother was at work, and then wondered whether *she* would take Jules there—to sail a boat, perhaps, on the Round Pond, or to feed birds at the Serpentine. But I expect I'll have to have a job of some kind, she thought. The parallel between her mother's life and her own struck her now with a sudden force. There had been glancing blows before, but she had managed to ward them off: now her own life seemed horribly to imitate her mother's in every respect. Her mother had been widowed in the last war. She, Zoë, had been the only child. When her mother had finally retired from the cosmetics firm for which she had worked for nearly twenty years, she had received three hundred pounds and a silver tray meant for the use of calling cards. She remembered her mother's pathetic attempts at finding some male companionship (no doubt, with the hope of marriage), and her own stony sabotage of them. Ever since Zoë could remember, her mother had always, as she used to call it, "fussed" over her, making her clothes, brushing her hair a hundred times every night, teaching her to look after her appearance, sending her to schools that, looking back on it, she must have found it a struggle to afford, and then, when Zoë had married Rupert, selling the small mansion flat which had been their home and moving to an even smaller one. And she, who had grown up taking everything her mother gave her for granted, had also grown up as much in love with her own appearance as her mother could ever have been with it. Her mother had brought her up to feel that *she* was the important one, the beauty who would go far. At school, it had been much the same. The other girls had envied her her lovely clear skin, her shining hair that curled naturally, her long legs and her green eyes; they had *envied* her but she had also been adored—spoiled—given the best parts in the plays at the end of term, introduced to parents visiting the school; some besotted girls had even offered to do her maths homework. She must not bring Jules up like that, she thought. Jules must go to a school where she would *learn* things. Four years of living with the Cazalet family had taught her that they counted appearance as nothing at all; it was never referred to, and with the Duchy, at least, there was the inference that vanity about one's looks or indeed anything else, was out of the question. She thought of Jules, who had the same thick, shining dark hair, the same creamy skin, the same slanting, moth-like eyebrows. Only her eyes were different as they were blue, like Rupert's, like most of the Cazalets'. She had been, and was now, the prettiest baby Zoë had ever seen, but that made no difference in the family. Ellen called her a little madam when she had her tempers; she was treated exactly the same as Wills and Roly. "How would you like it if someone took your teddy and threw it out of the window?" she had heard Ellen saying one day. "You'd be cross, wouldn't you, and it would make you cry. Well, you mustn't do things to other people that you know you would not like them to do to you." Nobody had ever said anything like that to her. If I hadn't met Rupert and all his family, I might never have grown up at all, she thought. She felt so different from the spoiled, vain, shallow nineteen-year-old who had married Rupert. Now, in two years, she would be thirty, her youth would be gone and nobody would want to marry a middle-aged woman with a child—thirty had always seemed to her the beginning of middle age.

Ponting's had the bust bodices, but not the camisoles. As this meant that there were a few clothes coupons left in her mother's book, and remembering the dank chill of Cotter's End, she bought her mother a pale pink woollen spencer instead. It was half past twelve—time to return to Charing Cross, find something to eat for lunch, collect her luggage and make for Waterloo to catch the train to Southampton.

She had lunch in Fuller's in the Strand: two grey sausages encased in what felt like mackintosh, a scoop of a paler grey mashed potato and carrots. Her glass of water tasted strongly of chlorine. For pudding there was steamed treacle roll or jelly. She was not used to lunching alone in public, and wished she had brought her book. But this isn't meant to be a treat, she thought. It is me doing the least I can do for Mummy. For now as on other occasions, the thought struck her that another kind of daughter would have left her in-laws' house, and made a wartime home for her mother. Even the faintest idea of this made her shrink with horror. Her mother's passive, humble attitude to life, and particularly to Zoë, irritated her beyond bearing. Her expectations, both drab and genteel, were confined to things being marginally better than she had thought that they would be: the milk turning out not to be off for her early morning tea would be a fair example, or the girl in the local hairdresser having enough solution to perm her hair. When Zoë brought Jules with her, her mother ceaselessly exclaimed at her prettiness—in *front* of her—and kept telling Zoë how much she should brush the child's hair or put Vaseline on her eyelashes at night: "You want to grow into a pretty lady, don't you, Juliet?" But even without Jules, the situation was irritating enough, as Mummy and her friend Maud had settled together by evolving a mutual admiration society, bickering gently as each disclaimed the qualities attributed to her by the other, and each appealing to Zoë to uphold their views. Exasperation was succeeded by guilt, and after twenty-four hours in Cotter's End, Zoë always found herself counting the hours until her release.

So it was this time. After the train, and then the ferry and then the little local train, she was met by Maud in her Baby Austin.

"Just wait until I'm in, my dear. The passenger door only opens from the inside.

"Your mother is *so* excited about you coming that I made her take a little rest after tea. Yes, she's as well as can be expected, but of course one never *knows* because, as you know, she *never* complains. Only last week, she slipped getting out of the bath and bruised herself black and blue, but I would never have known if I hadn't found her hunting for the Pommade Divine."

She pressed the starter, and the Baby Austin gave a startled lurch before the engine died.

"Oh dear! I left her in gear. Silly me. I expect you're exhausted after your long journey. I won't ask you for all your news, because I know Cicely will be dying to hear it. Here we go."

By the end of the journey, a mere mile and a half, she had been given all the local news. Commander Lawrence had broken his arm, his *right* arm, which had made his bridge-playing very difficult; there had been a severe shortage of potatoes—the shop had been rationing them; Lady Harkness had been so rude to the vicar's wife that the vicar had felt unable to call at the Hall although subscriptions towards repairing the church hall were desperately needed and Lady Harkness had always been a very good *source;* Prim, the tabby cat that they had thought was a male and had called Patrick, had suddenly had four kittens, "so now it's Primrose, Prim for short," she had explained. "She had them on Cicely's bed which was a terrible shock for her, but, of course, she was wonderful about it. I think that that is all *our* news," she finished. "You know that the Italians have surrendered, of course."

Zoë had seen it on a placard at Waterloo.

They arrived, eventually, at Cotter's End; the car was manoeuvred into the incredibly small lean-to built onto the end of the cottage that served as its garage, after Zoë had got out and her luggage had been wrested from the back.

Her mother came out of the sitting room to greet them. She was wearing her woollen dress of a dusty pink, with her graduated cultured pearls. She was carefully made-up, with blue eye shadow and mascara, bright lipstick and a peachy powder that came off on Zoë when she kissed her. It was like kissing a moth.

"How nice that you have got here," she said wanly, so that Zoë felt like a drab surprise.

She was expected to want to take her things upstairs, to unpack and "wash" before joining them in the sitting room, so this she did. "You are in your usual room,'' Maud called up the stairs—as though there was a choice. But with three bedrooms, there couldn't be, Zoë thought, as she lifted the stiff latch of the door that always stuck the first time you tried to open it and was assailed by a blast of cold damp salty air. The window was wide open: when she went downstairs they would tell her that they had been airing the room, and each would think that the other had closed the window. She would not mention it. The room was small and narrow with just room for the bed, a chest of drawers and a chair. It had dark blue curtains which she now drew, after shutting the window, and a further curtain arranged across a corner of the room behind which clothes could be precariously hung. There was a large coloured print of *When Did You Last See Your Father?* on the wall over the bed, and the same small pottery jar of crumbling everlasting flowers on the chest of drawers. She went to the lavatory, hung up her clothes, and with presents in hand went down to join them.

They all had a glass of sherry in front of the very small unwilling fire and Zoë answered questions about the health of Juliet and the Cazalet family, and her mother told her about the cat having kittens on her bed. Eventually, Maud said she must just go and see to their dinner, and had a brief argument with Zoë's mother about not needing any help. ''You two enjoy each other's company. I am perfectly happy in the kitchen.'' She shut the door upon them and there was a silence while both thought furiously about how to break it.

''Maud is wonderful.'' Her mother announced this before Zoë had thought of anything.

''She does seem kind.''

''She has *always* been kind. I don't know what I should have done without her.'' And then, as though she realized that this could be taken as some sort of reproof, she added: ''Of course I would have managed.''

''I'm afraid it will be very quiet for you here,'' she began again. ''Commander Lawrence has broken his arm, so I'm afraid our bridge evening won't be as lively as usual. He broke it trying to get into his loft.''

''You know, Mummy, I'm not very good at bridge.''

''But I thought with all that large family, you would have had a lot of practice by now.''

''They don't play much.''

"Oh dear." There was a pause: a piece of wood fell out of the fire basket and Zoë went to retrieve it.

"Zoë, dear, I hope you don't mind my asking, but of course I've been very worried for you—"

"There is no news of Rupert," she said quickly. "None at all." Every time she came, her mother asked the same question, in exactly the same way, and it was one of the things that she could bear least. "I'd have *told* you if there was any news. I promised to ring you up if there ever was, don't you remember?" In trying not to sound exasperated she sounded hysterical.

"Darling, don't be angry. I didn't meant to upset you. It's only that—"

"I'm sorry, Mummy. I'd just rather not talk about it."

"Of course. I quite understand."

There was another silence, and then she said, "You remember Lady Harkness? She came *once* to sherry when you were here about a year ago, I think it was. A very tall woman with very good skin? Well—she has been rather outspoken with our vicar, I'm sorry to say; he hasn't taken it quite the right way which has made things rather awkward. Socially, I mean."

At this point, Maud put her weatherbeaten face round the door and said that supper was ready.

This took place in a tiny room next to the kitchen at a rocky little gate-legged table and consisted of rissoles about the size of a trussed mouse—one each—with mashed potato and chopped cabbage. While they ate, Maud described in detail how the rissoles were made, using a mere four ounces of sausagemeat, breadcrumbs and herbs, and her mother said how clever Maud was with the rations. This was followed by stewed plums arranged in little glass dishes; there was nowhere to put the stones. Zoë had brought her ration book with her, having consulted with Mrs. Cripps about the appropriate contribution for three days. She thought gratefully of the packet of ginger biscuits in her room. The dining room had no fire and its white-washed walls were blistered with damp. After dinner, there was a faint squabble about the washing up, which resulted in all three of them crowding into the small dark kitchen, bumping into one another as each carried supper things out, and breakfast things in—Maud said she liked to have everything on the table for the morning as it was so much easier. By the time they got back to the sitting room, the fire had gone out. Bed began to be discussed—the question of who would or might have a bath: the hot water would only run to one and both of her hosts seemed anxious to accord this to Zoë. There was also the question of whether anyone wanted a hot drink and, of course, there were the hot water bottles to be filled. The kettle was so old and full of scale that it took an age to boil and was not large enough to fill more than one bottle at a time. All in all, the preparations for bed took up the rest of the evening and it was well after ten before Zoë was able to shut herself into her room. And this was only Wednesday, she thought; there is the whole of Thursday and Friday and half of Saturday, and she counted the hours involved as she chewed biscuits with her hot water bottle clasped to her stomach.

The visit, like all of them, was only different because she didn't have Jules with her; it was easier, but considerably more dull. They went for what her mother described as little strolls; they had Commander Lawrence and his wife and Labrador to tea. The Labrador stood politely if spoken to and wagged his weighty tail so that rock cakes were knocked off occasional tables and swallowed instantly by him as though they had never been. The Commander said he was a naughty boy who was not usually like that, but that there was nothing like the loyalty you got from a dog. His arm was in a sling, which made him feel, he said, after he had thoroughly described to Zoë the circumstances of it breaking, like Nelson.

Her mother was pleased with the bust bodices, but doubtful about the spencer. "I should really need two of them," she said, "to get the benefit. Otherwise, I might catch cold while it was being washed."

The paid the usual visit to Miss Fenwick and her mother, who Maud repeatedly said was marvellous for her age. She was ninety-two. It took Miss Fenwick the best part of the morning to wash and dress her and cram her into an enormous armchair which she filled like a vast sandbag. She was practically bald and always wore a red hat with a diamanté arrow stuck through one side of it. Below her ample jersey skirt her feet rested on a stool, encased in bedroom slippers, which were, as the family at home would say, the shape of old broad beans. Conversation with her was difficult, as she was stone deaf and did not remember who anyone was, although occasionally she would interrupt other people with a rather peevish enquiry about the next meal. "Mother does enjoy her food," Miss Fenwick always said on those occasions.

Conversation, on this occasion, when it was not concentrated on the marvel of Mrs. Fenwick's antiquity, was about what they most missed from peacetime, which mostly turned out to be food. Fresh cream, Maud declared, she did so love fresh cream cakes—not to mention strawberries and cream. Lemons, Zoë suggested, but nobody took much notice of her. Speaking of cream cakes, her mother said, she really missed a Fuller's walnut cake, and Mother, Miss Fenwick informed them, really *did* miss her bananas.

Eventually, this visit came to an end because Miss Fenwick said that Mother didn't like to be late with lunch. Goodness, Zoë thought, how awful it is to be old. I'd rather be dead than like Mrs. Fenwick, but she did not voice this view.

The sherry party was held, to which the Lawrences came, and the vicar, with his niece. Zoë's bottle of sherry was opened, and Maud made little pieces of toast with chicken and ham paste on them. They went shopping with Zoë's ration book and a tin of Spam was bought "as a standby" and Mrs. Cripps had also sanctioned the use of her cheese ration, and three ounces of cheese, Maud said, was a godsend and would make three meals if stretched. This occupied Thursday and Friday. Tomorrow I shall go home, she thought, and have the lunch with Archie on the way. She had said that she could not stay longer because of Juliet, who, they said, she *must* bring next time. The last evening, tiny pieces of cod in a sauce made with Carnation milk and mashed swede, they kept saying how sad it was that she had to go; Maud, in particular, kept saying how much her mother loved her visits, although Zoë could see no sign of it as they seemed to have nothing to say to one another. "I'll leave you two together while I just pop into the village for some bread," Maud said, after the early breakfast.

"She is *so* thoughtful," her mother said as they both heard the front door shut. Maud's kindness had become a kind of conversational walking frame.

"Is there anything you want me to do for you in London, Mummy?" she said desperately.

"Oh, I don't think so, dear. Unless you were to get me another spencer. Oh—and I *did* forget before, but I should be very grateful for another hairnet. For night, you know. Lady Jayne is the make I prefer. I'm sure Ponting's or Gaylor and Pope would have one. But only if you are going that way. I know how busy you are."

"Well, I shan't be able to do that this time, but next time I go to London, I'll remember. I could post them to you."

"But you'll be back soon, won't you?"

"Well . . . probably not until after Christmas. I do have my job at the nursing home, you see."

"Well, dear, *do* look after your hands. Nursing is not good for hands. And you used to have such pretty ones. Still have," she added hurriedly.

"You are quite happy here, aren't you?"

"Oh, yes. Quite happy. Maud is kindness itself, as you know. And, of course, I contribute to the housekeeping. I don't want to be a burden."

"Money is all right, isn't it, Mummy?" She knew that Rupert had arranged for the proceeds of the London flat to be safely invested, although that could not bring in much, but her mother also had her widow's pension.

But her mother, who considered money to be a vulgar subject, said hurriedly, "There is nothing to worry about. We lead a quiet life and manage very well. But that reminds me, I must pay you for the underclothes."

"Don't. They are a present."

"I wouldn't dream of it." She was fumbling in her worn leather bag for her purse.

"Please don't, Mummy, really."

"I would much rather pay you. Can you remember how much it was?"

This unrewarding argument and *fuss* about the whole thing, Zoë thought as she became more and more helplessly irritated—her mother wanted to know exactly what the things had cost, and she couldn't remember, and then her mother didn't believe her when she made it up, and then she only had a five pound note—persisted until Maud's return. *Maud* had change: her mother said that perhaps the bust bodices had a price ticket still on them if someone would just pop up to her room and look, and Maud, who knew where things were, offered to do this. By now her mother had become stubborn and Zoë felt sulky. The bust bodices turned out to be eight and sixpence each, so then her mother wanted a pencil and paper so that she could do the sum—"I've never been good at figures"—and then there was the question of the spencer. "That is twenty-five and six and?"

"Thirty shillings," Zoë said.

"So that will be—" She wrote and her lips moved as she counted and Zoë noticed the little lines of lipstick that ran upwards into her top lip, while Maud said in an operatic aside that they really ought to be off.

"Two pounds fifteen and sixpence! Maud! Can you manage the change for that?"

"Mummy, I'll have to go. I really mustn't miss the ferry."

"I'll give it to her at the station, Cicely."

"But I'm coming with you. I'll just change my shoes."

"We've got to *go*," Zoë cried. "There isn't time to change your shoes."

So in the end she stayed behind, and Zoë kissed the resigned powdery face.

"I shall have, as they say at the cinema, to step on it," Maud remarked, as she manoeuvred the Austin out of the shed. "Perhaps you had better take the money out of my purse. Cicely will never forgive me if I don't give it to you."

"I didn't *want* it, you know."

"I don't suppose you did, my dear. But we mustn't upset her—her heart's a bit dicky, you know."

"Why didn't she *tell* us earlier that she wanted to come?"

"I think it was just a sudden notion she had. She always hates it when you go, you know. She'll be all right after I get back. We'll have a nice cup of Horlick's for a treat, and play Pegotty, and go over all the events of your visit, and then I'll make her have a little rest—the last few days have been quite exciting for her. She's so proud of you, you know."

In the train, practically empty, and the ferry, which was only half full, these words came back to her, replayed themselves over and over in her mind. She had thought that a weight would be lifted once she had got into the train with the visit behind her, but the pall of boredom and irritation was quenched now only by guilt, as she thought of all the ways in which she might have given her mother more pleasure, been kinder, nicer, more patient. Why was it that, in spite of all these years during which she felt that she had grown from being a spoiled and selfish girl into a thoroughly grown-up wife and mother and responsible member of a large family, she had only to be with her mother for a few *minutes* to revert to her earlier, disagreeable self? It was her behaviour, after all, that made her mother so timid and conciliatory, made her, in fact, everything that she, Zoë, found most exasperating. Waiting in her empty carriage for the train to start for London she suddenly thought, Supposing Jules when she is grown-up feels like that about *me*? The idea brought tears to her eyes. She opened *Anna Karenina,* but she had reached the scene where Anna sees her son after he has stolen a peach and decides to take him away with her to Moscow. But she knew that Anna was not going to be allowed to have Vronsky *and* her son, and the mere thought of such a choice filled her eyes again and one splashed onto her book. She searched for and found a handkerchief in her bag. The train began to move, and as it did so, the carriage door was wrenched open and an army officer got in. He seated himself diagonally opposite to her having put one small, very smart bag with his cap on the rack. Now she wouldn't even be able to finish her cry in peace, she thought. A second later, he had taken out a packet of cigarettes and was offering one to her.

"I don't smoke."

"Do you mind if I do?"

She shook her head. "Not at all."

"You sound as though you have a cold coming," he said with a kind of sympathetic familiarity that confounded her. But he was American, she knew that—not only from his voice but from his uniform which was a much prettier, palish green, version of English khaki.

"I haven't. I just read a rather sad bit in my book, that's all." This excuse, which she had thought would sound lofty, sounded nothing of the kind when she said it.

"Is that so?"

"Not really."

"Perhaps you read a bit that reminded you of something in your own life and that's what did it."

She looked up from her handkerchief to find him regarding her. He had very dark, almost black eyes. He lit his cigarette with a large, rather battered metal lighter. Then he said: "Do you see yourself as a Russian heroine? As Anna?"

"How did you know—"

"I'm so well educated, I can read upside down."

She was not sure whether he was laughing at her, and said quickly, "Have you read it?"

"A long time ago. When I was at college. I remember enough to warn you that Anna comes to a sad end."

"I know that. I've read it before."

"Is that so? What is it like to read a novel when you know what is going to happen?"

"Once you know the story, you can notice other things."

A short silence. Then he said, "My name's Jack, Jack Greenfeldt. I was wondering whether you would have lunch with me when we get to London?"

"I'm afraid I'm already lunching with someone."

"Your husband?"

"Oh, no. A friend." She looked at her wedding ring. He asks a lot of questions, she thought, but that was probably because he was American—she had never met one before. If he does, I can.

"Are you married?"

"I have been . . . I'm divorced. How many children do you have?"

"How do you know I have any?"

"Well, if you'll pardon me, I can see that you are over eighteen and you're not wearing uniform: the chances are that you have children. Of course, you might also be some very senior or rare kind of civil servant as you call them here, but somehow you don't look the type to me."

"I have one child; a daughter."

"Show me a picture of her."

It seemed odd to her that he wanted to see a picture of the child of a total stranger, but why not? She took the leather folder out of her bag that contained her two favourite pictures: Juliet standing on the mounting block in the courtyard wearing one of the Duchy's garden hats (she adored hats) and Juliet sitting in the long grass beside the tennis court in her best white muslin summer frock. In the first picture she was laughing, in the second she looked very serious.

He looked at them intently for quite a long time. Then, shutting the folder and handing it back, he said; "She's very like you. I appreciate you showing me. Where is she?"

"In the country."

"So you don't live in London?" His disappointment was transparent. It made her feel kindly and old.

"No. Do you mind if *I* ask *you* something?"

"I don't think I'm in a position to mind. What do you want to know?"

"Well, is it because you are American that you ask so many questions of a total stranger?"

He thought for a moment. "I don't think so. I've always been inquisitive—more curious, about people, anyway. As you can see, I have the kind of nose that fits very easily into other people's business." This made her glance at his face. He smiled: his teeth looked very white against his sallow complexion. "I was hoping that you'd ask something more personal," he said.

There was a nervous silence. Once, she would have thought that he was flirting with her, and she would have known exactly what to do, or not do, could have chosen the next move. Now she felt utterly unsure—she had no idea what game it was, she had only the uneasy feeling that he knew more than she about whatever it might be.

"It is very difficult to be happy in a war."

"Why do you say that?"

"Because I sense that you are guilty about not being happy. Why on earth should you be? With people being killed all the time, slaughtered, murdered and sometimes tortured first, and then families being broken up, everybody without their partner, shortages of everything that makes life easier, a monotonous routine and a general absence of anything resembling a good time, why should you—or anyone else in this island—be *happy*? You may endure—the British seem to me to have gotten very good at that—but why should you *enjoy* it? I know the stiff upper lip is deeply embedded in the British creed, but you try and *smile* with one!"

He was generalizing; she felt safer.

"We've trained our lips," she said. "We're used to it now."

"I've found that it is very dangerous to get used to things."

"Anything?"

"Yes—anything. You cease to notice whatever it is, and, worse, you get the illusion that you've arrived somewhere."

"I don't feel that at *all*," she said, discovering this.

"Don't you?"

"Well, I suppose it depends what you mean by not noticing things or getting used to them—"

"Nothing about your life depends upon what I mean," he said, but it was not a harsh interruption.

"I think one can get used to some things and still notice it," she said. She was thinking of Rupert.

"That would make it a very serious thing."

"Yes. It would. It does." She was immediately afraid that he would ask her *what* would—would press her past that involuntary confidence—but he didn't. He got up and moved to sit in the seat immediately opposite her.

"I still don't know your name."

She told him.

"Zoë Cazalet. Would you have dinner with me tonight? I can see you're about to turn me down. Don't. This is a very serious invitation."

Reasons why she shouldn't do this crowded in. What should she tell the family? "I am having dinner with an American I met on the train"? Where should she stay in London, since she would be unlikely to get a train late enough afterwards? Where could she go between lunch and dinner? Why on earth was she even considering it?

"I've nothing to wear," she said.

Louise

October, 1943

Hasn't he finished yet?"

"He keeps falling asleep."

Mary, the new, very young, highly trained nanny looked disapproving. "Pinch his cheeks," she said.

Louise gave a gentle tweak. The baby squirmed, pushed his head against her breast and found her nipple once more, but after sucking once or twice, he gave up.

"I don't think I've got any milk left on that side."

"Oh, well. Have you winded him?"

"I tried, but nothing much happened, I'm afraid."

Mary leaned down, and took the baby from her. "Come to Mary, then," she said in a different, far kinder voice. She put the baby over her shoulder and patted the small of his back. He belched several times.

"That's a good boy. Your cup of tea's on the side there."

"Thank you, Mary."

"Say goodbye to Mummy, then." She levered the baby down so that Louise could kiss his face. He was pale, excepting for two blotches of bright pink on his cheeks; his mouth was pink and damp and pouting with a bead of milk on the protuberant lower lip. He smelled of milk and his eyes were shut. When they had gone, Louise buttoned up her nursing bra, putting fresh pads over her nipples. They were sore, but nothing like as bad as they had been. She reached for the cup of tea and drank it gratefully. The early morning feed was the worst. She was wakened from deep sleep by Mary, sometimes not until six o'clock, but sometimes even earlier, and the feed which, if only the baby would drink properly, need not take more than half an hour, always took twice as long. By the end of it she felt tired, but horribly awake. It took her ages to get to sleep again, and by the time she did, she had to get up for breakfast. At home, she would have stayed in bed, but at Hatton, where she now was, this was out of the question. She would have to get up, have her bath, dress and have breakfast with Zee and Pete, and soon after that it would be time for the next feed.

Michael had brought her down a week ago, and it had been made clear to her that, although, of course, he could not stay, Zee wanted to see her grandson, "really get to know him." So they were to stay three weeks, of which only one was nearly over. Michael had not been sure when he would be able to get down again, and Zee had begun to say that it would surely be best if Louise and the baby continued to stay until he *was* able to fetch them. This, she felt, might be weeks, even months hence. It was twenty to seven: she had better try and sleep. She turned off the bedside light but, as usual, the dark seemed simply to accelerate everything that had to be suppressed with people and the daytime. Sometimes, as now, she thought that if she abandoned herself to it she would understand it better.

It always began with a litany of her good fortune: she was married to a famous man who had chosen her when he might, according to Zee, have married anybody he pleased; she had had a healthy son which was what everyone had expected. She had her own house in London (Lady Rydal's in St. John's Wood, as her aunt Jessica was going back to live in Frensham when Nora was married). She had a nanny, which most young women with babies could neither procure nor afford these days. What more could she ask? She was twenty and she had been married for exactly thirteen months, and so far Michael had not been killed or even wounded. She had everything to be grateful for. She turned on her side, so that if her tears became sobs she could suppress them in her pillow. Zee, she had discovered, sometimes walked about at night and had on more than one occasion opened the door of her bedroom and stood there, once when Michael was in bed with her, and twice when she had been on her own. These visits were never mentioned, but apart from being rather frightening they invaded the privacy which her extreme sense of isolation made essential. She could only even *consider* her unnatural feelings when she was completely alone; the rest of the time, she had to play the part of happy young wife and mother—anxious about Michael being in the war, of course, but otherwise existing in a cloudless atmosphere. Because the awful thing was that she didn't have *any* of the feelings that *they* assumed to be the natural feelings that everybody was supposed to have. She knew that this was somehow her fault, but although she was sincerely ashamed and sorry to be such a person, she did not know at all how to change things for the better. She had tried once or twice, during the months of her pregnancy, to talk to Michael about how fearful she felt about having a baby. Not the *labour* of having him (he was always assumed to be male), but the fact of his existence. Michael, when he had listened, had brushed her anxieties aside, and told her that she would feel quite different the moment he was born. In the end she had clung to this. But she *had*—ever since his sorties in bombers over Germany (there had been several of them)—become more and more afraid when he went to sea and had his battles with E-boats. Other officers she met in Coastal Forces were killed, including very experienced ones, and there seemed to be less and less reason why Michael should not become one of them. Once, after they had taken a furnished house in Seaford and had been there for a few weeks, with him coming home to sleep when he was not at sea, he had returned one evening to say that the flotilla was being moved the next morning. She had burst into tears: "Then we'll have to give up the house!" she had sobbed, unable to voice her worst fears.

"It's not a very *nice* house," he had said. "We never really cared for it. We'll get another far nicer one, one day. Now, come on, darling, be a brave girl."

But she couldn't stop.

"We *never* have any time together: we never have a proper married life. We never have time to talk."

"Of course we do," he had replied. "Anyway, I can't talk to you if you're crying—you won't hear a word I say. This is what happens in wars. People *aren't* together. It's the same for everybody." Then the telephone had rung and he had answered it, and it was his Number One asking when he would be back on board. "They're loading the torpedoes," he said. "I must be there to be sure they are properly stowed. When you've shut up the house, I should go home to your family for a bit, darling. That would be best, until I know more what my lot will be on about."

"Can't you even stay for supper?"

"No, I've told you, I've got to go. I'd better pack my stuff now.

Cheer up, darling, and give me a hand with it. Sparky is sending a car in half an hour."

So he had gone, and she packed, and tried to empty the larder in which there wasn't very much, and rang up Home Place and said she would be coming. And then she had eaten the remains of some corned beef that had got left over somehow, and spent the whole night being sick and having diarrhoea. She thought she was going to die. In the morning she rang home and told her mother, who said she would come in the car to fetch her home. After that, she didn't try to talk to Michael about things that she was afraid of, or that made her anxious, or that she didn't understand. She clung to the notion that when she had had the baby everything would be different. She had stayed at home until about a month before the baby was to be born and then she and her mother had moved her into Hamilton Terrace. That had been exciting: there was a certain amount of furniture that had belonged to her grandparents, but the house was dingy, and needed redecorating. Also, she was able to unpack the wedding presents, and bring her own things, her books, from Home Place. She was in a fever to get everything arranged before the baby came, and Stella, who miraculously had a week's leave, arrived to help her paint the walls of the sitting room and the nursery. After a week, her mother had to go back to Home Place and Stella to Bletchley, where she worked at some job too secret to mention. It had been wonderful having her. Then Michael had arrived for a week's leave. They had gone to a film and had dinner out and then when they went to bed, he began making love to her. "I'm too fat!" she had said—she really didn't want him to—she didn't just not feel like it as usual, she positively couldn't bear the idea of it.

"Nonsense, you silly little thing, I don't mind how fat you are!" And he had gone ahead, and it had been extremely uncomfortable. The next morning he had had to go to the Admiralty, but said he would be back in the evening. Her labour had begun at lunch-time, when her mother was to arrive with some professor from the Royal College of Music who was to take away what remained in the house of her grandfather's manuscripts. She had prepared lunch for them—a great effort, but Michael had brought his ration book so she got a tin of Spam which she stuck with cloves, sprinkled with sugar and roasted in the oven. This, with boiled potatoes and a salad would have to do. After lunch, while the old man was sorting through the piles of paper in her grandfather's study, she told her mother that she thought something might be happening, although it didn't hurt at all and the stirrings, as she described them, only seemed to happen occasionally. Her mother said that, as the baby was not due for at least three weeks, she thought it very unlikely that labour had begun. "Anyway, Michael will be back quite soon—otherwise I would stay."

"Oh, no, you needn't. It was probably a bit of indigestion."

When her mother and the old man had left, she cleared up the lunch. Then she couldn't think what to do: she wandered up, down and round the house. It was not large: two little attic rooms on the top floor where she had once slept when she had stayed with her grandparents. The wallpaper had been small white clouds in a blue sky, and Lady Rydal had paper seagulls of different sizes that you could cut out and stick wherever you chose on the wall, but you were only allowed one seagull per visit. Below the attics were three bedrooms and a bathroom. The sunniest and largest was to be the nursery with a bed for the nurse and a family cot for the baby, although to begin with it would sleep in a basket. The other large room was hers and Michael's. It faced north and was bleak. It had been her grandfather's study where he had composed. The third bedroom, very small with not much more room than would hold a bed and a chest of drawers, had been his bedroom where he had died. The ground floor had a large drawing room with a french window and steps down into the small, square garden, and double doors that led to the dining room, served by a lift that conveyed food up from the basement. The basement contained a large kitchen with an old range that heated the water and an ancient gas cooker. There were two cramped, damp, pitch-dark rooms with small, heavily barred windows where Lady Rydal's unfortunate servants had slept. There were also a pantry, a larder and a lavatory. Louise hated the basement, and spent as little time there as possible.

By the time she had finished a tour of the house, her back ached. The July summer's day, which had begun with a pale blue sky and blazing sun, had now become overcast, grey, humid and oppressively hot. She decided to lie on the sofa for a bit and read, but the book she wanted was in the bedroom, and she couldn't be bothered to climb the stairs to fetch it. The curious stirrings had started again; they did not seem to be regular and they did not hurt at all. In the end, she decided to do some sight reading; one of her grandmother's pianos was still in the drawing room and there were shelves of music. But then she found that she had to sit so far away from the keyboard because of her now—to her mind—monstrous bulge that her back ached more than ever.

She couldn't remember much more about the rest of the day. She had made a kedgeree for herself and Michael, but the rice was overcooked and the fish stayed hard and salty: it hadn't been nice, but Michael had said he didn't mind, *he* was too fat anyway, which, she admitted, was true. She couldn't remember what they did after dinner, what they talked about, or anything. She remembered saying that she was tired; it went on being hot and she had a headache, and Michael said there would be a storm later. She *had* managed to say that she really didn't want to be made love to (she hadn't told him about the stirrings all day), but she said she felt rotten and he accepted that. They went to sleep, and some unknown amount of time later she was woken because she had unmistakable pains coming about every ten minutes. She woke Michael who pulled on his clothes with incredible speed and rang the nursing home where she was to have the baby. They said that it was far too early for her to be in labour, but she'd better come in, just in case. While Michael went to get the car, she put on the skirt and smock she'd been wearing all day, and then tried to pack her suitcase. This was to have been packed ready to go, but her mother had said there was no point in doing it until nearer the time. She put in two nightdresses, her sponge bag and some slippers, but every time the pains came she found she had to stop. The whole thing felt unreal at that point: she was neither excited, nor frightened —nor anything.

The nursing home was between the Cromwell Road and Kensington High Street. It was one of those immensely tall, grey buildings with a flight of steps up to the front door. They were received by a nurse, or sister, Louise didn't know which, who made her feel that she was making an hysterical fuss about what would undoubtedly prove to be nothing. "She'd better spend the night here," she had said to Michael, "and then Doctor can see her in the morning, after which I have no doubt but we'll be sending her home."

"Right then. Here's her case, sister." He seemed very eager to be off. She suddenly desperately wanted him to stay, but he brushed her cheek with his mouth, said what good hands she was now in, and disappeared out of the front door before she could say anything.

"We'll have to go right to the top: we weren't expecting you for another three weeks."

Louise followed her up the four flights of stairs. She got a pain half-way up, but she didn't dare stop as she already felt a bit afraid of the nurse.

She was told to undress and get into bed. "I'll just have a look at you. How long have you been having pains?"

"Since lunch-time today."

"Pity you didn't telephone earlier."

"I'm sorry. I didn't think it was the baby then."

The nurse did not answer this, but stood very patiently waiting for Louise to be in bed and ready to be examined; hostility leaked from her like a gas, and Louise dreaded being touched by her.

When that seemed to be over, she made one more effort: "Do you think you could tell me what happens next? I mean, you must know so much about it, and I don't know anything."

"What is going to happen next, young lady, is that as you're here, I'll shave you to be on the safe side, and then I shall give you something to make you sleep."

She went away and returned with a small basin of water, some soap and a razor that proved to have a very blunt blade, which hurt, and seemed to make her crosser than ever. Louise didn't dare ask why she had to be shaved. When it was over she swallowed a large pill with a glass of water, and the nurse departed, switching off the light as she went.

The best thing would be to go to sleep. Then she wouldn't be being a nuisance, and tomorrow morning she would be able to go home. The discomforting thought came that eventually she would have to come back here, but then it occurred to her that not all the nurses could be like this one. Quite soon she fell heavily asleep.

She woke suddenly because of a pain. The bed seemed wet and sticky. She reached out for the bedside light to see what was happening. The bed seemed full of blood, and immediately she thought that the baby must have died inside her. There was a bell on the table with the lamp by her bed and she rang it. Perhaps it is dead, and I am dying, she thought as another pain seized her. Nobody came. She rang twice more, for longer, but there was complete silence. By now she was very frightened. She heaved herself out of bed and opened the door of her room. "Please! Somebody come!" she called. In the end she screamed it, and heard footsteps and passage lights being turned on. The nurse appeared, and before she could say anything, Louise pointed to the blood.

"Ssh. Don't wake the other patients. Now you sit on that chair and I'll remake the bed." She went out onto the landing to a cupboard and came back with a fresh sheet.

"What's *happening?*"

"You just had a little show. It means the baby's on its way." The pains seemed to be coming about every four minutes and there was no doubt at all about them being pains. Her mother had told her that one did not make a noise during labour and this came back to her now.

"I'll send someone to sit with you. Don't worry. It'll be hours yet."

She heaved herself back into the bed. She had never felt so isolated in her life. Why had Michael abandoned her to this?

During the rest of that awful night she managed not to cry or scream. The nurse came back with another one who, elderly and woken from her sleep, looked sour and unfriendly as well. She asked when the doctor would come, and they said not until morning, at least, and possibly not then. They gave her a contraption that had a small rubber mask that she could put over her face and breathe from when the pains got too bad, but when she did this, it didn't seem to make any difference.

"I don't think it's working."

The midwife, who had positioned herself on a chair as far away from the bed as possible, came over and looked at it.

"It's broken," she said, and removed it.

Outside, the storm rumbled with enormous peals of thunder. In between the pains, she struggled with the agonizing desire to sleep that the pill had induced. Each time she felt herself sinking into oblivion, another pain seized her and she was tortured awake. If only she would *talk* to me! she thought, but the nurse went on reading a newspaper. When she could see that the sky was becoming pale from a chink in the blackout, and the thunder seemed more distant, she asked how long it would go on for.

The nurse, who did not even look up from her paper, replied that she was sick of people asking her that question. After that, there did not seem to be much point in asking anything else.

Eventually, things did happen; another nurse arrived and looked at her and then the doctor came and told her to push and then there seemed to be at least three people round the bed. Her mouth was so dry that she managed to say she was thirsty whereupon the doctor held a glass of water to her mouth but whipped it away before she had had more than a sip. "One more push," he said, "and then I'm going to give you something and you won't know a thing." And that was what happened. The last push was so agonizing that she thought she began to scream and the scream got cut off because he put a mask over her face and she disappeared or at least that was what it felt like—she simply ceased to exist. When she came to the nurse was bustling round her and the doctor smiled and said, a splendid little boy, but she couldn't see anything. "He's being bathed," they said. They were all smiling now. She asked what the time was and they said a quarter to twelve and somebody gave her a cup of tea. Then Michael arrived carrying the baby and gave it to her as though it was a present from him and she knew from the expression on his face that she should be overcome with delight. She looked at the tightly wrapped white bundle with its small, wrinkled, tomato-coloured face—remote and stern and fast asleep—and felt nothing at all.

"Six pounds twelve ounces," Michael was saying proudly. "You *are* a clever girl!"

They had brought her another cup of tea, but she said she didn't want it, she just wanted to go to sleep. "You must drink it first," they said; "you need to drink to bring the milk in." So she had drunk the tea; Michael said that he was going to ring up their parents, and the baby was taken away.

When she woke up she was crying. Michael came back in the evening, and said that he was popping down to Hatton as Zee wanted him to spend the rest of his leave with her. They poured liquids down her until her breasts were painfully swollen with milk, but the baby, being premature, did not want to suck, kept falling asleep—those early days she only saw him when he was asleep or crying. In the end they procured a breast pump, but by then she could not bear them to touch her. They told her how fortunate she was to have enough milk; there were mothers in the Home, they said, who did not have any to speak of. Couldn't she feed one of their babies, then? Louise had asked, but they looked shocked at the notion and said that it would not do. She cried for three days—from exhaustion, from pain—apart from her breasts she had had to have stitches—from thirst—one of the ways in which they reduced her milk was refusing to allow her anything to drink at all—from a kind of homesickness—although she did not know for what home—from the feeling that Michael had abandoned her—twice, once when he had left her at the nursing home, with the hostile strangers, and again when he had chosen to spend the rest of his leave with his mother rather than with her—and, worst of all, from the growing conviction that there was something wrong with her since she clearly did not love her baby as she was expected to, or indeed feel anything about him except a vague fear. They called it post-natal depression and said she would soon be over it, and after a few days told her that she must pull herself together and *get* over it.

A fortnight later, she was sent home to St. John's Wood with a middle-aged and garrulous monthly nurse, who taught her how to use Tampax and saw to it that she continued never to be with the baby unless he was feeding or crying. "He's as good as gold with *me!*" she would exclaim. She spent hours telling Louise about her last place that had been with a titled lady in a large house in the country where there had been a proper staff and she had not had to carry trays up and down stairs. Louise's staff consisted of a very old lady whom Zee had bullied out of retirement to come and cook for a month. She came up after breakfast for Louise to order the meals, but they never had what she ordered, either because it turned out not to be in the shops, or, Louise suspected, because Mrs. Corcoran did not want to cook it. Apart from being a snob, Nurse Sanders was also a bully: she insisted that Louise stay in bed for two of the four weeks that she was there, and made her have boring rests in the afternoons after that. She also had the terrifying habit of bringing the baby in when he was hungry and crying and dumping him in his basket on the other side of the room to cry for a good fifteen minutes before his feed. "Let him tire himself out, he'll sleep all the better after it," she would say as she left them so unhappily together. Louise could not bear it, but when she got out of bed to pick him up he would not stop crying (she was too frightened of Nurse Sanders to dare to start feeding him before she was allowed to). He did not seem to like her much, she thought: even when he was feeding, he seldom met her eye, and squirmed away from her when she attempted (when Nurse Sanders was out of the room) to kiss him. Half-way through each feed, Nurse Sanders seized him and banged him on the back until his head shook and eventually he belched.

"Doesn't that hurt his back?" she had ventured the first time.

"Hurt his back? Bless me, who do you think I am? Hurt his back? We have to get his wind up. Mummy doesn't understand you, does she? Poor little mite." And on and on, Louise counted the days until Nurse Sanders was to go. The nanny who was arriving to replace her could not possibly be so awful; she was young, for a start, and she had been trained in Aunt Rach's Babies' Hotel. Perhaps she would even be some company. But Mary, when she came, intimidated her with her quiet assurance and, because they were roughly the same age, both of them found it quite difficult to know how to deal with their relative positions. Mary adored the baby at once, and he seemed to like her, which was something. And Mary did not snub her. "He smiled at me!" she said to Nurse Sanders, on the morning that she was to leave. "Wind," said Nurse Sanders briskly. "It's nothing but wind." She left after lunch, and Louise felt her spirits rise for the first time in months. Stella was coming for the weekend, Mary would be able to look after the baby and they would be able to go out in between feeds. Meanwhile, she had the two o'clock feed, by herself, for the first time.

She remembered, sadly now, how she had run upstairs full of good resolutions: she would feed him and talk to him and cuddle him and without the malign presence of Nurse Sanders, he would respond. He was asleep, so she folded the Harrington square and the towelling nappy ready before she woke him. She had had very little practice at changing him. Then she lifted him carefully out of his basket. He was sopping wet, and started crying before she had got him onto her lap. Taking the wet nappies off was easy, but putting on the clean ones was another matter. By now he was screaming, arching his back and throwing himself about. She laid him on the floor in the end on top of the laid-out nappies, but it took her ages to fold and pin them as she was so afraid of pricking him. At the end of it he was scarlet in the face and, she felt, furious with her—so cross, in fact, that to begin with he refused to take milk, simply banged his head against her breast and went on roaring. Just as she was beginning to wonder insanely whether Nurse Sanders, as a parting shot, had somehow managed to feed him from the Cow and Gate tin she had insisted upon buying, he suddenly seized her nipple in a painful grip and started sucking, his slaty eyes fixed reproachfully on her face. Half-way through the feed, the telephone rang and, putting him over her shoulder, she went downstairs to answer it. It was Michael. He was able to get home for a couple of nights, and would be back in time for dinner.

"Stella's coming," she said.

"Oh, good," he said heartily. "It will be jolly to see her again. How's Sebastian?"

"Sebastian? Oh! He's just been sick on my shoulder."

"Poor chap! Well, see you later, darling. Has the dragon left?"

"Yes, just. The new nanny is due at tea-time."

"Splendid. I'll take you both out, if you like."

She went back to the nursery and gave him the rest of his feed. It seemed ridiculous to call someone that size Sebastian, she thought. She wasn't awfully keen on the name anyway, but Michael said it was a family name.

Mary had arrived soon afterwards, and in no time was sitting in her lilac and white striped cotton dress bathing the baby. But the weekend, somehow, wasn't fun at all. It was then that she discovered she was two different people, one with Stella and another with Michael, and with them both there, she didn't know which to be. Also, she had been hoping that she might bring herself to talk to Stella about her horrible lack of maternal feeling: she was the only person with whom, she felt, she could take such a risk. But she got no further than telling her how awful the nursing home had been and Stella had been sympathetic and said that her father had said all the good nurses were in major hospitals or overseas, and that private nursing homes were having to make do with the dregs. This made her feel better: it was a kind of acknowledgement that it had been a bad time, which she had not had from anybody else.

"Did it hurt frightfully?" Stella had asked, and she had been able to say yes, it did. Then it was time to feed the baby, and in the middle of that Michael arrived. She had the feeling, during that weekend, that although there was mutual goodwill, Michael and Stella did not really have anything in common excepting herself. He rang his mother the first evening and talked to her for a long time. "Mummy is longing for you to bring Sebastian down to Hatton," he said in bed that night. "I could take you down tomorrow. If Stella didn't mind."

She said she couldn't possibly leave the new house so soon; she must get things straight, and Mrs. Corcoran was not staying much longer; she couldn't leave the house empty. So it had been agreed to wait a month, which was now over, and here she was.

The core of the trouble was that while everybody at Hatton— beginning with Zee and Pete and going on to the servants, which even included Crawley the chauffeur and Bateson the gardener—all adored baby Sebastian, she, his mother, who was supposed to be the most besotted was nothing of the kind. Now, from having thought that she wanted children but not until she had got more used to being married, she had reached the conclusion that she should never have had a child at all, and her worthlessness in this respect weighed more and more heavily upon her. She felt guilty, ashamed and sometimes actually wicked. Alone with him, she did make efforts to forge some kind of link between them, but he seemed to be in the conspiracy: he plainly did not like her to kiss or hug him, and when she talked to him he simply regarded her with a kind of remote indifference. He seemed to know that she was a bad mother: she supposed that one of his earliest memories might be of his mother apologizing to him. So she spent the days acting the part expected of her and the nights—early mornings—struggling with her miserable confusion.

It was Friday, which meant that guests would be coming for the weekend. An endless stream of people came to Hatton; for lunch, for dinner and the night, for bits of leave, or short respites from London. Many of them were old and distinguished, a good many were young and promising, practically all were male. Zee seemed effortlessly to collect men around her, and by blandly ignoring that many of them were married usually and mysteriously seemed to get them to visit on their own. A good proportion of the older ones had been in love with her at one time or another—for all Louise knew they might still be in her thrall.

Everybody was expected to perform—to play, to sing, to act in charades or Dumb Crambo or, failing any of that, to tell of the extraordinary and entertaining things that had happened to them (this last was on the whole the prerogative of the very old and distinguished who had lived long enough, Louise thought, for enough of that sort of thing to have happened to them). People arriving for their first visit, usually the younger guests, were often rather silent, but Zee had a way of making them feel at their ease and at the same time particularly interesting, and they soon learned to play the games, laugh at the jokes, and generally enter into the rarified spirit of the place. The fact that she shone at the acting games told in her favour: this was a good thing, because—and it had only been apparent to her on this visit and then when Michael had left—there were other things that she felt were chalked up against her. Their arrival here, for instance. They had come down by train, as Michael did not have enough petrol to drive them, and the train had been interminably delayed because of repairs to the track. Sebastian had become hungry, was not appeased by water in a bottle, so in the end, in spite of a carriage full of people, she fed him. When this was announced at Hatton (by Michael who thought it all rather daring and delightful), it was clear that Zee thought nothing of the kind. "*Soldiers* in your carriage?" she said. "Oh dear, oh dear, I suppose *you* would call it Bohemian. What a disagreeable situation, is what *I* should have felt."

She had looked at Louise when she said this and wrinkled her nose in a kind of mock disgust, but disapproval, distaste, even contempt, was very clear to Louise. Then, she smoked, which Zee, who did not, disliked. However, there was not much she could say about this, since practically all her guests smoked, as did Pete and Michael. She also *drank*, not only glasses of wine but gin, and this, it was made plain to her, was not the thing for a girl. Louise knew, by now, that the real difficulty was that Zee did not like women generally, which was somehow worse than her disliking her daughter-in-law in particular. What it means is, Louise thought as she brushed her hair, that I can't win. Whatever I do she won't like me: she'll put up with me because of Michael and because she is so keen on babies. There was no doubt about her adoration of Sebastian. She spent hours with him, either nursing him on her lap, or pushing him gently about the terraces outside the house in Michael's old pram. When Michael was there he had drawn the baby asleep, but she had made an exquisite little wax head of him, and the Judge, Pete, apologizing for being unable to draw, had written him a sonnet. Zee was now engaged upon what she called "one of my stuff pictures" where she used every imaginable kind of material to appliqué and/or embroider to make a picture. This one was a kind of Rousseauish forest with wild animals lurking at every turn. It had great charm and was, Louise could see, just what a young child might enjoy hung in his nursery.

Michael ringing up was another matter that generated faint, but unmistakable tension. As Zee sat on a sofa with the telephone by her most of the day, she usually spoke to him first and at length before she handed him over to Louise, always said, "Tell him not to ring off. When you've finished I want to speak to him." With Zee present, Louise found it difficult to talk to Michael and could hear herself sounding inane and dull. Yes, the baby was well and had put on half a pound since he'd left, yes, Mary seemed to be satisfactory, yes, *she* was fine, felt far less tired. It was lovely early October weather . . . how was he? There would follow a long account of his most recent sorties in the Channel or the North Sea, then Zee would make motions and Louise would say goodbye and her bit about him not ringing off and they would settle down to a long chat about Michael's ship and shipmates, about the state of the war generally— wasn't it wonderful about the Tirpitz being torpedoed? Somebody called Jimmy—in the Navy, who was the son of one of Zee's admirers—had spent the summer in a tank in Welwyn Garden City in a miniature sub, could it be he? If so she must send a telegram to his father. And so on. Louise would pretend to read, or sometimes she would simply go out of the room, but whatever she did there was a sense of defeat and being excluded. At least letters were more private and she liked writing them—wrote at least twice a week, and Michael was extremely good and wrote at least once every two weeks, but she discovered one morning that even they were not inviolate. A letter from Michael lay on her plate at the breakfast table, but it had been opened. It was not that the gummed flap had become *un*gummed; the letter had been slit open at the top by a paper knife. Zee was not up for breakfast that morning; she was alone with the Judge.

"My letter has been opened!"

"My dear?" He looked up from *The Times*.

"My letter from Michael. It has been slit open."

"Oh, yes. Zee asked me to say that she opened it in error. She is so used to his writing, you see, that she did not look properly to see whom it was addressed to."

Louise put the letter back on the table. Her hands were trembling and she felt so angry that she could not speak.

"I am sorry. I see that it has upset you," the Judge said. His Roman coin face softened to concern. "Zee will be sorry if you are upset, and that will upset *her* which, as I know you know, is not good for her heart. Forgive her for me." He smiled gently and resumed his tranquil expression.

When Zee emerged later in the morning, she said nothing about the letter. Louise was furiously sure that she had read it all, and she did not believe for one second that it had been opened in error but, in a curious way, what she found most confusing about that incident was the Judge's behaviour. He seemed—and was—a man of the utmost honour, somebody whom she felt would be incapable of lying, cheating or betraying anyone. And yet he had clearly excused his wife to the point where he did not even seem to think an apology from her necessary. She came uneasily to the conclusion that Hatton was Zee's world, and that she made the rules in it.

Two other things happened during that visit which disturbed her much more, she realized afterwards, than she knew at the time. The Saturday before she was supposed to go, there was what she called a Distinguished Old Codgers' Luncheon: an admiral, an ambassador (retired), a general—with his wife—and a very doddery old thing who turned out surprisingly to have been an explorer, "but not any more," he told her during the soup. "Nowadays I'm hard put to find my way to my bedroom at night."

"And what do you do in the daytime?" She had learned that one was supposed to pursue the conversation and not simply acquiesce in what had been said to her.

"A good question." He leaned towards her and said in a stage whisper: "Explore the cavities of me own teeth. Those that are left to me. Haven't quite reached the sans everything, but no doubt I shall. My word, you're pretty, aren't you?" Something about the way he looked at her made her feel hot and she didn't reply.

As they were moving to the drawing room for coffee, Zee said, "Louise has to go and feed her enchanting baby. Louise, why don't you bring Sebastian to the drawing room and feed him there? I'm sure everyone will be delighted to meet him, and see you both."

"I don't think I will."

At first, she could see, Zee refused to believe that she meant what she said, and she was subjected to a kind of angry raillery while the company was appealed to. Yes, yes, they said—she noticed that both the admiral's and the explorer's rheumy old eyes were fixed upon her breasts, and got to her feet so suddenly that she knocked over her coffee cup in its saucer, and somehow, after that, she managed to apologize, to mop up the coffee and get out of the room.

Mary was waiting for her in her bedroom, walking up and down with Sebastian who was crying.

"I'm sorry I'm late." She seemed to do nothing but apologize, although it was only a quarter past two.

When Mary had settled her with the baby and left the room, the tears that had filled her eyes now fell—on the baby, on her breast, down her left arm that held him. When he had finished on one side, she put both arms round him and laid her mouth to the side of his little round head and he winced and turned his head away. Love is lost between us, she thought as she put him over her shoulder to get up his wind, but she did not know why and there was no one to ask.

When Mary came to fetch him, she lay on her bed overwhelmed with what she had always called homesickness, only now it seemed something more intangible—no longer a place . . . Michael, she wanted him, to be here, to take her away, to be on her side about not having to feed her child in front of a lot of lecherous old men, to tell his mother that she should not open his letters, nor stand in the open doorway at night for no reason on earth that bore thinking about . . . but just as her anger seemed to be making her feel better—which seemed odd to her but was true—she remembered Michael's expression as he had brought the baby in to her after he had been born. *He* expected her to feel about Sebastian as his mother so obviously had always felt about him. Despair engulfed her: he had no idea how horribly different she was; if he had, he would be the first to condemn her, and if she could not tell him, how could she be so disloyal as to tell anyone else? Perhaps it *will* change, she thought. When he is older, and I can talk to him, and play games with him, when he becomes a person. But the indolence of extreme fear prevented her pursuing that possibility, and she was back to Michael, and making an attempt to explain to him why she felt so confused. But when would she see him again? And for how long, and how much of that time would be spent alone? And even if she insisted on that—refused to come here to Hatton, for instance, when he had leave—how could she tell him these awful, unnatural things that so confused her and would undoubtedly shock him when, after a couple of days, he would be off again, back to his ship where he might easily be killed? Leaves for serving men were meant to be respites; you were not supposed to rock the home boat, as it were, rather to provide a calm and restful time and happy memories for them to take back to the war. If she was no good at being a mother, she must try even harder at being a wife.

The last thing that happened during that visit occurred the morning before she left Hatton. Michael had not returned, but she had insisted on going back to the house in London at the end of the three weeks. Zee had suddenly suggested that they go for a walk in the woods. It was a beautiful sunlit day, crisp and clear with a thin white frost on the ground. Michael had rung the day before to say that he had been awarded a DSC for one of the summer battles, and Zee was telling her that she must go to Gieves to buy the appropriate ribbon to sew onto his uniforms. "And, of course," she added, "I shall come to London to go to the Palace with him, and I think we should arrange a party afterwards." Then, before Louise could say anything, she went on, "Oh, my dear, *you* will come with us. He is allowed two tickets' worth of audience. I was saying to him the other day, that I really thought I should Present you, but we decided it would be better to wait until you have had the next baby."

"*What?*"

"Let us sit down, Louise, I have walked enough." There was a convenient fallen tree.

"You are not an awfully good mother, are you? I know when Michael was born I was unable to think of anything but him for months and months. But Mary tells me you are hardly ever in the nursery. It is therefore very important that he should have a brother to play with. Surely you can see that?"

She managed to say, "I haven't discussed this with Michael," but her throat was dry and she wasn't sure if Zee heard her.

"Michael is deeply in favour of a large family. It is the reason why he married you. Surely you knew that?"

"No."

"I told him you were too young, but he was sure you were the right wife for him, and of course I would want anything that he wanted that would make him happy." She rose to her feet. "I would expect you to want that too. But if," she ended, "I felt that you were—in *any way*—making him *un*happy, I should stab you to death. I should enjoy doing it." Her playful smile in no way concealed the chilling content of this remark. For some reason Louise remembered an historical novel of Conan Doyle's—*The Huguenots?*—where the woods in Canada had been full of murderous Iroquois who streaked through the chequered light and shadow of the trees exulting in death. The wood she was in now felt just as dangerous; her heart had stopped pounding, and she felt shiveringly cold.

They walked back to the house, emerging from the wood to the lawn on the edge of which were colchicum flaring out of the bare earth.

"How would you describe them?" Zee asked.

"They look like people wearing evening dress in the morning," she answered.

"*Very* good! I must remember to tell Pete that."

Already, the scene in the wood seemed unreal—so bizarre that she half thought that perhaps it had not happened at all.

The Family

December, 1943

Darling! Are those the only trousers you've got?"

"Sort of. I've got some breeches for work."

"But you must have had those for years! They're about six inches too short."

Christopher looked down his legs to the gap between the end of his trews and the beginning of his socks—full of holes, but he hoped his mother wouldn't realize that—to his uncomfortable shoes that he'd also had for years, hardly ever worn and now far too tight.

"They are a bit short," he said, hoping that agreement would end the matter.

"You can't possibly go to Nora's wedding in them! And your jacket's too short in the sleeves."

"They always *are* with me," he said patiently.

"Well, it's too late to *buy* you anything. I'll see if Hugh has something he could lend you. You're about the same height." But nobody could be thinner, she thought, as she went downstairs to find Hugh.

They were in Hugh's house, which he had kindly made available for any of the Castle family (Polly and Clary had gone to stay with Louise) for the night before the wedding. All the family, that is, excepting Raymond, who had rung to say he couldn't make it, but would take an early train in the morning. Angela had not arrived yet, but she was coming out to dinner with them—all arranged by kind Hugh. Which was a godsend, because she certainly couldn't have relied upon Villy to be of the slightest help. She suspected that it was Villy who had persuaded Raymond to take such a hard line about her returning to Frensham instead of remaining in London. The excuse that the house was needed for Louise seemed to her absurd: Michael Hadleigh had quite enough money to rent or even buy a house for Louise and had no need of the Rydal house, but it had been left jointly to her and Villy, and Raymond had said he was simply not prepared to deal with the upkeep of two houses. She had wondered, after an acrimonious telephone conversation with him, whether Raymond had somehow got to hear about Lorenzo, but really she didn't see how he *could* have: they had been pretty careful on the whole, she thought, although Lorenzo had once admitted that he could not bear to burn her dear letters. After that, she had been more careful about what she put in them, and she had kept all his notes—he never wrote more than a note—in the secret compartment of her sewing box. Since going back to Frensham, she had spent a good deal of time in the train going back and forth to London, but from now on this was going to be tricky, since Nora and her husband were coming to live in the house with her, and Nora had plans to turn the place into some sort of nursing home. Perhaps then she would be able to get a very small *pied-à-terre* in London which would be better: Lorenzo was often working so hard, and so busy, that sometimes, recently, she had made the journey to London in vain. She could tell Raymond that it was better for Nora to have the house to herself because, after all, hers could not be an easy marriage, although this would not be in the least true, since Nora was hell bent on turning the house into some sort of institution with other people in the same state as poor Richard to look after. If need be, she could suggest that either Villy or Michael Hadleigh buy her share of Mama's house which would give her enough, surely, to lease a small flat. She would be forty-six this year and she had spent over twenty years living for others, bringing up the children, cooking, washing, cleaning the series of horrible little houses that they had had to live in until Raymond's aunt had died and left them the house in Frensham and a fair amount of money. She had not *wanted* to live in the country, let alone in that Victorian museum, but Raymond had insisted. Coming into some money, being able to have servants like other people did (like Villy had always had), being able to buy decent clothes, have her hair done at a hairdresser, drive a new, instead of a second-hand car—things of that kind, and there were so many of them—had been quite miraculous at first. But as she had grown less chronically tired—God! she realized that she had always been exhausted all those years—and now having Raymond out of the way so that there were none of the tensions of being a buffer between him and the children, something had snapped in her, as though a butterfly had emerged from this chrysalis of domesticity: all she wanted was to have fun, to cease making do with anything that did not please her. The children, with the exception of Judy who they could now afford to send to a boarding school, were launched upon their lives. She knew that Villy thought her frivolous, and would intensely disapprove, well, *did*, so far as she knew the situation. Villy thought that either she should be making a home for Raymond at Woodstock, or be doing some war job. If Villy knew about Lorenzo she would go through the roof. She had said that once to him, and he had replied that she was a cold woman, who, he suspected, was a very English type where sex was concerned. (One of the things she loved about him was his almost feminine perspicacity.) When the war was over, she supposed she would have to go back to being Raymond's wife, whatever that then might involve, but meanwhile she would make the most of what she described to herself as an Indian summer.

Hugh, listening to the six o'clock news in his rather dusty drawing room (three Germans had been hanged at Kharkhov for war crimes), stubbed out his cigarette and said he was sure he could find something to fit Christopher, and why didn't she leave it to them to kit him out and would she like a drink?

"You are an angel. I'd love a drop of whisky if you have any."

"Help yourself. Where is Christopher?"

"Right at the top of the house, I'm afraid. But give him a shout: he'll come down to your room."

But she had hardly started to pour herself a cautious tot from the half bottle of Johnnie Walker when she heard the wail of dismay that undoubtedly came from Judy, sent earlier to have a bath.

"Mum! *Mum!* Oh, please come, Mum!

"I'm in here." She opened the bathroom door and, the moment that Jessica stepped inside, locked it behind her. "I don't want Uncle Hugh or Christopher to see me."

She was half in, half out of her yellow net bridesmaid's dress, struggling to pull the bodice down amid ominous splitting noises.

"It's too *small*, Mummy, I can't get *into* it."

"Stand *still*. Silly girl, you probably didn't undo the back. Stand *still*."

But even when she had levered it back over Judy's head, undone the hooks and eyes at the back and tried again, the dress was palpably too small.

"It's *stupid!* It's not my fault! I hate pink, anyway."

"It must be the dress made for Lydia, which means that she has got yours. Don't worry. I'll ring up Aunt Villy and we'll get them changed over. We'll have to mend it, though. I wish you'd waited and not tried to cram yourself into it."

"If I had, it would have been too late to change. Lydia would have gone off to church in mine, and I would have had to go in my beastly school uniform! It *is* unfair."

A great deal of Judy's conversation was conducted as though she was a child actress in a melodrama, Jessica thought, trying not to be irritated. Judy was going through a difficult phase, as *her* mother used to say. The school diet, presumably largely carbohydrate, had turned her into a pudding—a rather spotty one at that. She had grown a great deal during the last year, but that had not stopped her being podgy; her hair was always greasy, the down on her upper lip which had upset her so much in the summer had since been treated with peroxide by her faithful friend Monica with the result that it now glinted like brass shavings above which acne rioted. Of course, she would outgrow all these little disadvantages, Jessica thought, and meanwhile it was so lucky that, by and large, she seemed unaware of them.

"Put on your Sunday dress," she said, "and do tidy up the bathroom. It looks like a cross between an old clothes shop and a swamp."

"Mummy, you sound just like Miss Blenkinsopp at school. My Sunday dress is tight under the arms as well," she added.

"I'll see if I can let it out, but I can't do that for this evening. Now, mop up the floor and take all your clothes and put them in your room. Leave the bathroom as you would wish to find it."

"All *right*. Did you remember to bring my seed pearls?"

"Yes."

"And my christening present brooch?"

"Yes. Now get on."

Questions of this kind pursued her as she made her escape upstairs to change for the restaurant dinner.

Of course she was glad that Nora was getting married: she had thought for a long time that this would be unlikely. In fact, she had thought that of her four children it was Nora who would end up an old maid—matron of a hospital, perhaps. But seeing Christopher after rather a long gap—he seldom came home, and had never come to London when she lived there—she wondered about his future as well. He was desperately thin and did not look happy. He had not been called up, partly because of his earlier breakdown and the electric shock treatment he had undergone, but also because he had turned out to be very short-sighted and now wore glasses with very thick lenses. He had a high colour from working so much out of doors and his face always had minute scars where he had cut himself shaving. Almost his first question when he arrived had been "Is Dad here?" and when she had told him that he would not be arriving until the next day he had nodded, but she had seen the instant gleam of relief. Raymond had not been much of a success as a father: the three older children, although they did not feel the same, in their various ways had written him off—Angela despised him, Nora patronized him, but Christopher still dreaded and feared him. Only Judy was able to turn him into darling Daddy, doing very secret and important war work; Jessica could easily imagine that a certain amount of competition went on at school about fathers, and Judy's best friend Monica's father was a squadron leader and, vicariously, the source of all Judy's information about the war. "Monica's father says they had no business releasing Oswald Mosley from prison," she had written last term from school. "He says it is absolutely outrageous." To compete with this sort of thing, Judy had probably turned her father into a secret agent. She must tell Raymond that, it might amuse him.

Three miles away, Richard Holt was having what his best friend, his doctor, his parents and his sister kept calling his "stag night." Probably the most sedate affair of its kind there had ever been, he thought a trifle wearily. His back was hurting: the dope he'd had before dinner had worn off and he longed to be lying down flat, but they were just about to embark upon the dessert. He looked across the table to Tony, who instantly met his eye, so he smiled, and Tony smiled back, the sweetest smile—it made Richard feel better just to look at him.

"Richard would like chocolate mousse," his mother was saying.

"I'd like to choose, though," he said, making an effort to sound greedy and interested.

"Of *course*, darling," and she laid the menu in front of him.

"Creamed rice, apple pie, cheese and biscuits," he read.

"And chocolate mousse."

"*And* chocolate mousse. You're right. I'm a customer for that."

His chair was next to his mother's so that she could feed him. From tomorrow, Nora would be doing that, he thought, three times a day for ever. Before he was wounded, he had enjoyed food: in Suffolk, where his parents lived, they had a farm and the food had been plain but good. Apart from their own lamb, he used to go wild fowling; duck and geese had been on the menu and, in winter, hares that his mother had jugged or roasted or put into pies. In the Army he hadn't thought about food; it was simply fuel and a time when you could take the weight off your feet. But eighteen months of being fed everything with a spoon, food that was half cold anyway by the time it reached the ward, by a succession of nurses for whom the practice seemed to bring out latent, maternal and bossy feelings—whenever he said he had had enough it was "one more to please me" stuff—had really put him off food (although it was supposed to be an event in the patient's day). Drinks were OK because he could have them through a straw and not be dependent upon anyone.

They were a small family party, just his parents, his sister— widowed early in the war, but left with the twins (not present)—and Tony, who was to be his best man. He would not have asked him, but Tony had offered. The offer had been the last—golden—straw of his generosity and love.

The chocolate mousse had arrived. His mother was smoothing the napkin spread over his knees.

"I'm not very hungry," he said, meaning please don't make him eat all of it.

"You just have what you want," she said comfortably. "There's no sense in cramming food down you that you don't want." Her eyes, which had bleached from an intense blue to something paler than forget-me-not, had the same expression that he remembered as a child, a blend of wisdom and innocence that somehow went well with her weatherbeaten face—all fine wrinkles, like a brownish apple. Described by herself and his father as something of a tomboy when young (although in those days it had probably not meant more than not liking to ride side-saddle and refusing to wear stays), she looked as though she had made the most of what she knew and had learned, but her very innocence had always regulated the knowledge. Now in her early sixties, and with what she described as only a touch of angina, she was retiring gently from her hitherto active life. He could not possibly have imposed himself upon her.

"It's a pity Nora couldn't have been with us," his sister was saying.

"Oh, Susan, you know it's bad luck for the bride and groom to meet on the eve of their wedding."

"I do, but it is still a pity. It's all very well for you, Dad, you've met her—I haven't."

"She's a wonderful girl," his father said, not at all for the first time.

Wonderful to marry an old crock like me, Richard thought, when they had finally got him to bed. But *how* she had wanted to! He had met her when they had first started trying to operate on his back. She had come on duty one evening when he was sleepless and the pain was driving him mad and he was counting the minutes—a hundred and ten of them before he could have his next dose. She had known at once that he was desperate, had brought him a couple of pills with a hot drink, and propped him up while he drank it. Then she had rearranged his various pillows so that when she lowered him down again it all felt different and far more comfortable. "I'll be back when I've done the round," she said. "Just to see if we've got the pillows right for you." She had been gentle, assured, deft and wonderful, *un*cheery. A first-rate nurse. She never seemed in a hurry, as many of them did, and nothing was too much trouble. That had been the beginning of it. Months later, he had asked her how she had managed to give him a dose of pain-killer out of hours, as it were. "They weren't pain-killers," she said. "It was just some arnica in pill form. You needed to feel that something was being done."

By then, they knew each other quite well. When, after months, the time came for him to be moved to another home—that's what it was called, but really it was a hospital—and he told her, she went completely silent. She'd been pushing his chair round the grounds: it was her day off and they often spent it that way. He sensed, although he could not see her behind him, that she was upset, and when they reached the huge tree that had a wooden seat round it, she stopped the chair and sat down—sort of collapsed.

"I'll miss you," he said. This was true.

"Will you, Richard? Will you really?"

"Of course. I can't imagine what it will be like without you." This was not quite true: he could, but he felt she needed to hear it.

"I'll miss you," she said, so quietly that he could hardly hear her. Then she proposed to him, the last thing he expected—or wanted, come to that. He was both touched and appalled.

"Dear Nora. I'm not the marrying kind," he said. "I couldn't give you what you wanted."

"I could look after you!"

"I know you could. But that wouldn't be a marriage."

She started to speak, but then she suddenly put her face in her hands and wept. That was awful, because he couldn't put out a hand to comfort her—he couldn't do a damn thing.

"Don't," he said after a while. "Don't. I can't bear you to cry—just sit here and watch you cry."

She stopped at once. "Sorry. I see it's not fair. Not fair to you, I mean. I had to tell you, though. Because you might have felt—well, even if you had thought it was a good idea, you might have thought I wouldn't—anyway, I wanted you to know that I do love you."

That was the first conversation about it. He went to the new place, and she came to see him on her days off. The funny thing was he *did* miss her. She always seemed to know what he needed: she would read to him for hours if he wanted; she asked him about his childhood, his family, and one day she met his parents when they made the long journey to visit him. After they had left she asked him who was Tony. (They had asked whether Tony had managed to visit him, and he had said yes, but very seldom.) He was just a friend, he had said.

"I thought it might be an old girl-friend. You know, people sometimes call girls called Antonia Tony."

"No."

"Oh, well," she said, and he sensed how hard she was trying to be light about it. "I haven't got a rival, then."

He could never tell her about Tony. She knew after that that Tony visited him occasionally—took trouble not to come on the same day. "Nicer for you to space your visitors out," she had said. Tony could hardly ever come, anyway. His work took him all over the country: since he'd been invalided out of the Army, where he'd been trained as an electrical engineer, he'd got the job of servicing plant in factories. He had told Tony that there was no point in his writing, because his letters had to be read to him, but he did send postcards, and when he *did* come, he pushed the chair through the grounds and well out of sight so that they could feel as much as possible alone together. It was ironical, really, that they'd met because they were both such good athletes, that they were either in the same top team or competing, although differences emerged: Tony, for instance, was a sprinter, and he was long distance. Tony had copped it before he did, but he had ended up with comparatively minor damage; he now walked with a pronounced limp and had trouble with his lungs. When he was better they had spent Richard's leave together—ten unforgettable days in North Wales. It had rained almost all the time and even now he regarded rain with affection.

Shortly afterwards, he'd had his crash—prang, they called it in the RAF. Anyway, he'd crashed after being attacked by fighter aircraft, and a bullet had got him in the spine, so he couldn't use his parachute. All his other injuries had been from the crash: it was a miracle he had survived at all, they had said. He'd been unconscious —came to in a hospital bed, full of dope, disembodied; to begin with he thought he was dead and that this was the beginning of something else. It was some time before he realized, and they told him, how badly he had been hurt, and much longer before he had a chance to tell Tony. That was the first time that he understood what a lot hands had to do with affection and love: he could not touch, comfort or reassure Tony—just had to lie there and tell him. It would make no difference, Tony had said at once, none at all. At twenty-three, Richard believed that he would have said the same. But he was ten years older and, even then, the full implications of his state had not come home to him. He had been able to think that when he was better, he would need less nursing—would become more independent somehow or other. It was only as the months dragged by that he recognized this would never be so to any significant degree. Even so, he had not been able to disillusion Tony, or had not been able to bear to, since he was terrified that this might mean he would never see Tony again. But when they had discharged him from the original place and moved him to the second hospital, he knew what his options were. His parents wanted him to go home: his mother said she would look after him; "I'm sure they would show me what I need to do," she had said, "and your father would help me with the lifting." But he had known that this was out of the question. He would not, could not expect Tony to take it all on: he would be prevented from having any career, any job, even, any friends, any fun, and, last, but by no means least, any sex. He could not allow someone of twenty-four to commit themselves to that, could not condemn that faithful and loving heart to such an inevitable betrayal. Tony had been a Dr. Barnardo's boy: he had lived in institutions all his life, had never had family affection, let alone love, until he had met him, Richard. It was his first love: he would get over it. These resolutions had coincided with Nora's proposal. At first he had dismissed the idea as preposterous: he did not love her; he was not in a position to contract to a partnership of any kind with anyone. Much safer to stick to the institutional life, where nothing was expected of him, and where people were paid to see that he got from one day to the next. But his views, his opinions, his resolutions, seemed to make as little difference to Nora's feelings as they did to Tony's. There began to be a pattern to Tony's visits. Tony would talk about their future, and argue with him when he said that they wouldn't be having one— sometimes this would get to be nearly a row. Then he would make an effort to change the subject; there would be silences, filled inexorably by intense longing, by memories of fulfilment, which was all, he realized, that now they could ever have, and they would look at each other and there was nothing to say. And then, one afternoon at one of these times, Tony said: "There's one thing I'd like. Just once."

"You say."

"I could lift you out of your chair and put you on the ground."

"It would be no good, darling. I can't—"

"I know that. I just want to lie with you, hold you in my arms—be your loving and friendly lover."

He'd taken off his jacket to make a pillow, and then he'd lifted him up out of the chair and laid him down as gently as a leaf coming to rest. Then he'd put his arms round him over his shoulders with the miserable stumps that were what remained of his arms and cried until Richard felt that both their hearts would break. "That's it, then," he said, when he had stopped. He wiped his own tears from Richard's face before he kissed him. Then he had lifted him back into his chair, picked up his jacket and taken him back to his room. That was when he realized that Tony had at last accepted that there was no future for them. A month later, he agreed to marry Nora.

But now, with the wedding so near, he felt afraid. Not for Nora: nobody could know better than she who she was marrying; she was practical, she had nursed him for months, she could have no illusions about the prognosis. She said she loved him and he had come to believe her. They had had some pretty difficult conversations about no children, no sex, et cetera, and she had repeated steadily that she knew all that, she understood, it didn't matter to her. "Probably harder for you," she had said. No, he had replied: my libido seems pretty torpid. The one thing he could not bear to tell her was what he felt, still felt, for Tony. She simply thought Tony was a university friend; she was like his parents in this respect. In marrying Nora, he was doing, he hoped, the thing that would be best for everyone, but he would not betray Tony, who had continued to visit him, to care for him and about him, and who had accepted the news about his marriage with such gentle goodwill. "I do understand," he had said. "She sounds just the right person for you. I'm glad she loves you." He smiled then and added, "I'd have to win the pools to keep up with her." (By then he'd been told about her family and the house at Frensham and all that.) And even that, though it could have been, was not bitterly said. Later, he said, "You'll need a best man, won't you?"

"I suppose I shall."

"I'll be your best man," he said. "If you like." He smiled a second time; and Richard wondered yet again whether he was more beautiful when he was smiling, or when he was not.

"You'll always be my best man," he said before he could stop himself. "That sounds corny, doesn't it?"

And Tony, in their least favourite tutor's voice, replied: "I'm very much afraid, Richard, that it does."

Tony was not staying in the hotel, thank goodness. His parents had taken Richard upstairs and put him to bed. This meant that he was going to have to stay in one position all night—usually someone turned him, but he hadn't mentioned that. "You get a good night's rest," they said and, again, he knew that if he had gone back to live with them, they would never have had one. He lay, for what seemed like hours, making resolutions to be good to Nora, but in the end he gave up and went back to Wales with Tony.

Christopher had been standing for about twenty minutes just inside the church where the biting cold outside was taken over by a marginally warmer, but more compelling darkness. The lights from the brass chandeliers looked yellow in the twilight dusk. It was just after two, and already the day seemed nearly over. He was the only usher; it was not a large wedding and, indeed, it looked as though the attendants would be lost in the cavernous church. He had put Mr. and Mrs. Holt in the front seats on the appropriate side. It was strange how awkward most people looked in their best clothes, he thought. Even he could see that Mrs. Holt was not given to wearing a hat, nor Mr. Holt a dark suit. The bridegroom, in a chair, was wheeled steadily up the aisle by a marvellous-looking young chap with red-gold hair, dark eyes and a limp. Compared to him, the chap in the chair—his future brother-in-law—looked rather ordinary; his face, that is: the rest of him could certainly not be called that. Aunt Villy arrived with Wills, Lydia and Neville. Lydia threw her arms round him: "I'm wearing scent," she said; "I'm letting you smell it." She wore a winter coat over a long yellow dress. Neville had walked purposefully up to the top of the church, while Aunt Villy, with Wills trying to squirm out of her grasp, kissed him and said how nice it was to see him again. Neville returned.

"I suppose Nora *knows* he's got no arms," he said. "His coat is sort of draped, but you can see he hasn't got either of them."

"That is a personal remark, Neville," Lydia said in her most crushing voice.

"Children, children. No more talking."

Wills, having failed to remove his hand from Villy's, tried to sit on the ground. "When are we going to leave this place?"

"Where's Roland?" Christopher asked.

"He had a sore throat and I brought Wills instead to relieve Ellen. The Duchy sent her love to you, and said you must come and stay when you have a chance to get away. We'll find our way. You stay with Christopher, Lydia."

The organ began a rather meandering piece of Bach, and suddenly quite a lot of people arrived. Nurses who'd looked after Richard, his sister, who was fat and looked sad, and then the three cousins, Louise and Polly and Clary, all looking very grown-up in hats that tilted over their faces. It was lovely to see them and made him think of summers at Home Place. Then Mum with Judy, also in a dress like Lydia's. "I'm the bridesmaid."

"You're just one of them," Lydia said.

They eyed each other.

"I'm wearing my seed pearls. And I've had a perm."

"I can see." Lydia's hair, straight and shining, the colour of dark honey, hung down to below her shoulders, held back over her forehead by a yellow velvet snood. On this perched the narrow wreath of buttercups and daisies like a natural crown. On Judy the same thing looked embarrassingly inappropriate. But Nora had chosen the colours, and decreed what the wreaths were to be made of. Feeling sorry for her, he gave Judy a clumsy hug.

"Mind my dress," she said.

Mum returned to unpack the bride's bouquet from a cardboard box.

"She'll be here any minute," she said.

Angela arrived. It was ages since he'd seen her. She wore an emerald green jacket that made her shoulders look very wide, and a very short tight skirt that showed her lovely long legs in film star stockings. She had stopped plucking her eyebrows so much, so now she looked far less disdainful, and her mouth, which was so like

Mum's, was now painted a rosy pink instead of the pillar-box red she had worn when he had last seen her.

"You smell lovely," he said when she kissed him (Lydia's scent had been lavender water). "I wish you'd come last night." She had not appeared.

"I'm sorry, Chris. Something—came up. Where do I sit?"

"Anywhere along that side. I'll join you in a minute."

He turned back to the door, and there was his father, with Nora in her long white dress and a veil that very nearly obscured her face. He exchanged an uneasy, social smile with his father. "I say, Nora, you do look terrific!"

She nodded—he could see her eyes glittering with excitement behind the veil. A pause, while Mum arranged the bridesmaids behind Nora, she took her father's arm, and the organ struck up with the expected music. He could see the clergyman standing on the steps before the altar. Mum took his arm and they slipped round the side aisle to their seats, he with Angela in the second row, his mother in front.

During the service, he wondered if she knew what she was doing. He remembered the time when she had wanted to be a nun, a "bride of Christ." He hoped that she did not feel she was making a sacrifice—a lesser one, he supposed it would be—since Richard was not God, but possibly a sacrifice all the same. The idea of sacrifice made him feel uneasy: he felt that he would only be able to sustain a short sharp one, and Nora's would certainly not be that: it would continue until either she or Richard died. This made him think of Oliver—now probably about eight years old, and dogs didn't live much above twelve or fourteen. It was no good thinking about that. Often, when he had worried about things for ages they were not as bad as he'd imagined, or sometimes they did not happen at all. Like being called up: the moment he'd decided that he *ought* to agree to be a soldier or something, they hadn't wanted him. His eyesight wasn't good enough, apart from having had all that shock treatment. So then he'd gone to work for a farmer, who was more of a market gardener really. He grew acres of vegetables, some salads and some soft fruit, and he let Christopher have the caravan he used to use for holidays to live in for a very low rent. He and his wife had got quite fond of Christopher and offered him a room in their house, but he really liked the caravan, which he had turned into a home for himself and Oliver. The farm was just outside Worthing, and he had a bike to go and buy food and anything else he needed. He lived mainly on vegetables from the farm, plus potatoes and bread. He'd become a vegetarian, as he'd decided that you couldn't like animals as much as he did and then eat them, so he gave Oliver his meat ration. Once a week he had supper with the Hursts, otherwise he cooked on a Primus. He had an oil lamp and paraffin stove and a sleeping bag so it was quite cosy, even in winter, and Mum had given him a wireless for Christmas. He was all right. He worked hard and he didn't mind being alone, although he realized when he saw her today, that he did miss Polly rather. Gosh, she did look marvellous walking into the church just now! Louise, whom he'd never really talked to much, looked quite old in a grey squirrel fur coat (which he didn't approve of—it must have taken a frightening number of squirrels to make it), and Clary looked much the same as she always had only taller, and a bit silly wearing a hat, but Polly, in a coat the colour of dark blue hyacinths and with a blue straw hat tilted over her white forehead and coppery hair looked unapproachably glamorous—she had suddenly grown up so much that he felt he wouldn't know what to talk to her about.

Dad had left Nora now, and was walking back to sit in the front pew with Mum. It must be awful to be Richard, he thought, not having any hands and having to be grateful to people all the time. He looked at his own hands, spread out over his knees to keep his legs warm—he wasn't used to wearing such thin clothes. Mum had exclaimed about them when she was trying to get him kitted out in Uncle Hugh's clothes. They did look like hands that spent most of their life out of doors and did a lot of work: he couldn't get the earth thoroughly out from under his nails, and he'd had chilblains quite badly—on his feet as well, but he was used to them by now. They got better in the spring; this was the worst time of year for them. When he'd started at the farm, he used to get blisters too, but they soon stopped. Still, they weren't exactly hands for a party . . .

They had both said their vows: he could hardly hear Richard, but Nora's voice was clear and steady. He wondered if he would ever marry anyone; on the whole, he thought not. He couldn't imagine that anyone would want to marry *him*, but he was pretty bad at imagining the future altogether—he couldn't even think what it would be like when the war was over, if it ever was. Getting married if you didn't believe in God would probably be wrong. And he was pretty sure you couldn't marry a cousin.

There was a general movement. Richard, with Nora, was being wheeled into the back somewhere and Mum and Dad and Richard's parents were all following them. Soon they would all be going to some hotel for the reception, and then Nora and Richard were going to Frensham, till the end of the war, anyway, and Nora was going to earn money by nursing one or two other wounded chaps. It was quite a big house, but he supposed they'd have to live on the ground floor.

They were coming back. He hoped it would soon be over, because it was so cold and he was extremely hungry.

"Why wasn't Archie there?"

"He wouldn't have been asked. Nora doesn't know him, and even Aunt Jessica *hardly* knows him."

"Oh."

"Are you feeling sad too? It's funny how sad weddings make one feel. I even felt sad after Louise's, and that was a much starrier affair."

"I think this was a *particularly* tragic one, if you ask me."

"Clary, it wasn't *tragic*. Nora didn't *have* to marry him. She never used to do things she didn't want, so she obviously isn't now."

"Isn't what?"

"Sacrificing herself."

"Oh, Poll, she *is!* She wants to *and* she is. Don't you remember, Louise said she wanted to be a nun?"

"That was just a phase, as the aunts say. The female equivalent to wanting to be an engine driver."

"Neville was awful," Clary said, following that train of thought. "He asked Richard what he did if he had an itch."

"He *didn't!*"

"Oh, yes, he did. I told him he was both callous and tactless and he said if *he* was like that, he'd rather people asked him questions about it than pretended he was just like everyone else. But, of course," she ended loftily, "he can't have the slightest *idea* what it's like to be Richard."

"Well, *I* haven't. If I try to think about it, my thoughts just black out. I can't imagine that life would be worth living at all. Poor Richard! Goodness, isn't it lucky that something like that didn't happen to Archie?"

"I think crashes out of aeroplanes must be the worst. Look at that poor chap Zoë used to look after at Mill House."

"Does she still do it?"

"I don't think so. I think he may have gone back to his other hospital. What shall we do this evening?"

"We'd be warmest in a cinema. I'm not hungry after all those sandwiches and things. We could ring up Archie," she said, as though it was a thought that had just occurred to her.

Clary looked at her consideringly. "We *could* . . . I expect he'll be busy though—probably not worth it—"

"We could at least *try*," Polly said as Clary knew she would.

So they rang up Archie who said it was far too cold to go out, but as his flat was nice and warm, why didn't they come and have supper in it? "I know how awful it is after weddings," he said. "One does so need cheering up about ordinary life."

"Honey, the best thing you could do is to stop crying and tell me about it."

He handed her a glass of bourbon and a handkerchief.

She blew her nose gratefully. "I really don't know why I *am*. It was a *wedding*, after all."

"Find out," he said comfortably, settling beside her on the sofa.

"Of course," she said, "people often cry at weddings. And it isn't even as though I'm particularly *fond* of Nora. We never got on very well. She thought I was frivolous, and I thought she was a prig. She was awfully bossy, too. She told me once (it was supposed to be a secret) that she was going to be a nun and I just thought what a relief not to have her about criticizing my character all the time. The only times we ever ganged up were when Daddy was really awful to Christopher. He used to bully him and nag Mummy. I come from an awful family, I can tell you. Snobbish, and always trying to keep up appearances. But my father never earned any money much, and poor Mummy had to do the *cooking* and everything, which wasn't at all what she was brought up to. And by the time Dad's aged aunt died and left him the house and quite a lot of money, she was too old to enjoy it. Anyway, Dad expected Christopher to be a war hero and Nora and me to make good marriages."

"And what would that mean? Marrying into your Royal Family, that kind of thing?"

"Not quite that. But a title, or someone like my cousin Louise married—you know, famous."

"Golly! Well, I suppose parents are always ambitious for their children—"

"It didn't work in our case. Christopher works on a farm, and Nora has married a paraplegic—"

"And you are having an affair with an American who is old enough to be your father."

"Oh, they don't know *that*!" she said. "I mean, it's not because you're American, or anything, it's the having an affair part that they wouldn't like. People of their generation simply don't have affairs." She had begun to blush.

He put a bear-like arm round her thin shoulders.

"*American* people of their generation sometimes have affairs, as you know," he said. "It's possible you don't know everything about them."

She leant back against the warm wall of his shoulder. "I'm sure it's different in America. And the war and everything."

"You haven't told me why Nora's wedding made you cry."

"Oh! No. I suppose—it was really all the things that it wasn't. She wore a white dress and veil, and Judy and Lydia—that's another cousin—were bridesmaids. But when it was over, and she was walking down the aisle, she tried to wheel his chair, but the best man wouldn't let her. He was right, of course, it really would have looked like a nurse with her patient if she'd done that. But it was so *sad!* Her eyes filled with tears. I mean, she'll never be able to—to have children. She'll always just have to look after him."

"Perhaps she loves him," he said. "Perhaps she loves him and knows he needs her and she wants to be needed."

"You always look on the bright side."

"No. I'm just pointing out to you, honey, that there may be one."

"But supposing she finds someone else, some time in the future and falls in love with him?"

"That can happen to anyone."

"Oh, darling, I'm sorry! I didn't mean—"

"That was all a long time ago, and I know you didn't."

But at different intervals during the rest of the evening—while they got ready to go out to dinner, while they were dancing (he was a very good dancer), while they stood outside in the freezing cold waiting for the taxi he had ordered, when she fell asleep in the cab while he was holding her, when they were standing in the small lift on their way to his fourth-floor flat, when he had opened the door and they were assailed by the (to him comfortingly familiar, to her delightfully exotic) odours of the Chesterfield cigarettes that he chain-smoked and the Mary Chess scent of "White Lilac" that he had had posted to her from New York, when they had got to bed and he had made love to her, when he had given her a final kiss and reached out to switch off the bedside lamp that he put on the floor to make the light more cosy and romantic and she had turned her smooth bony back to him for sleep—during that whole evening Elaine Black thrust her way out of the past to confront them. Angela saw her as a large, dark-eyed woman with raven black hair and dazzling white skin, bosomy and with a low husky voice. He knew her to be small, red-haired, short-sighted and shrill. "A good girl," his mother had said when he had brought her home. "A well-brought-up girl." Her very plainness had appealed to his mother; certainly her appearance in no way prepared him for her going off with another man, a man he had never met or even heard of, a step she had taken with no warning or intimation even of dissatisfaction with her married state or with him as a husband. And then, two years afterwards, he heard that she had died—so suddenly that he thought it must have been an automobile accident, but in fact it had been a sudden and violent onset of diabetes. It wasn't until she died that he realized that he had never loved her and began to feel guilty. Eight years they had been together, and he had never known what she really thought or felt about anything, except that she had minded being unable to have children. He had been working his ass off during those years, first as a medical student, and then, after he'd qualified, in the big hospital in the Bronx. She'd worked as a receptionist for a psychiatrist but, even so, they'd been very short of cash. After Elaine had left, he'd decided that he didn't know enough about people and that was when he'd decided to qualify in psychiatry. Analysis had taught him how much of his life had been dictated by being his mother's son, and it was only when *she* died—just before Pearl Harbor—that he'd been able to accept that she'd done her best for him according to *her* lights. Her death had released him from the relentless campaign she had waged to find him another, more suitable, wife (Elaine's shares had dropped dramatically with her failure to produce a grandchild). By then, he was going quite well: had moved to a larger apartment in a better part of the city, shared a receptionist with two colleagues and enjoyed one or two unmemorable affairs (though never with patients). But Elaine's departure continued to haunt him: if she had not died, he might have been able to seek her out and talk to her, though he was never sure whether he would have taken the considerable trouble involved to find her and, if he had, whether she would have agreed to such an amiable post-mortem. As it was, the thought of her always provoked the sensation of unfinished business between them, and this, for reasons he could understand but not quell, induced guilt. Joining the Army, coming to England with the prospect of invading France, had made him feel free, isolated, and to begin with, and outside the context of the job, irresponsible. At first, although London seemed to be full of girls, he remained lonely. He went out on evenings with fellow officers where they ate the terrible food and watched couples dancing. Sometimes the others brought girls, and once a girl for him, but they hadn't hit it off: she told him dirty stories that made him feel embarrassed and sorry for her. Then, one evening, he'd gone out with John Riley who was in his outfit, and after dinner they'd gone on to the Astor (he realized afterwards because John knew a girl he was interested in was going to be there) and, sure enough, John located his lady and got her to dance with him. He'd watched them for a bit, and then just as he was thinking of going, he'd noticed that shit Joe Bronstein dancing with a tall thin girl in a green silk dress and a long page-boy bob. As they came round the floor nearer his table he could see that Joe was bawling her out and she was enduring it. He'd been in the same ship as Joe coming over and had disliked him as a bully who went for anyone weaker than himself. When they were about two yards away he saw that Joe was drunk, that the girl was precariously managing to keep him on his feet. For a second, she seemed to be looking at him, and her face, white, with a dark red mouth and eyes heavily fringed in black had all the mournful vulnerability of a clown . . . Then the music stopped and Joe, grasping her arm above the elbow, was lurching with her towards their table. Once there, he pushed her down onto her chair: he saw that she said something and rose to her feet, whereupon he seized her again and shoved her back so violently that she missed the chair and fell upon the floor. That was enough. He got up and went over to them. "Time you went home, Lieutenant," he had said, but he hadn't had to do much more, because the bouncers arrived and removed him. That was how he had met Angela. He had asked her whether she wanted a drink, and she had said, no, she just wanted to go home. Close to, she was younger than he had thought her. She started to thank him in her pretty, clipped English accent, but in the middle of it was overcome by an enormous yawn that she could hardly cover by her hand. She apologized and said she was rather tired. By then the cab he'd ordered had come. When she realized he was coming with her, she had shrunk into her corner and given her address in a voice that attempted distance, but sounded afraid. He would just see her safely home, he said, and she apologized again for being tired. (By the time they reached her flat, she had apologized four times.)

The next day he had sent her some roses with a card saying he hoped she'd had a good sleep and would she call him? He'd been faintly surprised that she had. He'd taken her out on New Year's Eve, and they'd drunk a lot, ending in a night club where her gin had been the worst hooch and she'd passed out.

Making love to her the first time had been disappointing: there was something both practised and impersonal about her that he found sad, and he sensed damage way beyond Joe Bronstein. She made love like someone who always had to catch the eight-ten in the morning and knew that they would be standing for the whole journey. But for the rest of the time, when he took her around, exploring London which she seemed to know as little as he, going for trips to the country when he could get something to drive, to the movies when the weather was bad, when they spent evenings in his flat eating tins of turkey breast or steak that he could get from the PX and he taught her to play chess, she blossomed. He kept himself very steady and patient and always gentle: he did not want her to confuse gratitude with love. He guessed she'd been in love with a man who'd been killed, but she did not tell him and he did not ask.

He caught the last train back to Oxford and she was waiting for him on the platform when he arrived, as he'd known she would be. It was bitterly cold, the train was late, and he limped along the platform stumbling nearly into her arms. They kissed: her face was freezing and she smelled of peppermint. Inside the battered little MG her family had given her years ago for her twenty-first birthday, they kissed more seriously.

"Oh, Raymond! I've missed you so!"

He had only been away for twenty-four hours.

"I came back as quickly as I could."

"Oh, I *know!* I wasn't blaming you!"

It was perishingly cold in the car; their breath was steaming up the windows.

"Let's get going, darling."

"Yes, of course. You must be frozen." She wiped the windscreen with her rather hairy scarf. She loved the way he said darling.

"Did it all go well?" she asked in as light and unconcerned a voice as she could manage. She was dying to hear every detail of the wedding; not that she was *jealous* or anything so idiotic, it was simply that she was interested in *everything* about him.

"Very well, I think."

"Did the bride wear white?"

"Oh, yes. It was all properly done. Bridesmaids, you know, in church and all that."

"It must have been lovely." I shall have to forgo all that, she thought. She had so often imagined herself walking slowly down the aisle, her radiance partly concealed by yards and yards of old lace like the end of all her favourite films. But now, when the war was over, and Raymond was able to leave the quite awful woman he was married to, it would have to be a registry office. However, what did a little petty detail like *that* matter compared to their wonderful, unique relationship?

"It must have been rather agonizing for you, though," she said. This was much later, after they had parked the car outside the huge dark red-brick Edwardian house in which they both had rooms. To begin with they had been with all the others, in Keble College, but after four people had broken into her room and tried to go to bed with her, Raymond had wonderfully arranged for them to live out. A bus collected them every day and took them to Blenheim. It was widely assumed by their colleagues that they were sleeping together; this, however, was not the case. They lived in a state of virtuous, romantic tension that made her admire Raymond more than ever, since she found it so intolerable. They had come very near consummation, but the value he placed upon her virginity seemed insurmountable. She would have liked him to be just as honourable, but at the same time overcome with desire. Then he could have regrets, make abject apologies, and she would be tender and magnanimous—she had rehearsed every detail of that scene without still, unhappily, having been called upon to perform it.

"I mean—the whole situation," she went on. They were in her room and she was making cocoa as Raymond's ration of whisky from the local pub had run out. She had lit the small gas fire, but they both still wore their overcoats. "I suppose you had to pretend to everybody."

"How do you mean?"

"Well—" She floundered. "I mean, that it was just a perfectly normal situation." She imagined him standing beside his wife, smiling glassily and shaking hands with the guests.

"Oh, that. Yes." He suddenly remembered watching the best man lean over to put the ring on Nora's hand since the bridegroom was not able to do it—a poignant moment that had somehow brought Nora's future state home to him as nothing else had. In spite of himself, his eyes filled with tears. "It was," he said huskily.

"Oh, my *darling!*" She flung herself down on her knees before his chair. "I didn't mean to upset you! Let's talk about something else!"

* * *

"You know Meccano?" Neville said in the train going back to Home Place.

"Of course I do, stupid. I've never cared for it myself."

"Well, if you made long bits, they could be attached to the top of his stumps—he did have them, I could see from his jacket, and they could have a little motor and you could make sort of hands, *claws*, anyway and then he would be able to pick things up. A bit like a crane," he added: Lydia had never been any good at mechanics.

"I think you're horrible to talk about poor Richard like that."

"Wrong, wrong, wrong," he returned. "I'm trying to think of things to help him, which is more than you have. Your mere sorrow isn't the slightest use to him."

She was silenced, and he spent the rest of the journey deciding whether or not he would be an inventor.

". . . and Daddy is *so* pleased that we are going to be at Frensham. If it had been requisitioned, goodness knows what would have happened to it, and anyway he thinks our ideas for it are far better than the Government's."

They were back in the hotel where he had spent the night, and Nora was to occupy the room that had been his parents'. The hotel had sent up flowers. Scarlet and pink carnations with gypsophila rioted in a cut-glass vase. There was also a plate of grapes, most of which they had eaten. Tomorrow they were to be driven to Frensham.

"You're tired," she said, before he could. "I'll settle you now."

Half an hour later, when that was done—his back rubbed with surgical spirit, his teeth cleaned, his pee collected in a bottle, his dope taken, his short-sleeved nightshirt on (much easier than pyjamas, she had rightly said when she bought it for him), his pillows, including his special one, comfortably arranged, she bent over and gave him a light kiss.

"I'll come in at three to turn you," she said, "and I'll leave my door open so you can call. I'll always hear you." When she had turned out the light and gone next door and he could hear her preparing to go to bed he was suddenly, overwhelmingly touched at the way she behaved exactly as though nothing new had happened.

Tony waited until Richard left the reception with Nora in a limousine that he could lift Richard into. He watched with the rest of the crowd until the car turned a corner and was abruptly out of sight, then he went back to the hotel cloakroom, collected his duffel coat, left the hotel, and found a pub where he got extremely drunk.

PART
---·---·---·---·---
THREE

The Family

January, 1944

THE HOUSE SEEMED horribly empty without Polly and Clary. He noticed it from the moment that his alarm went off in the morning. He would lie in bed listening to the silence; no thumps or crashes from above, no laughing, no imprecations, no light steps running down the stairs. He got up quickly, putting on his old blue dressing gown—the one Sybil had given him the first Christmas after the war had begun—and his leather slippers. Even so, the cold was very noticeable. He had had an Ascot installed in the bathroom on the half landing above his bedroom because there was nobody in the house to keep the range stoked. The Ascot unwillingly let him have a small bath, but the water ran into it so slowly, that in winter it was warm rather than hot. He had to boil a kettle for shaving. By the time he had bathed, shaved and dressed, he could turn the lights off, undo the blackout and reveal the bleak grey day without. He would descend to the basement, stopping on the way to collect the half pint of milk that was delivered every other day, and the newspaper that always came. 2,300 TONS OF BOMBS DROPPED ON BERLIN was this morning's headline. He tried to imagine 2,300 tons of bombs, but the mind boggled. When you thought of what *one* bomb could do . . . He ate breakfast at the kitchen table: it was handier, and he kept the gas grill on for warmth after he had made his toast. Toast and tea was what he had, with margarine whose foul taste was partly concealed by some of Mrs. Cripps's jam, or failing that Marmite. In the old days, he and Sybil would have breakfasted in the dining room next door, eating things like melon and boiled eggs and sometimes—his absolute favourite—kippers. Sybil had always sat with her back to the french window onto the garden, and on sunny mornings small tendrils of her hair had glowed against the light. Memories of this kind were no longer quite so agonizing, but they were essential: he couldn't get through the days without thinking about her, reminding her of some small private joke, remembering things she had said or thought or liked or worried about. Each time, he experienced a little surge of love for her that was momentarily untainted by the despair of loss. It kept him going, he said to himself. There did not seem to be very much else to do that. The business certainly used up the days, all right, but with the Old Man out of it—virtually, although he came up twice a week and sat in his office waiting for people to come and talk to him—and he and Edward at loggerheads about the new wharf in Southampton, it was hardly fun. It was Edward who had insisted upon buying it: the property was going very cheaply, it was true, but it still meant ploughing back not only the money they had got from War Damage but using every bit of spare capital they possessed as well. Edward had argued that after the war there would be a building boom, and that with more premises they would be in a much better position to house and process the hardwoods that had made their name, but it seemed to Hugh unlikely that they would have accrued the money to buy the huge amount of stock that would justify a second wharf. They had had a row about it—well, several rows—but the Old Man had taken Edward's side and so the new wharf had been bought and was going ahead. And then there was this large and now empty house. He supposed it would be sensible to sell it, or at least close it down, but he had to live somewhere, and this had been his house with her. If only Poll had stayed! But it had been he who had insisted that she should not. Louise had asked them both to share her house. Clary had wanted to go; Poll had demurred. "I'll stay with you, Dad," she had said. But he had known at once that she had not wanted to, even though she had said again and again that she did. In the end, he had taken her out to dinner to tackle her about it on her own. He took her to his club because he felt it was a better place to talk, and a little bit because he was so proud of her and enjoyed introducing her to his acquaintances there. "My word!" they would say, "what a stunning daughter!" and things like that. She *was* stunning. Her hair was like Sybil's had been when he had met her, a deep glossy coppery colour, the same white complexion, and short upper lip with the same flat, curving mouth that was as charming as

Sybil's, but her high forehead and her dark blue eyes were pure Cazalet, very much like Rachel's who in turn was like the Duchy. That was curious, he thought: one would not have said that she had the Duchy's eyes, rather her aunt's, but one would certainly attribute Rachel's eyes to her mother. But unlike her mother or her aunt, Polly had a way with clothes: she contrived to make glamour out of neatness. She had come out with him straight from work in a white jersey and a dark skirt with pleats in it. The jersey had a high rolled neck and she'd pushed the sleeves up to just below her elbows so that the wide silver bracelet he'd given her last Christmas was visible on her wrist. She looked as smart as paint. She had sat in a large leather chair opposite him sipping the Bristol Cream sherry that he'd got her and telling him about her and Clary going to be interviewed for joining the Wrens.

"It was so funny, Dad, all the things they asked us—either we'd never done them, like School Certificate, or we *couldn't* have, like produce references from our last job. When Clary said she was a writer, they simply didn't count it. But there was an enormous queue and they said the Wrens were nearly full anyway. It was rather a relief, really. I didn't want to have to go away from—everyone."

"So—what's the next move?"

"Well, Clary says there are hundreds of boring jobs. She says London is simply full of typing pools, so I suppose we shall be in one of them. Then, if you are fearfully lucky, you get asked to be a temporary secretary for someone because their proper one has got flu or something, and then if you are a success, you become somebody's permanent secretary." There was a pause, and then she added: "Archie says I should try to get into school. They have evening classes. I wouldn't be a permanent student, just go in the evenings. But I'm not sure yet whether you have to live in a particular part of London to be eligible."

"That sounds like a good idea," he said. He wished he had thought of it for her.

"It would only be about two evenings a week," she said. "Otherwise I'd be at home with you."

"I want to talk to you about that."

"Oh, Dad! We've talked about it."

"Yes, but not enough. I've been thinking and I've come to the conclusion that it is really a bad idea. You should be with people of your own age. Added to which, I may easily have to spend one or two nights a week in Southampton, so I wouldn't even be there and I'd hate you to be quite on your own at home."

"I'd be all right."

"The other thing is," he improvised, "I'm seriously thinking of shutting up the house. It's far too big for me, or even for the two of us. And if I go to Home Place every weekend, and to Southampton for two nights, it really begins not to be worth it."

"Oh! But where would you go, Dad, on the nights when you *were* having to be in London?"

"I can stay here. Or I might get a small flat. But," he added, with cunning bravery, "if I have *you* to look after, it all becomes more complicated. You know, a larger flat." He could see that he was winning; enabling her to do what he knew she wanted without feeling selfish about it.

"I do think, Dad," she said trying to sound considering and measured, "that *you* ought to go out more. Meet people of your own age," she finished demurely.

The implications of this last remark had been made to him before by others who, in most cases, had more or less delicately implied that he ought to marry again, and he felt the surge of irritation that this presumption about his private life—made worse because it was choked by generalization—always provoked. Then he looked at his daughter. She was without guile—or, rather, her guile concealing her excitement about going to live with Clary and Louise was so transparently concealed that it amounted to the same thing. She was not worrying about him, he thought, with a pang and with relief, she was just saying what she thought was a grown-up thing to say.

"I was joking," she said. "But people say that kind of thing to us, and Clary says that sometimes we should be the sayer for a change. Not that *you* meant it *seriously*, darling Dad."

"Well, but one day, you will fall in love and get married, Poll. And you have to meet people in order to find the right one."

He noticed that the faintest blush was rising to her forehead. "Let's go and have dinner," he said.

As they walked down the wide shallow staircase to the dining room, she said, "I think the chances of my marrying anyone are extremely small. Actually."

"Do you?" he replied. "Well, I don't."

The next week she and Clary had left, and the house seemed inexpressibly dreary without them, but he felt sure that Sybil would have agreed that he had done the right thing. In a way, it had been one of the easier decisions to make; the one about whether to close down this house was much harder. It would probably be *sensible*, but any alternative seemed to him such a business and so unrewarding that he wasn't sure if he could face it. It would be another link with her gone, because he was fairly sure that if he left the house *now*, he would not want to go back to it after the war. How often that phrase recurred! For years it had been something that everybody was aiming at—a time when a new life would start, when families would be reunited, when democracy would so much have prevailed that the pre-war social injustices would be all put right. Children of all classes would be educated for longer, the National Health Service would care for everybody's health, thousands of new houses would be built with proper sanitation; there had seemed everything to wish and hope for when peace finally did break out. Only now, for him—selfishly, as he was the first to admit—the zest for all this had gone: he could see nothing but years and years stretching ahead for him without her, and without her he felt he had nothing. In one sense this was nonsense, he would tell himself: he had a job, his family, his own three children who needed his responsible affection more than ever—but somehow above, or beyond, or inside that, a sense of futility prevailed. He felt now much as he had felt at the end of the other war, *his* war, that had lost him his health and a hand. And then he had met her, and everything had changed. That was over, he had had his miracle; then he had been waiting (although, of course, at the time he had not known it) for that amazing, marvellous chance that had brought her into his life. He had been incredibly lucky. But he had had, as it were, his luck. The rest of his life should, ought to consist of doing the best he could for the children, the business and the rest of the family. Although he missed her so much, he was sure that he had been right to let Polly go. Living with her cousins was a very good interim step for her towards total independence, and Louise, as a young married woman, would be bound to have her husband's friends to the house, and thereby introduce Polly to more people of her own age. Simon, who was leaving school at Easter, was much more of a worry. Simon had always been Sybil's, much in the way that Polly had been his. Since she had died, he had made efforts, but somehow they had only served to show him how little he knew his son and how difficult it would be to repair this ignorance. Simon parried any efforts he made by agreeing with anything he said, by a kind of awful docility in falling in with any suggestion that he made about what they might do together and by a distant courtesy that seemed only to underline their lack of intimacy. "I expect it is," he would say, or "*I* don't mind." He was due to be called up this year as he would be eighteen in September, and when Hugh had asked Simon what service he would choose to go into he had simply said, "It doesn't make any difference really, does it? I mean—it's all the same—learning how to kill people and that sort of thing." What should he *like* to do—after the war, Hugh had persisted.

"I don't know. Salter, my friend, is going to be a doctor and I think I might quite like to be one too. If he doesn't run a restaurant which is another thing he has in mind. He is very keen on food and cooking and all that. And he knows absolutely everything about Mozart. So he might write one or two books about him. He can do everything, really."

"He sounds interesting."

"He is, but I don't think you'd like him much. He believes in socialism and he has a ghastly stammer and once he had a fit and Matron thought he was just acting, which she *would*, and he might have died." There was a pause, then he added, "He won't get called up because of them—the fits, I mean—but of course I will so it's no earthly use our making any plans together. But I did wonder, Dad, whether I could have him to stay in London for a week because he lives in Dorset and there are a lot of things he wants to do in London, like go to concerts, et cetera. He wouldn't talk about politics—he knows you're politically immature but he quite understands because his family are too. He says it has just as much to do with generation as with class."

He had said, of course Simon could have his friend for as long as he liked. He was so delighted that Simon had a friend— none had ever been mentioned before—and that there was something he wanted that he, Hugh, could give him, and, above all, that perhaps the ice had been broken, that for several days he felt more light-hearted about his son. But after that burst of loquacity, Simon relapsed into politely fielding any shot that Hugh made of conversation between them.

With Wills he felt at sea in a different way. He simply never saw enough of him: a couple of evenings a week was not much, and although he did make attempts to play with him at weekends, Wills always gravitated towards the women—Ellen, of course, and Villy and Rachel, and Polly when she was there. He was terrified of the Brig, who had once pretended to be a lion, with disastrous consequences. He was nearly six now and rather spoilt and tyrannical. At Wills's age, and younger, it had always been Sybil who had coped with the children; he had come into his own when they were seven or eight, although he had always had a special relationship with Poll.

Villy had been a brick about Wills. It was she who was teaching him to read, who took him over on Ellen's days off, who cut his hair and bought or made his clothes. But when he thought of Villy, he came inevitably to Edward. He had always vaguely known that Edward strayed, as he put it to himself, but the extent and degree of his alliance with Diana Mackintosh had appalled him when he discovered it, which, of course, he did by degrees. He had nearly, he thought, persuaded Edward to give her up for Villy's sake, but Edward had reneged on that, and then the frightful blow of his having a child by her had come out. After that, he did not know what to say to his brother. He hated knowing about Diana because of his gratitude to and affection for Villy. He would never tell her what he knew, but knowing and not telling made him feel dishonest with her, which seemed a poor return for her kindness to his child. He felt she would be devastated if she knew and he did not trust Edward not to be so careless that his betrayal would be discovered. When he had tried to talk to Edward about it, they had reached a degree of tension that he knew would end in a pointless row: Edward's eyes became like blue marbles and in a voice that was chilly and trembling with anger he told Hugh to mind his own business. After he had tried once or twice to confront Edward, with more or less the same results, he gave up, but the unresolved situation silted up between them, damming any of the old easy intimacy that, nowadays, he missed more than ever. He even wondered sometimes whether he and Edward might not have come to some better agreement about the new wharf if they had been on generally better terms.

He was driving to the office; the day had hardly begun, and already he felt tired. "We're all tired, old boy," his friend Bobby Beecham had remarked at the club the previous night. "If Adolf sees fit to start another blitz on London, I think the situation could become really tricky. The average person has had about as much as they can take. Everything is either drab or terrible. It's all been going on too long. *We* need that Second Front every bit as much as the Russians do. Finish the blighters off while we've still got the strength, that's what I say." He had gone on to invite Hugh to visit the Bag o' Nails with him: "A bit of female company wouldn't do you any harm. Take your mind off things for a bit." But he hadn't gone. It wasn't that he had any moral obligation, he told himself, simply he didn't have the slightest desire to get into bed with a stranger, however attractive. He could all too easily imagine himself, unable to get it up, being drawn out by the girl to talk about himself. Even "my wife died" might open floodgates that it made him cringe to consider. Nothing would induce him to talk about Sybil to a total stranger.

"Darling, if what you are trying to say is that you want Thelma to come too, I *quite* understand."

"No, no, I didn't mean that." The thought horrified her. "I only meant that the timing is slightly awkward, because I'd promised to take her to Stratford for a few days and she'd arranged her leave to coincide with mine."

"The trouble is that I *can't* do the following week, because Ellen is having her holiday and I really shall be needed at home."

"I *do* understand. It's just a pity that you didn't tell me sooner." Then before Rachel could explain why she hadn't been able to do that, Sid added, "I'm sure that Thelma can make another plan about leave. I'll talk to her."

"Yes, do, but *do* bear in mind that I would perfectly understand if she can't, and then we could all three go, which might be the simplest thing in the end."

Oh, no, it wouldn't, Sid thought, when she had put the earpiece back. It certainly wouldn't. Thelma and Rachel had met but that had been nearly a year ago when the situation had been very different, when Thelma had been simply a protégée with every qualification for the post—young, penniless, friendless and reasonably talented. She had come from Coventry, was hoping to get into the Academy (violin, with the piano as her second instrument) but had had to give up the idea when her widowed mother had been killed in the big air raid on that city. The terraced house in which she lived had been reduced to rubble. It had been rented, and the small pension on which her mother had both lived and helped her daughter had died with her. Her eyesight had precluded her being called up, and dull domestic jobs had been the only available alternative. Shortly after Sid met her there had been a concert got up by the Station for a local charity, and Sid had asked Thelma if she would like to accompany her on the piano. It then transpired that Thelma did not have access to an instrument and Sid offered her a key to the house so that she could practise. To begin with Thelma had been scrupulous about going there when Sid was on duty, and she had been scrupulous in other ways. The first time that Sid came home it was to find the sitting room tidy, last night's supper tray removed, everything dusted; even the grimy glass of the french window looking on to the back garden had been cleaned, and (and this had touched her most of all) a bunch of rather mildewed Michaelmas daisies picked from the back garden had been put in a vase on the mantelpiece. When she had seen Thelma next day in the canteen and thanked her, Thelma had said, "Oh! Afterwards I was afraid you'd mind—think it was a bit cheeky of me," and started to blush. "I didn't know how to thank you," is what she managed to say at last. By the time they were rehearsing for the concert it had become a ritual for Thelma to provide all kinds of little domestic attentions: she had cleaned the old gas cooker so that the burners ignited properly; she had wrested a quantity of hair out of the carpet sweeper so that it now consented to clean the carpets; she had procured a washer for the hot tap in the bathroom so that it ceased to drip and she said she loved ironing. It was pleasant, Sid found, to have things done for you by someone who professed not only that they *liked* the work, but also intense gratitude for being allowed to do it. "It's so lovely to be in a proper *home*," she kept saying. And "I've never *touched* a piano half as good as this one."

When Rachel came to stay, which was not very often, the girl cleaned the spare room and seemed perfectly to understand that Sid would want the house to herself while her friend was with her. Rachel always asked after her and had thoroughly approved of Sid giving her lessons and befriending her. Then one day, after she had exclaimed about how wonderfully clean the kitchen had become (they were sitting down there finishing a bowl of delicious vegetable soup made by Thelma), she said: "And what do you pay her for all this work?"

"I don't."

"Not anything?"

"Well, she gets a free lesson a week and she has a key to the house so that she can come and practise whenever she likes."

There was a brief silence. Rachel was taking one of her Passing Clouds out of the pretty enamelled cigarette case that Edward had given her. She handed the case to Sid and then leaned across the table towards her for Sid's lighter, and Sid could smell the faint scent of violets that Rachel only used on special occasions.

"Do you think I should?"

"Well—I suppose it would be rather nice for her to earn a little extra. You told me she was pretty hard up."

"You're perfectly right, of course. I should have thought of it. The whole thing has just sort of slowly come about and I didn't think. Darling! What should I do without you?"

And Rachel had smiled and said, "You don't have to."

"I do. Most of the time, indeed I do." It had slipped out more bitterly than she intended; indeed she had not meant to say it at all.

"I think of you every day," Rachel said in her apparently casual but slightly unsteady voice that denoted deep feeling, and Sid experienced the joy—like sunlight flooding her heart—that these declarations, which did not even occur every time they met, invariably produced.

But then, the following week when she pressed a pound and a ten shilling note into Thelma's hand the result was not at all what she had expected.

"What's this for?"

Sid explained that it was for all the work she did.

"I don't want it!"

Sid explained that she couldn't let her go on doing all the housework for nothing.

"I thought I was your friend! How *could* you!" She looked at Sid with a kind of wounded consternation. "I thought you—*liked* me!"

Sid started to say that of course she liked her, but that that had nothing to do with it.

"It has for me." She put the notes on the kitchen table. "I don't want to be treated as a servant!"

Sid put her arm round her, and she burst into tears. "You've made all the difference to my life, and I can't give you things and I'd do *anything* for you, I'd have thought you'd have known that and being such a marvellous musician naturally you don't think about house things so I thought at least—"

Sid said how sorry she was, and she *was*. She invited Thelma to supper and said they would go out, but in the end they didn't, because she took Thelma upstairs and gave her some gin and for the first time asked her about her life, and by the time Thelma had finished telling her it was late and they had finished the gin. In the end they had dried egg omelettes in the kitchen, some cider and finally cups of tea by which time it was so late that Sid suggested Thelma stay the night. She lent her a pair of pyjamas and put her, now happy again and slightly tipsy, into the spare room. That night she reflected upon the poor girl's unhappy situation: she had clearly not at all recovered from her mother's death which had so suddenly swept away everything that she knew and had; her loneliness: she did not seem to have made a single friend in London; and finally Thelma's striking devotion to herself. This last, although she attempted to dismiss it as a schoolgirl crush with more than a little sentiment involved, still touched her. To be looked up to and admired—particularly as a musician—was a kind of balm that assuaged some of the pain and loneliness she suffered as a result of her love for Rachel that was never to be consummated. Her protective instincts were also aroused, and Rachel was seldom there to be protected: this girl responded gratefully to any care or affection. Her youth, too, was appealing: although she was not—as Sid put it to herself—conventionally pretty, there was something rather fetching about her hot brown eyes with the large dark pupils that peered at one with such intensity. She wore spectacles for sight-reading music, and Sid suspected that she could not see very much at any other time without them. She wore her straight dark brown hair parted in the middle and was always pushing strands of it back from her face. She was pale except when she blushed, which she did frequently and every time as though it was a new and embarrassing experience. She was small and thin with a high clear voice that if one did not see her—the telephone came to mind—could have been mistaken for a child's.

And there was nothing the girl would not do for her! As the weeks went by, the house, which she knew had been becoming quite squalid from neglect, was transformed. Curtains were taken down and washed or sent to the cleaners. Furniture was polished, paint was washed, kitchen cupboards were turned out, rugs were beaten in the back garden, even her clothes and the battered sheet music were carefully mended, and meals, which when she was alone had become minimal, a sandwich or opening a tin, had become civilized. Three evenings a week Thelma now cooked and stayed for supper after which they played violin and piano sonatas together and quite often Thelma stayed the night. She had early recognized that Thelma did not have the makings of a concert pianist, but she was turning into an excellent accompanist and continued to make steady, though unremarkable progress with the violin. With work at the ambulance station less pressing, Sid had returned to teaching two days a week in a large boarding school for girls in Surrey. This entailed being away for the night and it became routine for Thelma to stay in the house while she was away.

Then, it had been last September, she and Rachel had a long-planned three days' holiday on Exmoor and, on the Thursday before she was due to join Sid in London, Rachel had telephoned to say that the Brig had bronchitis and that she could not leave him. "The doctor says it could easily turn into pneumonia if he doesn't stay in bed and do exactly what he is told, and I'm afraid I am the only person who can make him."

The shock, the disappointment at not having this break with Rachel that she had looked forward to for weeks was so great that for a moment she was speechless—unable to reply.

"Darling, are you still there?"

"It's only three *days!* Surely there are enough people in the house to look after him for *three days?*"

"You couldn't be more disappointed than I am."

But even knowing that this was sincere, that Rachel would indeed be disappointed, did not then mollify her as so often she had managed to make it do in the past. She had wanted to rage and shout: "Oh, yes, I could! I can! You don't know how disappointed I am—you simply do not *know!*" What she said was, "But we've booked the rooms and everything."

"Well, I must pay for that, of course."

There was a pause, and then she heard herself say, "Don't bother."

"Darling! I can hear you're angry, and I *am* so sorry. It just can't be helped."

When she had put the earpiece back, she found she was crying. It seemed like the worst disappointment of her life. She found herself trying to equal it because it triggered off memories of when she had felt something of the sort: when Evie had taken her beloved rag doll and stuffed it into the kitchen range; when her mother had told her that, after all, there was not enough money for her to have the violin lessons she had been promised; when she had failed to get her first job teaching that had seemed certain; when she had saved and saved the money for a ticket to hear Hubermann and got mumps and Evie had gone instead . . . none of these things seemed to compare at all with what she felt now. She would never be first with Rachel. She would never be able to have her to herself. Even these pathetic, rationed little oases that she trudged towards for weeks could be turned, by Rachel, into mirages . . .

The telephone rang. "Darling! I've been talking to the Duchy. She says why don't you come down *here* for the three days?"

This offer seemed to illuminate, as nothing else had ever done, the hopeless gap between them: the years of longing and despair and keeping things comfortable for Rachel collected themselves into one implacable mass in her gorge; she felt sick.

"I think I'll go anyway, I really need the fresh air and exercise. Do thank the Duchy for her kind offer." She felt sick with *anger*. "I might take Thelma with me," she added.

"Oh, that's a good idea! It would be nicer for you to have company. I hope you have a lovely restful time, darling. Do ring as soon as you're back."

So she had taken Thelma. She had gone on with the holiday chiefly to show Rachel that she wasn't prepared to have her life disarranged all the time by Rachel's parents and her conception of her duty towards them. And yet once, she thought now, I would have been so grateful for the Duchy's invitation, I would have crept down there thankful for even a few minutes of Rachel's company when she could be spared. And once, I should not have dreamed of going on with a plan that had been made for her and me by myself. Once, I should have been desperately sad, but I shouldn't have been angry. And I certainly would not have considered for a moment taking a girl more than twenty years younger than myself on a holiday. Especially knowing that she was in love with me. For it was on the holiday that Thelma declared her love in such a way that Sid could no longer pretend to herself that it did not exist. She had been writing it off as what the girls at the school called a "pash," or as gratitude for help and support from one for whom these things had been in palpably short supply. But, sitting in the heather on that balmy September day, the step was taken. She had been starved for so long that it seemed miraculous to be wanted so much by someone so young, whose innocence was only matched by her passion.

For those three days it all seemed very simple: they were given sandwiches by the guest house, where they were the only occupants, and armed with a map they walked all the morning, found some private spot where they were concealed by rocks and heather from any footpath and when they had eaten, lay together on the springy turf. They were never disturbed. In the evenings after a substantial early supper—the guest house owners also had a farm and there were delicacies, eggs and chickens and home-cured bacon and blackberry pies—they would play bezique and Sid taught Thelma chess, at which she was unexpectedly good. They retired early, and Sid would lie in bed waiting for Thelma who would slip into the room in her dressing gown underneath which she wore nothing. For those three days it was easy for her to take everything that was offered so eagerly, to give Thelma all the attention she craved and to enjoy this wonderfully young, smooth white body abandoned to her. It was balm, too, to be told how much she was loved, to be with someone who thought that everything she said and did had so much merit. "I just adore you," Thelma would whisper as she lay in Sid's arms. "I'm so happy—just to *be* alone with you is perfect." It was easy at the beginning to confuse desire with love. To begin with, she did not even recognize this, felt simply happy that all her bitterness about Rachel had somehow melted, that she could see her as pitifully trapped by the duties expected of an unmarried daughter by parents who clung to Victorian ethics. She knew that Rachel must have been desperately disappointed, that she, too, looked forward to the rare breaks that circumstances would occasionally allow her to have with the person "she would rather be with than anyone in the world." "You couldn't be more disappointed than I am," Sid now remembered. This was on the last morning of the holiday with Thelma: they were to catch the afternoon train and Thelma wanted to repeat the walk they had done together on the first morning. Sid pointed out that there could not be time: it had taken them nearly three hours to get there, and they had no chance of getting back to catch the two thirty-eight train. Thelma had interpreted this as Sid not wanting to *go* to the place. There had been a small, fruitless argument that did not resolve anything. "Why do you want to go back *there* so particularly?" Sid had asked.

Thelma, who had been staring out of the window, suddenly turned from it. "Because—that was where I found out that *you* loved *me!*" she said. "Where you said you loved me." She began to blush, but the intense myopic eyes were fixed on Sid's face.

Sid opened her mouth to say she had never said that she loved her—and didn't, couldn't say anything. It was true, but it would be bitterly unkind to say so. That was the first jolt of reality.

"I'm truly sorry that there isn't time to go there," was what she did say.

In the train going back, with Thelma asleep opposite her in an otherwise empty carriage, she began to experience the first stirrings of anxiety—and guilt. She did *not* love Thelma: it was Rachel that she loved. She had been appallingly irresponsible towards someone far younger and vulnerable. The relationship could not possibly continue in this way. Somehow she must explain to the girl that she had succumbed to a madness that was wrong for both of them. They could continue as friends, go back to the situation that obtained before the holiday, but there could be no more going to bed. In the train, with Thelma asleep, this had seemed a perfectly possible solution. She had been unfaithful to Rachel, and that she would have to live with: she would, of course, continue to look after Thelma, teach her, play with her, take her to concerts, but she would not allow her to entertain any further thoughts of an affair between them . . .

Now, a year later, and struggling with the dilemma of either missing a few days with Rachel, or letting Thelma down, she wondered how on earth she could have been so naïve. Plans that involved other people were far from simple; they only seemed to be so when one was by oneself making them, but the moment the other protagonists appeared on the scene the simplest intentions became corrupted by conflict. She had not at all succeeded in regulating her relationship with Thelma, although she had certainly tried. But Thelma displayed a kind of rubbery resistance to accepting anything that she said or, rather, she fell in with any arrangement that Sid made and then seemed to turn it to her own account. Thus when Sid said her piece about ending the affair, beginning with the not entirely honest reason that going on with it would be bad for Thelma, the girl accepted the situation with a burst of tears, but then later came back to Sid saying that she did not care what became of her provided that they could continue together. When Sid, in great trepidation, attempted to explain that she did not really love her and could not live with the inequality of their affections, Thelma, with another burst of tears, agreed that this would be wrong. But then she returned with what she described as her second thoughts (her *deadly* second thoughts!), and said that (a) she did not mind whether Sid loved her as much as she loved Sid, and (b) that she thought Sid must love her more than she, Sid, realized to care so much about her feelings. She would do exactly whatever Sid wanted, she repeatedly said, as the situation continued with an uneasy compromise, or rather to be more or less what Thelma wanted, Sid now thought. She came and stayed for one night a week, when sometimes they went to bed. She continued to clean the house, to minister to every domestic need, to practise, to be given lessons and to play sonatas with Sid. Once, Sid had tried to get rid of her, had said that the whole thing should come completely to an end. That had been when Thelma had asked if she loved anyone else, "your friend Rachel Cazalet, for instance?" and Sid had lied. She had an instinct that to tell Thelma anything about that would be very dangerous indeed, but the lie further weakened her position. She kept them apart, although she sensed that Thelma's curiosity about Rachel was intense. This meant that Rachel coming to stay was a hazard: she could not absolutely rely upon Thelma keeping out of the way any more since she had turned up once when Rachel was there and, by the greatest good fortune, Sid had seen her coming in at the front garden gate. It was morning, and Rachel was having a bath. She had sped downstairs and met Thelma at the front door.

"I wouldn't have come since you told me not to, but I left my purse with all my money in it on the kitchen shelf. I'll just pop down and get it." Then, sensing Sid's displeasure, she added, "I honestly wouldn't have bothered you, only I simply can't manage for a whole three days without any money at all."

After she had gone, it crossed Sid's mind that Thelma had left her purse behind on purpose—an ignoble thought, but not unlikely.

No—there had not been, and still seemed not to be, any easy solution. The situation, rather, seemed to have developed a life of its own, and the only way in which she could put a stop to its insinuation would be to tell Thelma simply to go away and never come back. What stopped her from doing this? Because every time the thought of it crossed her mind all kinds of objections rushed in upon her, and while she might have been able to deal with one of them, together they made an insuperable barrier. That it was her fault the whole thing had started in the first place was one: she had only to have stood out against Thelma's attractions, have kept her faith with Rachel, for the whole thing to have been far more manageable; a pupil with a crush, something she had dealt with successfully before. Then she could not help putting herself in Thelma's place. She understood what it felt like to be single-mindedly in love: she knew, better than most, the agonizing frustration of it being unrequited. On top of that, she knew that in some awful way her vanity was engaged: it was both a consolation and a reassurance to be so cared for and wanted. Years with her sister Evie had effectively driven away any people who might have become friends; before Thelma's appearance, she had been used to a life that was essentially solitary except for her work; now she had become softened up—the thought of coming back to a house that was empty night after night, of losing the inestimable pleasure of making music with somebody with whom one could talk about anything from Schumann to the minutiae of daily life was bleak . . . It was a new and seductive experience to be cared for in the way that Thelma took care to care.

None the less, she thought now, she would be ruthless: she would *not* take Thelma to Stratford; she would go with Rachel, and she would simply say that Rachel needed a break. She would be firm about it: she would not change her mind when Thelma, as she knew would happen, erupted in tears. If she allowed Thelma to interfere with her precious time with Rachel, there would only be one course open to her: Thelma would have to go. The prospect of even this much truth in what she uncomfortably knew to be essentially a dishonest situation was both anxious and heartening. She decided to ring Rachel and tell her that she had fixed it with Thelma, and then deal with the latter that evening, and immediately thought, Oh God—that's another lie. I *won't* have fixed it with Thelma. Deceit, she thought, was becoming second nature to her.

Archie arrived, as he had been asked, at half past seven, which was pretty good considering how chancy Sunday buses could be. The walk from the 53 bus stop in Abbey Road had tired him—his leg had long since ceased to get any better. He negotiated the rickety wooden gate and limped up the path that was edged with ancient iris plant. The front door was the kind that had glass to the waist and, although it was frosted and therefore nothing inside was visible, the house was full of sound. A piano being played—extremely well, probably a gramophone record, he thought—a baby crying, the sound of bath water running out down the large iron stack pipe beside the front door, voices, somebody laughing—there was so much sound that he wasn't sure whether the bell he had pressed had rung. There was a knocker, so he used it.

"Archie! Oh, good!" It was Clary. "You *are* punctual," she added, as though he shouldn't have been. She gave him her usual perfunctory hug.

"Who is playing the piano?"

"Peter Rose. Louise's friend Stella's brother."

At the far end of the hall, Louise was sitting on the stairs. She wore a rather fetching housecoat of some striped material. Her hair streamed down her back and her feet were bare. She greeted him by blowing a kiss.

"You look like the heroine in an opera," he said.

"I'm sitting here to listen to Peter," she explained. "If we go in, he'll stop."

A girl appeared at the head of the basement stairs. "Where's the tin opener?"

"Haven't the faintest idea."

"Oh!" Clary said. "*I* used it to prop open the lavatory window."

"What, this one?" The girl indicated the door opposite her.

"No, upstairs. And Poll's having a bath."

"Well, you can interrupt her, Clary. You'll have to if you want any dinner."

Louise said, "Is Piers helping you?"

"Well, he's *with* me. Not exactly helping. I think he's the last person I'd have on a desert island."

"You're wrong. I'm wonderful at conversation, and you'd be surprised how quickly you'd feel short of *that*." He had loomed up behind Stella on the stairs.

"This is Archie," Clary said. "Piers. And Stella."

Piers gave him a tired smile. "I warn you there's nothing to eat in this house except cork mats," he said.

Clary had stumped upstairs in search of the tin opener. Archie looked round for a chair. His leg ached. Louise patted the stairs beside her. "Come and sit here, Archie."

"No. I'd never get up from there. I'd become a fixture. When you sold the house I'd go with it."

"Your baby is crying," Piers remarked, leaning over the banisters and stroking Louise's hair.

"He's teething, Mary says. But I'd better go and see what she is doing with him."

"Maternal love. Isn't it amazing? If I had to choose what was my bottom thing in this house I'd find it quite difficult to decide between Sebastian and that frightful soapstone of monkeys."

"It belonged to Louise's grandmother," Stella said.

Archie had found a chair with about six coats on it. He put them on the floor and sat down. The piano had stopped.

Clary reappeared with the tin opener and gave it to Stella, who said, "Is there really only one tin of corned beef?"

"I think so, because we used the other one for sandwiches for Hampstead Heath. We had a picnic yesterday," she said to Archie, "and we went to the Vale of Health. It's like a dear little village you suddenly come upon. Piers knows a painter who lives there, but he was out."

"It was lovely all the same," Piers said. "We sang the whole way. Sort of Handel recitative making extremely personal remarks about other walkers."

"We sang some jolly choruses as well. Nobody realized it was about them, though," Clary said.

"Did you want them to?" Archie asked.

"Well, it would have been fun if they'd looked a bit amazed, shocked, you know."

Louise reappeared with her baby on her shoulder. "Mary wants to eat her supper, so said I'd have him for a while."

"Let's go and sit in the *sitting* room," Piers said. "Stairs are not conversational for more than two."

"Who's going to finish cooking supper?" Clary demanded. "It really ought to be you, Louise, you're far the best at it."

"I'm no better than Stella—we learned just the same things. And, anyway, I've got Sebastian. I peeled all the potatoes."

"All right," Stella said. "Clary and I will do the rest. Just remind me of what we're aiming at."

"You fry the onions, mash the potatoes, and then you mash in the corned beef."

"Will one tin do for seven of us? It seems a bit mean."

"I brought a tin of peaches," Piers said. "All the way from sunny Bletchley."

"I daresay you did. But they won't be any good in a corned beef hash. They'll have to be pudding."

"Polly's made her Carnation Milk pudding."

"God! That sounds revolting."

"It isn't at all. It's a kind of whip. You'd never know it was tinned milk."

The sitting room was empty except for a young man sitting at the piano. He got to his feet as they came in, and Archie saw that he was wearing an RAF uniform.

"Leading Aircraftsman Rose," Louise said. "This is Archie Lestrange, and you know Piers, of course."

The baby, who had been staring at Archie in an intense impassive manner that he was beginning to find disconcerting, suddenly convulsed himself and began to cry.

"Give him to me," Peter said, and held out his arms; his rather heavy and haggard face was transformed by a tender smile. He carried the baby back to the piano, wedged him between his arms and began to play "Baa Baa Black Sheep." Sebastian stopped crying.

"Do play the variations, Peter," Louise called from the other end of the room.

Archie sat down on the hard little sofa and wondered whether he was going to be offered a drink. Clary had retreated to the kitchen with Stella, and Piers was leading Louise out of the french windows and down the steps into the garden.

Then Polly appeared, her coppery hair newly washed and shining. She wore her dark pleated skirt and over it a loose jersey of gentian blue that made her eyes look the same colour. "Sorry to be so long. I had to wait until Sebastian had had his bath and then the water wasn't hot for a bit. Nobody has given you a drink; I'll go and see what there is and tell you."

She went through double doors that led to the dining room. "There's a bit of gin, but there doesn't seem to be anything to put in it."

"Water would be fine."

She came back with a tooth glass and the gin bottle. "You help yourself and I'll get some water." When she had done that, she sat neatly on the floor a few yards away from him.

"Am I the only person having a drink?"

"Tonight you are. We don't awfully mind about it and the bottle got used up two nights ago when Louise had a party. We only get one bottle a month from the shop, you see." She gave him one of her quick little social smiles and then stared at her hands that were clasped round her knees.

"How's the art school?" he asked.

"Oh! The art school. Fine. Very interesting. The most surprising people seem prepared to be models. For life classes. I'm no good at drawing, of course."

"It's a bit early to know that, isn't it?"

"It may be," she answered politely.

The music had stopped as the baby had begun to cry again. Peter got up from the piano and walked about with him in his arms. "He doesn't really care for Mozart," he said, "he prefers the theme."

"He's teething," Louise said as she came up the steps from the garden. Piers was holding her hand. "I'll take him up to Mary."

It was a long time before they had their supper, which was eaten in the basement in the kitchen, and by the time they had had it Peter said he had got to start getting back to Uxbridge, and Archie, who had decided upon a cab for going back to his flat, offered to give him a lift to his station. He'd been on forty-eight hours' leave, he said, and Louise always let him stay whenever he wanted, but he only went when Stella got time off as his parents liked him to go home. "We don't tell them about these times," he said, "but you don't know them, do you, so it's all right. They'd kick up no end if they knew."

"I wouldn't tell them, anyway."

His white, rather haggard face softened, as it had when he had been dealing with Sebastian. "I'm sorry, I didn't mean you would," he said. "It's just that it would be awful if they knew." He had dark marks under his eyes, like bruises, and his uniform looked like fancy dress.

"Louise is wonderful," he said after a silence. "She's made the place so friendly and easy. And she lets me practise as much as I like when I go there."

"You're in the RAF orchestra, aren't you?"

"I know it sounds marvellously lucky, but it has its drawbacks. They don't think you need to practise at all, you see. I'm always travelling about, arriving somewhere and playing something I haven't worked up with practically no rehearsal on a usually quite awful piano that I won't have had a chance to touch before the concert.

"I suppose in a war one really has to choose between being frightened or being bored."

"Which are you?" said Archie.

"Well, after a spell of being frightened, I've been relegated to being bored."

After he had dropped Peter at Uxbridge, he thought about these alternatives: his job, certainly, was largely boredom. The hours and days and weeks he must by now have spent at staff meetings, in reading hundreds of Action Reports, and the endless flow of memos that were dumped in his in-tray every few minutes of every day in his office. He was really a kind of glorified clerk—condensing information for his superiors, making innumerable very small decisions about the selection of material that needed referral to the right department, sometimes trying to persuade people with bees in their bonnets to take them out. Since the window in his office had been blown out, they had made it very much smaller but it had also ceased to open—he felt he had been breathing the same air now for years. Still, he was lucky really—to be alive, to have something to do that was presumably useful in some sort. He did not have the kind of anxiety that Louise must live with: that her husband might be killed. He had not had to spend his extreme youth as the other girls were doing: Polly had a typing job in the Ministry of Information, and Clary, most surprisingly, was being a secretary for a very young bishop; "He hasn't asked me whether I believe in God, so I just don't say anything on the subject," she told him. But clearly, in that house, they were having some fun. They had a much played gramophone and the piano and they went to the cinema and on expeditions like the one to Hampstead Heath. In spite of funny food—and there hadn't been much of it—and no drink, they had a lot of silly jokes, and Louise gave parties. "Who comes to them?" he had asked. "Oh, we pick people up in the underground sometimes and Michael's friends from the Navy come when they are on leave and *they* bring friends—lots of people," Clary had replied airily. They had had a cook to begin with, a Mrs. Weatherby found by Villy in Sussex, but she had not been able to cope with the hours they kept, or the untidiness and noise, and had soon left. "It's much more fun without her and, anyway, we needed her bed for people who come to stay." On the whole, he thought, it was a good thing that the girls had gone to live with Louise, partly because it was time they had more independence, and partly because he had begun to sense that they were not any longer so close to one another as they had been. This had come up before: it no longer seemed to be the thing to invite both of them together for supper or a film. Clary had been quite open about it. "I'd much rather go out with just *you*," she had said. "Anyway, Poll has dozens of people in love with her—she could go out every night if she wanted to. Another drawback of working for the Bish. He's married and I can't see him taking me to anything except a Church fête."

"Are you jealous of Polly?" he had asked her one evening.

"Me? Jealous? Good Lord, no. I couldn't stand the sort of dreary people she has mooning after her. Frightfully old men in suits—far older than you," she added hastily, "who work in the same building as she does, and quite a lot of Louise's husband's friends—they all fall for her. It's her appearance—people stare at her in the Underground, and once, at the Arts Theatre when we went out with Louise and Michael when he was on leave, a man actually sent a note to our table to her. He can't have known at *all* what she is like, can he? Just across a room. Any more," she said after thinking about it, "than people could tell what *I* was like across a room. Or you, Archie." She had looked at him challengingly when she said this, but he decided not to disagree. But after that he took to inviting them separately, although he noticed that whenever he went down to Home Place for the weekend they both came too. On these occasions, Clary became rather noisily proprietary, and Polly withdrew. However, there was so much else going on there that neither of the girls could monopolize him. He had become one of the family, and was treated to all the small complaining confidences that might be expected from that. Villy did not approve of the frequency with which Zoë went to London—to see an old school friend who had just moved back there; it was hard on Ellen, she said, who was getting on and finding Wills a handful. Poor Rachel was pulled this way and that between the demands of her old aunt Dolly and the Brig, the one with no memory and the other with no sight, neither of them able to understand why she could not spend all of every day with them to the exclusion of the other. Lydia complained at not being sent to a proper school like Neville, of being treated like a child: "I am thirteen, after all, and they don't seem to realize that when they send me off to bed I've got nobody to go with. My foul cousin Judy who goes to a proper school is learning dancing and art and things and she goes on and on about team spirit and I don't even know what it *is!* You might point some of this out to them, Archie, because they listen to you. I don't want to go to the same school as *Judy* but any other old school would do."

Once, when he had finished playing a rather acrimonious game of Pelman patience with all of the girls, Lydia had suddenly asked: "After the war, Archie, will you be going back to your house in France to live?"

"I don't know. I expect I might."

"Because if you are, I thought of coming with you. Only I'd quite like to know if you are, because I won't bother with French if you aren't. So far, it is being a fearfully dull language where I can only say the sort of thing people put on postcards."

The other two came down on her like a load of bricks.

"Really, Lydia, you are the limit! You can't just propose yourself like that!" Clary said.

"He might not want anybody, but he certainly wouldn't want a *child!*" Polly said.

"And if he did, it would be up to him to say, not you," Clary said.

"And, anyway, he might not be going back to France at all," Polly said.

"He certainly wouldn't want someone as much younger than he is as you, anyway," Clary said.

"Shut up snubbing me! How old *are* you, Archie? We know you so well, I think I ought to know that."

"I shall be thirty-nine this year."

"That makes you twenty-six years younger, so you can see it is out of the question."

"What is? I wasn't considering *marrying* him! I just want to be an adventuress—like in *Bulldog Drummond.* I'd just live with him and he'd buy me frocks and strange exotic perfumes and I'd arrange parties."

"Oh, do stop talking about me as though I wasn't here!" Archie said with an exaggerated dismay that he hoped would lighten the situation. It didn't.

"He wouldn't want anyone so naturally rude and tactless," Clary retorted. "But if you do want someone, you know, to talk to in the evenings, I could always come and stay with you."

There was a pause. "And what about you, Poll?"

"I don't know." She shrugged her thin shoulders. "I really haven't the faintest idea. The war's not even over. I think it's silly to talk about—anything—till it is."

"Mr. Churchill said the hour of greatest effort is approaching," Clary said. "It might be nearly over."

"Only in Europe," Polly said. "There's still the Japanese."

Her face had become so pale, that Archie knew she had been blushing. She saw him, and began picking up the cards from the floor.

Then Clary put an arm round her and said, "It's all right, Poll. The Japanese will never invade *here*."

But Polly merely answered in a thin unfriendly voice, "I know *that*. Of course I know *that*." And Archie saw how Clary felt rebuffed, and suddenly wanted to put his arms round her.

That night when he lay in bed waiting for sleep, the house in France came vividly back to him. He had left one morning in such a hurry (he'd been offered a lift north in a lorry by a friend of the café owner who was taking a load of peaches to Paris, and some instinct had warned him to take the chance when it was offered), but it had left him no time to do anything but pack one bag of clothes; he'd even left his bed unmade, pots and pans in the sink and paintbrushes uncleaned—they might still be stuck, stiff and useless in the jam-jar with the turps long gone . . . He'd taken one final look at the kitchen, with its deeply recessed windows that looked out onto olives and apricot orchards and down onto the vine-covered veranda of the café below. The geraniums and basil that he had left on the window sill would have died quickly from lack of water. He had even left the book he had been reading—a huge American novel, what had it been called? *Anthony Adverse*—or, rather, that he had been struggling through, open on the pearwood table into which some long past wicked—child, probably, had cut initials. He'd walked through the wider door he'd made, which connected the kitchen with the larger room where he worked. It faced north over the valley, bathed at that moment in hot golden light. It wasn't really a house: he had two small bedrooms and a shower he had installed on the floor above, and then a steep staircase that led to the door that opened out onto the village street. But this separate entrance had made it seem like a house, and he liked the sounds and smells from the café where he often ate. It made him feel less solitary and, after ten years or so, he had become accepted as a reasonable foreigner. He'd left his key in the café, and perhaps the old woman who cleaned his place would have taken the plants although she would not have touched his brushes. It was odd. He missed the place—realized that he had a great longing for it, but at the same time so far as being solitary was concerned, he felt softened up. It would be an ordeal, of a different kind from what it had originally been when he first went there. Then, he had gone to try to forget Rachel; it had only been she whom he had wanted; if he could not have her, then he was able to endure without anyone. Now he would be going back with nothing to renounce, but he would be leaving this family who had taken him in and who had become a part of his life. This summer—the invasion was certain—it would be the beginning of the end of the war. And with France liberated, Rupert's fate would be certain. It was still possible, though very unlikely, that he was alive, but if he was not, then he would have to see to Clary. He might take her to France with him to help her through her loss, as years ago he had helped Rupert when Clary's mother had died. There was a kind of symmetry to that. It was the least he could do for Rupert, he thought defensively; he found himself smiling in the dark.

Clary

May–June, 1944

This is a weekend, and I'm not going home because I've just become an air-raid warden and I have to go to lectures which they tend to have at weekends so that people who are working can go to them. We haven't had any bombs lately, but everybody seems to think that we will—especially when the invasion starts which might be any day now. Louise has gone away to Hatton as Michael has leave and he doesn't much like spending it in London. She has taken the baby and Mary with her, but Mary is leaving soon to get married. We all earnestly hope that Louise will get another nanny because when Mary had a holiday the house got into a frightful mess and she never stopped washing nappies and sterilizing bottles and Sebastian cried an awful lot. He was cutting teeth and his face had sort of tomato-coloured blotches. Otherwise he looks rather like Mr. Churchill who is reputed to have said that all babies look like him, so you can see that my simile was not original. Anyway, this is Saturday morning, and the house is very quiet because Polly is still asleep. She has taken to sleeping later and later at weekends. So I'm sitting on the steps that go down to the back garden drinking rather cold brown tea and writing my journal to you. The trouble is, Dad, that by the time you get back there will be so much of it, it will take you years to read and you'll probably get bored which I wouldn't blame you for although it would hurt my feelings. I haven't told you about my job—my first job. It is a bit of an anti-climax actually: I work for a bishop called Peter. He's supposed to be young for a bishop, but that isn't awfully young. He has a rather bunnish wife—I suppose I mean dumpy (but she also has a bun) and she is always smiling but without much enjoyment. They live in a large dark house filled with bits of furniture that they don't seem to use, and the whole place smells of very old meals and clothes. People are always coming and Mrs. Bish makes tea for them, sometimes with biscuits, often not. Then the trays get left on tables until I clear them up, because she's run out of teapots. The garden is full of thistles and loosestrife and very ragged evergreens. They don't have time for the garden, they say. I work at one end of the dining-room table—well, it's where I do the letter typing, but I take down the letters in the Bish's study. I sit on a hard armchair that looks as though it is upholstered in *moss* and he wanders about the room making rather awful jokes that I keep putting into the letters by mistake. His favourite jokes are Spoonerisms, you know, like "Excuse me, Captain, your slip is showing" or "Hush my brat."

They have two children called Leonard and Veronica, but I haven't met them as they are always away. Anyway, I go in the morning to be there at half past nine and usually I go out to lunch at a local café and have chips and a fried egg or rather awful sausages that taste as though they are made from some animal that died in the zoo and then I go back and work until five and then I bicycle home. I have to answer the telephone as well, but that is in the hall, nowhere near my typewriter. Still, it is a job and I get two pounds a week. Everybody the Bish knows is described by him as a saint or splendid or a bit mad but enormously interesting, but when they come to the house they don't seem to be any of these things. So I am not learning much about human nature which is a pity.

This house is odd, largely I think because it doesn't feel as though it belongs to anybody. It still had quite a lot of Lady Rydal's furniture and things in it, and then Louise has added her wedding presents, and then we—Polly and I—have brought a few of our things. At weekends, when people come to stay, they have to sleep in beds in the dining room, because there are only five bedrooms and Louise and the baby and Nanny take up two of them. Poll and I have a little attic room each on the top floor.

Marriage doesn't seem to have changed Louise much. But in a

way, of course, she doesn't lead a very married life, with Michael nearly always away. Quite a lot of people who come are a bit in love with her and I think she enjoys that.

Poll worries me rather. She has become quite difficult to talk to. I know she finds her job awfully dull, but I don't think that is the whole problem. She feel guilty about having left Uncle Hugh alone in his house, but *that* isn't the whole thing either. I suspect her of being in love, but she gets furious if one approaches the subject, which I have done six or seven times with enormous tact. She goes to an art school two evenings a week, and I think it may be someone she has met there. Her not telling me probably means he is married and the whole thing is doomed. But she always *used* to discuss everything, and not doing so is making her much crosser than it makes me—the front door bell's rung, one of Louise's devoted admirers I expect, but I'll have to go and answer it.

This is *days* later because it *wasn't* one of Louise's men, it was Neville! He was wearing his school uniform (I told you, Dad, he'd left his prep school because he got too old and they sent him to Tonbridge). I knew he absolutely loathed it there, so although he said he'd come to breakfast, I knew he'd run away. He had a small suitcase with him which I knew wasn't his but I thought the best thing was to give him breakfast (he's got rather scraggy and always looks as though he's starving, even after a meal these days) so I didn't make any remark about the suitcase. He followed me down to the kitchen and I made him toast and he had marge and Bovril on that and then he ate the remains of the macaroni cheese Poll and I had had for supper the night before and some stewed apple and then he noticed a tin of pilchards that I didn't even know we had and wanted that. All the time he ate, he talked about Laurel and Hardy and the Marx Brothers' films. But eventually, even he had run out of things to say about them and he just sat drinking tea. Then he said, "Did you know, one can't get to Ireland any more? There's a ban. Idiotic. I didn't know till I got to London." I remembered that once before, when he'd run away, he'd said he was going to live in Ireland, so now I was sure he'd done it again. I told him he'd run away, and he said, yes.

"I really do definitely, absolutely inevitably loathe it," he said. "It's quite idiotic to go on being somewhere you hate so much." Then he looked at me in a surprisingly charming way and said,

"You've been miserable in your life, so I thought you'd understand. That's why I came here."

But if you'd been able to get to Ireland, I thought, you would have just gone. He was turning on the charm, and actually, Dad, in an awful way, he *can* be frightfully charming. I said: "Supposing I just hadn't been here. What would you have done then?"

"Waited," he said. "I've got some gobstoppers in my case, and some oats that a boy feeds his secret rat with at school. I took some of them."

"Of course you haven't told them at home."

"Of course not. They'd only try to send me back. I came here because I assumed you'd be different. Or have you," his eyes narrowed, but his voice was bland, "have you become one of Them?"

It was a jolly difficult question to answer, I found. Because I couldn't see what he could do if he *didn't* go back. On the other hand it did seem quite wrong to betray him. In the end I said I didn't know but I did promise not to do anything behind his back. "I shall keep my back permanently turned, then," he said, but he looked relieved, and it was then I realized that his usual expression these days is wary—a bit as though he is being hunted.

Then I thought of Archie. *He* would know what to do. To begin with, Neville didn't want me to ring him but when I guaranteed that Archie's behaviour would not be dastardly, he said all right.

Archie came in a cab. While he was on his way, Neville kept thinking of stupid things he could do: drive a taxicab—he said Tonbridge had taught him to drive but, of course, he's nothing *like* old enough—or be a keeper at the zoo—he knows quite a lot about snakes, but I really don't think that would help him—or be a waiter in a restaurant, or a bus conductor, which he thought he'd quite like for a bit, all hopeless careers for a boy of—he says fourteen but he isn't even that yet.

When Archie arrived, he hugged me as usual and gave me a kiss, and then he did the same with Neville, and Neville sort of shied like a horse and then frowned and frowned and I could see he was quite upset—he was trying not to cry. Archie didn't seem to notice and brought out a small parcel and said it was coffee and would I make some. While I was doing that Polly turned up in her dressing gown with her hair in curlers. She stopped in the doorway when she saw Archie and Neville, and said she'd just go and get dressed. I don't think she wanted Archie to notice her too much in her curlers. But he said why didn't she have her breakfast as he wanted to talk to Neville and they could do it upstairs. Neville said he didn't want to be told things to do, and Archie said, "I don't want to tell you, I want to hear you." And that seemed to make it all right with Neville because they went upstairs.

"Why didn't you tell me he was here?"

"I didn't like to leave him. He's run away."

"I didn't mean Neville, I meant Archie."

"He's only just arrived. I asked him because I don't know what to do." Then I told her how difficult I felt it was about what side to be on, and she was very understanding about that and said she would feel just the same. "I felt like that about Simon," she said, "he seemed so alone."

"If you think *he* was alone, what do you think it's like for Neville? He hasn't got anybody—with Dad—gone—away— Zöe's no earthly use as a *parent* and I don't think he would count me."

When I'd made the coffee, she took a cup up with her to get dressed. I made a tray for Archie and Neville and took it up to the sitting room, but the door was closed. I had to put the tray down to open it and I heard Archie's voice asking something quite quietly and silence, and then while I was picking up the tray again Neville suddenly burst out sobbing, the most awful sad sound I've ever heard him make. Archie saw me and motioned to leave the tray and shut the door which I did.

They were hours up there. I went back to the kitchen and washed up, and then cleaned things that hadn't been cleaned for ages because I felt so anxious and couldn't think what to do. He must be dreadfully unhappy, I kept thinking, and I felt I hadn't been at all a good sister to him—far too selfish and thinking about myself all the time, and not imagining what life was like for him at all. What I have found, Dad, is that those sort of ruminations are absolutely *useless:* saying to myself how badly I've done something only makes me feel awful and the actual thing simply feel harder than ever. I have to try and think what *else* I could have done, which sometimes means pretending I've done something in the first place. In this case I haven't cared enough about Neville—I haven't really even loved him much. I used to secretly hate him because I blamed him for your wife [here she crossed out wife and put "first wife"] dying. She was my mother, after all, and it didn't matter nearly as much to him because he never knew her. Then I suppose I got to tolerating him, and when you got left in France (and I have to tell you, Dad, that if I had been Pipette, I wouldn't have left you; I have to say that I care more about a single person than this country as a whole—in this case you), I was so worried about you and missing you that I didn't think what it was like for Neville. Because that left him with nobody—he didn't have a boy his own age like I have Poll. So from now on I am planning to love him. As you're not here I'll do it until you come back at least. The only thing is that he is turning into a sort of eccentric and in my experience people only like them when they are dead, or at least at arm's length. Eccentrics are people that other people like there to *be*—like giraffes and gorillas—but most people don't want one in the home, as they say. "Our lovely home" we call this house, particularly when it gets into a really bad mess due to lack of housework and maids to do things. So, from now onwards, my policy towards Neville is going to change.

Anyway, Archie was the tops. He rang up the school and said he would be coming back with Neville on Sunday evening and they seemed all right about that. They hadn't even noticed that he'd gone, so they hadn't rung up Home Place which was one good thing. He said he'd take us all out to lunch and then we could go to a film, but that after that he would take Neville back to his flat for the night. And he said that he told me that he didn't think that Neville was at the right school for him at all, and that he would find a better one. We went to two Laurel and Hardy films and Neville laughed so much that people turned round in their seats to look at him, and then he did all his ITMA voices for Archie when we had tea in Lyons. He was quite funny—no, he was *very* funny: he reminded me of you, Dad, when you do people. Then he had to go and be sick, which was a bit of a pity because he'd had quite an expensive tea. I would have gone with him but I couldn't because he had to go to the gents. But Archie went and when they came back Neville looked rather pale but quite cheerful and he had *another* tea including baked beans and some Battenberg cake—you know, that awful kind that is pink-and cream-coloured squares. Then we said goodbye at Tottenham Court Road, and Polly and I caught a 53, and Neville and Archie went off to Archie's flat. Archie said he'd ring me on

Sunday evening which he did. He said Neville was being horribly bullied at school and that the last straw had been that the friend who he'd had at prep school, who had also gone to this school with him, had joined the gang of bullies. He said he'd told the school that he was taking Neville away at the end of this term, and apparently he knows someone who knows the headmaster of a terribly good school called Stowe that he thinks would be right for Neville, and he's going to go and see them about it. Usually they don't take people at such short notice, but Archie's friend seemed to think that they might make an exception in the case of Neville. Archie is having lunch with Uncle Hugh about all this to get family agreement, but as everybody trusts him he's sure to get it. I told Archie that I wanted to help and he said, write letters to him and have him to stay a bit in London in the holidays. What would we do without Archie, I ask myself. I asked Poll that, too, on the bus on the way home, and she said, "But you don't have to, do you?" We were getting off the bus then and I dropped my purse, but afterwards I wondered why she said "you" in that way, but when I asked her she said she hadn't. She *had*, but I didn't want to have an argument with her.

6th June. This morning the invasion started. Oh, *Dad!* I hope they reach you wherever you are and you will be liberated. Everyone is excited—even the Bish has the wireless on to hear the news bulletins. They have not got anywhere near where you were last known to be, Dad, but I bet they will. The landings are in Normandy but obviously that's just a beginning. Louise is back, and Michael is in it and she is awfully worried. She went to a party on the night before it began and didn't come back all night. She said the party was out of London which she hadn't known and she missed getting a lift back and had to stay the night. That night Mr. Churchill said in Parliament that things were going well, but Archie told us that they are having rather bad weather. He said it must have been awful being in the assault ships, which are quite small, because they were in them for hours before they sailed and a lot of people must have been seasick. I can't imagine anything worse than feeling seasick and *then* having to scramble ashore and fight. (Actually, *I* hadn't imagined that, Archie imagined it for me.) Michael is in a frigate. We thought something must be happening the evening before, because planes kept on going over all night. Oh, Dad, wherever you are, I hope you know it's happening, because it must cheer you up.

For a long time after that, she didn't write her journal. She couldn't bear to because she had initially felt so *certain* that once the Allies set foot in France, he would be set free somehow. But nothing like that happened. There was still complete silence—no news of him at all. That summer, her heart began to fail her about him, and having to confront the idea that all these years he might not have been alive made writing to him that summer seem pointless and macabre. She told nobody, not even Polly, about any of this. Each morning she woke with hope which, throughout the day, ebbed away until, by evening, she was sickeningly sure that he would not come back. Alone at night, she practised getting used to the idea that he was dead and wept for him. And then in the morning she would wake and think that it was silly and wrong to think any such thing, and would imagine him suddenly turning up. Sometimes she longed to talk to someone, Poll, for instance, or Archie, but she was too much afraid that they would gently, kindly, confirm her worst fear, and, since she had gradually understood that she was the only person who believed he was still alive, to waver to anyone seemed a kind of betrayal.

She lost her job that summer for the perfectly respectable reason that the Bishop's wife's cousin was widowed the first day of the invasion, they wanted her to come and live with them and the Bishop said that the secretarial job would give her something to do. She did not mind in the least. She kept her promise about writing to Neville.

The V-1s started very soon after the invasion. The first time she saw one was when she and Polly were rather sulkily weeding the back garden. The warning had sounded and they heard anti-aircraft guns making the distant popping sounds like corks coming out of bottles. Then they saw what looked like a very small plane speeding overhead all by itself, which was unusual.

"It's on fire," Polly said, and she could see the flame coming out of its tail. "It can't be a bomber, it's too small," she said. There was something curiously unhuman about its undeviating course. It passed out of their sight, the noise of its engines becoming fainter and fainter until they could not hear it at all. But shortly after that there was the sound of an explosion. "It must have had at least one bomb," Polly said.

In the days that followed there were many more pilotless planes, doodlebugs they were called, and everybody became used to their small mechanical roar, and learned to dread the moment when the engine cut out, because that meant that they were about to crash with their cargo of explosive.

Dear Neville [she wrote],

I expect you've seen the V-1s coming over your school. As an air-raid warden I have to see to people going into shelters when the warning sounds which means counting them and, if there aren't enough people, asking the ones who are there who they think is missing. If anyone knows, I have to go to their house or flat and get them. Old people go to the shelters far more than the younger ones. You'd think it would be the other way round, wouldn't you? The warden post is in a room in a basement in Abbey Road (the road that the bus goes along). It is always boiling hot because of the blackout and windows never being open and it smells of coke and we drink tea there waiting for raids. When we are on duty we wear very scratchy navy blue trousers and jacket and a tin hat with elastic under the chin. Sometimes we have lectures. There was one last autumn about had we noticed that the tops of pillar boxes had all been painted a limey pale green? Of course we had. This was because there was reputed to be some awful new gas the Germans were going to use, and we were told that we would know when they had used it because the pillar boxes would change colour. We all listened quietly, and when the lecturer didn't say any more, I put up my hand and asked what we were to do about the gas once we knew it was there, and the man said—quite crossly—that there was nothing whatever we could *do* about it, it was lethal and our gas masks wouldn't work. *I have not told Polly* this because she happens to be particularly frightened of gas, but I know I can trust you to keep that kind of secret from her. Polly is thinking of joining up as a warden in spite of my discouraging her. Louise has sent her baby to Home Place because of the V-1s. Since I've stopped working for the Bishop I haven't been doing very much except I typed a play for a friend of Louise's which I didn't think was awfully good, but typists are not supposed to have opinions about what they type. Being a warden is taking up more time. We have taken to sleeping in the basement on mattresses now in rows—it's rather fun except for the silverfish that come out at night. I'll take you to lots of films in the holidays when you come to stay, and we go for lovely picnics on Sundays to Hampstead Heath or to Richmond Park. Archie sometimes comes with us. He says it is OK about your new school and he's going to take you to see it. I wish I could come too, but I won't ask him if you don't want me to. Louise knows someone who was at Stowe and they told her it was a civilized place and much nicer than most schools, and anyway, I'm sure Archie knows much more than our family about whether a school is bearable or not. I have to agree that our family don't seem to notice this. I often wonder whether Dad and the uncles had such an awful time that they simply think everyone does and that's that. Archie is more *modern*—it is one of the good things about him. Another warning has gone, I'll have to stop. Please do write to me. I'm not sure that having a shop to sell snakes after the war would be a terrific success because quite a lot of people aren't keen on them like you. [Then she thought that this was a bit discouraging, so she added,] But I suppose people who've been in the army in foreign climes might have changed their views and even miss them, so you may be right.

Then one day Archie rang up and asked her to have dinner with him. She had not seen him for several weeks because his job had taken him out of London. "Do you mean just me, or me and Poll?"

"I think on this occasion just you. I had dinner with Poll last week anyway."

"Did you? She didn't tell me."

When Polly came back from work she asked if she could borrow a shirt.

"OK, but you really should keep your shirts clean."

"It's not that. Most of them have reached the stage where even if I wash them, they don't look washed. So I'm always wearing the other one."

"All right, you can have my blue and green check."

"Couldn't I have your cream-coloured one? I'll have to wear my linen pinafore—it's the only decent cool thing I've got."

"Where are you going?" Polly asked while she was considering this.

"Archie's. He's asked me to supper."

"You never said."

"He only rang up after lunch. Anyway, you had dinner with him last week, and you never told me.

"I'll wash and iron it after I've worn it," she said, as she followed Polly upstairs to their attics.

"You're a rotten ironer, I'd only have to do it again. Goodness, it's hot up here."

It was baking. The heatwave had struck at the beginning of the week. People had begun by saying what lovely weather, but after a few days of it things like queueing for buses in the sun, working in hot offices, milk going off and even water seeming not cold enough out of the tap had frayed tempers. Conductors answered back, people became scarlet with sunburn from eating their sandwiches in the parks on the burned grass, cab drivers swore at pedestrians, pubs ran out of block ice and drinks became tepid, and above, in a sky leaden and suffused with heat, dozens of the small robot planes pestered and frightened people with their impartial death and destruction. Waiting for the engine to cut out, people sweated sometimes with fear as well as from the heat.

"It's a good thing we don't have to try to sleep up here," she said, trying to get Poll to be friendly about the shirt. But it was no good.

"The trouble is that you'll sweat in the shirt and then it'll never be the same again."

"I suppose I would," she answered sadly.

"Couldn't you just wear your pinafore with nothing? It would be cooler."

"If I try it on, will you tell me?"

"You'll have to shave under your arms, though," Polly said when Clary had paraded before her. "Otherwise it looks perfectly all right."

So she borrowed Polly's razor and put on her best sandals, and scrubbed her nails—she was getting slightly better about not biting them—and set off for South Kensington which meant changing trains at Baker Street. By the time she had walked to Archie's flat from South Kensington station, she knew her face was scarlet, which would not, she reflected sadly, as she waited for him to answer the bell, go at all well with her terracotta linen. But—

"Am I pleased to see you!" he exclaimed as he opened the door and she blushed with pleasure: luckily she was so hot she knew it wouldn't show.

He had put two chairs out on his small balcony that overlooked the square garden and brought her a gin and lime. She didn't actually like it, but it was the thing to drink.

"Well now," he said, "tell me your news. Have you got another job?"

"No. I did a bit of typing for a friend of Louise's. A rather bad play, I thought, but of course I didn't say."

"You could do better, could you? Well, why don't you?"

"Me? Write a play?"

"Well, what else are you writing?"

"Nothing."

"Oh."

"I was writing something, but I've stopped. What do you think of socialism?" she said, partly to change the subject and partly because it was something that she had planned to ask him about.

"I think we shall have quite a bit of it after the war."

"Do you?"

"I think it's on the cards. War is quite a leveller, you know. When practically everybody's life has been on the line, people are unlikely to take kindly to reverting to a class system where some people's lives matter more than others."

"But they don't, do they? I mean they can't have. Do you think that after the war, *women* will be taken more seriously then?"

"I have no idea. Aren't they taken seriously?"

"Of course not. Look at how women get landed with all the dullest jobs, and I don't think they even get paid the same as men for doing them. If men *were* doing them."

"Are you going to be a feminist, Clary?"

"I might be. The point about socialism is getting things fairer. I am in favour of that."

"Life *isn't* fair."

"I know it isn't—in some ways. But that needn't stop us trying to make it fairer in the ways that we could. Yes, I think I will be one."

"A socialist or a feminist?"

"I could perfectly well be both. Wanting things to be fairer for women is part of wanting things to be fairer for everyone. Isn't it? Archie, are you agreeing with me, or are you merely laughing at me?"

"I have an uneasy feeling that I'm agreeing with you. Of course, I'd rather laugh. You know me."

She looked across the balcony at him. He sat, with his long legs stretched stiffly out; his long arms with the shirt sleeves rolled up were folded and he was surveying her with his usual expression of suppressed amusement, but beside that she was conscious of a kind of intelligent looking, as though he was really seeing her without criticism or sentiment.

"I don't really," she said. "I feel suddenly amazed at how *little* I know you."

"The trouble is," she said much later when they were having tinned salmon and a salad made by Archie on the balcony, "that I think I have taken you for granted. I think all the family do. I mean, look at how you sorted out the problem with Neville. I can't see who else could have done it. Uncle Edward would just have said that all schools are awful and he must put up with it. Uncle Hugh would have gone to see them and got them to *say* they would stop him being bullied. Of course, it would have gone on. Aunt Rach would have taken him out in the holidays for an extra special treat."

"And what about Zoë? What would she have done?"

"Precisely *nothing*. She's taken to going to London more and more, and in between she spends all her time with Jules or altering her clothes. Neville and I simply don't count her at all."

"So what *are* you going to do? I mean besides embracing new ideas?"

"I don't know. Find some sort of other boring job, I suppose."

"Why can't you find a job *and* write?"

"I don't know what to write any more."

"What about the journal?" He knew about that, although she had never shown it to him.

"I've sort of stopped it." She knew he knew that she had been writing it for her father.

After a pause he said, "Well, one of the points of a journal is that it should go on, be complete. You might as well do the whole war."

"I don't feel like it."

"Ha! Well, in case you don't know, one of the differences between being an amateur and a professional is that amateurs only work when they feel like it, and professionals work whatever they are feeling."

"Then I'm not a professional, am I? It's as simple as that." She said it as aggressively as she could manage. "I'm going to the lavatory," she said, to escape. In the lavatory, she cried. "If I talk to him about Dad, he'll only try and tell me kind lies about what he thinks. *He* doesn't believe that Dad will come back. I don't want to hear what he doesn't think." She had to blow her nose on Bronco which from experience she knew to be stiff and unsatisfactory for the purpose.

By the time she had rejoined him, he had moved the supper things from the balcony and lit a lamp in the sitting room. He made her sit on the sofa and he perched on the arm at the opposite end.

"Listen, Clary," he said. "I know why you've stopped writing the journal, or at least I guess I know. You thought he'd come back the moment the invasion started. I think if I was you I would have thought that, but looking at it from the outside it is very unlikely. The Allies haven't got even to where Pipette left him, and, anyway, he might have travelled considerably since then. Communications in France will have got temporarily worse, not better. I'm not trying to comfort you," he said sharply, "so there's no need to look so cross. I'm telling you what I *think*—not what I feel. So if all these years you've been sure about him, I'm saying you've no reason to stop feeling sure just because we've set foot in France. We haven't liberated the wretched country yet, and even when we have there'll be chaos."

"You're trying to keep my hopes up," she said.

"I'm trying to get you to see that there's no particular reason why they should have changed."

"But wouldn't he just be able to go to wherever the armies are and join them? He must *know* the Allies have landed—it's weeks now. That woman who helped them—*she* must have been in the underground. Surely she would do something?"

He got up to fetch his pipe from the mantelpiece. "Well, except that he's almost sure to know about the invasion, the answer to the rest is no, or almost certainly no. The invasion has meant that the underground have been working overtime. It won't have been the time for them to be worrying about individuals. Much better for him to sit tight until things settle down."

"You *do* believe! Oh, darling Archie, you think the same as me, don't you? You *do!*"

"I don't—" he began, but when he saw her face he stopped. She could not see him because she was blinded with tears. He moved over to her, gave her shaking shoulders a small pat.

"Clary. It doesn't matter a *damn* what I think. You've hung on so long, don't give up now."

"Feeble of me."

"Yes, it would be."

"Not fair on Dad either."

"There you go again. Fairness doesn't come into it. We're talking about faith, not politics. Like a cup of tea?"

"Although, actually, you know," she said much later, when she was helping him clear up supper, "I think all kinds of things in life may be fairer than people think. Look at Greek tragedy. Wicked deeds get paid for—even faulty characters like King Lear pay for it. It's the other way round that worries me. I mean, if you cast your bread on the waters, *do* you get back cake?"

"Well, I suppose you might, without recognizing the cake," he replied, rejoicing in the speed of her recovery. "Now, I'm going to put you in a taxi."

"Got your latchkey?" he asked as he put her into the cab.

"Of course I have, Archie. I'm nineteen, I'm not a child."

"I was merely checking. I know you're not a child."

The next day, she resumed her journal.

The Family

April—August, 1944

Oh *dear!* I do *wish* he wouldn't answer the telephone."

Rachel looked at her mother with dismay. She was really upset, grinding her tiny lacy handkerchief together with her soft mauve fingers (her circulation was never very good).

"What's he done now?"

"He's asked Brigadier and Mrs. Anderson to dinner *again.*"

"They came only about ten days ago!"

"That hasn't stopped them accepting. Mrs. Anderson has lost her cook, so naturally she is mad keen on going out."

"And so is he, I should think, since she is such a crashing bore. Never mind, darling. We can have rabbit again, and there are lots of vegetables in the garden."

"Do you think we could *move* the telephone? Would he notice? Because if we took it out of his study, this sort of thing would not keep on happening. Mrs. Cripps has quite enough to do as it is."

"He'd really mind that. He thinks the telephone is *his.* We could get another instrument, and put it somewhere else, I suppose."

"Oh, I don't think we need go as far as that." The Duchy had always regarded telephones as a decadent luxury, and had originally campaigned that it should be installed in the back passage that led to the cellar, thereby ensuring that anyone using it would have to stand in what was probably the most powerful draught in the house. The Brig had prevailed, however, and now that he was blind lay in wait for its ringing all day.

"Well, I shall simply have to brave Mrs. Cripps. It is not simply a matter of two extra, it means trying to contrive at least one extra course."

"Shall I post your letters for you?"

"They are not mine. They are Dolly's. She has taken to writing to all her girlhood friends, some of whom married but I don't remember who, and most of whom are dead. Look! Mabel Green, Constance Renishawe, Maud Pemberton—and sometimes she hasn't even put an address!"

"It keeps her happy and occupied, darling."

"But nobody ever answers! And she asks me—several times a day—if there are any letters for her. It's so pathetic, it makes me feel *I* should write. I do hope, darling, that I shall not succumb to senility, and cause you this kind of anxiety."

Rachel reassured her, because, of course, she thought, as she walked down the drive and then down the hill to the pillar box, there was nothing else she could do. But the fact was that the old people in the house were beginning to outnumber the young and able. Everybody was stretched: Ellen's rheumatism had become steadily worse until now she had difficulty going up and down stairs and was generally hardly agile enough for the children in her care. Mrs. Cripps was having trouble with her legs: even the heavy support stockings she now wore only kept her varicose veins at bay, and the Duchy lived in constant fear that she would announce one housekeeping morning that things were too much for her. McAlpine was not only riddled with arthritis, but had lost practically all his teeth and, since he refused to wear the dentures provided for him, or to make any concession at all about the kind of food that he ate, suffered constant bouts of severe indigestion that shortened his temper even more. The Brig, as well as being blind, had an increasingly weak chest which was not improved by the cigars he refused to give up; in winter he was regularly bedridden from bronchitis and had twice had pneumonia when that new miracle drug M & B had saved his life. The Duchy seemed miraculously to be preserved: in spite of her age, seventy-four this year, her hair remained its dark grey, her back as straight as it had always been, but Rachel had noticed that she became more easily upset by small difficulties and the setbacks of domestic wartime life. Miss Milliment—whose age nobody knew, but Rachel and Villy suspected that she was in her eighties—had, it seemed quite suddenly, become rather deaf, a state that she made great efforts to conceal. She certainly pulled her weight, teaching the younger children in the mornings and reading to the Brig in the afternoons, but she would retire to bed immediately after supper and on Sundays she often spent the morning there. She still trotted lightly about in a meandering fashion, but Rachel had noticed that she sometimes made little faces when she ran into furniture, as though something—her feet, possibly?—hurt. The household still contained three children: Wills, Roly and Juliet, aged six, five and four respectively—but *they* could not be expected to help with the chores, although they were all given tasks to do by Ellen; then there was Lydia, who had reached the age of thirteen and was rather on her own during the term time, although she still played with Neville when he came home. She could not be relied upon to do the same chore two days running. In between, were Villy, who had become utterly indispensable, and Tonbridge, who had taken over a number of small jobs not usually within the province of a chauffeur (he was perfectly happy to whitewash the larder for Mrs. Cripps, but simply loathed doing anything about the horses, of whom he was plainly terrified, but with poor old Wren gone they had either to be fed and watered or put down, and the Brig would not hear of the latter). Zoë was not a great deal of use; Rachel had felt sorry for her immured in the country with the terrible uncertainty about Rupert. For a time she had worked at the convalescent home down the road, but for some reason she had stopped, and nowadays she went frequently to London to see some married friend who had moved there, leaving Juliet to Ellen. Rachel could not help feeling that this was a little *selfish*, although she made all the excuses for Zoë that she could—she was not yet thirty, had had very little fun and had a perfect right to have friends of her own outside the family. Still, Juliet was a handful for Ellen on her own, and when Zoë returned from her trips she slept even later in the mornings and often said she was too tired to take the children for their afternoon walk.

Well, they still had the invaluable Ellen, and Lizzie, who had to help with the housework when she was not working for Mrs. Cripps—they were a great deal better off than some. And I do my best, she thought, and could do so much more if it wasn't for my wretched back. In fact, it would be hard to think how much more she could fit into the day, even if her back had been all right. She looked after Aunt Dolly who had reached the stage where continued mobility and almost total loss of memory had turned her into a constant anxiety and sometimes a serious risk. She had recently taken to getting up in the night and wandering about. She had rung the gong for breakfast at four in the morning because she said the servants had not come when she called and she was hungry. At this time of year she was apt to wander off down the drive: she was going to meet somebody, she said, but they had not turned up. This would make her rather weepy, but she could be comforted with a boiled sweet. Rachel and Villy took turns at getting her up in the morning, and moving her downstairs to the morning room was, as Villy said, like moving a battalion. She had to have an extra cardigan, the book she said she was reading, her writing case, her work bag, her slippers in case her shoes got too tight, a hat in case she went into the sun, her spectacles. Her embroidery scissors had to be untied from the chair in which she sat in her bedroom and moored to the appropriate chair downstairs. If you kept scissors tied up, you did not lose them, she never tired of explaining. When she had read the death columns in *The Times* she would, with luck, settle to some needlework and could be left for a while. On bad days she would wander, and for someone whose movements were slow and shaky, she always seemed to get a very long way. The children had all been told that if they found her they were to say that Kitty wanted her immediately, and they were to accompany her home.

Walking more slowly back up the hill she reflected that Dolly must be very near the end of her life, partly because, with Flo dead, she had not got much to live for. She was two years older than the Duchy and five years younger than the Brig. But in whatever order, they will all die during the next few years, she thought. Then I shall be left. Then I shall be able to go and live with Sid. She was dimly aware that this prospect had turned into a comfort rather than a goal, and put the faint apprehension down to the blues. It was a warm and very windy day—not proper June weather at all. Mondays were always rather dreary, as Edward and Hugh left early in the morning for London and work. In the drive she met Tonbridge wheeling a barrow full of empty bottles down to the spring to be filled with drinking water. He wore his leather gaiters that somehow accentuated his small bandy legs, his grey chauffeur's breeches and a collarless shirt with the sleeves rolled up. Once he would not have dreamed of appearing before any of the family in this disarray, and he would not now think of driving them without his full uniform but, given the things he had to do these days that were definitely not normally his place to do, he would not waste his good jacket on them. Now, after she said good morning to him, he returned the salute with the sheepish smile of one caught out in a demeaning task. "What should we do without you!" she called and saw his damp pallid forehead turn cyclamen with pleasure. His mother can't have been very nice to him, she thought, and then that fearful wife. There were rumours of a divorce, and Lydia said that he seemed very keen on Mrs. Cripps: "I saw him put his arm round her waist. Not *right* round, nobody could do that, but quite a bit of the way."

When she got back, Rachel was immediately waylaid by the Brig from the strategic standpoint of his study.

"Is that you, Rachel?" he called. "Come in here a minute, would you? The very person I wanted to see."

He was sitting at his immense desk with nothing to do.

"Most extraordinary thing," he said. "Telephone rang. A woman called Eileen or *Isla*, it sounded like (damn silly name), said she wanted to speak to Mr. Cazalet. 'Diana's had a fire in her cottage,' she said. I said I thought she must have the wrong number, but she seemed positive. Turned out to be Edward she wanted. Lives at Wadhurts. Said she was going over to rescue this Diana woman— can't see what it's got to do with Edward. Tried to call Villy, but she doesn't seem to be within earshot . . ."

Rachel said, "It doesn't sound as though it has anything to do with Villy. I'll ring Edward, if you like."

"Well, let him know, though what on earth he's supposed to do about a fire in some unknown woman's house beats me. Damn cheek! Well, get on to him, then."

Wishing she could get rid of him while she rang Edward, yet knowing that she hadn't a hope of doing so, Rachel made the call. She got through to Miss Seafang who said that Mr. Edward was not in his office at the moment, but that she would find him and could they ring back? "I trust you are all well at home," she added in the tone of voice that betrayed she had faint hopes that somebody wasn't.

"Fine, thank you, Miss Seafang," Rachel replied, and then, anxious that she might be giving the wrong impression, she added, "but I should like him to ring me back as soon as possible. Will you tell him it is rather urgent?" Miss Seafang certainly would.

"Brig, darling, I think it would be quite a good thing not to mention any of this to Villy at all."

"Would it?" he said. "*Would* it!" Then he got ponderously to his feet. "Give me that damn silly little stick," he said. "I think a spot of fresh air would do me good."

When Edward rang, which he did almost at once, she heard herself telling him that it sounded like a storm in a teacup, but then she realized that it wasn't at all. Edward was silent for a moment, then he said: "Has he told Villy about this? The Brig, I mean?"

"No. I asked him not to."

"Good. What a balls-up! I can't think what possessed that wretched sister-in-law—of course, Villy's met Diana, but years ago and she probably wouldn't remember her. Her husband was killed, poor thing, and she's rather on her own."

"Edward, I think I'd rather not know anything more about this." She could not bear to hear him trying to cover his tracks.

"Right. Well, thanks for telling me." He rang off.

Edward has always flirted with any attractive woman he met, Rachel thought, but she thought it uncomfortably. Her experience of Edward with women really went back to before his marriage, when, after he came back from the war, he was constantly going to tea dances, playing tennis, choosing trinkets and chocolates for a bevy of girls. When he married, he was regarded as having settled down, but now she knew from her immediate reaction to the Brig this morning, that somewhere she had always known that he hadn't. Of course it wouldn't be *serious*—all the same he had clearly been anxious about Villy knowing about the telephone call . . . The fact that he did not always come home for weekends now impinged—about one in four he was unable to come. For reasons that had not been clear to her, he had stopped living with Hugh in London. At the time it had not seemed odd, because Clary and Poll had gone there, but now that they had left . . . But Villy had stayed in his flat in London; she had said it was a horrid little anonymous shoe box, but she had stayed there—once or twice . . . Although she had never found Villy a particularly *easy* person, she had become very fond of her and admired the way in which she seemed able to turn her hand to anything. She was certain that Villy would be extremely upset if she discovered that Edward was flirting with anyone else. Perhaps, she thought, it would be a good idea to get Hugh to have a word with him. As she went in search of the Duchy to see if she had survived her housekeeping with Mrs. Cripps, she suddenly saw that she had not given a thought to the person called Diana whose husband had been killed and whose cottage had caught fire. The sister-in-law must have been fearfully worried or she would not have tried to ring Edward. After all, Diana, whoever she was, might be the widow of one of Edward's fellow officers in the RAF. It would be like him to have said that he would keep an eye on her. And Edward might simply be *afraid* that Villy might be jealous, even if she had no cause . . . The idea of anyone looking after anyone else made her feel much better about the whole thing.

"So I've been told."

"How do you mean?"

"Your sister-in-law rang Home Place this morning to inform them."

"She *can't* have!"

"I assure you she did. She got my father—luckily he told my sister rather than my wife. Rachel rang me."

"What can have possessed her to do such a thing?"

"How did she *manage* to do it? You must have given her the number."

"Edward, of course I haven't. She must have got it from Directory Enquiries."

"You must have told her about the fire."

"Of course I did. I had to. The place is such a mess, I had to see if she would take the children while I try to sort it out." There was a pause, and then she said, "The sitting room's nearly a foot under water from the fire brigade."

"How did it happen, anyway?" he asked; he still sounded angry.

"It was the chimney, a large cross-beam caught fire, or rather smouldered. I went upstairs because I thought I heard Susan and found the children's rooms full of smoke. It was incredibly lucky I went up when I did—they might have died."

"Oh, Lord! What beastly bad luck! Where are you now?"

"At the pub in the village. My telephone isn't working. Isla came over and took the children, thank goodness."

"I hope you told her to stop ringing up my home."

"I couldn't *tell* her not to. For one thing I didn't know she had, and if I did now, she would suspect something."

"She must do that already, or she wouldn't have tried to make trouble. You'll *have* to tell her. She can't *do* anything to you, after all."

"Edward, I didn't get any sleep last night. I'm dead beat, the children might have died and the house is in an indescribable mess. I really do think you might be a little more—" She was cut off. He wouldn't have done that surely, she thought. She waited a minute to see if he would ring back, and then realised that of course he wouldn't—he couldn't—didn't know the number. But somehow, pride stopped her ringing *him*—she was afraid if she did, he would say things that would make her resent him more. I couldn't cope with that, she thought wearily, as she bicycled against the wind back to the cottage.

The cottage smelt strongly of burning wood. Some of the water had seeped away, but the filthy residue lay everywhere on the ground floor—the sitting room, the small kitchen and the downstairs lavatory. She got the mop and a bucket and set to work.

She mopped and mopped, moved furniture and staggered to and fro to empty endless pails of dirty water. Resentment at Edward fuelled her energy: she reflected that every advantage (to him—privacy, secrecy and so forth) that had made the cottage seem ideal was a disadvantage now. She had no near neighbour and could therefore expect no offers of help, nor was there anyone in the village a mile away whom she knew well enough to ask, or even to borrow the use of their telephone. The cottage, originally built for a gamekeeper, lay at the end of a cart track with a wood behind it. It had no electricity and water was pumped by a noisy dogged little engine from a well, but it was extremely cheap which was the main reason why she had agreed to take it. Even with Angus's parents paying half of the older boys' school fees there was still their clothes—uniform for school, sports things—and then their dentists, their pocket money, their train fares to Scotland for holidays, and all this before she began to pay for herself and Jamie and Susan. Money was very tight indeed, with no prospect that she could see of getting better. And although the war did show signs of beginning to end, she was no nearer marrying Edward than she had been the day that she met him. She was forty-four and trapped in this isolated hideout, and he, at forty-eight (quite different for a man), was virtually living apart from Villy, on his own in London and all too likely to find someone else who was younger and more available. Edward did come and see her every week on his way to Home Place, and about once a month he contrived that they spend a weekend together. But it was plain, on these occasions, that he found the cottage uncomfortable and dull, and wanted her to come to London to be with him. She could only do this if and when she could drum up someone who would look after the children: Isla occasionally if she sucked up to her enough, and once or twice an old nanny who had looked after the older ones when they were babies. But often these plans fell through, and Edward had to put up with the cottage and her cooking meals and privacy only when the children had gone to bed at night. This made her think that probably Isla had cottoned on to the situation because Jamie had talked about Edward coming to the cottage—perfectly natural, but unfortunate.

By the time she had cleared up the water, and seen that the floor would need scrubbing, it was afternoon, and she felt faint from exertion and no food. She opened all the windows and the front and back doors to try to air the place and went to the larder to find something to eat. There wasn't anything much—she had been going to do her weekly shop that morning—simply the heel end of a loaf of bread and the remains of a packet of Grape Nuts but no milk because she had given it to Jamie and Susan for their breakfast. She made herself a cup of tea and ate the Grape Nuts with water, which was fairly horrid. She would have to go shopping if she wanted any supper, but she had become obstinately fixed upon the idea of getting the floor clean. Half-way through this, the water from the kitchen tap gave out, and when she tried to start the pump to get more, she found that it would not work. Water must have got into the battery, she thought, but that simply meant that she couldn't finish the floor. Nor could she have a bath and she was filthy. And it was now nearly six o'clock and the shops would have closed long ago. She went to fetch the floor cloth and scrubbing brush, left in the sitting room, slipped on the remains of a bar of soap she had been using and twisted her ankle. It was too much. She collapsed on the floor and burst into tears.

It was thus that Edward found her (she had not heard his car on the cart track as so many aeroplanes were thundering over the cottage).

"My dear girl! Darling! Diana! What is it?"

The shock of seeing him, of his suddenly being there, made her cry more. He bent down to help her up, but when she tried to stand, her ankle hurt so much that she gave a cry of pain. He lifted her onto the sofa.

"You've sprained your ankle," he said, and she nodded—her teeth were chattering.

"The water ran out. I couldn't finish scrubbing the floor." This seemed to her so sad that she went on crying.

He fetched her coat, which was hanging on a peg by the door, and covered her with it.

"Have you got any whisky?"

She shook her head. "We finished it last time."

"I've brought some. It's in the car. You stay put."

All the time, while he was getting the whisky, finding a glass, giving her his dark green silk handkerchief and drawing up a chair to sit by her he was making encouraging, comforting sallies: "My poor sweet, you *have* had a rough time of it. I came as soon as I could. By the time I'd discovered the telephone number of that pub—*couldn't* remember the name of it—you'd gone. I don't know how we got cut off. I was a *beast*—after all you'd been through. No sleep, and I bet you've had no lunch. What you need when you've drunk that, is a nice hot bath and then I'll take you out to dinner."

But she said, almost irritably, "I can't! I couldn't get into a bath. Anyway, there's no water left. Not a drop."

"Well, then, I'll put you in the car and take you to an hotel."

She felt the resentment that had dissolved into a pure relief at his appearance begin to crystallize. He seemed always to think that everything could be resolved by a few, passing creature comforts. He would take her out, and then bring her back to this desolate place where she would continue, without any adult conversation beyond exchanges with the shopkeepers and the man who would hopefully repair or replace the pump battery. Everything would be as it was before: she would be lonely and poor and increasingly anxious about the future as she got older, and one day, she knew it, he would leave her. She wanted to say, "And then what?" but some innate caution stopped her. She felt she was fighting for her life, and decided there and then upon a false, rather than a wrong, move.

She looked up at him, her hyacinth-coloured eyes still swimming. "Oh, darling, that would be so lovely, you can't imagine!"

Ever since their first meeting in the train Zoë felt as though her life had been split—unevenly—into two, not halves, but pieces. There was Juliet, Cazalet family life with its privations, its routine, its duties and affections—and there was Jack. There was far less of Jack—a matter of irregular snatched days and nights but these so crammed with excitement, romance and pleasure hitherto unknown to her that they seemed to occupy most of her attention—could invade her thoughts at any time to the exclusion of anything else. To begin with, of course, it hadn't been like that; changing her mind about going straight home and staying in London to have dinner with him, an attractive stranger who made his interest so plain, had certainly been exciting and, she told herself, it would be fun—it had been years since she had gone to a restaurant with any man and she had regarded it as a slightly wicked treat. No more. The fact that she was lunching with Archie—something that she had looked forward to for much the same reason—suddenly didn't seem to count. They *had* lunch, but after she had resisted a passing urge to confide in him about the stranger, she felt *distrait* and could not think of anything much to say. Archie had been kindness itself: he had brought a present for Juliet, and he had been understanding about the boring visit to her mother. When they were drinking bitter little cups of coffee in the coffee room of his club, and there had been rather a silence, he had said, "Poor Zoë! You are in an awful kind of limbo, aren't you? Do you want to talk about it? Because I can quite see that you can't at home."

"I don't know what to say. Except—you don't believe that Rupert is alive really, do you?"

"No, I don't think I do. It's too long now. Of course, he *might* be . . ." He left that in the air.

"I suppose I feel I *ought* to believe he is. And I can't. But I wish I *knew*. It makes me feel quite—well—oh, *well*—"

"Angry, I should think," he said. "Sorry this coffee's so awful. Would you like a brandy to wash it down?"

The urge to tell him recurred. She said that she would.

She waited until the waiter had brought the drinks before telling him. "I just felt like having dinner with him," she finished. "You know, it seemed like a bit of an adventure."

"Yes."

"Do you think that's bad of me?"

"No."

"The only thing is that I shall miss the last train."

He fumbled in his pocket and produced a key. "You can stay with me, if you like. If you turn out to need to."

"Archie, you are kind. You won't tell—anyone—will you?"

"I wouldn't dream of it."

On the steps of the club, he said, "What are you going to do with yourself until your dinner?"

"Oh—I thought I'd try and find a dress somewhere. I didn't take one to Mummy's—a suitable one, I mean." She felt she was beginning to blush.

"And your luggage?"

"I've put it in the cloakroom at Charing Cross. Except a very small case." She'd repacked in the ladies' at the station, so that at least she had make-up and her best shoes.

"Well, if you want to change at my place, you're welcome. By the way, do you know my address?"

"What a good thing you said that. I don't."

He took out his diary, propped it against a pillar of the portico and wrote it down for her.

"Elm Park Gardens. It's near South Kensington. Keep my key safe, won't you? Don't bother to ring. Just come or not, as the case may be." He leant down and kissed her cheek. "Have a nice time anyway."

Afterwards, in a taxi going to Hermione's shop, she wondered at the way in which he seemed to think she might not come. Did he think she was the kind of person who spent the night with a total stranger with whom she was simply going to have dinner? She felt quite indignant at the thought.

Any doubts he might have had, were, as it turned out, well founded. She spent the night—or what remained of it—in a studio flat in Knightsbridge. "My intentions," he had said at dinner, "are strictly honourable. I want to seduce you."

At dinner, that had simply seemed a wild, though flattering, notion; she had had no intention of his succeeding. "I don't go to bed with people the first time I meet them," she had retorted.

"And *I* don't want to do anything with you that you usually do with people," he had replied equably.

After dinner, he had taken her to the Astor, where they had more champagne and danced. The dress she had bought at Hermione's proved a perfect choice, a sheath of soft black silk, cut to just above the knee with a low square neck and wide shoulder straps; it was cool and glamorous and worth, she felt, every penny of its twenty-two pounds. She had availed herself of Archie's offer to change in his flat, spent a delicious hour and a half bathing and dressing and making up her face, putting up her hair, taking it down again and finally putting it up with the string of pearls—the only jewellery she had with her—twined into the knot on top of her head. She had no scent, no evening bag and only her winter coat to wear over the dress, but it would have to do. At this point, as much as anything else, she was enjoying the whole business of getting herself up for a party and when Archie turned up she paraded before him as though he was a parent to approve her before her first dance.

"My word!" he said. "That's a dress and a half, or I suppose you could say half a dress. You look *extremely* pretty in it, anyway. Do you want a drink before you go?"

But she didn't. She was due to meet him at seven. She left her overnight case with Archie and took a taxi to the Ritz.

He was waiting for her, rose from a sofa, greeted her with a small nervous smile.

"I had begun to imagine you weren't going to show," he said.

"You said seven."

"And here you are." He took her arm and led her off for a drink.

During drinks and subsequently dinner he asked her dozens of questions—about her family, her childhood, friends, interests, what countries she had been to, what, as a child, she had wanted to be when she was grown up, but these questions were slipped in between others—What food were they to eat? What about food in Britain in wartime? How did she feel about the war? Had she been afraid of the air raids? No, she had answered, she was far more afraid of spiders and he had laughed—his nearly black eyes that were sparkling when, as nearly all the time, they were fixed upon her, softened, he was silent and she was conscious of a momentary, tender affection that went straight to her heart. This happened several times and each time it created a small fresh shock of intimacy.

At the end of dinner, he offered her a cigarette, and when she refused, he said, "I wasn't sure whether you don't smoke, or whether you simply don't accept cigarettes from strange men."

"You *are* fairly strange. You don't tell me much about yourself."

"I answer your questions."

"Yes, but . . ." She knew by then that he was a reporter, a photographer as well, apparently, attached to some part of the American army and that he had been brought up in New York, that he had been married and was divorced (he'd told her that in the train) and that his parents were also divorced. "You don't *tell* me anything."

"What do you want to know?"

But then she couldn't think. Or, rather, the kinds of things she felt curious about seemed wrong to ask of someone she hardly knew. She felt herself beginning to blush and shrugged.

When the waiter came with the coffee, he asked for a large cup and some hot milk and offered her a liqueur.

"Now," he said, when the waiter had come and gone again and they were on their own, "I need to ask you something. Is your husband a prisoner?"

"What makes you think that?"

"I don't know. Just a feeling. You don't talk about him at all. That's unusual. All the time you were talking about your family, you didn't mention him."

"It's because I don't know what to say."

There was a short silence, and then he said, casually, "I suppose you could just say what *is?*"

So she told him. Beginning with Dunkirk, and his getting left in France, and all their hopes of his being taken prisoner, and no word for two years, hopes fading, she had thought he must be dead then, and then the Frenchman arriving with his news and everyone jubilant. And now two more years without a word or a sign.

"He's never seen his daughter," she said. "If he hadn't twisted his ankle jumping into the ditch because of the German lorry, he would have. So I don't *know*—anything. I suppose I've sort of got used to it."

She looked up and again met that silent, expressive regard. He said nothing.

"But really, I suppose I've come to think that he is dead."

He was silent for a moment; then he said, "I understand now what you said about getting used to something and still noticing it."

"Did I say that?"

"In the train, this morning. It's kind of unfinished, isn't it? You can't grieve, and I suppose you can't feel free—it's a kind of devilish limbo."

Yes, she had said. She was thinking how odd it was that he should have used the same word as Archie when all these years no one had said it—the situation had somehow never been discussed, let alone defined.

Then he leaned towards her over the table. "Zoë! Will you come dancing with me?" and before she could answer, he had taken one of her hands before saying, "Off we go then."

Much later that night, he said that a night club was the only legitimate way he could think of for taking her into his arms.

They danced for hours. They did not talk very much: in the first few seconds, she found that he was a very good dancer and abandoned herself to following him and thence to anticipating every move that he made. She had almost forgotten how much she loved it: had not danced with anyone since before Juliet had been born. He was barely taller than she—occasionally she felt his breath touch her face—if their eyes met he gave her an absent, dreamy smile. When the band stopped for a break, they went back to their table and drank the champagne that gradually ceased to be cold in its bucket of melting ice. There was a small lamp on their table, on every table, with a dark red shade; it gave enough light for each to see the other but not to discern the features of the people at other tables: it made a kind of romantic privacy as though they were sitting on the shore of a tiny island. Out on the floor the spotlights from the ceiling, which varied in intensity, made the dancers' faces and the women's bare shoulders livid; their eyes glittered, diamonds and medals winked and went out as the dancers shifted in and out of pools of smoky light.

The music began again. She turned to him, ready to rise, but he put out his hand to make her stay. "This is when I court you," he said. "I haven't told you how beautiful you are because you must know it. You dazzle—you *blind* me, but you must be used to all that. I've been falling in love with you since about eleven o'clock this morning—and that's a long way down. I got past your appearance hours ago in the restaurant, when you told me about Rupert. You look like the kind of girl who plays games, who tries to turn men on to comfort her vanity. But you don't do it. I've been waiting all evening for any of that and you simply don't do it."

"I used to," she said, suddenly recognizing the change. "I used to." She stopped—the recollection struck her with a kind of confounding violence. Once, she remembered, her whole satisfaction in such an evening would have rested upon her partner's responses to her appearance. If these had not been frequent enough to satisfy her vanity, she would have put out little hooks to catch more extravagant compliments. Thoughts of this now revolted her.

". . . so, will you? I didn't mean to ask you like this, but I just have to know."

She started to say that she didn't know how she felt, whether she was in love, that they had only just met, but the words crumbled, became meaningless as she uttered them. She fell silent and simply gave him her hand.

When she woke, the next morning, it was light, the telephone was ringing, and there was no sign of Jack. She was drowsy and her limbs ached from so much dancing and making love. She turned to the empty pillow beside her and there was a note: "The telephone will be me. I had to go to work." Getting out of bed to answer it, she found she was naked, but he had left his dressing gown draped over the chair by the telephone.

"I hate to wake you, but I thought you might need to know the time."

"What is it?"

"Just after ten. Listen. Can I call you at home?"

"Call? It's miles away—Sussex, I told you."

"Telephone—ring, as you say."

"I think that might be difficult. The only telephone is in my father-in-law's study and he's nearly always in it."

"Can you call me, then?"

"I might be able to. There's a telephone box in the local pub, but it's not very private."

"Can you spend next weekend with me? We can establish communication arrangements then. Could you, do you think?"

"I could try. I'll have to let you know."

"This is my number at work. Might have to be rather formal. I'm Captain Greenfeldt in case you have to ask for me. Isn't this ridiculous? Having to behave like a spy or a wicked child."

"But we do have to."

"Are you wearing my dressing gown? I put it there for you."

"Yes, I am, over my shoulders."

"Please come for the weekend. I don't often get them free."

"I will try. I'll think of something somehow."

"You *are* the only girl in the world," he said—and then, "I've got to go."

That was the beginning. It was the beginning of lies, inventions (she fabricated an old school friend with three children who constantly invited her to stay). The Duchy looked at her kindly and said she thought the change was doing her good. It was the beginning of coded telegrams, calls made to his office where he was sometimes chillingly formal, but after the first time, he had said he would always call her John when there were other people in his room. She wrote to him at the studio when the gaps between them meeting became unbearable—he wrote back only once. His energy was astounding to her. He worked hard—he frequently went for trips in planes to visit American troops dispersed about the country. When they met, for the rare weekend, they would fall into bed desperate for each other: she realized how starved she had been for love as well as sex. Then they would bathe and dress and he would take her out—occasionally to the theatre, but more often to dinner and then on to dance until three or four in the morning. Back in the studio, a bare place with a piano, a low, rickety divan, a table and two chairs and a huge north window that was always half blacked out, he would undress her slowly, take the pins out of her hair, stroke her and talk to her about making love until she was mad for him. She had forgotten, or perhaps, she thought, she had never known, that aftermath when the body seemed becalmed, its weight so evenly dispersed on the bed that it seemed weightless and sleep took with such an insidious stealth that she was gone before she knew it. Waking on Saturday morning was a voluptuous business; the one who woke first would watch the one asleep with such tender intensity that they could not remain uncon-

scious of it. Lovemaking on those mornings had a different quality—
it was light-hearted, playful, full of the intimacies of affection, they
felt rich with the prospect of two whole days together—it was the
time of purest happiness for her. As autumn became winter, the
studio was very cold: there was a stove, but no fuel for it—he
grumbled cheerfully about the lack of heating or a shower; there was
a small bath with an Ascot that reluctantly provided small quantities
of hot water at uncertain intervals. They lunched off tins that he
brought from the PX—beef stews, corned beef, turkey in tins,
Hershey bars. On fine days they walked all over London while he
took pictures—of bombed churches, bombed houses, abandoned
shops with sandbagged windows, air-raid shelters, camouflaged
anti-aircraft gun sites, the cabmen's Gothic hut at Hyde Park Corner,
where, he said, the cabmen went to gamble—he was a mine of
information in that kind of way. "They go to Warwick Avenue if they
want a good meal," he said, "and here to play cards." And he took
pictures of her, dozens and dozens of them, and once, because she
said she wanted it, he allowed her to take one picture of him. It wasn't
very good; her hand wasn't steady enough, and his eyes were
screwed up against the sun, but when he had it printed, she kept it in
an envelope in her bag. In the afternoon they would go to a movie,
she learned to call it, holding hands in the dark. At weekends, in the
daytime, he would wear mufti, but in the evenings he put on his
uniform. Gradually, she brought clothes up from the country to keep
in the studio. They spent Sunday mornings in bed with the papers
and he made coffee which he also seemed able to procure. But on
Sundays, the shadow of parting was there, and this always seemed to
lead to a tension. He was capable of black moods when he became
very quiet, agreed with anything she said, but seemed to have
withdrawn from her. Once they had a row, about her daughter. He
wanted her to bring Juliet up for a weekend with them, but she would
not. "She's too old. She would talk about you—I couldn't stop her."

"Would that be so terrible?"

"I think it would be difficult. I can't tell them about you. They
would be shocked."

"They wouldn't like the idea of your being in love with a Jew?" It
was the first time he had referred to his race.

"Jack, of course not. It isn't that."

He said nothing. They were walking by the Serpentine. It was a
bitterly cold Sunday afternoon, and suddenly he flung himself down
on one of the iron benches facing the water.

"Sit down—I want to get this clear. Can you honestly tell me that if I were some British—lord or earl or whatever you have here, you wouldn't take me home to meet your family? By now? We've known each other for nearly three months and you've never once suggested it."

"It's nothing to do with that," she said. "It's because I'm married to Rupert."

"I thought you loved *me*."

"I do. It's *because* I love you. They'd know that at once, and—and, can't you see? They'd feel I was betraying him. They would feel I ought to wait in case Rupert *does* come back."

"I see. And if he does, that's the end of us, is it? You're trying to keep your options open—"

"You aren't *trying* to understand me—"

"I'm afraid to. Either it *is* that, and faced with the choice you'd settle for your upper-class life in a large country house with all those servants rather than risk your luck with a middle-class Jew who doesn't own anything except a classy camera—or you've already got some alternative arranged. You'd marry that friend of his, Archie whatever, and your precious family would approve of *that*. He goes to stay, doesn't he? You've told me that—and what a member of the family *he* already is."

She was shaking with cold, and fear; she had never seen him like this, so angry and bitter and implacable, and, she felt, wrong.

She said, "When I told you about Rupert that first evening, you seemed to understand—exactly what it was like—the situation I was in. What has changed?"

He turned and seized her hands in a painful grip. "I'll tell you what has changed. Or what I thought has changed. We've fallen in love. I *thought*. Really in love. That means not just now, today, it concerns the whole of our lives. I *thought*. I want to marry you. I want your children. I want to live with you, for you to be mine. I can't bear the idea of anyone else *touching* you. You're not a child, Zoë. You're a grown woman—you can make your own choices—you don't have to go through life doing what other people expect of you. Or isn't any of this true for you? I really need to know."

She was so confounded by his anger and these resentments so suddenly and savagely presented and so confused at being attacked about a future that, she realized, she had most carefully never considered that, for a moment, she simply stared at him, unable to speak.

"I do love you," she said at last. "You must know that perfectly well. And it's true that I haven't thought about the future—at all. It *isn't* true—" Her voice was shaking and she tried again: "I *haven't* had secret options as you call them. I *do* love you. I'm not sure about anything else at all. I suppose I've been living on a kind of island with you—I haven't thought about anyone else." She was silent a moment, and then, but hardly audibly, she said, "I shall—now."

He released her hands and she covered her face with them to cry as though she was with a stranger. She wept and wept, as though all the years of pent-up grief and uncertainty and downright anguish were suddenly released in her, as though one world had come to an end and there was now no other to take its place. He put his arms round her and held her through it. At the end of it he was gentle and tender—and contrite—taking her hands from her face, stroking the tears with his fingers, kissing her, asking her to forgive him. They made it up: forgiveness was the easy part, but the pure, unalloyed happiness she had known became fugitive, uncertain, its present leaking into the past, infected by the future. The row made her understand both how much she loved and how little she knew him.

At Christmas she felt especially divided, unable to leave the family, and knowing that he would be alone. "Haven't you got some Army friends you could be with?" she asked, and he said, yes, he had, but he didn't want to be with them. "Christmas doesn't mean all that much to me anyway." But he bought a present for Juliet—a little turquoise heart on a chain. They had the New Year together and he showered her with presents—stockings and a black evening bag sent from New York, and a scent called "Beige" from Hattie Carnegie, and a bunch of red roses and a man's silk dressing gown that she thought must have cost a fortune and two novels by Scott Fitzgerald. She had spent weeks making him a shirt: it took a very long time partly because she had to make it more or less in secret from the family. "You *made* it?" he said, in amazement. "You actually sewed this yourself?" He was deeply touched and put it on at once.

That seemed to be the right moment to suggest to him that they might go and see Archie. She told herself that she wanted this in order to defuse any jealousy of Jack's about him, but there was also the desire to show her lover to someone, and Archie was trustworthy and discreet, and, anyway, the only person who knew of Jack's existence.

And so, later that day, there they were in Archie's flat (where she had only been once before to change for her first meeting with

Jack—*years* ago, it seemed) and Jack and Archie were getting on perfectly well. She didn't listen to what they were saying because it all sounded like the usual war talk. Instead, she examined Archie's room—the dead white walls, the large picture of a half-naked woman lying on a sofa beside a bowl of roses, an ugly person, but the colours were marvelous. There was a table with a pot of hyacinths on it and also a lamp made out of some old black glass bottle. The shelves each side of the fireplace sagged from the weight of the books: one short wall by the door was filled by the worm-eaten oak chest in which he'd told her the spare bedclothes were kept. Its top was covered by a piece of silk, purple and green, with embroidery and pieces of glass sewn into it. Opposite, the rather dirty, widely striped curtains of red and cream hung each side of his window with its balcony that looked out onto the square gardens. That evening when she had changed into her black dress, she had noticed none of this.

The meeting broke up because Archie was going out to lunch in Chelsea, "a very late lunch as my hostess is Spanish, but even with her, it is possible to be late."

He had kissed her cheek and thanked them for coming, and she noticed then how he had never, once, alluded to Cazalet family life or Home Place, or, indeed anything that might have made Jack feel left out.

In the street, Jack took her arm and said: "I'm glad to have met him. It's good to see something of your family."

"He's not actually *family*."

"He feels like it. Anyway, he's a good friend for you to have."

It was a mild new year, dry and bright, it never seemed to rain. Afterwards, she could never remember when they had the first conversation about it—they did not often talk about the war, but the impending invasion of France, the Second Front, was constantly referred to at Home Place, in newspapers and people talking in the train. "When do you think it will happen?" she asked him idly one day.

"Soon, I hope. We shall need good weather, though. And over here that seems to mean summer. Don't worry, darling, it won't be just yet."

"Worry? Why? Will *you* be going?"

"Yes," he said.

"To France?"

"Darling, *yes*."

"For how long?" she foolishly asked.

"For as long as it takes," he said. "Don't worry. I'm just a reporter—only a kind of witness. I shan't be fighting."

"But you might—" Terror possessed her: she couldn't go on.

"I went to Italy in January. To take pictures of the landings."

"You never told me!"

"No. But I came back safe and sound. It's my job. We should never have met if I hadn't had this job." He gave her shoulders a little shake. "That's enough of that."

"But will you tell me—warn me—before you go?"

He was silent.

"Jack! *Will* you—please?"

"No," he said shortly, "I won't."

Then he said, "We shall have a row about this if we're not careful. So let's not talk about it."

Two months passed, then three and the summer began. There were wild roses in the country, the willowherb growing out of bombed masonry in the city started to flower. As the train crossed the river before coming into the station, it slowed down on the bridge as it often did and she watched the silver barrage balloons swinging abruptly in the sky, which was also crowded with long banks of scudding clouds casting hasty shadows on the pewter-coloured river below. The train got in at six in the evening; she had time to catch the number 9 bus to Knightsbridge and still get to the studio before him. It was Monday, not a day that she usually came up but their plans for the weekend had gone wrong: he was working longer hours and making frequent trips to the south coast—and the weekend that they had had a fortnight before had been interrupted by a call for him to report for duty. But this Monday she was coming up in order to go to an early appointment next day with the dentist, and when he spoke to her in the week they had made the plan that she should spend the previous night with him.

There was the usual queue at the bus stop, and when the bus did come and the old lady ahead of her lost her hat in a sudden gust of wind she had to get off the bus to chase it, but the conductor waited for her. "Can't have you without your titfer," he said, and while she was wondering what on earth he meant, a fat old man sitting opposite her said, "Tat. Hat. Rhyming slang—very amusing, what?" and gave her a smile that showed his glossy apricot artificial gums, and then lowered his eyes to her legs where they remained for the rest of the journey.

The studio smelt dusty. The big window would not open; she had to open the small ones in the kitchen and in the bathroom to get any air. Jack never opened them: he liked hot houses, he said, and cold drinks—he couldn't get over the lack of ice and refrigerators. She opened the windows now to air the place. Everything was very neat, the bed made, no dirty coffee cups, although there was a half bottle of milk that had turned in the small meatsafe that served as a larder. She made herself a cup of weak tea. Then she decided to have a bath and change before he got home. Home it had become, she thought. It had become less bare, with books that he had accumulated, the clothes she kept there, a couple of Shell posters that he had bought—a Ted McKnight Kauffer and a Barnet Friedmann.

By the time she was changed it was nearly half past seven, and she left the door ajar so that she would hear him on the stairs. There was a pile of *New Yorker* magazines that he had sent to him, and she tried to settle down with them, but she had begun to feel anxious. She waited until eight o'clock and then tried his number where he worked. It was a direct line, she did not have to go through a switchboard, but she let it ring and ring and there was no reply. He was on his way, she told herself, but already she had begun not to believe this.

She waited and waited and he did not come. At half past eight she poured herself a stiff bourbon and water, found his battered packet of Lucky Strikes that he kept always in his dressing gown pocket and smoked one because the smell of it was comforting. He must have got called away—he wasn't going to turn up. The sky became lavender and the wind seemed to have dropped although there were still clouds. She sat by the window and watched the light drain away until it was dark. It wasn't until she heard the—very distant—sound of Big Ben on somebody's radio from the kitchen window when she was getting herself a second drink that the idea occurred that it might be the invasion. The thought that this might be so, that he might have gone without even saying goodbye to her, gone for an unknown amount of time to God knew what danger—she had no illusions about that. How could thousands of men get out of boats and walk up beaches where Germans must be waiting for them without fearful loss of life? And whatever he said about just being a witness, if he was there they would shoot at him just as much as at anyone else. She knew that she couldn't just sit alone in the studio all night not knowing. She would go to the pub at the end of the mews and buy herself a drink, and ask about the news: someone there would be sure to know. She had never been alone to a pub in her life, and ordinarily it would have been an ordeal, but now she was too desperate to care, and when every man in the small smoke-ridden bar looked at her with that mixture of curiosity and disapproval reserved for women who came to such a place without a partner, she ignored them, went straight to the bar, ordered a small whisky and, when she had paid for it, asked the barman if there had been any news. Not what he would call *news*, he said, of course she knew that we were into Rome. King Victor Emmanuel, whoever he may be when he's at home, has abdicated in favour of someone whose name he couldn't remember. "I can't say I care. Foreign royalty's a closed book as far as I'm concerned."

No news. She could have kissed him. She swallowed her drink, and left. When she got back to the studio, she undressed, wrapped herself in Jack's dressing gown and slept.

It wasn't until she was in the dentist's chair with her mouth full of cotton wads that she learned that the invasion had indeed begun that morning. She shut her eyes to try to keep her tears from escaping, but in vain.

"Now, now, Mrs. Cazalet, this isn't going to hurt, and I haven't even begun yet. Just a little injection and you won't feel anything at all."

Louise

Winter, 1944/5

Y<small>OU STAY PUT.</small> There's absolutely no point in you getting up. I'll just shave, dress and be gone."

"Don't you want me to see you off?"

"I'd rather you didn't. There might be other people on the train."

He disappeared and she heard water running: it was a flat that had been made out of one huge room and the partition walls were very thin. His alarm clock went off: it was half past five—he was taking no chances about catching the train. She fumbled to silence it. I will wait till he's gone, she thought, and then I will get up, wash and put my clothes on—and go.

When he returned, half dressed—his black socks had holes at the toe and his trousers were shiny with wear—she said: "When shall I see you again?"

"Not for some time, I'm afraid. I rather think it's going to be madly war for a bit now." He seized his not very clean white shirt, thrust his arms into it and began buttoning it up. "And I suppose it depends a bit on your husband."

"*Does* it? Why?"

"He's my boss. For the next few months, anyway. There's a certain irony in that, isn't there? Where the hell's my tie?"

"On the floor." It was a greasy black affair, worn with being tied in the same place for too long. He scraped a bit of it with his thumbnail. "Damn! I seemed to have got something on it. Funny, isn't it, how it always looks like egg when there isn't an egg in sight." He came over to the bed. "Darling! I hope you will always look at me like that—especially when there are other people present." They frequently used lines from the play that had been the subject of the first conversation they had had.

"Well," she said, trying to respond, "the suspense is terrible and I hope it *won't* last."

He was putting on his jacket now, worn and shiny like the rest of his uniform, his left breast heavily sewn with ribbons. He had a DSC and bar, and had been five times mentioned in despatches. He opened his battered attaché case, disappeared and returned with a sponge bag, which he crammed into it with a jar of Brylcreem.

"Your alarm clock."

"Well done." He felt in his top pocket and withdrew a broken comb which he scraped through his heavily creamed hair. She hated the smell of it, but had not liked to say so. Then he came over to the bed, sat on the edge of it to kiss her. He had cut himself shaving—she said there were little beads of blood on his cheekbone like a curved dotted line.

"Shaving in cold water," he replied. "And my razor blade's had it, anyway." He put his hands on her bare shoulders, stroking her long hair off them and gazed at her with his beautiful large intelligent grey eyes.

"It was good, wasn't it? Look after yourself."

"Do you—"

"Of course I do. I should have thought after last night you would have noticed that." He kissed her again. His mouth smelled now of peppermint instead of whisky. "I'm afraid I really must go and win the war."

"Win it," she said; she felt a sudden danger of her crying, but it passed.

"In the train I shall think of you lying there—all voluptuous, like a thin Renoir. *Very* nice." He straightened, ran a hand through his hair that had flopped forward, picked up the briefcase and went.

She had thought she might cry after he had left, but now found that she didn't want to. She simply felt sad and flat. Last night after Rory had rung she had got ready to go and meet him, full of excitement: she had felt reckless, daring, stirred by the whole idea of going to meet her lover and spending the night with him in some unknown flat. In spite of trying she still didn't *enjoy* being made love to, but she had decided that that was simply one more thing that was wrong with her to add to the mounting others: rotten mother, ungrateful wife, failed actress, undomestic altogether useless person that she seemed in the last two years to have turned into. She seemed to herself to spend all her energies acting the same old part of Mrs. Michael Hadleigh, having sore throats (they seemed to get worse and worse), and generally going through the motions of being a happy, successfully married young woman. But privately, with Michael, things had been going wrong for ages.

She had begun to notice that it had all started, she supposed, quite soon after the day that the door bell rang at home in London and she had answered it to find a very lanky, dark young man in army uniform.

"Excuse me. Does Michael Hadleigh live here?"

"Well, when he's on leave, he does."

"When's he coming on leave?"

"I'm not quite sure—"

"Oh well, I'll wait," he said, stepped into the house and put his bag on the floor. "You must be Louise Hadleigh. I saw a picture of you getting married in *The Times*. I was overseas when you got married, or I'd have been there like a shot." He smiled engagingly, as he added, "Rather an overworked analogy, these days, don't you think? I say! Have you got anything to eat? I had a sort of poison pie in the train and I thought I could fancy it, but could I keep it down? I'm a kind of cousin, by the way—my name's Hugo Wentworth."

By now, she was delighted. She took him down to the kitchen and made him toast with Bovril on it and cups of tea. He chattered away, seeming able to have about three conversations at once, telling her about his journey from what he described as a Catholic stronghold in the north, interspersed with mock news bulletins about the war and extremely personal remarks about herself. "Trains are either boiling hot or icy cold these days, have you noticed? I say, you really are distractingly beautiful—I suppose if I had a larger *frame* I could have contained that poison pie," and here he made a hideously funny face saying, "Goering: with just a touch of indigestion. It's funny about Bovril, isn't it? I mean do you think it's the *whole* bull, or just that intensely reliable face you see on the jars? You don't look at *all* as though you've had a baby, I must say, perhaps you just had a very small one . . . Is there any more toast? Although what I should really like would be a lobster. Life in Yorkshire with my dear mama was one long wartime scone and as she's never cooked until the war they were like small hand grenades. You won't mind my staying for a bit, will you? I can doss down on the floor, I'm lamentably used to discomfort.

I can't tell you how glad I am that Michael has married you. I was afraid he never would marry anyone . . .''

"He painted a portrait of you, didn't he? I've just remembered."

"He painted several. I used to stay at Hatton a lot when I was at Oxford. The Judge was a very splendid godfather. Have you got a piano here? We could go and sing sentimental duets. It might cheer you up. You know things like 'My true love has my heart, and I have his'—pure pale treacle if you ask me."

"I shouldn't think people get a chance to ask you much," she said.

"Ah! That's my Latin temperament. My mother is French, a tiny little black widow: naturally I call her *maman.* My father was English, though—some sort of cousin of the Judge. Got badly knocked up in the previous war and died when I was born, so I've always been a precocious only child. You aren't one, though, are you? You come from a very large family, I'm told."

"Only four of us, but there are a good many cousins."

"Then you'll hardly notice one more, will you? Should I go and view your baby?"

"He's not here. He's in the country with my family. Because of the V-2s."

"Oh, well, I can't, then. Actually, I'm not mad on babies. They're nearly always *damp* and they *look* so depressing. It amazes me that they're so popular with people."

"They're not particularly popular with me," she said, and felt at once a shade lighter for being able to say it.

"*Really!* That's most interesting." He took her hand. "Poor you having one, then."

Although he talked—very largely nonsense—most of the time she quickly discovered that he noticed a great deal and was not as inconsequent as he made out. By the time Polly and Clary came back from work, she felt as though she had known him for years and hoped he would stay for weeks. He was immediately popular with them as well, and after a hilarious supper they spent the evening being the Gaumont British News with action and music, no words— Hugo excelled at this game: race commentators, Queen Mary, war reporters, even Mr. Churchill blowing out seventy candles on his birthday cake; when he was not doing these things, he was playing the sporting heroic music with some lavatory paper and a comb.

He stayed about a week the first time, but thereafter, he turned up at irregular intervals, becoming one of the family, and particularly an indefatigable escort for Louise. They went to the Old Vic at the New Theatre; usually, she bought the seats, he never seemed to have any money—largely, she thought afterwards, because he kept giving her presents—he had an eye for good things in junk shops, and once arrived with a Pembroke table that he'd lugged for miles. "It cost nine pounds and is really rather pretty—nicer than that awful old card thing with mothy green baize," he said. Another time he turned up with his hair slicked forward and a small black moustache.

"*Heil, mein* Eva!" he cried, enfolding her in his arms. "I just wanted to see what would happen," he said. "But the people on the bus just looked, and then seemed frightfully embarrassed and looked away. Funny, I thought that ladies would shriek and men would try to arrest me." On this occasion he was in mufti. "Regulation number one thousand seven hundred and sixty-four stroke five nine is pretty sure to say don't dress up as the enemy," he said.

When Michael rang during the first time he was staying and she told him that Hugo was there, he seemed rather deliberately hearty about it. "Good-oh! Sorry I shall miss him. Tell him to behave himself and give him all the best," was really all he said.

Eventually, they did coincide—for one evening, and she noticed, more sharply than she had before, how the silly house jokes that had evolved withered in Michael's company; either he sat with a set good-natured smile on his face, or, more embarrassingly, he attempted to cap them, and there was either dutiful laughter, or someone changed the subject. He and Hugo seemed awkward with each other, Hugo attempting to rib him, and Michael snubbing and then being conciliatory. "Why are you in London so much?" he asked Hugo, who replied that he was doing a stint at the War Office.

"Are you living here, then?"

"Well, yes, just while the job lasts. Louise very kindly said I could."

When they were going to bed that night, Michael said, "I think you might have asked me about Hugo. He can be a bit of a parasite."

"I'm sorry. I thought you'd be pleased. Anyway, he isn't being a parasite, he's always bringing nice things. Those glasses we drank out of at dinner, he brought them and that lovely glass dome with flowers in it. He's awfully good at picking things up and he always gives them to me—to us," she amended.

"Well, be careful he doesn't try to pick *you* up."

"That's an idiotic idea," she had answered sharply. She had felt angry then—and innocent.

That was round about Christmas time. Her sore throats persisted—

they were always worse in winter and were accompanied by depression that she found it harder and harder to conceal.

One evening, Hugo got back early from his office to find her in tears. She'd been trying to paint her throat with some disgusting brown stuff that hurt and she'd put the brush too far down her throat and it had made her sick. He found her hanging over the basin in the bathroom, feverish and in tears. He put her to bed, got her a hot drink and some aspirin and came and sat with her. "I'll read to you," he said. "Then you won't have to hurt your throat by talking." He was so matter of fact *and* kind and read to her so beautifully, that she actually began to feel not well, but happy, and fell into a peaceful sleep.

When she woke, he was still there.

"What's the time?"

"Past the witching hour," he said. "You've had a good long sleep." He took her temperature and it was nearly normal.

"Have you been here all the time?"

"Most of it. Polly brought me a sandwich. I've been reading. But I didn't cheat and go on with *Hadrian.* I read something else."

"Hugo, you are the kindest person I've ever met."

"You are the person I love most that I've ever met," he replied.

There was a complete, trembling silence.

It was not a shock: it seemed the most natural thing in the world. It was what *she* felt, and she told him.

For a few weeks after that she was conscious of a light-hearted happiness that seemed entirely new to her. When he left to go to work each morning, the knowledge that he would return in the evening sustained her all day. Her energy came back: she decorated the house, she tried far harder to make good suppers (he had an enormous appetite—ate everything in sight and remained bony). Occasionally, she bicycled downtown to lunch with him, coming back uphill in the Edgware Road straphanging on lorries. At weekends they went to junk shops together picking up things for the house—it reminded her of going down Church Street with Polly before the war. Indeed, she felt as though she had suddenly become much younger, was hardly grown up at all: he was her brother, her friend, the best company in the world to her—and she loved him. Once, she took him home to Sussex for the weekend where he was an instant success. She had used to go every two or three weeks to visit Sebastian who was now staggering about and looked exactly like Michael. These visits usually caused her much pain, made her very anxious and guilty: she knew that she was expected not to be able to bear being parted from him, knew, too, that there was no real reason why she should be. She did not have to live in London; it was convenient for Michael to have her there, but secretly she knew that if she had said she must be with their child, he would have agreed to it. It would also have meant prolonged and regular visits to Hatton and that she couldn't face.

During these weeks there was no talk of love: it was simply taken for granted between them, but she did tell him something of how she dreaded and feared Zee's animosity. He listened; he knew that she did not like women, he said, so some of all that wasn't even personal. "And I suppose, after the war, you'll have Michael to protect you from her," he had ended. When she was silent, he suddenly blurted out, "But he won't, will he? He does whatever she wants."

She stared at him, recognizing the awful truth. "Does he? Yes, he does."

"Louise! I haven't asked you—swore I never would, but here I am doing it. Do you love him?"

"I don't *know!*" she said: "I thought I did, but I don't know. I feel as though all my feelings are wrong and I ought not to feel them. I try not to have any, but it gets worse and worse. Last time he came up I couldn't bear to—" Suffused with shame, she could not go on.

He looked at her with love. "I sort of knew," he said. "Really— from the first day I saw you—" There was a kind of suppressed anguish in the way he said that. He cleared his throat. "Well, anyway, you have me," he said.

"But I don't, though, do I?" she cried and then flung herself into his arms. That was the first time that he kissed her, began to kiss her and could not stop; they clung to one another for comfort, for reassurance and then passion, which for her came as a joyful shock, as though her whole body was discovering love for the first time in her life. "So this is what it is!" she said during a lull. "Both people want it."

"My poor darling. Both people."

But they did not go to bed. For a few nights, after the girls had gone to bed they met in the drawing room, lay together on the floor in front of the fire locked in each other's arms, kissing until their mouths were sore and they were exhausted with longing. But it was by some unspoken mutual consent that they did not consummate, and eventually they would creep upstairs, bare-footed and hand in hand, until they reached their separate rooms when they would part without a word.

On a walk the next weekend, he said that they could not go on as they were, and that the only honourable thing for him to do was to speak to Michael. At first she was aghast at the idea, was sure that it could not lead to any good solution, but he was unwavering, and gradually—although she felt very frightened at the prospect—she began to feel that he must be right. After all, she was usually wrong in what she thought and felt; she trusted him, and she also felt that they could not go on as they were. She loved him and he must know better than she.

Michael turned up for a forty-eight-hour leave the following week. She and Hugo had arranged that she would go down to the kitchen to prepare lunch while he talked to Michael.

All that day—the day of Michael's return—she had existed in a kind of nervous euphoria: she was unable to imagine what Michael's reaction would be and this was frightening; on the other hand as long as Hugo was there she felt that everything must in the end be all right.

It was not at all long before she heard Michael calling from the top of the stairs telling her to join them. She walked into the drawing room to find them both standing, Hugo by the window—he turned to face her as she came in and she saw that he was very white. Michael stood by the fireplace with his forearm resting upon one end of it; his face was flushed and the moment that he began to speak she knew he was very angry. What he *said* was breezy, patronizing and dismissive. He'd never heard such nonsense in his life—they were behaving like spoiled children, although he would have thought that Hugo, at least, was old enough to know better (he was a year older than she which made him twenty-three). What on earth was he supposed to say to such an utterly idiotic proposition?—and so on. It was pretty odd if one was away fighting this war, which perhaps they had not noticed was still *on*, if one came back to find that one's cousin, who had spent so much time with his family, had been making trouble with one's wife, and quite extraordinary that she should apparently forget her position . . .

Here Hugo said, "For God's sake stop talking about Louise as though she wasn't there!"

He would stop talking about it altogether, Michael said. It simply wasn't *worth* talking about. He must go, or he would be late for lunch.

What lunch? she had asked, before she could stop herself.

Lunch with Mummy and the Judge. He thought he had told her: when Mummy heard how short his leave would be, she had suggested coming to London for the day to see him. Now, given the circumstances, he didn't feel like taking her with him. He ended by telling Hugo that this was his house and that after what he had been told, he naturally expected Hugo to leave at once. "I shall expect you to be gone by the time I come back. And don't ever, ever consider coming back."

When Michael had gone, some of the implications of what they had done began to be apparent to them. He would have to go, he said. He could not possibly stay in Michael's house after this. It would be thoroughly dishonourable. Could she not go with him? No, he said. He had not enough money to keep her and they had nowhere to live and he was tied to the Army. "I have to send money to the little black widow," he said. "I wouldn't have told you, but she hasn't enough, and that really only leaves me with pocket money."

Michael was being horrible, she said; she felt then that their honesty should have been in some way rewarded. "We did tell him the truth," she kept saying. "Or at any rate you did."

"The truth isn't always jolly for other people," he replied. "*He* loves you, too. You can't leave that out."

"How do you know that he loves me?"

"He wouldn't have been so furious if he hadn't."

"We shouldn't have told him, then," she said some time later.

"Oh, darling, we should. Anything else would just be lies, deceit— awful stuff . . ."

During all this they went down to the kitchen to have lunch, but neither of them felt like eating. Hugo said he must pack things up a bit and while they were hunting for his things, and searching for something to put them in, the question arose of where on earth he was to go. He hadn't thought, he said, he'd find somewhere—she was not to worry about that. But of course she did: could he go to Uncle Hugh, she wondered. But if he did, what reason for it could they give the girls? Thank God they weren't there that weekend. When he had packed, she thought of Archie. Hugo had met Archie, and they had got on well, Louise thought. "But I don't know him well enough to go and plonk myself on him," Hugo said. She did, she said. But when she rang him up, he wasn't there. By now it was nearly three o'clock, and Hugo said that he'd better just go.

"I can always go to a Turkish bath," he said. "And on Monday I'll be able to find someone at work who'll know somewhere. You really are not to worry about that."

"But you'll ring and tell me where you do go?" she had said.

"I'll ring you on Monday evening—after Michael has gone, I promise."

The fact that they were to part now impinged. His luggage was in the hall—they did not know when precisely Michael would return and Hugo said he would not risk being told again to go. He put his arms round her and kissed her gently on the mouth.

"It's a hell of a mess, isn't it?" he said. There were tears in his eyes.

"Shall I come with you to the bus?"

"Better not, I'd rather say goodbye to you here."

"I love you so *much*."

"You are the person that I love most that I've ever met," he said. He stroked her hair back from her forehead and kissed her again. "Goodbye, dear darling Louise."

After the front door had shut, she heard the garden gate click. She could not hear his receding footsteps, and the house was silent. She went upstairs to the little room that had been his, flung herself on his bed and cried until her throat ached.

But that was only the beginning of what turned out to be the blackest time of her life.

When Michael came back, she knew, without being told, that he had discussed things with his family—with Zee. He had a kind of cold schoolmasterish resolve now. She was to join him in the port where he was taking command of a new destroyer. She would stay in an hotel there and he would sleep ashore. They would be leaving on Sunday afternoon. And he required only one undertaking from her. She was not to write to or to communicate with Hugo in any way at all. That was to be that. She was so stunned by these arrangements that she agreed—and then realized that when Hugo rang her on Monday evening, she would not be there. She asked if she might write just one letter to him explaining what was happening, but he said no. "The Judge will make clear to him what is happening," he said. "It is quite unnecessary for you to do anything about it at all."

And so, just over twenty-four hours later, she found herself standing in the dark and cavernous hall at the reception desk of the Station Hotel, Holyhead, waiting with listless patience while Michael signed the register and the key to their room was found. The porter then conducted them into the lift, onto the second floor, along a wide dark passage studded with doors, until eventually he stopped in front of one of them, fumbled with the key and opened it. When he had dumped the cases and received his shilling from Michael, he went. They were alone again—more so than in the train where there had been other people and noise.

"I'll leave you to unpack," he said when he had washed (it sounded like a concession). "Meet you in the restaurant in half an hour." The door clicked heavily shut after him. For a moment she simply sat on the side of her bed. Already the place felt like a prison. Her head ached from the long journey in a close smoke-filled carriage: she had slept some of the way because she had not slept the previous night—Michael had insisted that they go out to dinner with another naval officer and his wife. The men had talked naval shop during dinner and the wife had talked about babies and how lucky she— Louise—was to be going to stay in an hotel with her husband safe and sound every night. Then they had gone dancing for what seemed to her hours. She had thought she would be glad that this interminable, awful day was to be over but by the time that Michael, with wordless, perfunctory speed, made love to her (why did people call it that? she wondered) she was unable to sink into oblivion— something else she had been looking forward to all evening. She had lain in the dark rigid and wakeful: she had not stopped thinking of Hugo since the moment that he left, but it was as though the shock of their sudden separation had frozen her heart, had paralysed her thoughts so that all day, all the evening, the pain had seemed distant, she knew that it was painful, but she was out of earshot, as it were. But with Michael asleep, the thaw, the misery began. She missed him, she loved him, she could not imagine how she would get through life without him—it was very like the consuming homesickness that had dominated her childhood. If I could just be with him, she thought, I wouldn't mind anything else. During that day, and the day after, Michael managed somehow to make her feel guilty about what he called her behaviour; alone, the guilt was easily overwhelmed by her misery. It seemed extraordinary and awful that she should find out about love too late.

Dinner, in the dining room that had such enormous windows and such a high ceiling that there was no way it could ever be warm. They sat at a table with one carnation and maidenhair fern and had tinned tomato soup, cold ham and potatoes and pickled beetroot followed by a choice of apple pie or a prune mould. Michael said the breakfasts were the best meal there. The dining room was about half full with naval people and others who, Michael said, were catching the midnight ferry. After dinner, they went and sat in another enormous room where, after lengthy periods of waiting, people could have coffee or afternoon tea or gins and tonics brought to them. They had coffee and Michael talked about his new ship, and she thought about Hugo ringing Hamilton Terrace and finding she was not there. She had managed to leave a note for Polly and Clary in which she said that Michael had suddenly insisted upon her leaving with him on Sunday, that Hugo had also had to leave but that he would be ringing, and would whichever one of them answered the telephone explain to him where she was? This was better than nothing: she knew that Hugo would know that she had not *wanted* to go away, and if he knew where she was, perhaps he would write her just one letter, even if she could not reply to it.

She got through the evening by pretending she was acting in a rather dull play, and she noted, with a kind of objective interest, that Michael responded to her performance as though it wasn't one at all. He expected her to be as interested in everything to do with his ship as he was himself; therefore, she thought, he would have been more surprised if she had been bored. By the time they retired for the night, he had become far less schoolmasterish, and altogether warmer and more expansive. There was the usual performance in bed but, after initial repugnance, she decided to continue her performance and discovered that this meant that she did not need to feel anything at all. But afterwards when she could feel alone because he was asleep, the tide of homesickness, of longing for Hugo engulfed her: recalling his voice—from the first day, "I say, you really are distractingly beautiful . . ." "What I should really like would be a lobster . . .", the day he brought the table and they spent all the afternoon polishing it together with proper beeswax, the day he found the glass dome— "Miss Havisham's wedding bouquet," he had cried, "we simply must have that!" His kindness to her when she had stuck her throat-painting brush too far down and had been sick and was so miserable (nobody in her life had been as kind as that): her mother had always seen that she was nursed, but the implication had usually been that if only Louise had been less careless, she might not have caught whatever it was in the first place; her father had always visited her when she was ill in bed—and as far back as she could remember she had felt both ungrateful and uneasy at the attention . . . but Hugo had been there when she woke in the night, after reading to her for hours, that extraordinary book about an ordinary man becoming Pope, a very interesting exposition of the writer's personal fantasy, Hugo had said, when he told her about the strange author who called himself Baron Corvo. He had found *Hadrian the Seventh* on a second-hand book-stall; he was always finding books—never ones that she had ever heard of—bringing them home and reading bits to her. Then his telling her that he loved her, "the person that I love most that I've ever met": he'd said it twice, the second time in their last few seconds together. Then "It's a hell of a mess, isn't it?" He had never been in love before, he had told her once, when he was helping her to wash her hair. "I've liked girls, and sometimes I've thought they were far from plain, but my feelings about them were quite minor."

"You smell of apples," she had said to him one evening when they were lying together, and she remembered how, after he had gone, and she had flung herself onto the bed he slept in, the pillow had that same—faint—scent. Every night she lived with him during those hours and when she finally slept she would hold her own hand and pretend that it was his.

The dreary and aimless regime of living in an hotel with nothing to do was quickly established. In the ensuing weeks, she went for lonely—and usually wet—walks, she lunched alone with a book, sometimes—because in spite of doing nothing she felt perpetually tired—she would go up to the room and lie on the bed and cry and then fall asleep. Before dinner, there would often be drinks, parties aboard one ship or another: she struggled down slimy iron ladders set into the dock walls onto the faintly rocking decks of gunboats, Michael's old refitted destroyer, or either of the frigates that were also there. Down other ladders to saloons of various sizes, but always smelling of diesel fuel, cigarettes and damp jackets. Then back to the hotel for dinner; she knew the menus by heart quite soon. In the evenings, Michael would draw—fellow officers, sometimes their wives if they were staying for a day or two, and failing that herself. And night after night he established his possession of her, without it seemed any particular pleasure, more as a necessary ritual.

The whole of January went by: Hugo did not write. At weekends, when he did not go to sea, Michael went shooting at a nearby estate. The owner, with whom he had been at school, was away at the war, but he had told his agent to look after Michael if he wanted any sport. She met the agent, Arthur Hammond, one evening when he brought Michael back after a day's shooting. He was a gentle, dark, melancholy man with an old-fashioned drooping moustache. Louise liked him; his wife was having a baby, he said, which surprised her because he looked as though he was at least fifty. She thought then that this was a childish notion, but she often had ideas of the kind. The last few weeks of living in the hotel with Michael seemed somehow to have turned her into a child living with a grown-up (Michael, too, seemed to have changed, or perhaps she was seeing him for the first time), a great deal of whose behaviour and conversation was incomprehensible and therefore dull: he seemed to be in charge of her life and she was too unhappy to question or resist.

So when he returned one evening after a day's rough shooting and said that Arthur had been summoned to London by his employer, who was too briefly on leave to get to Anglesey, that he was worried about leaving his wife alone for the night and had wondered whether Louise would be so awfully kind as to stay with her, her response had been to ask Michael whether he thought she should go.

"Yes, I think you should. The poor chap is beside himself with worry. She's had the baby, but she doesn't seem to be at all well."

"All right. Of course I will." She started to say that she wasn't much good at babies, but stopped.

"Oh, good! Well, you pop up, darling, and get whatever you'll need for the night and I'll tell him. He's telephoning a neighbour of her mother's. If he can get hold of her, he's sure she'll come tomorrow. But be quick, because he's got to drive you there and then come back to catch his train."

Ten minutes later, she was sitting in the car beside Arthur, driving through dark, narrow, winding roads.

"Baby was premature and she's had some kind of fever, you see. Very depressed. Don't know what it is. But the doctor will come tomorrow. And her mother's coming, so it's only for the one night. Awfully good of you, I must say."

"I don't know very much about babies," she said.

"I don't know *anything* about them," he said. "Married rather late in life. This is her first."

"What is her name?"

"Myfanwy."

He stopped the car beside large iron gates at the entrance to a drive. Without the car lights, everything was pitch dark, and he took her arm to guide her through a side gate and into the small lodge. The front door opened straight into a sitting room with an open fireplace; the logs in it had almost burned out, but there was a light from a small lamp on a stool. As they entered there was a slight whirring sound from a very large grandfather clock, whose height was almost that of the ceiling, before it broke into its stately quarter-hour chime.

"She's upstairs," he said.

She followed him up the steep and narrow staircase that opened onto a square landing on which there was barely room for both of them to stand. A door on the left was ajar, and he knocked upon it gently before they went into a bedroom almost entirely furnished by an old brass-headed double bed, the room lit by another lamp placed on the floor beside it.

"Myfanwy, I've brought Louise. She is going to stay with you."

The girl, who had been lying with her back to the door, turned to face them with a sudden, restless movement.

"You said to get my mam!" she said. Her face was flushed and her eyes glittered with tears. She tried to sit up, then threw herself back on the pillow. "I want her to come, I told you that!"

He went up to the bed and stroked her tangled dark hair.

"She will come. She will be here tomorrow morning. Louise is going to look after you tonight. You remember. I told you I had to go to London for the night."

"To see his nibs," she said. She pushed the bedclothes from her and one strap of her nightdress fell down her white arm exposing one breast, round and taut with milk, and also a tiny baby tightly wrapped in a shawl that lay as silent and motionless as a doll beside her.

It won't be able to breathe under the bedclothes, Louise thought, and the awful notion that it was already dead occurred to her.

The girl seemed to notice Louise for the first time. "He won't take anything. He doesn't want me," she said and the tears began to slide slowly down her face.

"There's some medicine the doctor left this morning. She is to have it every four hours." He indicated a bottle standing by the bed. "Will you see that she takes it? She has a fever, she may not remember. I have to go now," he said more loudly, but she seemed not to hear him. He leaned down and kissed her, but with another lunging movement she threw herself away from him.

"Might be better to get the baby away from her for a bit," he said quietly. "But you know best, of course."

Then he was gone. She heard him shut the door and moments later, the car start up and leave. She experienced a moment of absolute panic, in which the baby already being dead and its mother insane with fever and grief assailed her. She looked at Myfanwy who was picking at her nightdress making small moaning sounds when her careless fingers knocked against her breasts. One thing about the poor girl that had been slowly dawning upon her was that she was not much older than herself. Please, God, let me do the right things, came to her. She edged round the bed and picked up the baby. It was far smaller than Sebastian had ever been, but it was not dead. Its swollen, almost transparent eyelids flickered and then were still again.

"Owen," Myfanwy said. "He's going to die. I know that," and she began to rock and cry in the bed.

"No," she said. "I'm going to give you your medicine and you will have a good sleep."

"If I go to sleep he *will* die," she said in tones of such heartrending certainty that Louise, whose pity had been paralysing her, felt a sudden strength.

"I will look after him for you while you sleep and then he won't die," she said with all the assurance she could bring to such a wild promise.

But Myfanwy seemed to accept this; she nodded, her eyes fixed trustfully on Louise's face.

"Is there a spoon for your medicine?"

"I have to take it in water. The bathroom's next door."

She retrieved the sticky, much-fingered glass beside the bottle and took it into the bathroom, rinsed it out and measured the dose. "Two teaspoonfuls," it said, "every four hours." When she returned, Myfanwy was trying to make the baby take her milk, but he turned his head away from the nipple and began making weary, thin, mewling little cries. Louise took him gently away and put him at the end of the bed. He was still crying, but she felt she must get the medicine into the mother before anything. She helped her to sit up, smoothed the long strands of hair off her face and burning forehead and gave her the glass. When the medicine was drunk, she turned the hot pillows and arranged the sheet over the blankets.

"Owen's room is next door to the bathroom," Myfanwy said. "His things are all there; my mam and I made all his clothes, and there's a kettle there if you want to make yourself a cup of tea. You won't sleep though, will you? You'll watch him for me?"

"Yes, I will. I'll stay awake if *you* promise to go to sleep."

When she nearly smiled, Louise saw that she was beautiful.

"I'll put some water by your bed, in case you're thirsty," she said. But when she came back with it, Myfanwy was asleep.

The night alone with him began. She boiled a kettle and put some water in a bottle with a teaspoonful of glucose. Then she put the rest of the water into an enamel bowl, and put the bottle in it covered with a nappy to keep it warm. The room was tiny, containing a camp bed, the baby's basket and a table on which his talcum powder and safety pins were arranged. She felt to see if he was wet, and he was, so she laid him on the camp bed and knelt by it to change him. He was so pitifully small that she was frightened of hurting him, and he started his weary cries while she was doing this. She shut the door and prayed that Myfanwy would not hear him. She had been going to put him in his basket, but his face was so pale and his hands and feet so cold that she changed her mind. She took off her jersey and got into bed, propping herself up with the pillow and her overcoat. Then she unwrapped him from his shawl and laid him in her arms so that their flesh touched. But the room was so cold that she felt this would not be enough to warm him, so it was out of bed again and back to the bathroom where she remembered seeing a hot water bottle. When she had filled it, she wrapped it in the baby's shawl, and then, because she was terrified of burning him, in her jersey. In bed, she held him so that he was sandwiched between her and the hot water bottle. Once she was still, the silence was broken only by the distant chiming every quarter of an hour of the grandfather clock below. She kept the light on so that she could watch him: the room was very cold, and she could see her own breath. So she sat, staring down into his tiny wizened face, trying to pour life into him, willing him to survive, and after a while, as he became warmer and his skin was suffused with a faint flush, he opened his eyes. For a second they wandered, unfocused and then they came to rest and they were looking at each other. She spoke to him then: endearments, encouragement, admiration for his fortitude and he watched her with a kind of grave attention. She felt his body move, his foot lurched uncertainly against her rib-cage, the fingers of his free hand unfurled and then closed again as tight as a bud. When he began experimenting with his mouth, smacking and mumbling his lips, she tried feeding him with the sugared water. He would not suck or even hold the teat, but if she squeezed it onto his mouth he seemed to accept the drops although the taste of them induced a flurry of little squallish frowns. He took very little—not even an ounce, but it was something. After it, when he opened his hand again, she gave him her finger and was rewarded by his instant grip which loosened only when he fell asleep.

That was the pattern of the night: she came to listen for the chimes below of the hours—two, three, four. Once, she got up to make sure that Myfanwy still slept, but she carried him with her, and once she boiled another kettle and refilled the hot water bottle and warmed up his drink. Twice more he consented to take a few drops: awake he looked at her all the time, but mostly he slept.

As the night wore on, it became harder and harder not to fall asleep, but she was determined, and the knowledge that he became cold so quickly helped, and anyway she did not dare to lie down although her back ached from sitting up in the same position. But chiefly it was her growing conviction that his life was a painfully fragile business, that he needed not only her warmth and nursing, but her constant determination that he should live: by then she loved him.

Soon after seven she heard Myfanwy get up and go to the bathroom and then she was standing in the doorway asking after him. "Oh, he looks fine!" she said. "I've had such a sleep thanks to you. I'm dying for a cup of tea. I'm going downstairs to make one."

"You go back to bed and take your medicine. Then I'll bring you the baby and I'll make the tea."

"I will."

He slept while she wrapped him in his shawl: she half wanted him to wake so that they might gaze at one another again, but he did not. She carried him and settled him with his mother. "*She* is the mother," she said to herself as she went downstairs to make the tea. It was still dark and she could hear the rain against the small pointed Gothic windows.

At eight o'clock the district nurse arrived on her bicycle. Louise went down at the knock on the door and found her divesting herself of her mackintosh cape and its hood.

"Raining cats and dogs, it is," she said. She spoke as though English was not her first language. "Dr. Jones told me to come as early as I could. Puerperal fever, he said it was. Upstairs, is she? Don't worry, I'll find my way."

And that was it, really. She accepted the thanks, the offer of a bicycle to get back. When she bent over the baby to kiss him, the nurse advised her not to wake him, so she didn't. "I'm so grateful to you," Myfanwy said, but had become shy in the company of the nurse.

"It was nothing," Louise assured her.

But battling home on the bicycle through the rain with her muffler, which was quickly soaked, over her head, although she felt light-headed with exhaustion, she was somehow exhilarated as well. The image of his gaze with its trust and dignity stayed with her all the five weary miles. I'll see him again, she thought. I'll have to take the bicycle back anyway. It occurred to her then that she had never felt like this about Sebastian, but the idea was painful and she was too tired to consider it.

She had thought she would go straight to bed, but the smell of breakfast stopped her and she realized that she was ravenous. No dinner the night before, she remembered.

In the dining room a captain of one of the MTBs in Michael's flotilla was breakfasting with his wife. She always wore demure frocks with white Peter Pan collars—came up about once a month and Louise had never liked her.

"Goodness!" she called across the room. "You look as though you've been out on the tiles! I wondered why your poor husband was all on his own at breakfast."

"He said to tell you that he had to go to an early meeting," the husband said.

"Oh. Thank you." She had hung her dripping coat on the back of the spare chair and was spreading a piece of toast that Michael had left with margarine. It was leathery toast, and the margarine tasted awful but she was so hungry she didn't care.

"Where *have* you been? Or can't you tell us?"

Resisting the urge to invent some wild night of dancing and debauchery, she said that she had been staying with a friend who had had a baby. This silenced Barbara, who murmured something to the effect that she hadn't thought that babies were much in Louise's line.

When she had eaten as much breakfast as the menu afforded, she went upstairs planning to have a hot bath and then a sleep. But on the bed was a note from Michael: "Darling. I do hope everything went well. Arthur was so worried, but I'm sure you made all the difference. Shall be back for dinner. Love, Michael." His confidence that she would have been of some use warmed her as she got out of her damp clothes. Michael had the thickest dressing gown and she decided to put it on while her bath was running as she was beginning to feel shivery. Even her hands were cold. She thrust her hands into the pockets and felt a letter. Pulling it out, she recognized Zee's writing. She knew that Michael wrote a good deal to her, but her letters went straight to the ship so she never saw them and now she felt curious.

After detailed comment on his naval activities and pieces of news of people barely known to her, the letter was signed "always with love as you know, my dearest one. Mummy." But there was another sheet of paper.

Just received yours of the 10th and thought you would like to know that Hugo has been sent to join his regiment in Germany, so he is safely out of the way. I do hope, my darling, that this relieves you, as in spite of Pete exacting a promise from him that he would not communicate with Louise *in any way* you must feel that neither of them are entirely to be trusted. Pete was *appalled* to hear that he had written in spite of the promise. How lucky that you were able to intercept it. Of *course* I think you were right to do so—the whole business must have been most distressing for you, as indeed, it has been for me, since any trouble of yours, my darling, becomes mine also. Again—love and blessings. Mummy.

She read this last sheet of paper twice, but the tumult of emotion it evoked was no less from a second reading. Anguish that he had left the country and she had not known it; fear that he would be killed; relief that he had *not* obeyed the family injunction, but had written to her none the less; an agony of impatience to find and read the letter he had sent; and through all this, rage at the horrible collusion. She began to search for the letter—through his chest of drawers, in the pockets of his clothes hanging in the wardrobe—but she did not find it. The thought occurred that he might have destroyed it, but she could not bear to consider that. She wanted the letter so much that it had to exist—somewhere. When she could think of nowhere else to search, she threw herself on the bed and wept until she had no tears left and her exhaustion overwhelmed her like a fog.

She woke to find Michael standing by her bed telling her that it was dinner-time. "You must have been asleep for hours," he said.

That was the beginning of the first, and most terrible row that they had ever had. She had read his mother's letter, she said.

She should not have done that.

Why not? *She* read other people's letters.

Silence.

She knew about Hugo. She wanted her letter from him.

That was not possible. He had destroyed it.

After reading it, she supposed.

No. That would be dishonourable. He had simply destroyed it. It was a promise, after all.

She had been made to promise not to write; she had not promised not to receive a letter. It was only *one* letter, she had pleaded. (She had never had a letter from him; it would have been something to keep—some comfort when otherwise there was none.)

It was much better to make a complete break. She would get over it sooner that way.

How did *he* know that she *wanted* to get over it? She *loved* him. In all these weeks it did not seem to have occurred to him that she loved him.

And what did she think this made him feel? She had loved *him*—enough to marry him and have their child. Did she not take that seriously? These weeks had not been easy for him either. He had tried to make allowances—knew she was very young. Marriage was difficult when one partner had to be away so much of the time. She *would* get over Hugo—but it would happen far sooner if she would just make some effort and not give way to everything so easily.

Had he really destroyed her letter?

For God's sake, *yes!* He was not a liar—surely she knew that?

He was not a liar, she said, but he did not tell the truth.

That sounded very clever: he couldn't think what she meant by that.

She meant that he simply didn't *tell* her things.

What things?

She couldn't be bothered to *tell* him.

Silence.

She looked at him as though she had never seen him before.

"I shall never forgive you for destroying my letter."

The row, like all the worst rows, did not end here, or, indeed, at any particular moment thereafter; she discovered that the cold resentment with which she had said she would never forgive him had struck him as no pleading, no attempt to say how much it mattered to her, had done. He had been treating her like a child—a badly behaved one—punishing her for her fault, discounting any reason or feeling that might have generated it. She thought then that even his bedding her night after night was some form of punishment, since he did not seem to enjoy himself either. She refused to go down to dinner with him, and when he rejoined her much later in the evening, she pretended to be asleep.

The next morning she woke with a headache, a very sore throat and some fever, and for several days after that, the aftermath of the row was masked by her illness and his efforts to look after her when he was not on duty. He got a doctor, who prescribed the usual horrible throat paint, plus aspirin and the injunction to take plenty of fluids.

He also pronounced her tonsils severely infected, and said that, in his opinion, they should come out. Michael brought her books and flowers. "I do love you, you know," he said. He also suggested that perhaps while she felt so rotten, and was probably pretty infectious, he'd better sleep on board. So for three days she had the bed to herself, although she felt so awful that the days and the nights ran together into what seemed like an endless tract of time when either she was mercifully unconscious or lay in a kind of stupor about Hugo—where was he, when would she ever see him again, was he missing her, did he indeed still love her? But what would be the good of it if he did? She was married to Michael, and she had a child, so nothing could really be changed. Most of the time she felt too weak to think about any of this, and when she cried, it was about not having his letter—it was as though she no longer expected to see *him*.

Michael came before dinner each evening giving her news of various kinds. "The Allies are closing in on Berlin," and "I rang Home Place and your mother says Sebastian has cut two more teeth and the new nanny is a great success. She sent her love and hopes you'll soon be well again, darling."

On the fourth evening, he suggested she get up for dinner.

"I've asked the new Number One from Martin's boat to join us. Do you good, darling, to have a little company. You can pop off to bed immediately afterwards."

So that was when she first met Rory. They had a long talk about Oscar Wilde, and she liked him at once.

Polly

1945

IN THE YEAR—or a bit more—that she'd been in Louise's house she had managed to make her little attic room more or less how she wanted it to be. She had got rid of the paper and its clouds with seagulls stuck onto it and painted the walls a rich green. Then she had painted the furniture white. The result was airy and refreshing to look at, although in summer, the room being next to the roof, and only furnished with one small Gothic ace-of-clubs window, it was still rather stuffy; she had to sleep with the door open to make some kind of draught. And in winter, of course, the reverse was true: it quickly became the coldest room (except for Clary's, which was identical next door) in the house. It was Hugo who suggested that she hunt for an old kilim carpet to hang on one of the long walls to warm things up, and she went to one of the big markets and eventually found just the thing: threadbare in places but beautiful with oranges and pinks and browns in it. After that, she kept finding things and changing the room until it felt exactly right. Hugo was awfully good at making things look nice and he even seemed to get Louise interested because the drawing room got a lot less impersonal. It was Hugo who had helped her to make a simple shelf to run down the other wall on which she could put her Delft candlesticks and other pieces of china she had acquired over the years. "I suppose you're falling in love with him," Clary had said rather accusingly after she had come to inspect the shelf.

"No. That's the whole point. He's just like one of us. There's none of that worrying stuff."

She was alluding to the confounding regularity with which men she encountered seemed to fall in love with her. In the last year she had had (or felt she had had) to change her job three times in order to escape everyday encounters with people who had expressed undying love for her. They always began by asking her out and, to date, she had always been taken in by their deceptively casual manner. Even if she didn't particularly want to, she never had the heart to say no. The first evening, or lunch, or walk, or cinema or whatever it was, was usually all right: they told her a lot about themselves and ended by saying how much they had enjoyed talking to her. But by the third, or even, once, the second time, the climate had changed, was thundery with suppressed emotion until the cloudburst of their declarations. On top of that, she had Clary's inquisition to face afterwards. "As absolutely nobody proposes to me, you *must* tell me. All novels have proposal scenes in them. I really need all the material I can lay my hands on."

She could no more say no to Clary than she could to anybody else so she went patiently through the declarations, the proposals, the subsequent alleged ruination of the proposer's life . . .

"Honestly, Poll, you're a bit of a menace. I know you don't mean to be, but the fact is you *are*. It can't just be because you're so frightfully pretty, it must be some ghastly weakness in your nature."

"I know it must. But it is such a worry. And sometimes a bit boring."

"It wouldn't be boring if you loved them back."

Before she could stop herself she said: "I shall never do that."

"Well, why don't you *invent* someone you're engaged to? You could wear your emerald ring on the right finger as a sign."

"Would that work, do you think?"

"Except with absolute *cads* it would. And even you ought to be able to tell which they are."

"Oh, no," she said sadly. "I've no idea how to tell which they are. You invent someone, then." She knew that Clary loved that kind of thing.

"Right. Well, he's about twenty-five with wonderful thick curly hair and he's fairly arty but also good at games and he's been madly in love with you ever since he first saw you—oh, yes, like Dante he first saw you when you were nine (that shows how much in love he is) and when you were eighteen, he asked your father for your hand and naturally ever since then you've been engaged."

"Surely I would have got married by now, wouldn't I?"

"No—because of the war. Your father said you had to wait until the end of the war. How's that?"

"I don't care whether he's good at games—it wouldn't make the slightest difference to me."

"But you don't mind him being arty?"

"No, I don't mind that. I wouldn't want him with fair curly hair. I prefer dark hair on men."

"I never said he had fair hair."

"Well, I don't like curls. And I think he should be older."

"Thirty, then."

"Older than that."

"How old?"

"Round about forty, I thought."

"Don't be so stupid, Poll. You couldn't possibly be engaged to someone of *forty!*

"I don't see why not. Mr. Rochester. Mr. Knightly," she offered.

"Jane and Emma were both older than you are. You've completely spoiled my person. *Nothing*'s the same. I can't think why you asked me at all."

"Well, he's still a painter."

"I never said *painter!* I said arty. You're beginning to make him sound like Archie!"

"Of course I'm not!"

"Forty, dark, unsporty, a painter. It sounds exactly like him."

"Well, it wouldn't matter if it *was,* would it? I mean, it's all a made-up business."

"I think it would matter." She thought for a moment and then added, "Archie might not like it."

She didn't reply. She had a sudden urgent desire to be alone, which was difficult because they were both making a special supper to welcome Louise back from Anglesey. She finished slicing the cooking apples and put them in the pie-dish ready for the pastry that Clary was making—she was the best at pastry. Then she remembered that Clary was always touchy if her advice was not precisely taken.

"OK," she said. "You're probably right. So he's twenty-five, with curly hair and I've known him for ages and he's always been in love with me."

"And you with him. Otherwise he'd be just like they are."

"And me with him. What's his name?"

"Henry Ascot," Clary said, her good humour entirely restored.

Louise came back. She looked pale and somehow *older*, Polly thought. She didn't have much to say about her stay: except that hotels were boring and there hadn't been much to do. She was glad to be back, though. She was going to try and get a job with the BBC, reading poetry or something, and now that the V-2s seemed to have abated, she thought she would get Sebastian and his nanny back. Otherwise, she wouldn't know him at all, she said.

It wasn't until they'd all gone to bed that she was alone and by then she had become nervous about what any examination of herself might uncover. For months now, almost since she had come to live in Louise's house, she had lived a secret double life, one with her family and the people she met and worked with, and one that contained only herself—and him. This second life was hardly a *life* since there was no continuity to it; it was more like playing selected pieces of film again and again. It had started by recollection of real life events; like the first time he'd invited her to have supper with him on her own, without Clary. "I don't get enough of either of you when you are together," he had said. Quite soon she had dropped the "either" from this memory. Then when he had advised her to go to an art school. "You have talent," he had said. "I don't know enough to know what direction that will take you in, but if you don't go and learn more about it you won't know either. I don't want you wasting yourself." The first time she told him about Mr. Fairburn at work proposing to her. "Well, Poll, you *are* immensely pretty and attractive, so you must expect that kind of thing." "Other people don't seem to have so much trouble," she had said—pushing it. "Well, other people probably aren't as pretty as you are." But she had fished for that compliment so it hadn't been as good as the unsolicited ones were.

Then, one time—it was after Clary had borrowed her silk blouse and then spilled salad dressing on it—she had complained to him about the way that Clary kept borrowing things and then ruining them, "especially if she's spending the evening with you," she had said, and he had given his little snort of laughter and said that Clary regarded him as a sort of substitute father, which was why she wanted to look her best for him. "Whereas, as you have a perfectly good father of your own, you can regard me simply as a kind of uncle, and one doesn't have to take anything like as much trouble over them."

After that, she dropped pure memories and started to make things up.

The fantasies, which began tentatively (What would it feel like if he put his arms round her? If he told her that he longed to see more of her? If he asked her if she would mind mending his shirt?), gradually became bolder, but they were inhibited, she discovered, by the increasing disparity between what she thought about him when he wasn't there, and what actually happened when he was. Thus, after a tensely romantic evening with him enjoyed by her in her green and white bedroom where he told her how he thought about her all the time that she wasn't with him, he kissed her (they had reached the kissing stage) and then they had settled down to a luxuriously despairing discussion of what kept them apart—she was not sure what this was, but there must be something, the course of true love not running smooth and all that—it was quite difficult to meet him outside at Tottenham Court Road tube station and, after a cheerful peck on the cheek, be asked for all the family news, and told, as he limped briskly ahead of her down the windy street, to "Hurry, Poll, or we'll miss the trailers." Sometimes she felt herself blushing, when, so far as he was concerned, there had been nothing to blush at. The last time she had seen him, he had been full of the Americans sinking Japan's biggest battleship and when she had asked him why it was so important, he had said that as soon as the war in Europe was over, it would all be shifting to the Pacific, "the Navy, anyway. The *Yamamoto* is a bit like knocking out the Queen in a game of chess."

"*You* wouldn't be going there, though, would you?"

"I'd quite like to, but I doubt it. Don't tell Clary that. I don't want to upset her unnecessarily." (At the time, she had minded that; later it got transmuted to, "I know I can trust you with a secret; in fact, you're the only person I can trust.")

He had then said, "Would you miss me, Poll?

(When she was alone, this got changed to: "I can't bear the idea of going: I should miss you so much." She went to sleep in his arms.)

What he had said about the war disturbed her. It was true that people were talking about when it would be over, but she had not thought of this simply in terms of Europe and the idea that it would still go on, but thousands of miles away, was deeply depressing. The war seemed now to have been going on for most of her life: it was quite difficult to remember things before it clearly—there was just a jumble of wonderful summers at Home Place, and her cat being alive and Wills not even born. Clary felt much the same.

"Although sometimes I wonder whether *our* lives would have been very different if there hadn't been a war. What we're doing, I mean, not our feelings. I suppose you might have been made to be a deb and that would have been different for you, but I'd probably have the sort of job I've got now while I'm practising writing." She had recently been taken on as a secretary for a literary agent, who ran a very small firm with his wife, and was enjoying it. "They really treat me as an *adult*," she had said after the first week. "He's a pacifist and she is a vegetarian, but except for the ghastly nut cutlets she gives us for lunch sometimes it's terrifically interesting. It's a pity you can't find something that you really enjoy."

"I can't think of what it would be," she replied truthfully. "I mean, if one is simply typing letters and answering the telephone and making appointments for people, it would be pretty much the same whoever they were." She now worked for a doctor in Harley Street, sitting in a dark room with high ceilings and fake Dutch pictures and a reproduction dining-room table covered with very old magazines.

"And you're quite sure you don't want to be a painter?"

"Absolutely. I'd only paint awful nice *careful* pictures that people who don't like painting would want."

"Oh, Poll, *do* watch out. You'll fall into the *trap* of marriage if you don't. Look at Louise."

They both fell silent. They had discussed Louise soon after her return and come to no very cheerful conclusions. Clary said Louise was depressed; Polly said she thought she was actually unhappy; they had agreed that Michael was not very easy to talk *with*, "He simply tells you things he's doing all the time and Louise must know all that by now."

"I think marriage is very bad for most women," Clary said.

"Who told you that?"

"Noël." Noël was her employer.

"*He's* married," Polly pointed out.

"Only to stop his wife being called up. It was a thoroughly *adult* arrangement. In the ordinary way, he doesn't approve of it at all."

"Do you think," Polly said tentatively, "that perhaps she fell a bit in *love* with Hugo? And she was so sad when he had to go away so suddenly that she couldn't bear to be here any more?"

"I think it's the other way round. I think Hugo fell in love with *her*, and as the whole situation was hopeless, she decided to go and join Michael, and then *he* didn't want to be here."

"What makes you think it's that way round?"

"Because of how Hugo was on the telephone that first evening when we got back from Home Place. When I said she'd gone away, he sounded sort of stunned."

"*She* left a message for him."

"Of course," Clary said. "I suppose the whole thing could be really awful and they were *both* in love with each other. That must happen quite a bit, because a good many novelists write about it. I do wish I could ask her."

"For goodness' sake, don't do that!"

"Don't be stupid. But it all goes to show that marriage is an extremely tricky business and you, particularly, ought to be careful, Poll."

"I suppose it's all right if you find the right person."

"*If* you do. And then you might find them, and they don't want you. And, then, men go for much younger women."

"We *are* much younger women—"

"We are *now*—"

"Perhaps the thing would be," Polly said as casually as possible, "to marry a much older man *while* one is young."

"Louise did that," Clary said.

This silenced her.

She found herself more easily silenced by Clary these days: it had something to do with the fact that she wasn't confiding in her—couldn't, she felt, although she was not absolutely sure why not. Although she did not know exactly *how* Clary would disapprove—with ridicule, resentment, incredulity, even—she did not feel that she could bear whatever it would be: it was almost as though telling Clary would dissolve the whole thing, and, almost as bad, make it impossible to face him in real life. And if she would not tell Clary, she could not tell anyone else. But this withholding produced a kind of conciliatory attitude in her towards Clary that somehow, she felt, weakened things between them.

Then, one Friday morning in the middle of April, when Louise was still in bed and she and Clary were sleepily making toast in the kitchen for breakfast, the telephone rang.

"You answer it. I'll watch the toast."

"Bet it'll be for Louise." Clary pounded upstairs to the hall.

"Friday the thirteenth," she announced when she returned. "Wouldn't you know?"

"What about it?"

"Zoë wants me to go down to look after Jules. She's *got* to go to

294

London to look after her friend's children because the friend is ill or something."

"Can't Ellen cope?"

"Apparently Wills has had earache all the week and she's had no sleep and she's exhausted. And Noël was going to take me to a play-reading of a frightfully interesting verse-play by a Communist on Saturday evening. He'll be awfully cross; he simply can't bear having his arrangements altered."

"Couldn't Zoë bring Jules to London and then Nanny would help look after her?"

"They're going to Hatton with Louise. It's her monthly weekend there. Oh, it's all so *boring*. It isn't as though I get asked to a Communist play-reading every day."

"Do you want me to come with you?"

"Jolly nice of you, but no. You went last weekend, after all."

It was true that she did go every other weekend to be with her father and Wills.

"OK," she said, "but I did offer. What about Anna?" They had been going to have supper in Anna's new flat. Clary said she would have to go on her own—a prospect that she found faintly unnerving.

Anna Heisig was the lady who had briefly been a fellow student at Pitman's. They had eventually approached her and found her friendly and seemingly pleased to know them in an amused kind of way. Apart from the fact that she *was* foreign (in itself exciting: they did not know any foreigners), she remained mysterious: she came originally from Vienna, but had lived some time in the Far East—Malaysia, where she had been married, again, it seemed, briefly. They had the impression that a great many things had happened to her, but none of them for very long. They were fascinated by her appearance; her look of dishevelled nobility, her voice, which varied in tone from a caressing, almost sly confidence when she was telling them some extraordinary story, to a kind of deep, almost jeering baritone when she was denying them any amazement at her tales: "Oh, *yers!*" she would exclaim with a good-natured impatience at their disbelief. ("Surely, Anna, all those women wouldn't travel all the way from Holland to Kuala Lumpur to marry just any man who chose them!" But, oh, *yers!*) She seemed to enjoy shocking them.

"You must have been very beautiful when you were young," Clary had once said to her.

"I was fabulous," she replied. "I could have had anyone I liked. I was very, very spoiled," and she smiled with reminiscent sensuality.

"It's as though all the *really* exciting things are secret," Clary had complained when they were walking home together after one of Anna's evenings.

She had been learning to type in order to write a book. She needed to earn some money, she said, as she had virtually none. In spite of this, she seemed to get lent, or be offered for next to nothing, a series of flats, and she was always strikingly well dressed in a style that was her own. Sometimes she came to Hamilton Terrace, sometimes they went to her where they had interesting food that was new to them: yoghurt, pickled cucumbers, strange pieces of sausage and nearly black bread. Once, Polly had arranged for them to take Anna to dinner with her father at his club, but the evening had not been a success. Her father had been scrupulously polite, and asked her rather stilted questions, to which Anna had responded in a manner both superior and enigmatic, so that conversation was a series of small cul-de-sacs. Afterwards, he said that she was unusual, and she said he was typical, verdicts that put the lid on any further intercourse.

"Anyway," Clary had said, "you simply couldn't imagine them *married*. Socialists and Conservatives don't marry each other—think of the rows they'd have every time they opened a newspaper. And they are both far too old to change—about anything, poor things. When Noël married Fenella, she simply had to change to Conservative or he wouldn't have done it."

That Saturday evening, as she was to have Anna to herself, Polly resolved to see if she could find out some things that she couldn't find out if Clary was also there.

She took a bunch of daffodils and some chocolates: Anna loved to be given flowers and sweets and had once regaled them with a tale of her home being so overwhelmed with bouquets brought by suitors after a dance that she and her mother had had to hire a cab to take them to the local hospital. "Oh, *yers!*" she had said. "There *were* dozens and dozens of them: lilies, roses, carnations, gardenias, violets—all the flowers you can imagine."

"Clary couldn't come," she said, as she followed Anna up the stairs of the little mews house.

"So!"

"She said she'd ring to tell you."

"I was out much of the day."

A large piece of sacking was laid upon the floor, and beside it a heap of balls of wool and scraps of material.

"I make one of my famous pictures," Anna said.

"Can I help you? I'm quite good at sewing."

"You may knit me a piece four, five inches long of this, if you like. To be the ploughed field."

She was handed some thick speckly wool and a pair of very large needles.

She had a box gramophone, that you had to wind up, and played records while she got supper. "Mahler is not understood here as he should be," she said. "You perhaps do not even know this piece."

Later in the evening, she got around to what she wanted to ask. Should one, if it was a very serious matter, tell somebody something if ordinarily one had always confided in them, but in this instance had not because one was afraid of what they would say?

Anna was immediately engaged. "Is it something about them that you wish to tell them?"

"No—not actually. It's about somebody else."

"Does the somebody else know?"

"No, no, they don't. I'm pretty sure," she added.

"Then why do you not tell *them*?"

"I couldn't do that." She felt herself grow hot at the thought.

There was a short silence. Then Anna, lighting a cigarette, said calmly, "When I have been in love with people, *always* I have told them. It was always a staggering success."

"Really?"

"Really. Oh, *yers!* They had many times been afraid to tell me—it was a load of bricks off their mind. You mustn't be so English about love, Polly."

There was more in this vein, punctuated by a number of stories to prove her point. But Anna did not pry, or try to trap her into any admissions, for which she was grateful, and this gratitude somehow gave added weight to Anna's opinion. She walked home from Swiss Cottage that evening full of nervous resolution.

At first it seemed as though everything was in her favour. She rang him in the morning; he was there, he was free; he suggested that they take a picnic and go on the river—"Only bring warm clothes, Poll, it will probably be cold."

They discussed what each could contribute to the picnic and agreed to meet at Paddington station. She dressed with care: her dark green linen Daks trousers bought in a sale at Simpson's, her gentian blue jersey with a white shirt under it in case it got hot and her duffel coat. It was a fine, sunny morning with small white clouds—a perfect day, she thought for such an outing.

He was waiting for her at the ticket office. He wore his old navy blue roll-neck jersey with grey flannel trousers and an extremely old tweed jacket and he carried a huge straw basket bulging with stuff.

"I've brought some things so we can both draw if we feel like it," he said.

In the train going to Maidenhead they exchanged news about the family, and he did his usual tease about her ignorance of what was going on in the war. Did she even know that Roosevelt had died, for instance?

"Of course I did." It had been on all the placards of the evening papers two nights ago, but she had to admit that she and Clary had not mentioned it.

"So, who is the next President?"

"Mr. Truman. But I don't know anything else about him."

"I don't think you're alone there. Jolly bad luck on Roosevelt, though, going through all the Second Front and everything, and then missing all the fun of victory by such a narrow squeak."

"*Is* it going to be victory so soon?"

"Pretty soon now, Poll. But it will take a long time to get back to normal."

"I don't think I really know what that will be like at all."

"That's probably better than having a lot of fixed notions about it."

"Anyway, one's own life never seems exactly normal, does it?" she said.

"Doesn't it?"

"Normal lives are something other people have. Although I expect if you asked them they would say they didn't."

"Do you mean like one of those terrible bores who something extraordinary has always happened to?"

"They're boring, because they're so boring *about* it. Some people" (Hugo had come to her mind) "can tell you about losing the soap in their bath and you can't bear them to stop. Uncle Rupert was like that."

"Anyway," he said, after the short sad silence that her last remark had engendered. "Do you equate normality with enjoyment?"

"I don't know. Why?"

"Because if you do, it might just be that you haven't had enough enjoyment because of the war. In which case, dear girl, you'll be in for a series of delightful surprises."

She glowed at the notion of delightful, and smiled inside at the idea of it being a surprise.

When they had walked from the station to the river and chosen a punt ("but we certainly want paddles as well, I'm not up to much punting") they set off up river. Archie said that he would do a bit of poling until his leg got tired.

"I suggest we just go and find a really pretty place to tie up and then we can have our picnic and draw." She agreed with all of that.

They found the perfect place, a little grassy promontory with willows in their fresh green dripping down to the olive-coloured water.

It was not until they had nearly finished lunch that she brought the conversation round to what he would do after the war. He had been talking about Neville, now in his third term at Stowe, and saying how interesting it was that in less than a year somebody could change so much as there now seemed to be so many things he liked doing.

"He does go through interests rather quickly," she said. "I know Clary is worried about that. She's afraid he will have tried everything by the time he is twenty, and there won't be anything left. The first term he came back it was playing the trumpet. He wanted to do it most of the time, and the Duchy had to make him do it in the squash court. Now it's the piano, but he'll only play by ear, he won't learn to read music. *And* he's mad about buildings. And says he wants to be an actor when he's not exploring. And he brought a friend back last holidays who *only* thinks about Bach, just when he'd begun on moths, so they did Bach all day and moths in the evening. Lydia's very hurt. Since his voice broke he hardly takes any notice of her."

"They'll get back together when he is a bit older. And it's a good thing he is exploring so much. I think that means that by the time he is twenty, he *will* know what he wants to do."

There was a pause, and then she said, "He loves you very much. He told Clary. In case you didn't know."

He was refilling their glasses with cider. Now, as he handed her her glass, he said easily, "Well, I've become a sort of stand-in for his father."

When he had lit his cigarette, he leaned back on the battered plush cushions. They were opposite one another with the remains of the picnic between them.

"And what are you going to do with your life?"

"I'm not sure. I get rather confused about that."

"Well, you shouldn't worry, my pretty Poll. Sir Right will come along and sweep you off on a white horse."

"Will he? How do you know?"

"I don't absolutely *know*. And you may not want simply to get married. You may want to do something on your own. *Until* Mr. Right turns up."

Her heart was thudding; she sat up; it felt like now—or never.

"Well, I would quite like to get married."

"Aha! And have you chosen the lucky chap?"

"Yes." She fixed her eyes just to the right of the top of his head. "It's you. The only person I should like to marry is you." Anxious to prevent any response, she began speaking rapidly: "I've honestly thought a great deal about it. I'm completely serious. I know I'm quite a bit younger than you are, but people of different ages do get married and I'm sure it works out all right. I'm only twenty years younger and by the time I'm forty and you're sixty, it will be nothing—nothing at all. But I wouldn't consider marrying anyone else and you know me quite well, and you've said you like my appearance. I've been practising cooking and I wouldn't mind if it was France or where we lived—I wouldn't mind anything . . ." Then she couldn't think of any more to say, and made herself look at him.

He wasn't laughing, which was something. But by the way in which he picked up her hand and kissed it, she knew it was no go.

"Oh, Poll," he said. "What a compliment. I've never had such a great and serious compliment paid me in my life. And I'm not going to hide behind all that crap about me being too old for you, although in some ways it may be true. I love you very much, I regard you as a serious friend, but you are not my love, and the awful thing is that unless you were, the whole thing wouldn't stand a chance."

"And you don't think you ever could be?"

He shook his head. "It *is* the kind of thing one knows, you know."

"Yes."

"Dear Poll. You have your whole life before you."

"That is what I was thinking," she answered: it seemed interminable, but she did not say so.

"I suppose you think I shouldn't have told you," she said.

"I don't think that at all. I *do* think it was extremely brave of you."

"It hasn't made any difference, though, has it?"

"Well, at least you wanted to know something and you asked."

And moved from hope to despair, she thought, but again she did not say so. She did not know how to be without him for the rest of her life, and she did not know how to be with him now—trapped in this wretched punt miles from anywhere.

She was saved by a sudden heavy shower. The sky had been becoming greyer, and—hours ago it now seemed to her—they had wondered whether it would rain. Now, she could be occupied in packing up the remains of lunch, getting into her duffel coat, and untying the painter from the willow, while Archie wielded the punting pole. All the same, by the time they reached the boatyard, they were both soaked. The sun came out, but intent upon its appearance rather than its warmth, and Archie wanted to go to a pub to get a whisky to warm them, but the pubs were closed. There was nothing for it but to go back to the station and wait for a train.

Standing on the platform, she said, "I haven't told anyone—what I told you. Not even Clary."

"I wouldn't dream of telling Clary—or anyone else," he replied.

They had a carriage to themselves on the slow Sunday train that stopped at every station. He talked to her—about her drawing, about painting in general, about life at Hamilton Terrace, about anything but her confidence or her feeling about it. She felt he was trying to prop up her dignity and did not like it: it prompted her to efforts of her own.

"What I shall probably do," she said, "after the war, that is, is to find someone who is building houses and be the person who does the inside of them. I don't mean just the paint or wallpaper, I mean the inside architecture—doors and floors and fireplaces—" but then she found that she was starting to cry, so she pretended to sneeze and turned to the train window. "Oh dear! I bet I've caught a cold," she said.

At Paddington, he asked her what she wanted to do, and she said she thought she would just go home. "Would anyone be there?" he asked, and she said yes, she was sure someone would.

In fact, she thought she knew that there would be no one, but she was wrong. She saw Louise's coat flung on the hall table at the same moment as she heard her sobbing from above. Michael has been killed, she thought, as she ran up the stairs.

She found her in the small spare room lying face downwards on the bed.

At first Louise was incoherent with grief—or was it anger?, she didn't know which—

"It slipped out!" she said. "Someone who came to lunch just said it—in a sort of what-a-pity voice . . . no warning! And *they* all knew and they never told me. *She* must have known! What a shock . . . I *couldn't* stay after that. I just left the table and then I ran. Oh! *Polly!* How can I bear it! And it was supposed to be nearly the end of the war!'' A fresh paroxysm overwhelmed her.

She sat on the edge of the bed and put a timid hand upon Louise's arm. Eventually Louise became quieter, rolled over and sat up, arms clasped round her knees.

''It was ten days ago,'' she said. ''It was in *The Times*, they said, but *she* knew I didn't know.''

''Who are you talking about?'' she asked, as gently as she could.

''Zee! She hates me for it.''

She knew now that it wasn't Michael.

''Are you talking about Hugo?''

She flinched as though his name had struck her. ''I loved him so much! With all my heart. And now I've got the whole of the rest of my life without him. I don't know how to manage that at all.'' She looked up. ''Oh, Poll! You are so comforting—to cry with me!''

The Family

April–May, 1945

TONBRIDGE GOT BACK from fetching Mrs. Rupert from the station in nice time for his elevenses with what he described to himself as "my intended." He had tried to pass a few interesting remarks to Mrs. Rupert on their way back from Battle, but she hadn't seemed interested. He'd mentioned the American President passing away and the Allies liberating Vienna—not that that could be expected to interest British people much, and he had added that it was his considered opinion that the war could not last very much longer, but Mrs. Rupert hadn't really *conversed* with him about any of it. She had been looking very pale lately—peaky, Mabel had said when they discussed it—and he wondered whether she was not feeling herself but naturally he passed no remark about that.

Anyway, when he had carried her case in for her, and put the car back in the garage, he walked across the courtyard to the back door and through the kitchen to the servants' sitting room, but although there was a tray set with some drop scones and two pieces of gingerbread and the miniature toby jug full of top of the milk, she wasn't there. That was funny, because she hadn't been in the kitchen either when he passed through.

He went back to the kitchen where Lizzie was up to her elbows washing spring greens in the sink. She was the kind of girl who always gave a start when you spoke to her and then you couldn't hardly hear what she said. *She* didn't know where Mrs. Cripps was. This was annoying, because he had something very important to tell her and he'd been saving it up for the appropriate moment of peace and hot tea that they usually enjoyed in the morning. He went back to the sitting room and sat down in his usual chair to wait for her.

Mrs. Cripps had been having a very unusual morning. Dr. Carr, who was paying his weekly visit to poor Miss Barlow upstairs, had been taking a look at her legs. They had hurt her something awful lately, and matters had come to a head after one of the morning sessions with Miss Rachel, as Mrs. Cazalet Senior was feeling a bit under the weather. She had stood, as she always stood with Mrs. Senior, while the day's meals were discussed—not that there was very much choice these days, but Madam had always ordered the food and there was such a thing as standards, so she had stood as usual—taking the weight off her feet by leaning one elbow on the back of a kitchen chair. But that morning, when she had shifted to give the other leg a rest, the chair-back had given way, just splintered to the floor, and she had gone with it. This had hurt her so badly that she had not been able to help a shriek of pain, and what with that, and the fact that she couldn't, at first, get *up* from the floor, she had altogether given way. She had *cried*, in front of Miss Rachel who had been ever so kind as indeed she always was. She had helped her up and taken her into the sitting room and made her sit down with her feet up and told Lizzie to make a cup of tea, and it was when her legs were up on a stool with the cushion on it that Miss Rachel had noticed them. She was ashamed for anyone to see them, and she was only too glad that Frank had had to take the car to the garage for the morning and was safely out of the way.

Anyway, the upshot was that Miss Rachel said Dr. Carr must look at them, and meanwhile she had gone to Battle and bought her some heavy elasticated stockings that had been a great comfort. Dr. Carr had seen her in her own bedroom, as she had told Miss Rachel that the men might come into the servants' hall at any minute and it wouldn't be right. Dr. Carr had said that she should have come to him before, and she really needed an operation, and she hadn't worried too much about that at first because, being on the Panel, she didn't think they did them. But then, when Miss Rachel came in she had said that she would pay for it, and then she had felt really frightened, because the only time she had been to a hospital in her life had been when her father was dying. And then Dr. Carr had asked her how old she was, and telling him—fifty-six in June, she would be—she was suddenly overcome with shame, with remorse, because she had not told Frank this at all. She had told him that she was forty-two when he asked, and she'd stuck to it. He'd believed her, of course, in spite of her saying she was over ten years younger than she really was. Naturally, she wouldn't tell a lie to a *doctor*, but telling him the truth made her suddenly feel that it was very wrong to conceal it from Frank. She'd been afraid he wouldn't want to marry her if he knew—hadn't even been sure whether he envisaged children, but when she had told him forty-two, he had said, "Well, it doesn't sound as though our troubles will be little ones," and he'd gone red when he said it, and they'd changed the subject. Well, she might have an operation in a hospital and die, but she did want to be married first, and she didn't want to die with a lie on her lips to her husband. So she would have to tell him.

He was waiting for her in the servants' hall—wondering where she had got to, he said. Then, just as she was going to tell him, Lizzie brought in the tea, and then, when she had let it stand and was pouring it out, he pulled a brown envelope out of his pocket and said that he had had a letter from the lawyers saying he had got a Decree Nice Eye, whatever that might mean. It was to do with the divorce, but it wasn't the end of it, oh dear no. After the Nice Eye you had to wait for something called the Absolute. *Then* it was over. But that, he said, was only a matter of weeks . . .

She was opening her mouth to tell him, when he stopped her again, by producing a small box, pressing a little knob on the lid which flew open to expose a *ring*—two, what looked like diamonds, not large, of course, you wouldn't expect it with diamonds, each side of a smaller dark stone.

"Rubies and diamonds," he said, "and it's nine carat gold."

It was a real engagement ring and quite took her breath away, but when he tried to get it on her finger it was too small—wouldn't go above her second knuckle. "I'll have it enlarged," he said, but she could see he was disappointed.

"It's really lovely," she said. "Frank, you shouldn't have. It's ladies that have engagement rings."

"And you are a lady," he said, "if ever I saw one."

Perhaps it would go on her little finger, she suggested, just for the time being, but it wouldn't even do that. Don't put it away, she said, she wanted to look at it, and she laid it on the palm of her hand with the diamonds winking if you caught them right in the light.

"Are they *real*, then?" she asked: she did not think they could be, but he said of course they were.

"They must be ever so valuable."

"Well, they're not exactly . . . cheap," he had answered in tones that showed he agreed.

She was entranced. It was the most valuable thing she'd ever *touched* in her life, and he'd gone and bought it for her.

"Oh, Frank!" she said. "Oh, Frank!" There were tears in her eyes, and she gave a series of short, sharp sniffs. "I'm so pleased! I'm *ever* so pleased. I really am!" And then she told him—quickly while he was on the crest of her gratitude.

He didn't seem to mind at *all*. "I knew—really," he said. "I mean—that you might not be quite the age you said you was. No self-respecting lady would tell a gentleman *exactly* her age." He looked at her with his mournful brown eyes that were now far less mournful than usual—were almost glowing with satisfaction at his generosity. "For me," he said, "you will always be young."

He picked up the ring and put it back in its box. "It is only," he said, "a small Token of my Esteem."

After all the trouble that she had taken to get away to London at such short notice, Jack had only stayed for Saturday night; he had left to fly to Germany very early on Sunday morning. There was nothing new about this situation: it had been going on more or less ever since D-Day nearly a year ago. He was abroad practically all the time, returning only for the odd night, or sometimes two or three days, usually at short notice, although not as short as this last time when he had literally rung up on Friday afternoon to ask if she could come up that evening. In spite of the fact that he had come through these last months unscathed, she could not get rid of or in any way diminish her sense of anxiety about him, so that each parting had a kind of double-edged anguish about it. Their meetings were still charged with excitement and joy, and for the first few hours they could be entirely engrossed by each other; the world and the war seemed hardly to exist, but somehow, always, something—often small— happened that breached their magic circle and brought them back to a dreary, and to her nerve-racking, reality. In the winter after the invasion it had sometimes been the V-2s. Even when they fell miles away you could not ignore the explosion; it shook the stomach as no other bombs seemed ever to have done, although she had not experienced very many of any of them. Her association with Jack brought her face to face with the war in a way that nothing had, excepting Rupert's disappearance, and that had happened so long ago now that it had become like a piece of sad history. Sometimes Jack would say, "I must call my office," and listening to him talk to unknown people whom clearly he often knew well, but whom she had never met, made her realize that nine-tenths of his life was unknown to her.

She did slowly discover more about him. Once, a few weeks after the invasion, he brought her back a box that contained a set of exquisite embroidered silk underwear—a camisole, a petticoat and French knickers all in pale turquoise silk edged with creamy lace; she had seen nothing like it since before the war. "The shops hid them," he said. "They kept them for when we would come." But later that time, when they were having dinner and she had asked him about Paris and whether it had been fun to go there, he had said no, it hadn't been fun at all.

He had been cutting up some meat before eating it with his fork and, feeling her attention, he looked up, and for a fleeting moment she saw a look of utter despair in his eyes—two black fathomless wells. This disappeared so quickly that she wondered whether she had imagined it. His mouth smiled, he reached for his glass and drank. "Never mind," he said. "There was nothing I could do about it."

In bed, when it was dark, she put her arms round him. "What happened in Paris? I really want to know."

He said nothing, but just when she began to think she shouldn't have asked, he said, "My best friend in New York—he was a Polish Jew—told me that if I ever got to Paris, I must look up his parents who had been living there since nineteen thirty-eight. They'd sent him to America, because he had an uncle there, but his sister had stayed with his parents. He wrote the address down for me, and I kept it, although I didn't know if I'd ever get the chance to use it. Well, I went to his street, to the house where they used to live, and they weren't there. I asked around and I discovered that they'd been taken off to a camp a few months before the invasion. All three of them. They were collected one night and nobody ever heard anything more."

"But if they went to a camp in Germany, you'll still be able to find them, won't you? I mean, we've nearly got to Berlin."

It was odd: she could not remember what he said in reply, but the next day he had been withdrawn, in one of his unreachable sombre moods that she did not understand, and that made her feel vaguely frightened.

There came to be a kind of tacit censorship of what they talked about: once she had tried to find out about his marriage, but he had only said, "She wanted me to bully her, make all the decisions, order her about—no, correction, she wanted a *rich* bully and that bored me. We brought out the worst in each other. Will that do?" And after that Elaine, she was called, was never mentioned again. They never talked about Rupert, although he always asked after Juliet. They talked about their own brief past with each other but never, since that time on the bench by the Serpentine, about the future. They talked about books that he had given her to read, and films they saw, discussing the characters in these as though in lieu of the mutual friends that otherwise they did not have. Bed became the safest place. There was no censorship there: familiarity enhanced pleasure and the smallest discovery about the sensuality of either became an added joy. Sex was not so much taking off one's clothes as getting into one's body, she said to him one night.

A second Christmas apart. "Oh, I wish I could ask you home," she had said, and had then been afraid that he might say why didn't she? But he didn't. He would be working then anyway, he said, "sending pictures of the boys at Christmas to the folks back home."

After that, she didn't see him for nearly a month. And after that, their times together became fewer and further apart. So that, in spite of the terribly short notice, she had managed to get Clary down to look after Jules and gone to London on the Saturday morning as early as possible, and they had spent the day and the night together. He hadn't told her that he was going away on Sunday morning until after they had made love for the first time.

"I'm sorry," he said, "but I have to go."

"Where? Where are you going?"

"Somewhere east of Bremen. A place called Belsen."

It didn't really matter *where* he was going, she wept, it was the fact that he was going at all. Why hadn't he told her?

He hadn't been sure: he was substituting for someone else at the last minute; he'd pulled strings not to go this day in order to see her. He would be back. The war was nearly over, and, anyway, he would be back.

He left at five in the morning to catch a plane. She hated the flat without him. She got up and tidied everything and wondered what on earth to do. She couldn't go back to Sussex so soon (she was supposed to be returning on Monday). Then she suddenly thought of

Archie, and rang him, but there was no answer. It was awful, the way she could think of nobody, not a single person, she could go and see. She spent the day walking about the streets as sometimes she used to do with Jack, eating some spaghetti in the small Italian restaurant that they used to go to together and afterwards returning to the flat where she lay on the bed to read, but almost at once fell asleep.

When she woke, it was nearly seven o'clock. There did not seem to be much point in getting up, since she had nowhere to go. She longed for someone to talk to about Jack, and started to dial Archie's number, but then changed her mind. He was Rupert's best friend, after all. She got up in search of food. There was half a packet of biscuits and some of the powdered orange juice that Jack drank in the mornings. She made herself a glass of this, and ate the biscuits, and went to bed again where she lay for hours, wakeful, worrying about where he was and whether he was in a safe place, and when he would return.

Early on Monday morning she rang Home Place and said she was catching the early train back so that Tonbridge would meet her.

She heard nothing from him that week, and then the following Friday he rang—at lunch-time, thank goodness, because it meant that the Brig was not in his study. Rachel had answered the telephone. She did not say who it was, but Zoë knew somehow that it would be Jack.

"Sorry to call you at lunch-time. I was wondering whether you could get away for tonight?"

"Oh, Jack! Why can't you give me more notice? I've just said I'll look after the children so that the nurse can have the weekend off."

"It wouldn't be for the weekend. Just for tonight." There was a pause, and then he said, "I'd really like to see you."

"You make it so difficult. You know I want to come. I can't, though. I really can't."

"OK. That's it, then."

There was a click, and she realized he had rung off. She rang his office, but they said he was not there; had not been there for some days. She rang the flat, and there was no reply. She went back to the dining room and pretended to finish her lunch.

All the afternoon, when, after their rests, she walked the children up to the shop in Watlington and back, she felt sick with anxiety. Now, if he were able to ask her, she would have dropped everything, and simply caught the next train—*walked* to the next station, if need be. Why had he rung off like that? It was not like anything she knew of him. But he had sounded strange: as though he knew something, or was concealing something—was angry—with her? Oh, *God!* Why had he rung off like that?

"We want to go back through the fields," Wills was announcing. They had reached the gate that opened onto the road from the field where the Home Place land began.

"No, we're going by the road today."

"Why are we? Why, Mummy? What good will it do?"

"We want to go back to the field with the charabanc tree."

This was a fallen pine tree where the passengers sat on the branches while one person drove holding the upturned roots as a steering wheel and the other walked precariously up the trunk dispensing tickets (oak leaves).

"Clary let us last weekend," Roly said.

"Yes, and she played with us. She didn't just stand about like Ellen talking about clean hands and meals."

"Grown-*ups*," scoffed Wills. "I'm just not going to *be* one, they are so boring."

"When you're a hundred, you'll be an awfully old child."

One of them was climbing the gate now. She'd either have to give in or stop them.

"I shall. The oldest child in the world. People will come for miles to see me. I shall be quite small but extremely wrinkly with specs. And a white beard."

"You'll be a dwarf, then," Roly said.

"No, I shall not. I hate them. I hate their pointed red caps."

She gave in. It seemed easier at the time.

"You can have ten minutes playing charabancs," she said, as they trudged through the long wet bright green grass.

"Ten minutes! Ten *hours* is what we want."

"Ten days."

"Ten weeks."

"Ten hundred years," said Juliet, pre-empting any further crescendo.

She looked at her pretty daughter, who was wearing a tweed coat, cast off by Lydia some years ago as too small for her, black wellingtons and a scarlet beret that was currently her favourite thing, and for the first time, the thought that in some unknown distance of time they might be in America together lingered in her mind. It seemed so extraordinary, and yet, what else could happen? One day, she thought, I shall look back on this house and the family as distant landmarks, which she supposed was how she now thought of Rupert. Then she thought of the family—particularly the Duchy—of how completely they had taken her in and made her one of themselves, of how this place, and she used to be bored in the country, had become her home in a way that no place she had lived in with her poor mother had ever been. She would have to leave *her*, too—and curiously, although she had endured three further visits to the Isle of Wight since the one she had returned from to meet Jack—"Don't you dare speak to any strange man you may meet on that train," he had enjoined her the first time she went after they had become lovers— curiously, that seemed hard, because she knew it would be hard on her mother, whereas leaving *here* would be harder for her than for any of the family. She would take Jack to see her mother, for *her* sake. And, of course, they would return to England to visit.

"How far are you going, madam?"

"America," she said without thinking.

"America? *America?* We don't *go* there, madam. We go to Hastings and then we go to Bexhill. You can go to both of them if you like." A damp leaf was thrust into her hand.

When she felt that everybody had had a turn at being the driver, the conductor and a mere passenger, she said it was time for tea. The person who was the driver—Juliet—said it wasn't fair, she hadn't been driving nearly as long as the other two, but the other two, having had their turn, sided with Zoë about tea.

"Yes, you have," they said brutally, "long enough for your age."

Tea had begun by the time they got back. It took place in the hall where the long table was spread with a cloth and the Duchy presided at one end with the teapots. Jack was sitting at her right hand.

"Here she is," the Duchy was saying as she came in with the children, tearing off their coats and boots to get at the tea. "Captain Greenfeldt has called on us, darling. Your friend, Margaret, told him where we were and as he was passing by he thought he would call. Isn't that nice?" And as she met her mother-in-law's frank and penetrating eye she knew that the Duchy knew.

Jack had risen as she came into the room. "Just a quick call," he said. "I hope you don't mind."

"Of course not." Her mouth was dry, and she sat, almost collapsed, into a chair opposite him at the table.

"If you were a proper American," Lydia said, "you'd have rushed round and pulled out her chair for her. That's what they do in films. But we don't do it here. Perhaps you knew that."

"Mummy, my socks have come off with my boots so could I just be in my feet for tea?"

"He *is* American," Wills said. "You can tell by his uniform." He was eight and very interested in soldiers.

"Don't talk about people in front of them as 'he,'" Rachel said. She was pouring mugs of milk.

"Is this your daughter?" Of course he knew that she was.

"Yes."

Juliet had slipped into the seat beside her and was now gazing at Jack with unblinking intensity.

"Captain Greenfeldt was telling us that he is just back from Germany," the Duchy was saying as she passed Zoë a cup of tea.

She suddenly remembered him saying "a place called Belsen" which, during the last ten days, had been much and horribly in the news.

"Did you go to take photographs at the Belsen camp?"

"I did."

"Oh," said Villy, "that must have been simply horrifying. Those poor, poor people!"

"I think," the Duchy said, "that perhaps *pas devant les enfants.*"

"Not in front of the children," Lydia said. "We all knew that ages ago."

Wills, who often quoted him, said, "Tonbridge said it was a death camp. But he said it was mostly Jews in it. What are Jews?"

Jack said, "I am a Jew."

Wills looked at him gravely. "You don't look at all different," he said. "I don't see how they could tell."

Lydia, who did not read newspapers or talk to Tonbridge, now said, "Do you mean it is a camp for *killing* people? What happens to all their children?"

Villy, in a voice of icy authority, said, "Lydia, will you please take all three children upstairs to the nursery? At once!"

And Lydia, after one glance at her mother's face, did as she was told, the others following her with surprising meekness. The tension in the room lessened—but not very much. Villy offered Jack a cigarette and while he was lighting his and hers for her, Zoë, who discovered that she had been pressing the palms of her hands onto the carving of her chair so hard that she had nearly broken the skin, looked mutely at Jack as though to implore him to help them to escape.

The Duchy said, "Zoë, why don't you take Captain Greenfeldt to the morning room for a little peace and quiet?"

"Your daughter is very like you."

The small room, with its gate-legged table, had four chairs ranged round it. He had sat down in one of them. Now she could look at him and was shocked. She had wanted to fling herself into his arms, tell him how sorry she was that she hadn't immediately said she would come to London, but instead she sank into the chair opposite him. He was reaching in his pocket and drew out his packet of cigarettes to light one from the Goldflake that Villy had given him. She noticed that his hands shook.

"It was all in front of the children there," he said. "They were playing round an enormous pit—eighty yards long, thirty feet wide—piled high with the bodies of their mothers, grandmothers, aunts—naked *skeletons* piled on top of each other—four feet high."

She stared at him aghast, trying, and failing to imagine such a scene. "Would you like me to come back to London with you?"

He shook his head. "I have to go back very early tomorrow morning. It wouldn't be worth it."

"Back to that camp?"

"No, another one. Buchenwald. Our troops are there. I've been once, but I've got to go back." He stubbed out his cigarette.

She said, "But when you rang, when you called me from London, you wanted me to come then."

"Ah, well. I had a sudden urge to see you. Then I thought that I'd like to see you in your home—with your family—before I went."

"When will you be back?"

He shrugged. Then he tried to smile. "Your mother-in-law is one nice lady. You're in good hands." He lit another cigarette. "But thanks for offering to come."

There was a kind of bleak courtesy about him that frightened her. Searching for anything that might comfort either of them, she said, "But those poor people will be all right now, won't they? I mean they are safe now and people will look after them and give them food."

"Some of them. Six hundred are dying and being buried every day at Belsen. And they say over two thousand will die at Buchenwald—too far gone. And those aren't the only camps, you know. We haven't reached all of them, but they'll be like that. And millions *have* died."

There did not seem to be any comfort.

He looked at his watch, and got to his feet. "My cab will be here by now. I mustn't miss that train. I'm glad I've seen Juliet, at last."

"Are you really going to be away a long time?"

"Yep. Better count on that."

She was standing now, facing him, between him and the door.

"Jack! You're not angry with me, are you?"

"What makes you think that?"

She wanted to cry, "Everything!" but all she said was, "You haven't kissed me. You haven't touched me, even."

For the first time, his black, bleak eyes softened in the old way: he took a step towards her and put his hands on her shoulders. "I am not angry with you," he said. He kissed her gently on her lips. "I've gotten rather out of touch with love," he said. "You'll have to bear with me about that."

"I will, I will! But it will come back, won't it?"

Still holding her shoulders, he pushed her a little away from him. "Sure. Will you say goodbye to them for me? And thanks, for everything? Don't cry." It was a command rather than a plea. "I left my cap in the hall."

"I'll get it." She didn't want the intrusion of other people. But the hall was empty, and the cap lay on the table. When she returned with it, he had already gone the other way to the front door, which he had opened. He took the cap and put it on. "I'm glad I came." He touched her cheek with two fingers.

"Look after yourself and—Jules, you call her, don't you?" He bent and kissed the cheek he had touched—his lips were as cold as his fingers. Then he swung away from her and walked, very fast, to the gate and out of sight. She stood, listening to the taxi's engine starting, the door slamming and then the sound of it going down the drive until she could not hear it at all.

Villy, in town for a day and a night, was having lunch with Jessica in the little house in Chelsea she had rented in Paradise Walk. They were better friends again now that it was common knowledge that Laurence (they no longer called him Lorenzo) had left his wife to live with a young opera singer. They had even had a cautiously commiserating talk about poor Mercedes and what was to become of her, and had come to the uneasy conclusion that although she was desperately unhappy, she was probably better off without him. (Of course, Villy thought, Jessica did not know about her frightful evening.)

It was a Monday. Villy had spent the morning at Lansdowne Road and apologized for arriving dishevelled.

"The news is so good, you'll soon be back there, won't you?" said Jessica as she showed her the tiny bathroom.

"Edward thinks it's too big for us now that Louise is married and Teddy is launched, so to speak. I shall be very sad." She had taken off her watch and was rolling up her sleeves. "I'm so filthy, I really ought to have a bath."

"Darling, do, if you want to. Lunch can wait—it's only a sort of pie."

"I'll just wash."

"What a pretty house it is!" she exclaimed as she came down the stairs again to the sitting room.

"It is rather a doll's house, but it suits me beautifully. *So* easy to keep. All I need is a daily for the housework."

"Has Raymond seen it?"

"Not yet. It seems to be more and more difficult for him to get away. But he so loves being important, and he seems to have made friends in Oxford and, of course, I go to Frensham at weekends to help Nora."

"How is that going?"

"Very well, I think. I don't find *him* very easy to *know*, but she seems utterly devoted. It's rather a weak gin, I'm afraid. I've run out and my local grocery rations everybody—one bottle a month." She took her gin and sat with it in the second armchair.

"The news *is* good, isn't it?" said Villy. "We'll be in Berlin any day now."

"Except for those awful, dreadful camps. I simply couldn't believe it! It's obscene!"

"It seems so extraordinary that it could all have been going on and people didn't *know*."

"I'm sure they knew. I've always loathed Germans."

"But Daddy had such a lovely time there when he was a student. Do you remember how marvellous he said it was? Even the smallest provincial town had its concerts."

"I agreed with Mr. Churchill. Words can't express the horror."

"Yes." They could neither of them think of anything else to say about the camps, and there was a short silence while Villy smoked and Jessica watched her. She had got much older: her hair was nearly white now; her skin had become weatherbeaten and dry, the slate blue veins on the back of her hands much raised, her neck an old woman's neck. She is only a year older than me, Jessica thought, only forty-nine, but she does look older. The war has taken its toll of her, she thought, whereas for me it marked the time when I suddenly had more money and far fewer chores. And, of course, the affair with Lorenzo (she still called him that to herself), even if he was rather naughty in the end, *was* fun while it lasted. Actually, she was quite dreading the peace with Raymond about all the time wanting regular meals and having nothing to do. On her own, she hardly ever cooked—even the pie in the oven at the moment had been bought, and when Judy came home for the holidays, she either stayed with school friends or at Frensham. Nora was fully occupied, and Christopher seemed to like his strange hermit-like existence. Angela . . . That was the reason that she had wanted Villy to come to lunch, to have the chance to air some of her feelings about Angela. She waited, however, until they were sitting at the small table laid for lunch at the far end of the room.

She began by asking about Louise, who, Villy said, seemed rather under the weather. Dr. Ballater, to whom Villy had made her go, said that she really ought to have her tonsils out—she was in fact going into hospital some time this week. Teddy, in Arizona, had finished his training as a fighter pilot, but had been kept on there, thank goodness. "With any luck, he won't have to be in the war, and Lydia—" And then, realizing from her sister's face that she was bursting to tell her something, she stopped and said, "Come on, Jess. What is it? You're looking quite tragic."

"I feel it. I really want your advice. I simply don't know what to do!"

"What is it, darling? Of course I'll help in any way that I can."

"It's Angela. She rang me last week and told me that she was going to get married."

"Well, darling, isn't that rather—"

"Wait! He's American!"

"Well, that seems to me perfectly—".

"*And* he's nearly twenty years older than she is, *and* he's been married before. He's got a daughter nearly the same age as Angela who is a *tap* dancer! And when I asked what he does in peace time, she said he was psychiatrist!"

"Have you met him?"

"She brought him here last week for a drink. He's a funny little square man with a face like a pug and very *hirsute*. He calls her Hon."

"You mean, as though she was *German*?"

"No, short for honey. And she calls him Earl."

"Why does she do that?"

"It's his *name!* Earl C. Black. She wants to become Mrs. Earl C. Black. The Second."

Her distress was so operatic and she reminded Villy so much of their mother that she nearly burst out laughing.

"Darling! Don't you think you are being a tiny bit narrow-minded?" (Snobbish, she wanted to say.) "Does Angela love him?"

"She *says* so," Jessica replied, as though this did not make it more likely to be true.

"Well, then, I can't see what you are worrying about. I mean, of course, it will be sad that she will be so far away, but you will go and visit her. And you've always worried that she wouldn't get married at all."

"Oh, but, Villy, you *know* what I mean! She was such a lovely girl and I must confess that I had pinned my hopes on her making what Mummy would have called 'a good marriage.' You know, as your Louise has done. It does seem such a fearful waste. Mummy would have been appalled!"

"Darling, we can't *choose* who our children marry, and Mummy was simply appalled at both of *our* husbands, don't you remember? I think you should stop worrying, and be glad for Angela. When is it to be?"

"*She* wants it to be at once, but he wants to wait and see whether when the war here is over, he gets sent to the Pacific to finish off the Japanese."

"Well, that seems very thoughtful of him." She continued in this vein until Jessica seemed to have run out of objections. Privately she thought that Jessica should thank her lucky stars. There had been rumours about Angela—Edward said that a friend of his in the RAF had actually *picked her up* in a bar, but on seeing her uncle Edward, she'd beaten a hasty retreat. It was clear that she had been leading a rather rackety life, and although naturally Villy did not dream of telling Jessica any of this, it made her more robust in her advice than she might otherwise have been.

"I'm sure it will all turn out well," she said, as she left after lunch to do some shopping before she met Edward at the club for dinner. "Thank you for a lovely lunch. Do keep in touch. And do look on the bright side about Angela, darling."

She had reason to remember this last admonition with some bitterness when she met Edward in the coffee room for a drink before dinner. She could tell at once that something was up, that he had something—not good—to tell her and for one frightful moment she thought it might be Teddy . . .

"It's Teddy," he said. "No, no, he's quite all right—oh, darling, sorry. I didn't mean to frighten you. But he sent this." He produced an air mail letter and held it out. "Have a swig of your gin before you read it," he said.

Dear Mummy and Dad,

This is rather a serious letter and I do hope it won't be a shock to you, but I have met the most marvellous girl and we want to be married. Her name is Bernadine Heavens and she had to give up her career in Hollywood to marry some brute but he left her quite soon with two children and she had an awful time till we met. She is a really wonderful person, very funny and gay, but also extremely deep and a serious person underneath. You would like her if you saw her. The thing is because of my age we have to have your permission to marry. She wanted me to write to you the moment we got engaged which was the second time that we met, but I felt it might be too much of a shock. She is the most wonderful person I've ever met in my life. I honestly never thought of being married until I met her and then—bang! I just fell for her, and she for me. She has had a really sad life as her father left her mother when she was quite small and her mother made her live with an aunt as she couldn't be bothered. But Bernadine has come through it all in the most wonderful way: she bears no malice to anyone she says. She would write to you only she says she is not much of a hand at letter-writing.

The thing is that actually we *did* get married last week, only Bernadine can't get a passport until we've been married again with your permission. Isn't it amazing? If I hadn't been asked to stay on helping to train other pilots, I wouldn't have met her. She works in the canteen here, but she only started a month ago so I might have come back to England and we would never have met. It gives us the shivers to think about it, but as she says, it must have been Meant . . . You see what I mean about her? She is actually frightfully thinking and deep—not a shallow person at all. I do hope you will be understanding and write back to me quickly.

Your loving son, Teddy.

"Good God!"

"I know." His eyes were like blue marbles, and she could see that he was very angry. "What was his commanding officer up to, for God's sake? *He* must have had to give permission."

"I suppose he may not even have known. They may just have slipped off somewhere. It's far easier to get married in America, isn't it? I mean people in films are always waking up Justices of the Peace or getting married in drawing rooms. Oh, Teddy! How could he do it!"

"Completely irresponsible. He's old enough to know better."

"I bet it was the girl. I bet she trapped him. She's clearly older than he is."

"How *much* older, I wonder?"

"He doesn't say how old the children are."

"I expect he went on about Home Place and the house in London and she thinks she's on to a thoroughly good thing. Well—she'll soon find out. She won't find it fun living on his pay, and when the war's over, and he *does* go into the firm, he'll have to work his passage— like anyone else."

She had been reading the letter again while he was talking. "He's completely *infatuated*. And even so, he manages to make her sound awful."

"I expect she *is* awful. Supposing we simply refuse to give permission?"

"He'll be twenty-one in October. He's only got to wait until then."

He snapped his fingers at the waiter.

"Two large martinis, George, if you would. *Really* large."

When they were having dinner, she said, "Was that what you said you wanted to talk to me about this morning?"

"What? Oh—yes—yes, it was."

"I can't think how you managed not to tell me on the telephone."

"Oh, well," he said. "I wanted you to see the letter. And it would only have spoiled your day. How was Jessica, by the way?"

"It's quite funny, really. She was worried about Angela marrying an American, and I was telling her to look on the bright side of things. It serves me right. I think I'd rather have Earl C. Black than Bernadine Heavens."

"Good Lord! Is that what he's called? What a pity we can't pair them off."

"Although, darling, she *may* be very nice. One can't go on names."

"We *aren't* going on names. I'm going on the fact that although she's older—probably a good *deal* older—she married a mere boy behind his parents' back. At best, she's a baby snatcher. At worst a gold digger. Probably both," he ended gloomily.

"It's extraordinary, isn't it? We don't actually *know* a single American. At least, I don't. Perhaps you do." Then she thought of Captain Greenfeldt, whom she had thought rather charming in a haunted way, but decided not to mention him.

During coffee he reverted to the question of moving house. He thought she should come to London for a few days to start looking for something smaller and more suitable. "We can store the furniture at the Wharf and put the house on the market," he said.

"All right, I will." For some reason the whole idea filled her with a vague dread, but she did not say so. "It isn't," she said as she poured them a second cup of coffee, "it isn't at all her being American. It's his marrying the first girl he has anything to do with."

"It's funny you should say that. I was just wondering how many parents are sitting over coffee in America reading letters from their twenty-year-old sons saying that they've fallen in love with Grizelda Wickham-Painswick-Wickham or Queenie Bloggs and how much they are looking forward to introducing them to the family. I'm sure we're not alone, if that's any comfort."

She smiled at him. He did not often indulge in such flights of fancy: the remark was much the kind that dear Rupert would once have made . . .

"Now. Whereabouts are you going to look?"

"Look?"

"For your house. This would be a good time to buy, although we'll need a bloody good surveyor—I should think at least a third of the houses in London have suffered some sort of war damage."

"Edward, I can't see that we have to move at all. Lansdowne Road isn't all that big. Lydia could have Louise's old room, and Roly and a nanny—I'll have to get one—can share the top floor with the servants. And Teddy's room can be a spare."

But he was adamant and in the end she gave way, and then a friend of Edward's came to offer them a drink to celebrate Hitler having shot himself, a piece of news that in any other circumstances would have dominated their evening.

* * *

Michael took Louise to the hospital on Sunday evening, before catching his train back to Portsmouth. It meant leaving her there rather earlier than originally planned, but he wanted to see her in, and he *had* to catch the train.

"Shall we go out to lunch?" he said to her that morning.

"If you like." She did not seem exactly enthusiastic, but, then, she did not seem to be that about anything these days. Mummy had written two immensely long letters about Louise running away in the middle of the weekend at Hatton, and had said in both of them that, of course, she had had no *idea* that Louise had not known about Hugo's death, and he was sure that Mummy would not say that if it was not true, although Louise said, "She hates me and she knew perfectly well that I didn't know. I wouldn't have gone to stay at all if I'd known," she had added, but he put all that down to hysteria on Louise's part. Of course it had upset her; the death of anyone one had known was upsetting. *He* felt sad about it—in a complicated sort of way. Indeed, whenever he thought of Hugo, which was more often than he liked because it aroused a whole lot of conflicting feelings that he didn't want to go into, he felt this clash of jealousy, and sadness, nostalgia for a halcyon time of his life before the war when Hugo came to stay in the vac for weeks on end and Mummy treated him like another son, encouraging them to do everything together. They had played tennis and racquets, and shot and gone hacking and taken a boat out on the lake and he'd done one of the best portraits of his life of him. And Mummy had been so sweet—never interfering, only every week or so she seemed to have to have various daughters of friends of hers for lunch or the weekend, and there had been a family joke about *how* desperately plain/dull they invariably were. It quite put him off girls, but Mummy, kind as always, had said that one must be sorry for them, poor things. She called him and Hugo Ancient Greeks. She had been very kind to Hugo's poor mother, sending her money quite regularly and Hugo had been very touched by that: he, too, was fond of his mother. He had, actually, fallen a bit in love with Hugo and for a long time he had said nothing about it to anyone, but eventually, it came out. Hugo hadn't felt as he did, which at the time seemed awful and they'd almost had a row. Of course Mummy knew: she seemed to know everything that mattered to him. "Oh, darling, what rotten bad luck," she had said: she was wonderfully *broad-minded*; most mothers would have got tremendously worked up, but Mummy was not like that. After that, Hugo hadn't come at all to Hatton for a bit, and by the time he had found Rowena and was a bit in love with her he didn't mind Hugo being there at all. But it had never been the same with him again. But then, Hugo had ensconced himself in *his* house and seduced his wife—a really dirty trick. And she wouldn't have another child, although Mummy said really she ought to—a son and a brother for Sebastian. But lately, Louise had even been difficult about bed, said she didn't want it and she was tired. He thought that that was probably because, poor little thing, her throat had made her really run down. After her operation, he was going to see to it that she had a proper holiday—he thought the Scilly Isles might be good for her. Sea air and a quiet life, if her friend Stella could go with her. He so wanted her to get well and happy again.

Meanwhile, he had his problems. They were very likely to offer him the command of one of the newer destroyers to take to the Pacific which was a pretty exciting thought. It would make a triumphant culmination of his career in the Navy. Not many Wavy Navy officers had got that far. But Mummy, who said she had given the matter a good deal of thought (and, of course, she had discussed this with the Judge), said that this was the moment for him to go into politics. There would be an election once the war was over here, and Mummy said the PM was keen on getting Conservative candidates from the Services, and obviously, with a bit of a name already, he stood a good chance of getting in. He wasn't sure that he wanted to become a Member of Parliament, but it might be a bit of a lark to go for it and see what happened. He'd told Louise about all this over dinner, which had been rather a dreary affair as so many restaurants were closed on Sunday evenings. But they'd gone to the Savoy.

"If you stayed in the Navy, how long would you be away?" she had asked.

"Darling, *I* don't know. Until the Japanese surrender. We're doing quite well out there now, taking Rangoon and all that, but it could be anything up to eighteen months or so, I should think."

"And if you went into politics?"

"I'd come out of the Navy, we'd buy a nice house in London and, with any luck, you'd become an MP's wife."

"Oh."

"What do you think?"

"I thought you wanted to be a painter."

"Darling, I shall never stop *painting*. But, as you know, I'm a vulgar sort of chap who likes to make his mark in other ways as well."

"I don't know. You'll have to decide. After all, it's your life."

"It's both our lives," he said, wishing that this had already occurred to her. "The first thing is to get you well again."

In the train he could minutely recall her face, although, funnily enough, he couldn't *draw* her from memory. But he knew how the creases in her eyelids made a pretty curve over her eyes (but also how they were different from one another), how her cheekbones ran into the top of her ears so that her face was almost pointed, how her eyebrows had a sharp angle on them so that they were almost like shallow roots over her eyes, how her hair sprang from a widow's peak which to her chagrin, was just off centre but, as he had pointed out, would only matter if she had happened to live in the sixteenth century, how she would bite the inside of her bottom lip when she was thinking, and, above all, what an extraordinary contrast her face presented full face, from her profile when her large rather beaky nose predominated. Full face, one had no idea of its prominence (she hated her profile), but this made her most interesting to draw from a three-quarters angle. He loved her appearance, and although she was turning out to be a more complicated creature than he had first thought her, he was glad that he had married her.

When he had left her at the hospital, Louise had felt pretty nervous. The last time he had done that everybody had been horrible, which had been almost as bad as the pain. But the hospital was quite different. She was taken to a bare little room that contained nothing but a high bed, a washstand basin, a small table beside it, a chair and a small wardrobe for her clothes. She was invited to undress and get into bed. Thereafter a series of people came to see her: a nurse to take her temperature and blood pressure, the anaesthetist who asked her if she had any false teeth and finally the Sister, who was both formidable and reassuring. "Sorry we have to starve you this evening," she said. "But Mr. Farquhar's operating at eight o'clock. What I should like you to do now is to get a good night's sleep. There's a bell there if you want anything."

"Does the operation take a long time?"

"Oh, no. It's very quick. You will have rather a sore throat afterwards, but that will soon wear off."

When she had gone, Louise lay, listening to the distant traffic in Tottenham Court Road. She did not feel nervous any more. These nurses seemed kind and efficient and as for the operation—she did not care about that. She would not, she felt, even care very much if she died from it. Ever since she had learned of Hugo's death she had felt a little mad: as though it simply wasn't possible to be responsible for herself, so if a very expensive doctor killed her by mistake she would merely be relieved of the seemingly endless efforts of pretending to be somebody who had interests, opinions and feelings. She was quite good at the pretence; it was, after all, simply acting, something that was becoming second nature to her, and it didn't matter very much, but it was an effort and she felt tired all the time.

She had *not* forgiven Michael for destroying Hugo's letter, but as the weeks had gone by in the Station Hotel, she had come to see that he, Michael, had absolutely no idea about how much it had mattered to her, and although he had done this awful thing, he had not at all known how awful it was, which somehow exonerated him—and made her feel that her resentment was irrational. But when she knew that she would never see him again, that there never could be another letter, then, locked in the impotence of her grief, she raged at Michael, attributing actual malice to his destruction. None of this was apparent: it was her secret life; *he* did not tell her things—he had not told her about Hugo and it transpired that he *had* seen the newspaper, though not when it came out. She had been *sickened* by his attempts to exonerate Zee, and when, one day, he had started to say he was sorry *he* hadn't told her about Hugo, she had cut him short saying that she never wished to speak of Hugo with him again in her life. She would not go to Hatton either, she said. He had accepted these strictures with surprising meekness, but he had gone on in bed as though everything was the same.

When she knew that Hugo was dead, after the first few awful days—when both Polly and Clary had been really good to her; indeed Polly had cried that first evening almost as much as she—she came out of it heartless, as though she had literally lost her heart. This made one thing seem very like another—she could not put a value upon anything more significant than having an amusing evening, or people flirting with her. And so, when Rory turned up at her house one day on leave and made clear how much he had wanted her ever since their first meeting after her flu, she went to bed with him without a qualm. She found, also, that really not caring at all beyond the mild satisfaction of being admired and having attention paid to her, she became better at the bed side of life, as she put it. Rory had the added attraction of not knowing anything about Hugo, of not, indeed, knowing anything much at all about her. He also did not seem to notice that she was acting. For a few months she pretended to be someone who was having an exciting affair with a dashing, courageous young man who certainly amused her. They could not meet often, and usually not for long, and then, shortly after the night she had spent in his friend's flat, she met a girl at the Arts Theatre Club who had said she believed Louise knew Rory Anderson.

"I only asked, because the girl who shares my flat is mad about him. He's taking her to Scotland for his leave. I have the feeling he's a bit of a philanderer, and she's *so* serious. What do you think?"

And that was the end of that. He never even wrote to her, but she did not really care. Her vanity was dented, but she felt it was hard to see what she had to be vain about. She had been available and he had availed himself. "Can't even keep a lover," she said to herself in the jeering, worldly voice she now used for internal dialogue.

In the morning they gave her an injection and soon she felt wonderfully carefree and even more irresponsible. By the time she was wheeled to the theatre and put into some sort of reclining chair she felt as though she was going to a party.

Mr. Farquhar leaned over her: the bottom of his face was covered, but his eyes looked full of merry bonhomie. More anaesthetic—she felt herself drifting away—could scarcely determine his face above her and then there was one terrifying instant of shrill scorching agony—and then nothing.

When she came to she was back in bed and her throat hurt so much that she longed to pass out again. In the evening, Polly and Clary came to visit her, bringing *The Diary of a Nobody* and a bunch of grapes.

"It's a nice little book you can read lying on your back." Clary said. They said that peace had been signed. "Eisenhower signed it. I must say I thought it ought to have been Mr. Churchill, but there you are," Clary said. "Anyway, the Germans have surrendered—unconditionally."

"Well, they couldn't have any other way," Polly said. "And tomorrow there'll be Victory celebrations. It's making people awfully jolly and nice in the streets—as though it's everyone's birthday."

"It's jolly bad luck to be in hospital, poor Louise."

As she really couldn't talk much at all, they didn't stay, but said they'd come the day after tomorrow.

"Oh yes. Some people called Hammond rang and they wanted to come to see you. I told them where you were, and they said they would come tomorrow and hoped you'd be well enough to see them."

"Hammond?" she whispered, and then she remembered the agent, and Myfanwy and the baby. She had almost forgotten them, because Myfanwy's mother had taken her and the baby away with her the next day and she'd never seen them again. She wondered why they wanted to see her.

"Well, if you feel too ropy, I'm sure they will understand."

After they had gone, Sister came in and said that Commander Hadleigh had rung to ask how she was, and to send his love.

"I told him you were doing very well," she said. "You can have a little jelly or ice cream for your supper."

On her own again, and not up to reading, she felt feverish and horribly depressed. For years the end of the war had been a time to look forward to, when everything would be better and, indeed, wonderful. Now its immediate prospect seemed to her to hold the most dreary alternatives: becoming an MP's wife (she saw this as sitting on hard chairs at meetings for hours while people talked about mining, or having endless careful teas with strange people), *or* she would have to live on her own in a house with Sebastian and a nanny, waiting for Michael to come back from the Japanese war . . . She realized now that she did not want either of these. For the first time she faced the frightening possibility of not being married to Michael . . . She was not the right wife for him—no, that was a weak way of putting it, she wasn't up to being anybody's wife . . . She didn't love him: he seemed at once too old and too young for her and she found his relationship with his mother both despicable and frightening. Perhaps she was not capable of love—but this reached something so painful in her that it blocked any further thoughts. Somehow, somewhere, she seemed to have gone wrong, to have made a mess of things that could not now be unsaid or undone . . .

After lunch—ice cream—the next day, the Hammonds arrived. The nurse who brought them in said she would fetch another chair and a vase for the bunch of pink tulips that Myfanwy laid upon the bed. She looked very pretty in a brown dress with a cameo brooch on her white collar, and her hair—that Louise remembered as lying in disordered profusion on the pillows—was now piled neatly on top of her head.

"We were in London for a couple of days and felt we must see you," he said. His name was Arthur, but he was so much older than Myfanwy that she thought of him as Mr. Hammond.

"Myfanwy's never been to London," he said. "And I always promised her we'd come. We've certainly picked the right time for it. Awful bad luck for you being laid low on VE-Day."

Myfanwy seemed very shy, although she smiled whenever she caught Louise's eye.

Mr. Hammond asked after Michael, and then her child. Then Myfanwy said, "I never knew you had a baby. No wonder you were so good with Owen."

"How is he? Is he with you?"

"He's fine. He's with my mam—just for these few days."

Her husband said, "Myfanwy was so sorry not to see you again, but her mother took her home to look after her and the baby and there was no chance. But she wanted to thank you." He paused and looked at his wife, who blushed and then suddenly took Louise's hand.

"I do indeed thank you. You were so good to me. And the doctor said he thought you may have saved Owen's life. He told me afterwards how very poorly he was. There is no way I can thank you enough for that."

Soon after that, they left.

"I can see it tires you to talk," he said. "We shall never forget you."

"No, indeed. It's very glad we are to have seen you." She took Louise's hand again. "I am so grateful," she said, "for your goodness."

When they were gone, she lay looking at the two chairs. It was she who was grateful, because if they hadn't come to tell her that she would have continued to feel completely worthless.

When he was sure that Clary was safely tucked up in his bed and asleep, Archie limped painfully back into the sitting room and took off his shoes. He had taken Clary to see the celebrations outside Buckingham Palace, Polly having gone with her father. "I can't see why we can't all go together," Clary had said, "but Poll didn't want to."

"You'll just have to make do with me," he had replied, and she had said: "It won't be making *do*. You're not a making do sort of person, Archie, much more people's first choice." A remark that, coming from her, had given him inordinate pleasure.

He turned off the ceiling light. Then he fetched himself a whisky and decided to have it on his balcony where there were two chairs. He could put his bottom on one and his feet on the other. He was completely done in: not surprising, really, as they'd walked miles that evening. All the way to the Palace and then, eventually, back. And before that . . . One way and the other, he'd been on the go since

Friday, which seemed a very long way away now. On Friday morning, he'd been at his desk, the office buzzing with the news of the Germans' imminent surrender in Holland, Denmark and northern Germany when the Wren who brought his post had come in with it.

"And this was delivered by hand just now," she said. It was an envelope with something else in it—money, or a key, he thought, as he slit it open. Before he read the letter which was written in pencil, he looked at the signature. Jack Greenfeldt. Greenfeldt? Oh, yes, the American, Zoë's young man. She had brought him once to the flat for a drink, a saturnine, rather haunted-looking fellow, but he'd liked him. The object, wrapped in paper, proved to be a key. Oh, Lord, he thought, when he'd unwrapped it, I bet now the end is in sight he's hopping it back to the wife and kids at home and hasn't got the guts to tell her himself.

It was headed Dachau 2 May.

Then he read the letter. It was quite short, and he read it twice.

I am sorry to bother you with this [it began] but I couldn't think who else to ask. I have made several efforts to write to Zoë, but I couldn't find any way of telling her.

Anyway, by the time you get this I shall be dead. I have two days' work to do here taking pictures, then I shall put the film with this letter on a plane on Thursday morning and then I shall come back here and put a bullet through my head. She will ask you why. Tell her I couldn't live with what I've witnessed in the last two weeks—I can't be a survivor of what has been, literally, a holocaust. I'd go crazy, out of my mind at not being *with them* in it. I couldn't make her happy—not after the days here, and at Buchenwald and at Belsen. The key is to the studio I rented, and she may want to collect things from there. Rent paid until the end of this month and perhaps you would give the key back to the agent in Sloane Street—Chestertons I think it is. Tell her I loved her and thank her for that—oh, hell—tell her whatever you think best. I know you'll see her through it—and maybe that husband of hers will come back?

Jack Greenfeldt

When he had read the letter a second time he found himself folding it up and putting it back into its envelope. He felt stunned by it—which meant, initially, that he had no feelings at all. Early in the war he had had to face up to the possibility of losing his own life, but the idea of taking it was so alien to him that he was completely unable to imagine the state of mind that might lead to such an act. Then he thought, Supposing he wrote this letter and then, when he got back to the camp, changed his mind, or someone found him in time to persuade him against it? Telling Zoë would be bad enough, but telling her and then discovering that it wasn't true would be worse. Or would it? Perhaps he ought to try and find out. He took the letter out of its envelope and read it again. This time it engendered hostility, respect and finally, pity—in equal quantities—what a shocking waste and selfish, too—what courage to do such a thing in cold blood and poor chap, what he must have seen and heard and experienced that could drive him to such an act . . . but he did not doubt it. He picked up his telephone and asked for a line.

He asked for the Duchy and after struggling with the Brig who neither seemed to know who he was nor could understand how on earth anyone could want to speak to his wife ("some feller on the line seems to want to talk to you about something or other") he got her. He said he wondered if he could come down for the weekend? He was always welcome, she said, if he didn't mind where he slept. He asked whether Zoë would be there, and she said, yes. Then she said in her most level tone, had he bad news? Not about Rupert, he replied. There was a pause, and then she said, Ah. If he came on the four twenty, she added, he could be met with the girls.

So that was what he had done. He had waited until after dinner to tell Zoë, because it was the first opportunity for having her on his own. He took her into the morning room, and made her sit down. She sat upright, with her hands on the table: he saw that she was trembling.

"What is it? Is it—Rupert?"

"No. It's Jack."

"*Jack?* How do you know—*that?*"

"He sent me a letter."

She looked at him mutely.

"He died."

For a moment she stared at him as though she had not heard; then she said: "He sent you a *letter*—to say he was dead?"

His mouth was suddenly dry. All day he had wrestled with what he should tell her, how much, and how. "Tell her whatever you think best," Jack had written. When he had finished washing his hands before dinner, and had straightened up to comb his hair in the small glass and had seen his face, weak with indecision and potential evasions, he had suddenly known that only the truth would do. So he told her—as gently as he could, but there was nothing gentle about the tale.

She sat still, upright and silent, until he said: "He said to tell you that he loved you and to thank you for it," when an expression of extreme pain came and went on her face. She swallowed and then asked if she might see the letter and he gave it to her, saying he was going to get them both a drink and he would be back.

On the table in the hall there was a tray with two glasses and decanters of whisky and water on it. Blessing the Duchy, he waited a few minutes, none the less, to give her some time to herself. When he returned she was sitting just as he had left her, and the letter lay on the table—she was not crying as he had half expected. He poured the whisky and put a glass by her hand. "I know this is the most awful shock," he said, "but I felt I should tell you the truth."

"Yes. Thank you. The funny thing is that I sort of knew—not that *this* would happen, but that it was an end, somehow. He came here two weeks ago—without any warning—and after tea we sat in this room. And then he went and I had the thought that I would not ever see him again."

He put the glass into her hand.

"My poor Jack," she said, as she began to cry.

Much later she had said, "I expect you think it was very bad of me—to go off like that—to have—an affair."

And he'd said no, he didn't, he thought it was very understandable.

But she had answered, "Understandable, but not good. But I *don't* believe that Rupert is going to come back. If that was going to happen, it would have happened by now."

Later she said, "I think *he* came here to make sure I would be all right."

"That showed love," he said.

"Yes, it did, didn't it?" She cried a bit more, and then she asked him why he thought that he'd done it.

And he had answered slowly, not exactly picking his words, but trying to imagine being Jack: "Perhaps he thought it was the only thing he could give those people—to show that he loved them and cared—"

"His own life?"

"You can't give more."

By the time they parted for the night, the house was dark and silent.

It was half past two and the war had ended officially over two hours ago now. There were still sounds of distant revelry in the streets, outside the nearest pub—people singing, cheering, laughing. He got up from his chair and went back into the sitting room. His leg ached, as he supposed it always would do from now onwards, if he overdid things. So many people had come to stay with him during the last months—the children, mostly—that he had given up the sofa as a temporary bed and bought himself a divan. He undressed, fetched his pyjamas from the bathroom and got into bed.

For a long time, he was unable to sleep. He felt so beset by the quantity of confidences bestowed on him by the family—always on the grounds that he was part of it, or had become so, but really because he was not, would never be quite that. He was anything from a catalyst to a general repository. Hugh, for instance. Hugh had asked him to accompany him to Battle to collect some cases of beer. The moment they were in the car, he had known that this was a pretext, and had hoped that he didn't want to talk about Polly. But it had been Edward. He was worried about Edward. They weren't getting on at all well, and the chief reason for that, Hugh thought, was that Edward knew how much he disapproved of what was going on. Archie had long since realized that Edward had affairs and had wondered idly from time to time whether anyone else in the family was aware of this.

"He's always been a bit of a—*ranger*," Hugh said. "But this time it's more serious. You're part of the family, really, so I know I can trust you. The thing *is* that he's had a child by this woman. And in spite of saying he was going to end the whole thing, he hasn't. And now he's talking of selling his house in London in order to buy a smaller one. Well, putting two and two together, I don't like the sound of that at all."

Why, Hugh had gone on, would he sell a perfectly good house, that he knew Villy was fond of, just to buy a smaller one unless he had no intention of being in it himself? That was what was worrying him. It transpired that he, Hugh, wanted him, Archie, to talk to Edward. "It's no good me even trying any more, old boy. He simply flies off the handle and it makes office life harder. But I thought perhaps you might . . ."

He'd said he'd think about it, but he didn't think that anything he said would make much difference.

Then, when they had collected the crates of beer—ordered by the Brig for the servants to celebrate the peace when it came—and were driving home in the rain, Hugh had suddenly said: "What's up with Poll, do you think?"

"How do you mean?"

"Well, she seems in a funny mood. I wondered whether perhaps she's fallen in love with somebody."

He had waited: he had promised Polly silence, and she should have it, however many lies were entailed.

"I asked her what was the matter, and she said nothing, in the kind of voice she always uses when it *is* something. If I'm right, it's clearly not going very well, and she hasn't got Syb to talk to who would have been wonderful with her. I thought, possibly, she might have confided in you. Or you could have asked her."

"Better not," he had said.

"Oh, well. I want her happiness more than anything else, and it's awful to have to stand by and feel so helpless."

"I hope it's not that bloody doctor she works for," he said as they turned into the drive. "I mean, he's foreign, for a start, and far older, and almost certainly married. Or if not, he certainly ought to be. Just thought I'd ask. I know she loves you."

"Eh?" This had startled him.

"My dear old boy, we *all* do. You're one of the family. In a way."

He could see no way of saying anything at all to Edward that would in the slightest degree influence him. Better keep out of that.

Zoë had not appeared at lunch-time. She had a very bad headache, the Duchy said. After lunch, she had tucked her arm into his and asked him to come and look at her rock garden.

"Really I wanted to thank you for breaking that dreadful news to poor Zoë," she said. "I'm afraid she is very unhappy. Of course I've known about the man—all those visits to London suddenly. She is so young, and she's had a very hard time. It seems to me that something must be done about her state."

"You mean—"

"I mean that she cannot continue indefinitely neither a widow nor a wife. Naturally, she will have a home here for as long as she wants—" She stopped speaking and walking and turned to look at him.

"Or do you believe," she said unsteadily and in a voice that reminded him sharply of Rachel when she was moved, "do you believe that he *still* might come back to us?"

He looked at her, unable to say what she wanted to hear. Her gaze did not falter.

"There is nothing in the world that I want more," she said. "But I was so fortunate in the last war with the other two coming back—"

He had said that he would find out what needed to be done or found out.

There had been some light relief. Lydia had buttonholed him after tea. "Archie, I have one extremely serious thing to ask you. It's very small really—for you, I mean, to do something about—but for me it may well be life or death."

"What now?"

"You say that as though I ask you things from morning to night. What it *is* is could you explain to my parents that it is absolutely essential for them to send me to a good school? I thought the one that Judy goes to, actually. I know she's awful, but I don't think that that is the school's fault. She learns interesting games like lacrosse and hockey and they do ballroom dancing and a play at Christmas every year. And she's got a pash for the geography mistress who is simply marvelous—and I know her mother told her it was only a phase but I'm not having a chance to go through it because it really isn't possible to feel like that about Miss Milliment."

"Why don't you ask them?"

"I have, and Dad just says talk to Mummy and *she* says things like 'we'll see'—which means we never will. You could say that you were appalled by my ignorance," she added.

"I could. But am I?"

"Also I've been through quite a lot of *Who's Who*—it's a kind of telephone directory only full of famous people you've never heard of—and it *always* says 'educated at'—and then the name of a school."

"Are you planning to be famous?"

"I don't wish to rule it out. Oh, Archie, *do* talk to them: you're one of the family now—they'll listen to you . . ." And so on.

And then—and not at all light-hearted—Clary. This evening, which they had spent together beginning with supper in a Cypriot restaurant just off Piccadilly that she loved because it always had lamb chops and those little dumpling things fried in honey for pudding and thick sweet coffee. She had met him there and arrived looking unexpectedly smart in a black skirt and a man's collarless shirt and dark red sandals and her hair glistening.

"It's wet, I'm afraid," she said when he kissed her. "I thought I ought to wash it for the peace and there wasn't time to get it dry."

"I like your shirt."

"Zoë gave it to me at the weekend. The collar and cuffs are all frayed, so it wouldn't be any use to him, but with the sleeves rolled up you wouldn't notice."

"You look very nice. Attractive."

"Do I? I don't look anything like Poll, though. She's got a new dress, a yellow one—a kind of lemon peel colour—it looks super with her hair. She's gone to the Reform Club with Uncle Hugh." She had looked at him searchingly then and looked away when their eyes met. He had offered her a drink and she had said could it *not* be gin and lime? "I know it's what girls all seem to drink, but I've always hated it, so I've decided to change."

"What to?"

"What would you advise? Whisky tastes of rubber, if you ask me, and the only time I had vodka it was like an electric shock and I don't know what else there is. Oh, I know. I like dark *brown* sherry. I really like that."

"Did you go to work today?"

"You bet! Noël doesn't consider that it is a particular day at all. They aren't even celebrating. They are spending the evening reading somebody called H. L. Mencken aloud to each other. It is a very mature way of dealing with peace, don't you think?"

"A bit dull, too, I should have thought."

"Me, too. Are we really going to go to Buckingham Palace and wait for the King and Queen to come out? Will they, do you think? I've never actually seen them, except on news reels."

"I thought we might. It is a night to remember."

But by the time they'd had dinner (which he had thought they'd had quite early enough), the crowds were so thick that it took them ages to get anywhere near the Palace, although everyone was so good-tempered that it was possible to edge nearer by degrees. Showers of golden stars from rockets occurred in the lavender-coloured sky and the Palace was floodlit, and round the statue of Queen Victoria an enormous snake of people were dancing the hokey-cokey, singing and stamping their feet, and beyond, near the railings, people were chanting, shouting for the King. There were *thousands* of them, so many indeed and sometimes so tightly packed that they had held hands all evening in order not to get parted, and sometimes they had to shout to each other to be heard, but sometimes they simply sang whatever everyone else round them was singing: "Land of Hope and Glory," "God Save the King" and bits of the hokey-cokey. When they had seen the Royal Family standing on the balcony and waving, he thought that perhaps they should call it a day, but she wanted to wait for them to come out again, and she was so excited that he had not the heart to refuse her. Eventually, long after it was dark, they did come out again—just the King and Queen this time—no princesses. "I suppose they've been sent to bed, poor things," Clary said. After that, she agreed that they'd better start for home.

"You'd better come back with me," he had said. "I live nearer than you, and we'll never get a cab."

At Hyde Park Corner, he said he would have to sit down for a bit, so they went into the bit of park that ran down to Knightsbridge and found an empty bench, and he smoked, and that was when she told him that she knew about Polly.

"It came up because I couldn't understand why we couldn't all spend this evening together," she had said. "Poor Poll, she made me promise not to laugh. As if I would about anything that was so serious to her. It's a good thing she told me because I'd known for a long time that things weren't all right, and tonight I reminded her that we'd made a pact—ages ago—to tell each other things that were important. And, of course, when she remembered that, she had to tell me. It's funny, isn't it? You can know that something is completely ridiculous, but if you see it isn't to the other person, it almost seems not to be."

"Is that how it struck you?"

"Well. Well, not that *somebody* shouldn't be in love with you, but they ought to be more your age, oughtn't they?"

He had opened his mouth to say a whole lot of things and then shut it again. "I suppose I seem incredibly ancient to you."

"No, not incredibly, at all. In fact, you don't seem to have aged at all since I met you."

"Thanks for that."

They could not see each other as it was now dark and the nearest street lamp yards away. After a short silence, she said, "Sorry."

"What for?"

"I don't know how, but I *feel* I've hurt your feelings. I *did* say to Poll that I thought you weren't the marrying kind."

"Did you?"

"Well, I mean, here you are not married to anybody. It was to help her get over it. Of course she will, but she doesn't believe that. People do, don't they?"

"Get over being in love?"

"If it's hopeless."

"Oh, yes, I should think they usually do. I'm really sorry about Poll. I'm very fond of her, you know."

"She knows, but she says it's the wrong kind of fond . . . I can see that. I can see that burning antagonism might be a better start."

A moment later, she said, "You have got a funny croaky laugh, Archie."

Without thinking, he said, *"You* have."

"Have what?"

"Aged since I met you."

"Oh," she had said at once. "I see what you were minding. You were minding me implying that you were old. All I meant was that you were far too old for *Polly*."

He'd suggested then that perhaps they'd better resume hobbling home.

When, at last, they had got back, she'd wanted to make some cocoa, so he told her to go to bed and he'd bring her some.

She was sitting up in his bed, wearing his pyjama jacket, her face looking as though she had scrubbed it with soap and water.

"I used some of your toothpaste and my finger," she said. "I didn't think you'd mind."

He put the mug into her hands and sat on the edge of the bed—to take the weight off his feet.

"Do you know what this reminds me of?"

"Of course I don't. What?"

"When I was quite young—well, about thirteen—Neville had an asthma attack because he said I'd woken him up because I had a bad dream and went into Ellen. Well. Dad came in with a mug of hot milk and I didn't want to drink it because of the skin, and he picked it off and ate it for me. That showed love, didn't it?"

He looked at the crinkling top of her mug, put out two fingers, picked it off and ate it.

"There," he had said. "You're still loved."

"Copycat," she said, but her eyes sparkled with affection and pleasure. She drank some of the cocoa, then she put the mug aside on the table.

"There is something," she said slowly, almost as though she wasn't quite sure what it was, "something—about Dad that I wanted to talk to you about. Well—*discuss*, you know?" She drew her knees up and clasped her arms round them: holding herself together, he thought, as anxiety stirred in him.

"Right," he said with an assumption of cheerfulness and calm.

"You needn't be anxious, Archie. This is what it is." She took a deep breath and said rapidly, "After the invasion last year, I thought, you see, that he would be *bound* to come back: I mean there would be no Germans to stop him. And then, when he didn't I thought that probably he had got some sort of war job—I don't know what, but something—which meant that he had to stay until the peace. And now, we've got that. So what I thought was, that it might be best if I made a sort of date, and if he hasn't come back by then, I will have to understand that he never will. I've been thinking about this for a long time, and when Zoë tried to give me all his shirts last weekend, I only took the really worn ones, because taking the others would be like giving in. So I thought if I made a sort of pact with you, and set a date, that this would be sensible." At the word sensible her eyes filled. She cleared her throat. "I thought as this would be an easy date to remember for both of us, a year from now?"

He nodded. "Good idea," he said.

"It is odd. I used to mind about him so awfully because of me. Because *I* missed him so much. But it seems to have turned into something different. I *do* miss him, of course, but I mind it more for *him*, because I wanted him to have a good life and *all of it*—not be cut off. It isn't that I don't still love him."

"I know. I know it isn't. I think," he said; he was finding it difficult to say anything, "that what's happened is that you've grown up, and your love has grown up with you."

"You mean, more adult?"

"More mature," he said, smiling at her favourite word. "I've known quite a few adults who weren't remarkable for their maturity."

"Really?" He saw her savouring this new and clearly pleasing notion.

He remembered now how, when he'd suggested that he leave her to sleep, she had said, "After all, darling Archie, I've always got you," and turned her face up to him to be kissed good-night—like someone not far off thirteen.

His leg ached—perhaps he *was* getting old: was he? With the war over, he could go back to the sun, to France and painting: would he? For so long he, like, he supposed, everyone else, had thought of the end of the war as the beginning of a new and wonderful life, or at least the resumption of an old and comfortable one. Now he wondered whether for most people it would be either. He thought of what Hugh had said about Edward, and tried to imagine how Villy would deal with being abandoned if that were to happen; he thought of the Duchy having to leave her beloved garden if they resumed living in London—and surely that house would be too large for them once the descendants had all gone back to their own houses? He thought of Zoë coming to terms with both her husband's and her lover's deaths: he had been moved by her courage, but then he thought that they were all a brave lot: the Duchy with her stoic acceptance of losing Rupert, the Brig with his gallant determination not to be beaten by blindness, Polly with her courage in telling him that she loved him and in her response to his rejection . . . and finally Clary, asleep next door, whose love, unquenched by time or reason, had transmuted from need and fantasy to some purer and more enduring substance that in its turn could only inspire admiration—and love.

Lying in the dark he made a pact with himself. If Rupert did not return, he would pledge himself to taking his place so much as was possible. If Rupert came back, however, he might embark upon a very different course.

He had refused the offer of a bunk in one of the two cramped little cabins below, and now sat forward with his back to the wheelhouse which protected him from the following wind. It had been dark when they left Guernsey (just as well, since he had no papers of any kind and it had been easy to slip aboard with the seaman who had befriended him). "Just keep your head down, and do as I say," he had admonished. He had been stowed below until the boat sailed, and very stuffy it had been—he'd sat on the bunk, which was covered with a heavy damp blanket in pitch dark in the cabin that reeked of diesel oil, wet oiled wool and English cigarettes. They'd sailed at four o'clock in the morning and when they were well out of the harbour his friend rapped on the door and said it was all clear. It was good to get out into the fresh, salty air, and he watched the small yellow light in the harbour master's hut twinkle and recede and go out in the increasing distance. After about an hour one of them came round with thick white mugs of tea with milk and sugar in it—he hadn't drunk tea for nearly five years. When he said that, they smiled: they'd treated him with a kind of patronizing protectiveness ever since he'd mentioned Dunkirk—he wasn't sure whether they believed him, were sorry for him or thought he was mad. The seas ran slap on their quarter in strong, but not steep waves, and the small boat chugged and plunged steadily forward. Soon after it was light, he fell into a stupor: he had hardly slept since he left, which was thirty-six hours ago now; his skin itched with fatigue. They woke him for dinner at noon: some sort of stew with mushy peas much in evidence and a thick chunk of rather grey bread. The sky was overcast, although far away patches of sea glittered fitfully from distant sunlight. He slept again and woke in the late afternoon to a watery sun and a fresher wind. They had spread an oilskin over him and he realized that it had been raining—his hair was wet. He was ravenously hungry, and grateful for another mug of tea and a huge sandwich with some sort of tinned meat in it. They also gave him a packet of Weights to smoke. They watched him light his first one, and then one of them said, "E's bin to sea all right. Wouldn't only use one match else." They had left him alone after that and he'd been grateful. He thought he wanted to think, to imagine what he was going back to, to envisage a little of the future but he seemed incapable of thought and his imagination ranged wilfully from Zoë's face at his return to *her* face when he had left her—lying in the high carved old bed against the big square pillows that were cased in coarse white cotton—her long dark hair combed out after her labour, the baby tightly swaddled beside her. She had tried to smile at him as he stood by the door and that effort had so poignantly reminded him of Isobel when she had been dying after Neville was born, that he had gone back to her, to take her once more and for the last time in his arms. It was she, after kissing him, who had pushed him gently away, had propelled him into this future that he was embarked upon. She had kept her word, had not tried to make him stay: she had simply wanted him to see the child. Leaving had not been easy, and returning, although it had all the trappings of a happy ending, would mean the reunion with a number of people he loved, some of whom must have become strangers. Clary, for instance, would be nineteen? No, nearly twenty! A young woman— far removed from the little girl who had so passionately needed him. And Neville, he must now be at public school, his voice broken, his asthma perhaps outgrown. But Zoë—how would she be? Had she waited for him all these years, or had she succumbed to somebody else? He must not expect too much: and then he remembered that that was what he had always said to himself about her. She would still be beautiful, he was sure of that, but he had learned to discover beauty in other aspects. Would his parents still be alive? Could he bear to go back into the wood business—to the house in London, the dinner parties, the business entertaining, the family weekends, the occasional holiday abroad, to giving up the idea of painting for the second time in his life? *She* had found him some materials, to draw with, at least, and once a small box of watercolours that he had used until there was nothing left. He would have gone mad during those first years, when she had constantly to hide him and he could not go out or go far or speak to anyone, if he had not been able to draw.

But in all these random speculations, it was Zoë that he kept coming back to and with the most anxiety, because, he realized, it was the part of homecoming that would exact most from him, and it was also the part where he was afraid he had least to give. There was, of course, another child, a son or a daughter, provided all had gone well, which it hadn't last time for her, he thought, with a pang of guilt. It was odd how he had not been as miserable when that baby had died as he felt he should have been, but then, nor had she. That was when he had found it most difficult to love her: whatever he did, or said, however he was with her seemed wrong, rousing no more in her than small sparks of irritation . . . Motherhood had not come easily to her, he had thought then, perhaps she was not cut for children at all. Then, when she had started the second baby, she had seemed different, excited, the symptoms of pregnancy that she had complained about so much before had been lightly borne that second time. But he had never known the outcome, and when he had sent the notes to her and to Clary by Pipette (and, of course, he did not know whether they had ever received them), he had not dared to mention the baby in case she had lost it.

There was no sun now: the breeze had died down, the sea and the sky were all a dusky dark: rain fell, as lightly as mist, and he put on the oilskin. One of the crew walked past him to the bows to empty a pail of potato peelings—the wind, what there was of it, was still on their quarter. I suppose I'm still officially in the Navy, he thought, and wondered how long it would take for him not to be. Then he wondered whether they would consider him, for the last ten months or so, to have been a deserter—a confusing thought. But it was not the Navy he had deserted during those months, it had been Zoë. And now, as the boat took him further and further away from her, it was *she* who was to be deserted—for good. He could not think of her without such senses of loss and longing that he knew he must not think of her at all, and so escaped again into sleep, or rather, patches of sleep.

He was woken at dawn by spray: the wind had backed round to north-east, but the sea, a livid pewter from the rising sun, was calmer, a heaving surface with only the occasional wave slapping at the starboard quarter.

They brought him a mug of cocoa and said they would soon sight land. He lit his last cigarette and watched for it. The low bank of cloud on the horizon that seemed to separate the sea from the sky resolved itself into a paler streak of mist. He watched as the mist solidified to swatches of brownish green above the chalk white of cliffs and then the small blocks and rows of darker detail presented themselves suddenly as buildings that became steadily paler as the sun rose, until the scene resembled a very distant stage set. He was cramped from being in the same position for so long, and damp from the showers and spray. He continued to watch and his heart felt as cold as ash from a fire deliberately put out. It was possible to do that, he thought: it was the rekindling that seemed insurmountable. But if one knew anything about love, he supposed, it should be possible. He picked up his mug. God! How he *loathed* the skin of hot milk! He took it off with his fingers and then, without knowing why, he ate it before he drained the mug. Somehow, he thought, I must find it in me to make a start.